WHEN THE DEAD
COME CALLING

WHEN THE DEAD COME CALLING

THE BURROWHEAD MYSTERIES

HELEN SEDGWICK

POINT
BLANK

A Point Blank Book

First published in Great Britain, the Republic of Ireland and Australia
by Point Blank, an imprint of Oneworld Publications, 2020

Copyright © Helen Sedgwick 2020

ISBN 978-1-78607-569-7 (hardback)
ISBN 978-1-78607-570-3 (ebook)

Typeset by Geethik Technologies
Printed and bound in Great Britain by Clays Ltd, Elcograf S.p.A.

Oneworld Publications
10 Bloomsbury Street
London WC1B 3SR
England

Stay up to date with the latest books,
special offers, and exclusive content from
Oneworld with our newsletter

Sign up on our website
oneworld-publications.com

MIX
Paper from
responsible sources
FSC® C018072

For Hazel

TUESDAY

BREAK OF DAWN

My hiding place is not a cave. It is a shrine.

I can see that, now I've stopped running. I see it in the twigs bound together with twine, in the scratched crosses on the walls. Prayers barely legible chipped into stone: PLEASE HELP MY MAMMY; PD & RT 4EVER; RIP, everywhere RIP. I edge back to the entrance. Don't want to be here. Can't be. We used to whisper about this place – the cave that doesn't exist – but here it is, cold and dark and stale, filled with the marks of people who have found it before me. Their words scrape the back of my neck but at least there is air at the front. My toes touch the pebbles of the beach, my heels the cave's floor. My feet cross the threshold.

The cliff face is steep either side of my head. Jagged. Rusting like tetanus. I don't know where the red comes from in these rocks, only that the walls get closer as they rise, make a pointed cavern the width of my arm span and the height of a block of flats – emptied for demolition but left standing, to rot, repainted on the inside with bird shit. Shouldn't have left those windows open. My breath is a staggered echo, distant, so close it makes my skin shrink. I don't want to look behind me, don't want to see inside. RIP. Gouged, carved. PLEASE HELP. Alone. Desperate.

On the horizon: a military carrier. Fat and full. Smoke belching from the back of it, the waves useless against its hull. It's a darker grey than the grey above and below it, charcoal deep, while the clouds are bruised and the sea below frothy and spitting. The waves

and I are separated by dunes of rock and shingle, barnacled, sharp
when you least expect it – I should know, I ran the miles over them
to get here. Keep low to the stone, graze your knees, let broken
shells puncture your soles, just keep moving. The rain will wash the
blood from these rocks.

Legs planted apart, stretching my arms out, one to the left, one
to the right. This shaking has to stop. I keep my palms pointing
outwards and close my eyes, control my breath. Roll my head back
as far as it will go. Something clicks; joint, bone, cartilage. I open
my eyes again. Straight ahead I can see through the gash of the cave's
entrance all the way to the sea.

But they will not be coming from the sea.

They will be coming from the cliffs.

I press myself as flat as I can, peer back out the way I came. My
hands are grazed and stinging now with the salt from the sea and
my sweat. The wind scratches at my eyes but the beach is empty.

Then, to my surprise, I see colour. There is a crate, a cage, for
catching crab or lobster, blue rope, turquoise, with tendrils of black
seaweed tangled through the holes. Abandoned. I think some of the
rope has been broken. A creature has eaten its way out. So there it
is, unexpected colour on this grey beach: soggy blue rope. Seaweed
like matted hair. Messages scratched into stone. Whispers. Escape.

BACK A SEVEN

Georgie and Fergus sleep with their curtains open so they can see the sky, so they are wakened every morning by the sunrise. It's so beautiful out here, they always say. But today Georgie has dozed, because it is a Tuesday and Tuesdays are usually the calmest days, the kindest sort of days, and so she is still a little sleep-muddled when Fergus kisses her forehead.

'I made you some bacon, hon. And scrambled.'

Georgie sits up in bed, just waking. 'What's the time, love?' She feels a gurgle in her tummy; that bacon smells delicious.

'Back a seven.'

'Back of seven?'

'Aye.'

'I slept in.'

She reaches up and strokes the side of his big, familiar face. He's wearing the checked pyjama bottoms she got him last Christmas, and his favourite green T-shirt with the fox on it. Little tight round the waist nowadays, but that doesn't bother either of them. You get to an age when you learn what's important, and what's not.

'Smells good.'

Georgie stretches, like she does every morning, full down to her toes to start, a circle of the ankles, before pulling her legs up to her chest, stretching out her spine. Fergus kisses the top of her head as she lies there, bundled and content. 'Mmm,' she says with the stretch, arms up over her head now, and he turns the handle of the mug on the bedside table towards her.

'Tea first, hon?' he says.

'Tea first.'

The tray is balanced on the chest by the door, and he reaches for it as she sips her tea. Fergus thinks breakfast in bed is a good thing, and there's always time for a good thing. That's one of his sayings. Georgie can hear it now, though he doesn't say it out loud today. No need, between them. She tucks into her bacon, which is just the right side of crispy, and speaks with her mouth full, because there's fun in that and certain rules can be bent, especially before you're dressed in the morning.

'Nice lenticular clouds this morning,' she says.

They are her favourite type of cloud. Always pleased to see them. Though today they are distant, away at the gold strip of horizon, and the sky is dark and bloated closer in. Windows already streaked with rain.

'What're your plans for today, love?'

'Might walk over to the hill at Burrowhead Cross. If the weather lightens.'

'Mmm?'

'See if I can't get some aerial photos, looking down over the village. You know, for the website. Or there's the motte at Mungrid...'

She raises her eyebrows. 'It's steep,' she says, 'that motte. I need the rope to climb up the side of it.'

'I'll use the rope too, hon, to get up it.'

They sit together for a moment, Georgie under the covers and Fergus on the edge of the bed.

'Any members signed up yet?' she asks, though she regrets it as soon as she sees his face.

'I'm going to bring my tray up,' he says.

'What?'

'Breakfast in bed together, eh?'

'Oh yes, of course.'

She reaches for his hand and gives it a squeeze.

'Those clouds…' she says, staring away to the horizon. They are beautiful, smooth as satin, with the way they catch the morning light and glow, actually glow, beyond the charcoal overhead. It is understandable, to Georgie, that people might believe there's more going on up there than air and water. She listens to Fergus's footsteps down the stairs, hears the familiar almost-whistle under his breath that is the sound of him when he thinks no one is listening. He doesn't make that whistle in public because his mum told him it was rude, when he was a little boy – what a thing to do. A child should be allowed to whistle all he likes. But then there is something about it being just for her.

She chases the last of her scrambled eggs around her plate, picks up a final crunch of bacon with her fingers. A good way to start a day. Especially a Tuesday. Then her phone flashes beside her.

The tone of Simon's voice makes her heart sink down to her belly. She has to ask him to repeat the details, to let the full meaning sink in. It's too awful. His words are fragmented, confused – the shock. Worse than that, too. She could hardly have believed it but for that terrible crack in his voice. She pushes back the duvet, stands for a minute looking towards the window, the rain beating against the glass. Stuff like this isn't supposed to happen here. That's why they chose it when they moved down from Scotland, her and Fergus. She's standing on something small and sharp, bare feet on cold wood. God, why'd it have to be Simon who got there first? She can hear the shriek of the wind up on the cliffs.

'I'm on my way, Si,' she says. 'You need to keep your distance. Don't do anything till I'm there.'

'I know.' His voice is gravel and pain.

'I'm… I'm sorry. Cal will be on his way too. We need to get the scene secured, and fast.'

The call disconnects.

She reaches for her towel and meets Fergus at the top of the stairs on her way to the bathroom. He's holding his tray of breakfast. He's brought up a crocus from the garden in a little water glass.

'Oh, love,' she says. 'Something awful… I've got to get to work, right now.'

'What is it?'

She swallows.

'They've found… they've found a body.'

He stands there, holding the breakfast tray.

'What?'

'They've found a body, under the swings.'

'But what do you mean?'

'They've found a dead body, love. Someone's been killed.'

'Not here in the village?'

'I think so. I don't know any more than that.'

'It can't be… Not here, in the village?'

His throat's turned red – that happens when he's upset.

'Guess it's not much like a Tuesday after all.' She shakes her head. 'I've got to get to work.' Turns to the bathroom, then back again. 'This is lovely though.' She nods at the flower. 'Thank you. Such a pretty colour, that purple.'

'Seemed a good morning for it. But now…'

She reaches towards him then stops.

'Do they know who it is?' he asks.

Georgie nods.

'Young Dr Cosse.'

'Oh, Georgie…' He shakes his head, like he doesn't want his next thought to settle. 'Oh my God. Simon?'

'He's there.'

He closes his eyes against it. 'Is it to do with all this stuff about, you know…'

'I don't know, Fergus.' She leans forward and rests her forehead against his. They breathe, in unison. 'I don't know.'

She straightens up and gives him a quick kiss, already backing away.

'Will I get some coffee on?' he says, with something hopeless in his voice.

'I've not got time for coffee.'

It's an accidental snap, but she leaves it hanging.

In the bathroom she locks the door, turns the shower on and steps in too soon. Ice-cold water hits the back of her shoulders and for a second it feels like the strike of a baton. Then she tilts her head back and lets it cascade down her face.

08:15

Burrowhead playground, the only one in the village of Burrowhead, has its back to the houses and its gaze out over the clifftop and beyond the rough shingle beach to the sea. From time to time the villagers get together for a meeting to discuss how this setup is unhelpful for the safety of the children: what if they swing too high and jump off, go cascading down the cliff's edge? What if they're dizzy from the roundabout? What if they fall? Georgie has been along to the meetings herself, once or twice. It's important, when you're part of a community, and perhaps they have a point. The bedrock itself seems barely attached to the rest of land, especially on a day like today – it would not be a surprise, to Georgie, if the whole headland were to slip over the edge any minute. The smudged, sodden grass around the roundabout, the faded English Wildlife information sign and all. Gone. It could happen. These things do happen.

As she approaches, she has to hold her hat down over her eyes, the wind has got such a whip to it this morning. It's carrying the rain like nettles. Dark too, the sky, the sea – none of that morning light left on the horizon. Spring takes a while to arrive after spring has supposedly arrived, up here in the borderlands, and there's the salt in the air this side of the village. No wonder the roundabout squeaks and the swing chains are rusted. Cal and his team are already at work, the pale shapes of their suits hunched, crouched, hoods pockmarked by the rain. Beyond the cordon, at knee height, are two animals: a horse and donkey, attached to the ground via spiral springs of metal. Their chipped red and yellow paint makes a disturbing contrast to that angry grey sky. The roundabout, squeaking the way it does, seems to answer the wind. There's no one on it, of course. It spins all on its own. It's lasted though, that's the thing. Still clinging on.

Simon is standing a way off, but he's staring over at the swings. His coat is open, fighting against the wind, his hair plastered across his forehead. And that shape he's staring at on the ground. That's the body. The angles of it look all wrong, even from here. Everything about it looks wrong. She keeps away though, lets Cal and his team do their work. Besides, she needs a minute with Simon, just the two of them. She puts her hand on his arm.

His breath is ragged and his eyes are unable to hold her gaze.

'Will you come over here with me, Si?' she says. She has to raise her voice to be heard over the wind and those furious waves. God but this weather.

He looks at her with his eyes such a pale blue she finds them unnerving, even now, but she doesn't look away. He's drenched but unflinching, like he's not even aware of the rain.

'Over to this bench here, okay?'

The bench is dedicated to Abigail Moss, whom nobody knows. It faces away from the swings, out over the beach that on a summer's day can be pebbled with red stone and yellow quartz but which today is a reflection of the clouds themselves, the black nimbostratus, all churned up and bitter.

'I'm so sorry, Si,' she says. The rain intensifies, stinging her face. She holds her hand up as a kind of shield, and water spills from her cuff down her arm. 'What an awful thing. And for you to find him... You must be in shock.'

Simon doesn't reply. For a second she thinks she sees something soggy and misshapen out by the tideline with the seaweed and the drowned feathers, that dirty froth – but no, it's just more of the rubbish that's washed up with the storm.

'I know how close you were,' she says.

She touches Simon's hand, once, twice, then away. His fingers are like ice, like the sea itself. She pulls out her gloves and offers them to him. He's got big hands, but then so has she, and she reckons the gloves would fit him nicely. He shakes his head, eyes down, and she puts them on herself instead, lets them absorb the water from her skin. They're good gloves, padded and lined with that thermal insulating stuff, the same kind they use for mountaineers. Make her hands look giant, and she likes that too. She taps his hand again, her gloved palm dwarfing his fist this time.

'You need to head home,' she says, kindly.

He looks up at last. 'Please no,' he says. 'I want to… I don't want…'

'No choice, you know that.'

'I can't be at home right now.'

Georgie sighs. 'You can wait for me at the station, if you like.'

'Thanks.'

She shakes her head.

'We'll need to take your statement, Si. That's all.' The squawk of seagulls sounds like it's always been there, but Georgie is fairly sure the gulls were silent when she arrived. She watches them circling the putrid line of seaweed that marks the high tide, here, whatever the time of day, whatever the season. The smell of it down on the rocks is sickening but up here it barely reaches them, just a waft, now and then, of something rotting, something carried on the wind.

'Can you see anything down there?' she says with a frown, and Simon stares up at her, pleading. 'Look,' she points, standing. 'The way they're circling.' The rain's in her eyes now, dripping down her neck.

'Could be a dead crab or something.' His voice sounds like he has to force it out of his throat. 'They like to pick the carcass.' He swallows.

Georgie hears a car pull up behind her, the slam of a door – Trish, good, they need to get to work.

'You head off, Si. It's important.'

He stands, starts to walk away. God, but he looks broken.

'Jesus, Si,' says Trish, watching him. Her padded coat is zipped from her knees to over her chin, the huge hood hiding her cropped hair. 'This is…' She moves towards him like she wants to give him a hug but he shakes his head, starts the walk back to the village alone. 'Fucking hell,' Trish says, once he's out of earshot. 'This is the worst thing…' Her hands are in fists. 'Where do we start?'

Georgie's hat is soaked now, not keeping the rain off so much as bathing her head in it.

'See down at the shore there, Trish?' Georgie's voice is gentle. 'Can you see anything?'

Trish holds her hand over her eyes, trying to keep the water out. 'What, down there?' she shouts over the wind.

The path to the beach is a long scratch of stones and mud zigzagging down the cliffs. You can slip even in the summer but now… Well, Trish is steady on her feet, and keen too.

'Shall I head down?'

Georgie shakes her head. 'I'll get Cal to send a couple. You're with me.'

He hears her say it – Cal's good like that – and already two of his team are ducking under the cordon and heading to the cliff's edge. They move fast; the rain is against them, the wind, the tide. Still, Georgie gives herself a moment to look over at the swings. To take it all in.

Dr Alexis Cosse, whom she knew, who was a part of their village, whom she's fairly sure Simon was in love with, is lying dead in Burrowhead playground. She nods at Trish and they walk closer. For a second the only sound is waves breaking.

His tanned face is soaked, but strangely perfect. Washed clean in the rain – not a speck of blood on it. Like he was lying down here to get a better view of the sky. Except for how his eyes are gone. It's pooled above his collarbone, though, the blood. His shirt is slashed where the knife went in and came out again. In and out five, perhaps six times. She doesn't know. Hasn't seen anything like this for years. She'd hoped never to again. There's a flap of what was the pale green fabric of his designer shirt – he always liked to be smartly dressed, took pride in it, though some people laughed about it behind his back. His shirt is stained dark brown now, drenched and torn, and his chest hair is thick and matted, showing in places through the shirt's ripped front. Matted with blood, of course. Sticky with it. Like the St Christopher around his neck on a slim gold chain. One of his arms is pointing straight up at the sky. His wrist is entangled in the triangle of metal links that attaches to the swing seat. Georgie follows the line of his arm up to the desperate clouds and to something lying beyond them. It feels to her like they're being watched. It is not a good feeling. There's a flock of geese flying in a jagged V, so high above the wind they're nothing but specks of grit. As the wind gusts, the swing curves around and the seat is forced almost vertical because of how it's attached to his body. There's the taste of ancient salt on her lips. The noise: a rising groan of wind as it hits the cliffs and is channelled into the village, and the screech of the swing's metal chains against its rusted bolts. Georgie doesn't want to look back at the eye sockets.

Cal stands. His team are preparing to move the body.

'What have we got?'

'A bloody storm that's making our job a nightmare.'

Georgie looks down at the streams of muddy water running across the brown rubber surface below the swings, the rain streaking across the frame, the sodden mess of Alexis's clothes. Grass and dirt beyond, heavy with puddles.

'Any chance of footprints?'

Cal snorts.

'Blood spatter? Tyre tracks?'

The car park is potholed tarmac and gravel, flooded.

'We're looking, Georgie. I did find this. Seems it had fallen out of his pocket.'

She takes what is being offered. Inside the evidence bag is a stylish black Moleskine day planner. It's lying open. The page is wet, but the writing is legible. She stares at it.

'He used to make house calls,' says Cal. 'As well as working out of his front room.' He grunts, could be clearing his throat, could be something else. A lot of the village folk took against the idea of a psychotherapist when he moved in. Georgie doesn't know why. He was just another kind of doctor, wasn't he, trying to help people. Though it was a PhD he had. He was very proud of it, too. He'd told her once that he was saving up for a proper office to work out of; he'd always had big plans.

'Probably used his phone for most stuff, like everyone else.'

She looks at him, hopeful, but he shakes his head.

'No sign of a phone. Still, you'll know who that is. Yesterday's appointment. Worth checking out.'

Monday. His last day. 11 a.m. Walter Mackie.

'Walt?' she says.

'Aye.'

'Well.'

'I know.'

'It's a start. Thanks, Cal.'

They both stare out at the waves for a second. It looks dark green today, that sea. Like it's infected. She doesn't know where the colour comes from. Maybe algae. Can algae grow in the sea, or does it need something stagnant?

Her hair in her eyes, pushed back a fraction too late, leaving a sting of salt.

'Well,' says Cal, 'I'll let yous know what we find.'

'Good. Thanks. And can we try to keep this quiet for now? Avoid the gossip. Last thing we need is meddling from—'

'Course. But you'll be calling in some help?'

She nods. Maybe they'll send someone from the city. She's reported it to headquarters already, had to leave a message, for crying out loud – though she's never got the impression any of them care what happens in Burrowhead. 'I've called some extra uniforms down for starters.'

They are lifting the body now. They've untangled his wrist from the swing chain. And something else. A shout goes up, a sudden rush of scrambling and Cal moves fast, stamps it underfoot to stop it from blowing away. A bit of paper, pushed under the body or fallen there. As he slips it quickly into a bag, she sees the words she was hoping not to see. *Go home*, it says. Nothing more. Her lack of surprise makes her throat ache.

'Fingerprints,' she says. 'Ink. Paper. Anything.'

Cal nods. She can see the flashing lights of the car from Crackenbridge making its way through the village. Not subtle. But at least they're here.

'Right, I'll check out Walt,' Georgie says. 'Then see what I can find at Dr Cosse's flat. Trish? You're with me. I want a door-to-door coordinated.'

'What, now?' Trish says.

'Yes, right now.' Georgie turns and strides past the horse and the donkey, rocking back and forth in the wind like the inane creatures they are. 'I don't know what's happening to the world,' she says. But her words are snatched by the wind, to be coated in salt and preserved for the apocalypse. Like jerky.

ABOUT TEN

Walt pulls his dressing gown close, like he's cold, but he can't be cold, not in this greenhouse.

'Will I open a window, Walt?' says Georgie.

He looks nervous, but that's Walt. You can see him sometimes, in the village square, sitting in the fountain. Legs hanging out the side – can't fit a whole man in there. Says he remembers when there was water in it, but that doesn't explain much to Georgie. He'd still be sitting in a fountain then, with his legs dangling out the side, only his bottom would be all wet. There's something about the memory, though. That fountain's always been empty, for as long as she's been here, at least. She doubts if it's plumbed in. But there is something good about the memory.

She pulls at the sash window, straining her back.

'You've not painted this shut, have you, Walt?'

His knee is jigging up and down. He's skinny as a scarecrow, Walt Mackie, old skin like sacking and freckled from head to toe. Trish is watching him. Stony, like she is sometimes. Georgie's a bit worried about her, truth be told – it's why she invited her along. She gives the window a final yank, feels the catch in her back, gives up and sits back down. Georgie and Trish on the sofa, Walt in his once-comfy armchair. It looks like something's been nibbling at it.

'So, Walt.'

'They've gotta stay shut, see,' he says. 'Got to keep everything locked and bolted, in case they come.'

'Who's coming, Walt?'

'Don't you understand?' he says, pleading eyes at Georgie, ignoring Trish. 'Don't you see?'

Georgie looks round the room, seven, eight, nine lights on, all different shapes and sizes. Ceiling and wall lights, floor standers and desk lamps. Every corner lit. And then there are the heaters, electric heaters, plugged into every socket. She didn't know he'd got this bad.

'The thing is, Walt, we were wondering where you were yesterday.'

'Yesterday?'

'That's right.'

There are plants everywhere. Spider plants and geraniums, dragon trees and cacti and aloe vera, succulents cascading from tables. Georgie looks for signs of dehydration, wilting in the heat, but they are all green and lush. Good leaves. He must spend a long time watering them. Caring for them.

'Yesterday was a bad day,' he says.

'Did you go out, Walt? See anyone?'

'They were hanging round by my fountain,' he says. 'The big gang of them. You've seen them, Georgie?'

'You mean the kids?'

'Not kids any more, that lot. No.'

'Were you heading somewhere other than the fountain?'

'I had to go all the way round, past the butchers. Don't feel safe when they're hanging round at the fountain.'

'They're not going to hurt you, Walt.'

Trish is staring at her. She's got one hand clasped around her wrist, tight.

'You went to the doctors, didn't you?' says Trish. Butting in, blunt and to the point. It's her way. 'Who did you see at the doctors?'

'Not the doctors, no. Went to see Alexis. He doesn't believe me, though, so not much point in going back.'

'You go to Dr Cosse every week, don't you?'

'Aye, most weeks. You know, most of the time. Depends. I'll not be going back though. Probably not, anyway. He doesn't believe me.'

'Doesn't believe what?'

'That they're coming.'

'Who?' says Trish, leaning forward now, her gaze fixed on Walter.

'Them,' he says. 'Them.' Pointing up, up at the ceiling, up at the sky. His face breaks and he's looking at Georgie, looking and staring at her like she knows the answer, like he needs her to understand. 'They might come for you too, Georgie.' Whispered to her, like if he turns his back to Trish and keeps his voice down she won't be able to hear a word.

Trish hears though, of course she does.

'Please tell me this isn't about the Others again, Uncle Walt.'

Walt looks at Trish like he's never seen her before, like she's a total stranger to him and not his brother's grandchild, the closest thing he's got to family left in the village. But sometimes those closest to us are not the ones we need. Georgie knows that. Thirty years of police work have taught her that.

'There was this bright light, see,' Walt says, turning away from Trish by swivelling in his chair and reaching out to Georgie. 'It was all around, like I was looking up and there was this light surrounding me.'

'He was at the dentist,' Trish snaps.

'Trish,' says Georgie. 'Why don't you put the kettle on for us? I could do with a nice cup of tea.'

'Yeah,' says Trish. 'Yeah okay, you're right, Georgie. I'll get the biscuits. I put some custard creams in the cupboard the other day.'

'That's smashing. Thanks, Trish.'

So Trish leaves and clatters about in the kitchen, and Georgie and Walt are left alone in the heat with the succulents.

'Lights out to sea, too,' he says now, conspiratorial. 'Hovering low.'

'I see,' says Georgie. 'It could be the navy out there, though. Patrol boats, submarines. Helicopters, maybe.'

Walt sniffs, puts his finger to his lips.

Georgie can hear a noise. While she's waiting for him to speak, below the clicking of the central heating and below the tap filling the kettle, there's a noise from out in the hall, sort of a scurrying but lighter, more erratic. She's trying to place it, blocking out the other sounds of the old house and listening, leaning forward and listening. But after a minute, during which both of them stay perfectly still, Walt leans back and starts humming to himself.

She'd thought he was going to tell her something important, at least something that was important to him. Something he didn't want Trish to hear. But now it seems more like he's forgotten why she's here at all. She feels her phone vibrate in her pocket. Must be headquarters, calling to say they're sending a team over, some help. She'd not refuse some help.

'Georgie,' says Cal down the line. 'Couple bits of news for you.'

'Go on, Cal,' she says, moving to the hall and out of earshot.

'Two more entries in the day planner you'll want to be aware of. Firstly, we've got a Kevin Taylor.' Georgie recognises the name; can't picture a face. 'Three months back. Four sessions.'

'Okay, that's something.'

'More intriguing is an entry made in pencil, then rubbed out by the looks of it. Not too well though – easy enough to read. It's the initials N.P. Six weeks ago.'

'N.P.?'

'That's what it says. Someone's name, I guess—'

Georgie smiles. 'New patient,' she says. 'It could stand for new patient.'

Cal grunts. 'Should have thought of that one myself.'

'But it might not…'

'Well, other than that, diary's been empty for months except for a few sketches of trees. Not sure why he'd even bother carrying it around.'

'Right, thanks. What about time of death?'

'Body temp puts it about 9 p.m. After dark, but not so late as I was expecting – that early there'd have been a risk of someone walking by. It was stupid, is what I'm saying. Possibly unplanned.'

'Good. That's helpful. Thanks, Cal.'

'I'll call when I've got more.'

As Georgie walks back into the living room, Walt's head jolts upright as though he'd been asleep.

'Are you round for tea?' he says.

'Not really. Look, Walt,' Georgie tries again, 'we need to know if you saw anything unusual when you went to meet Dr Cosse yesterday.'

He looks at her, confused. It's heartbreaking to see old people looking so lost.

'Someone hurt him, Walt. Someone hurt Alexis. That's why we need to know. Did you see anything strange yesterday?'

He frowns as he's trying to remember.

'Them at the fountain,' he says.

'Anyone else?'

He shakes his head, but he's still frowning and she can tell there's something he knows. He just needs a minute to find it.

'What is it, Walt?'

'He looked very smart, is all. Even smarter than usual, like he'd made a special effort. Showed me his new cufflinks. Gold they were, these little gold clovers. Meant to be lucky, them.'

'Did he need extra luck for something yesterday?'

'Oh no, he'd already had the luck, see. He'd got his citizenship – came through that morning, he said. I figured he'd be off to celebrate. Smash some plates and whatnot. But he didn't understand.'

Georgie leans forward. 'Didn't understand what?'

'That they're coming for me.'

'The Others?'

'Aye, Georgie. Aye. Coming to take me away again.'

His dressing gown is clasped too tight around him now, his knuckles white with holding it and Georgie knows he believes it, with everything he is.

'Again?'

'Like last year, you know? When I went missing? But of course they're going to come back. Not going to leave me here, are they? Are they?'

'It's okay, Walt. You've been very helpful.'

'Have I?' His eyes hopeful now as Trish arrives back with the tea.

'Yes, Walt. Yes.'

'Have a custard cream,' Trish sighs. 'There now. You like a custard cream.'

Georgie sips her tea and it reaches half past ten and they all listen to the striking of the cuckoo clock as the pendulum swings and the cuckoo grinds out of its house – just once, and the mechanism is old, you can hear the cogs turning – then retreats back inside.

'What about when you left?' Georgie says.

'Left where?'

'Dr Cosse's office. Yesterday, Walt.'

He looks down and notices the biscuit crumbs caught in his dressing gown, in the dip of fabric above his stomach. He moves to brush them away then thinks better of it, collects them on his index finger and pops them into his mouth. His hand is shaking.

'Remember yesterday?'

'Yesterday?'

'After you left Alexis. Did you see anything then, anyone on the street, anything outside?'

He closes his eyes, and Georgie isn't sure at first whether he is thinking or has fallen asleep. But then he speaks, still with his eyes closed.

'Butchers was closed for lunch. Sign on the door, back at two. A bicycle chained to the lamp post over the street. Alexis's car parked in front of the Spar. No one in the Spar but Pamali. She

22

waved. I like Pamali. I walked home the long way, avoiding the fountain. Nothing else.' He opens his eyes. 'Nothing else,' he says again.

'That's really good, Walt,' says Georgie. 'Thank you.'

He's looking down at his chest again, shaking his head, seeing more crumbs.

'Really,' she says, standing up and going to kneel by his chair. She takes his hand and he looks in her eyes. 'Thank you, Walt.'

'Is he dead?' Walt says.

'Yes, Walt,' says Georgie. 'I'm afraid he's dead.'

Walt shakes his head, shakes it like it's too heavy for his neck to keep on holding it up. 'This place,' he says. 'There's evil in the ground here, Georgie. Down in the soil.'

For a second – only a second, mind – Georgie thinks it's true, feels it so close she could touch.

But all the villagers are used to death, in a way. Georgie too. It's a part of living in the country, accepting death. And there's an ageing population here, no doubts about that – often enough people die at home, in Burrowhead. This murder, though, it's a new kind of darkness. Georgie shakes her head, same as Walt. She's not equipped for this. Not any more. Doesn't want to fall back into it.

'Should we get going?' Trish says. Then, under her breath, 'He'll be needing his nap after that.'

Georgie stands and says thanks to Walt again and checks her phone but there's nothing – no reply from headquarters, no word from the city. She has this sudden feeling like she's all on her own, like no one is coming to help.

'I'm sorry,' Trish says once they're back out on the street. 'He's lost in his own world.' She says it like she's angry with him for having such a bad sense of direction.

'But we passed the Spar on the way here,' says Georgie.

'Well, he can just about make it to the Spar on a good day.'

'No, I mean... Dr Cosse's surgery is above the Spar.'

'His surgery was his front room, Georgie, in his *flat* above the Spar. And he wasn't a real doctor.'

'I know that. But there was no car parked outside, was there? So where did he drive to, in his smart suit with his gold cufflinks – that he wasn't wearing when we found the body – sometime after noon yesterday? After he got his good news and refused to believe your Uncle Walt about the Others, where did he go?'

TWO HUNDRED AND FIFTY YEARS
AFTER THE VILLAGE MISFORTUNE

The village of Burrowhead has three roads, and a number of inadequately paved side streets. The three roads are called High Street, Main Street and Church Street. They form a triangle of sorts, a little lopsided as it is, that encloses the village square, which is not really a square at all.

In the village square there is a fountain with no water. Grass covers the ground from the edge of the fountain to the kerbs of the three roads, though whether it was originally planted to be a sort of small village green or if it has grown up over the years, as weeds tend to do, is unclear. Beyond the corners of the triangle each road continues for a while and then ends in a different way.

Main Street turns gradually from a maintained road with central road markings to a potholed track as the houses along it become further apart with noticeably fewer roses in the metre strip of front garden assigned to each. After a while there is a gate, which is always open, followed by a cattle grid, beyond which the track is made of mud and gravel. You are now on the land of Ricky Barr, farmer, widow, and father to seventeen-year-old Andy, work shadowing at Burrowhead police station.

Church Street leads out of the village for half a mile and straight to the church, which is not a functioning church but a ruin, abandoned by its congregation, who moved to the larger church five miles away in Warphill at some point in the late-eighteenth century. It is thought there was a scandal, something to do with a minister and a boy, or perhaps a girl, or something to do with an abandoned baby or something maybe to do with a slave. The villagers tend not to tell the story, truth be told, but parents will give snippets to the children to keep them quiet or, more likely, to keep them away from the church with the threat of a haunting – twenty-five years ago a bit of the roof fell in and crushed a sheep that had been loitering there to chew the grass. It had to be shot later, to put it out of its misery. The ruined church, along with the rusting playground, is considered a danger to the children of Burrowhead. The children of Burrowhead are not afraid of the ruined church, or of the rusting playground.

Then there's High Street, where Georgie and Trish are currently standing outside the Spar and looking at an empty parking space – in fact an entirely empty road. There are no cars parked on this stretch that leads from the butchers on the far corner up past the Spar and Dr Cosse's flat and on to the village square with its fountain. But if they were to turn around and follow the street back past the butchers, past the lane Walt must have used to avoid the village square, and out of the village altogether, then they would find themselves where they started this morning, at the village playground. More specifically, the road leads into a car park next to the playground that could probably fit twelve cars at least, though Georgie has never seen it with more than half that number, and usually there are none at all. And that is the end of High Street: a car park next to a rusty playground at the top of Burrowhead cliffs, facing out over the froth-marked pebble beach to the sickly green sea.

Coincidentally enough, the playground was built the same year Georgie and Fergus arrived in Burrowhead, which is to say that all three have become familiar fixtures of the village but are not quite from the village either. In fact, no one really knows where Georgie is from at all. No one in the village can quite place her accent – there's a bit of Scottish in there, for sure, so maybe she spent time north of the border, but it's mingled with something from the Deep

South of the United States, they think. Bobby the taxi driver suspects she's lived in Australia, which she hasn't, though what he actually said was that there looks to be a bit of the Aboriginal in her. No one felt the need to comment. And they say maybe she's the daughter of diplomats; maybe she's spent time in Singapore, maybe she has relatives in Africa. She's not from here though, that much they know. Brown-skinned. Tight dark curls. But originally? Well, where Georgie became Georgie is a mystery no one has been able to solve. A bit like why she married Fergus. Big Fergus with his pointless projects and his collecting of other people's junk, Fergus who's Scottish as the day is long and ginger to boot. But marry him she did, for her own good reasons, and Fergus, meanwhile, has followed Church Street beyond the church, at which point it becomes simply the B8629 and leads up to Burrowhead Cross, where there is a crossroads beside a hillock on which he is standing.

He's been upset all morning, unbalanced and sick. Such an awful thing with Dr Cosse – and right here in the village. He can hardly believe it, though the moments when it seems untrue are quickly replaced by nausea as he remembers Georgie's face when she told him. He spent a while thinking about what he could do to help, but he didn't really think there was anything he could do, so he pulled himself together and got on his bike and now here he is.

He's wearing his Lycra outfit, bought when the cycle shop in Crackenbridge closed down and got rid of all their kit. CLOSING-DOWN SALE AT POUND-SHOP PRICES, the sign said, before they locked the doors for good and dumped what they couldn't sell in the old quarry. It annoys Fergus, the way people dump things in the old quarry. What a pointless thing to do. To litter. He doesn't understand the urge at all. It's not as though the old quarry is convenient – people must actually travel there in order to dump what they don't want into the greyed-out dip in the hill where they used to dig for limestone. Now he goes there to dig through the possibilities that other people have discarded. Once, a few weeks back, he saw Farmer

Barr dumping a deep chest freezer in there with the digger bit of his tractor. He saw Fergus watching him do it, but didn't seem to care. There's an anger about the village these days that Fergus doesn't understand either – the anger and the littering. They don't make any sense to him. But, to go back to the closure of the cycle shop in Crackenbridge, Fergus bought all the cycling outfits he could ever need in that sale and then some. He just didn't like the idea of it all going to waste.

It is Fergus's deepest fear that his life will be a waste, though he's never told anyone so, not even Georgie. She'd only worry about him, and she's too protective as it is – something to do with how he reminds her of her brother. But how do you know what bits of a life are worthwhile and what bits are wasteful while you're in the middle of it all? It's not so easy as taking your litter home with you. Though, when he thinks about it, taking your litter home with you seems like a good way to start.

From where he stands on high, he can see both the village of Burrowhead to the south and the larger neighbouring village of Warphill to the north. That's where the congregation from the old church moved, back in the late-eighteenth century. On the road to Warphill, not far out of Burrowhead, is a derelict block of flats, council housing scheduled for demolition twenty years ago. It was a mad place to build a block of flats in the first place – he was an engineer once, he could have told them that. The village of Warphill is a place Fergus rarely goes to, or rather, it's a place no one really goes to, unless they have relatives there or friends they particularly want to visit. Unlike Burrowhead, it doesn't have a semi-famous beach, and so it doesn't have a tourist season to speak of. It does, however, have a standing stone that seems to suggest a line to the coast, passing through the woods with their half-buried stone of the cup and ring, and ending with the cliffs near Burrowhead playground. He wishes he could get higher up; imagines himself soaring over the fields and dense hedgerows, the glassy twists of the river, to approach the standing stone from above, feel it rising from the land, connecting him to the ancient rock bed below the surface. In fact, a series of photos and a map would make a good introduction to his new archaeological society on the homepage of his website. So many people have lived and died here, over so many thousands of years. He finds that strangely comforting.

NOT YET NOON

Georgie pushes the door next to the Spar on High Street and it opens, easily, and without a sound. The hinges must be well oiled. She leads the way, with Trish following close behind, up the dark staircase – there are no windows and the door has swung shut behind them; the lower of the hall lights seems to need a new bulb – until she is standing in front of another door, this one painted a pleasing sky blue, which does not open when she pushes it. The nameplate on the door is brass and polished and it says DR ALEXIS COSSE, PSYCHOTHERAPIST. God, it's no wonder folk didn't like him, round here. Most of them farming, or retired, or working in whatever shop can stay open long enough to take on staff for the season. Crackenbridge has more boarded-up shopfronts these days than Burrowhead has sheep, and Warphill is ... well, no one really goes to Warphill, unless they're from Warphill and haven't yet found a way to get out. But Alexis was proud of what he did, and Georgie liked that about him. A wave of loss hits her, more real standing here than it was when she was looking at the body.

She kneels in front of the door and checks under the mat for a spare key.

'No such luck,' she says to Trish.

Then she checks the mat for signs of mud or visitors or disturbance, but she sees nothing out of the ordinary. It is just a doormat. WELCOME, it says. She shakes her head, and briefly places her hand on the mat. It prickles. It is coarse.

Standing, she looks next for a flowerpot – almost everyone in the village keeps their spare key under a mat or a flowerpot. It's such a safe place to live, they say, when visitors are surprised. And true enough, there are very few break-ins here, very few burglaries. Though that's not the only type of crime, Georgie knows, and it would be a foolish villager to rob his own neighbours in a place so small as this. She finds herself leaning against the banister, staring down towards the dark of the ground floor, trying to catch the tail end of a thought, when a person-sized thump echoes through the enclosed hallway.

Trish, it seems, is ramming the door with her bottom. Having failed to break through the first time, she's stepping back now, checking the height of the lock against her body. Taking aim. This time her hip smashes against the door, to the sound of wood splintering and a creak of hinges. Quite a thud she makes, for someone so small.

'I'll call a locksmith,' Georgie is trying to say, but she doesn't try very hard, because this might be exactly what Trish needs just now. There has been something going on with her for a few months now, maybe more, maybe it's been building slowly for a year or two. Georgie wonders if she should have said something before, but it's not really her way; Georgie tends to wait for people to ask for help before offering it. Besides, she thinks Trish doesn't like her very much. They have a different approach, a different temperament. If Trish wanted help, Georgie is fairly sure she wouldn't be asking for it from her.

Still, that's got to hurt, on the hip bone like that. That's going to bruise. And Georgie knows, though she would never comment on it, that Trish doesn't have anyone at home to run her a hot bath, to help with that later. Georgie moves fast, once she's made up her mind to do it, and stands in front of the door before Trish can ram into it again.

'It's okay,' she says – though it does look a bit like Trish might ram the door through Georgie, if it came to that. 'I think you've done enough,' she says. 'That was really good.' She smiles and Trish relaxes a little, breathes back into herself. 'I'm impressed.'

'Was nothing,' says Trish, with a shrug, but one she looks kind of pleased about.

Georgie turns, waits for Trish to come and stand next to her, and then she tries the handle again.

This time, the door swings open. It is splintered all down the inside; the lock no longer reaches the mechanism. It sort of hangs there, lopsided on its hinges.

'We're in,' says Trish.

Georgie hangs back and lets Trish stride her way in first. She admires her, actually, the way she can be so forceful about things. Georgie doesn't tend to be so forceful. Georgie would have patiently waited for the locksmith. She's not sure, when she thinks about that, whether it's a fault or a virtue. And Trish is petite, that's the funny thing. Pale as can be and that spiky hair, fringe down to her eyebrows, nails neatly filed. Georgie glances down at her own big hands, pulls on a pair of latex examination gloves. Passes another pair to Trish.

'The thing is,' Trish is saying, 'I knew something bad was coming. Something terrible. Didn't you? Georgie?' She's standing round the other side of the desk now, repeatedly pressing the power button of the computer to see if it will start up. 'Of course you did,' she says. 'Even *you* must have seen it. Been building for years. Or maybe it's always been here.'

A pause while a circle spins on the computer's grey screen.

Georgie has noticed certain things, actually. She notices a lot of things, and there has been a sort of bubbling, recently, like people are starting to reach the boil. Though there have always been the comments. Then there was the day when Fergus unplugged the radio from the socket in their bedroom and moved it out to the garage, where it now lives untouched. No more the days of listening to the news together of a morning. Now they have the birds. He says he likes it better, with the birds. They have such an extraordinary variety of song.

'You heard about that boy, down south, that foreign boy they hung from a tree?'

At the mention of it Georgie feels her insides twist. There are no words for it, for the awfulness of it. She doesn't know what it would have done to her, if she'd been running the case.

'Animals,' Trish says, her voice low, cutting. 'Fucking animals.'

But it's people who did it, thinks Georgie. That's the awful thing; it was human beings who did it.

While Trish continues furiously jabbing at the keyboard, Georgie walks round to the small filing cabinet behind the sofa. She stands still for a minute, waits for the sting in her eyes to die down some. The sofa is where his patients would have sat. Above it, there are three different pictures of trees – a pencil sketch, a watercolour and an oil painting. The oil is all silvers and dark olive greens, abstract lines with the unmistakable sheen of frost and moonlight. It's the watercolour she's pulled to, though, a softer palate, springtime perhaps, and there's something about it she recognises. Then she sees the name. It's one of Pamali's. It's lovely, delicate, warm. Alexis was into art, she'd seen him out sketching sometimes. The pencil drawing could even be his – there's no name on that one. She steps back, glances over at the door that, presumably, leads to the bedroom. She's never even been in here before. He was private, in a way, tended not to invite folk round for tea. But then he would have needed to keep patient confidentiality, wouldn't he, and what with his office being right here in the front room, well, maybe other visitors weren't a good idea. With that thought comes the knowledge that this is his whole home; that she will be going through his whole home.

'Such an awful thing,' she says. 'I don't understand it.'

Though she's not sure herself if she's talking about the boy, or Dr Cosse, or all of it. The whole mess of things.

She leaves the cabinet for a second and walks over to the door, gives it a gentle push. The mood through there is completely different, richer somehow – the front room is for his clients, clearly, but the bedroom is his own. Pristine white sheets cover the bed, topped with a quilt of embroidered velvet, deep red and blue and gold, the luxurious colours reflecting a tiny gold icon hanging on the far wall. There are photos too, on the chest of drawers: an old woman with a creased, tanned face, dressed head to toe in black, his grandmother perhaps; Alexis and Simon together, their faces close to the lens, a white blur of sky and coastline behind them. Simon's laughing, holding the camera, looking straight at it but Alexis isn't – Alexis is staring at Simon, his expression serious and genuine and vulnerable and Georgie backs quietly out of the bedroom and kneels down behind the sofa, closes her eyes, gives herself a moment before getting back to work.

The filing cabinet opens as soon as she pulls a drawer – it isn't locked or anything. But she was expecting notes in the cabinet drawers, records of his therapy sessions, contact details for his patients, that kind of thing. That's not what it is, though, not at all – it's his household filing. Electricity bills. Council tax. She tries the next drawer down. Bank statements. They'll have to go through all that, of course. Might be something in there. She pulls out her phone and texts Cal to send someone over. *Right away*, he replies immediately. But she'd assumed she would find something else. Not personal finances or the change of an energy supply company.

'Got it.'

Trish's voice is hard as concrete, and Georgie closes her eyes. She knows, somehow, that it's going to be bigger than the death of one man. Something harder to comprehend, harder to defeat.

'Fucking. Animals.' That's what Trish says.

Georgie looks at the note Trish is pointing out to her, lying in the open drawer of his desk. Scans the words with an increasing feeling of dread. *FOREIGN SCUM.* Just two words, just like the note

34

under the body. Capital letters. Blue ink. It's not even personal; it's
so impersonal it almost doesn't seem real. Like a cliché of a racial
threat. Except the stab wounds, they weren't random. They were
deliberate. They seemed personal. That's how they looked to
Georgie: close up and personal. Something moves between her
fingers, sticky, wet, the slip of blood; a memory so vivid it knocks
the air out of her lungs. She looks down – there's nothing there.
Takes a deep breath and gives herself a second to focus. For years
she used to reach for Fergus's hand when that happened, the solid
warmth of him enough to bring her back to the present. Today all
she's got is her own gloved hand resting on the edge of Alexis's desk,
and beneath it a small pad of Post-it notes lying next to the computer's keyboard. With writing on the top one: *Kingfisher 8 p.m.*

'He had a dinner reservation,' she says. 'That's a restaurant, isn't
it? The Kingfisher, up at Crackenbridge?'

Trish looks at her.

'I know,' Georgie says. 'I know. It looks like a hate crime.'

'I can write you a list of all the people in this village—'

'We don't need a list, Trish.'

'Let's start with Ricky Barr then.'

'Got no reason to that I can see.'

'Well, he's a fucking racist. And he beats Andy often enough, too.'
Georgie looks up at her then. 'I didn't know that,' she says.

'Everyone else knows,' says Trish. 'Does nothing about it. That's
why I offered to help him. I thought...'

It was Trish's idea to let him do his work experience at the station.
Georgie had been reluctant. She'd only agreed because things were
quiet, figured he could clean the place a bit, wash the windows –
God knows the station could do with it – maybe help prepare their
community stall for the spring fair on Saturday. Though things have
changed now. She'll phone, tell him not to come in today. Maybe
cancel the whole week. The school won't blame him for that, surely.

'Was Andy seeing Dr Cosse? Is that the connection?'

Trish thinks for a minute, and Georgie isn't sure whether she's trying to remember the truth or trying to formulate a lie. Luckily Trish isn't a very good liar, and she knows it; she opts for the truth.

'I don't think so,' she says.

'There was no mention of Andy, or any of the Barrs, in his day planner.'

'Did you see the advert he put up last year, for summer workers? British only?'

Georgie takes a deep breath, the way she's learned to over the years. 'It was unpleasant, that. And he was warned. But we follow the evidence here. It's all we can do.'

'Fingerprints. Ink. Paper,' Trish says, reusing Georgie's words from earlier that morning. 'I'll call forensics.'

'They're already on their way. I think we've got a lead to follow.'

'You'll not find anything at the Kingfisher.'

'No harm in giving them a call.'

She's got her phone out already, Georgie, she can move fast when she wants to and she has this feeling that there's something to find, in the Kingfisher. Could be Trish's certainty that there's not, could be something else. Maybe it's an easier route to take, a way to avoid the nastiness – that's what Trish thinks of her. Perhaps that's what they all think of her. Is that what she's become, to survive? A coward? She doubts herself for a second, then makes the call.

Trish watches her as she's talking on the phone. As she asks about the reservation last night in Dr Cosse's name. As she listens to the reply that comes a bit at a time, that yes there was a reservation, for two, at 8 p.m., and no, it looks like he never arrived. She's quite glad Trish can't hear the other side of the conversation; she's careful not to repeat the information she's being told. She just listens, with that same feeling of dread, as they call over a waiter who was on last night, as he describes the man waiting at the table for someone who never showed up, waited for a full hour, tapping away into his phone all the time. He says they didn't get his name, since he hadn't booked the table, but yes, he looked distinctive enough. Blond hair. Piercing blue eyes. Upset he was, when he left, the waiter says, knocked the chair right over as he grabbed his jacket from the back of it. Looked like he was ready to do someone an injury.

'Thank you,' says Georgie. 'You've been really helpful. Thank you.'

'It can't have been him,' says Trish, quietly, once Georgie's hung up the phone. 'I mean, whatever happened between them at the Kingfisher, it can't have anything to do with the murder. This note, this is racism...'

Georgie lets her get to where she knows she's going.

'It wasn't Simon,' Trish says. 'He'd never hurt anyone.'

'But you do know it was Simon who Alexis was supposed to meet at the Kingfisher?'

Trish nods. She looks worried. In fact, unusually for Trish, she looks like she could be hurt. 'But he didn't kill Alexis. He's not capable of that.'

'They never are,' Georgie replies.

GONE ONE

When Simon left Burrowhead playground that morning, he hadn't walked back to the police station as he'd told Georgie he would. She and Trish were working the case anyway, which meant he'd have been as alone at the station as he would have been at home. Something about being inside and alone – he can't handle that today. Needs to be out in the storm, closer to the brutality of it. He'd turned off High Street once he was out of view, cut down past the old community shed and looped back to the coast further out of the village. The sea was calling him. Maybe that was it. Or the rain wasn't enough inland, he needed the force of the wind, the scream of waves hitting stone. He'd scrambled over the rocks, boulder-sized and slimy with seaweed on that strip of coast, scraped his hands on the barnacles when he fell. And he did fall, more than once – was glad of it, too. Some bit of him needed to feel the pain. He didn't care that stale water had seeped through his shoes and soaked his socks, didn't care how the wind was making his ears throb, his face burn with the sting of salt rough as sandpaper. He slipped and ran and forced his way to the tideline, where the rocks gave way to shards of shells and the grit of sand, and he fell to his knees in the freezing cold and he stared down at the brownish grey froth of the waves. He didn't even know he was doing it, when he let out a cry. It came from somewhere down past his lungs, somewhere nearer his stomach; a shout that wrenched something out of him – that belonged to the crashing sea and the jagged cliffs, and to the cave hidden somewhere within them. He didn't know it was behind him. Couldn't see it when he turned, so he didn't know he was being watched. He thought he was alone and it was a desperate, pleading noise he made, and he stayed there, kneeling on sharp stones in the waves, letting his body retch until there was nothing more to come out. When he finally stood up again the cliff's edge was impenetrable and his expression closed. It's still that way now as he trudges back to the police station with the cold moving past his wrists, past his elbows and curling in around his chest. He keeps walking only because the world has disintegrated into the movement of parts and the basic functioning of the human body. He thinks about a breath, and he breathes. If he didn't think about it, he wonders if it would happen. Standing still doesn't seem like an option, so he lifts a foot and places it ahead of his body, then shifts his weight. Repeats it again, on the other side. And again.

He's been sick that many times there's nothing left in his stomach. He retches again, brings up nothing but a string of yellowish fluid. He leans over with the cramp of it though, notices for the first time that his trousers are wet. A dark stain around the knees where he knelt on the beach. A bit of seaweed stuck to the fabric. Brown and bulbous. He watches nothing but the ground, thinks of nothing but each footstep. But the shame, that clings. He'd been so angry.

Georgie has probably worked it out by now. He hadn't meant to hide anything, just couldn't find the words earlier. Up half the night, pacing back and forth along High Street, then at home, lying awake and playing it over, the possibilities of what went wrong. The sick feeling of jealousy, lodged in his belly. And the noise in his ears, wailing like a siren that won't stop.

He stares at the ground and tries to think about the last time he saw Alexis.

No, not the last time. Not there at the playground, when everything was too late and broken. The last time they spoke.

Alexis was nervous.

He wasn't normally like that. So well put together and precise, the way he held himself you'd never think he could be nervous underneath it all. Underneath those perfectly pressed shirts. Simon used to take the piss out of him for those. It became a thing they did. Not a joke, exactly, though it amused him to exaggerate his role every time, it was just that Alexis got smarter and smarter, with his cufflinks and his straight ties and the hanky he used to fold into his top jacket pocket, an equilateral triangle of coloured fabric. And Simon would turn up in a creased black T-shirt and jeans, hands rough from being out all day. Police work, he'd say, voice fake-gruff as he kicked off large muddy shoes. But that last time, Alexis didn't have his suit jacket on at all.

He'd taken all the exams already, for the citizenship, sent them all the documentation they asked for. Filled the forms out perfectly. They were spotless, even though they were filled in while raging. Simon had seen them, he could confirm everything – every *i* dotted and that. And somehow, stupidly it seemed now, blindly, Simon had always thought everything would be okay. They'd joke about what they'd do, fight the bastards in court, make a campaign out of it; they'd share their anger over dinner. But underneath, Simon always thought they couldn't *not* give Alexis his citizenship. The last couple of years there had been stories in the papers about deportations, but no one from around here, no one Simon knew. It didn't seem like it could be real. It didn't seem like a thing that could actually happen.

But then Alexis got called for the interview.

It was a last chance. They both knew that; you got your citizenship or you got called for the interview, and after that, usually, you were gone. It was happening to them. It was insult and threat and exam all rolled up into one. Talk of fighting the bastards in court didn't seem to cut it any more, so instead they got pissed.

He'd always thought it was great, the way Alexis got drunk. Simon was basically the same sober or drunk, and it took a lot of beer to have any effect at all. Just a gift he was born with. Simon was tall and broad and he had the nickname Simon the Viking at school. He'd been proud of that. He rowed. He climbed. Of course he could take his drink. But Alexis completely transformed. After the first few sips he'd lean back and loosen his tie, grinning like anything could happen, and his eyes got that sparkle of amusement at everything he saw, as though once his professional persona was dropped (and he didn't drop it easily, he kept it up day and night, everyone found him so sure and so serious) he couldn't keep the laughter in. Simon would see him like that and feel this sudden need to mess up his hair, rip open his shirt, grab him inside all those ironed clothes; he can feel the ache of it in his mouth now, how much he wanted him. Not that night, though. That night was different.

Screw it, Simon had said. Screw them. I want to go to Greece.

And he'd meant it too – of course he'd go to Greece. What's not to like about Greece? True, he'd never actually been, but he could imagine it, the sun and the sea and the tavernas and that.

No, Alexis had said, closing his eyes against it. Don't be stupid.

Simon had gone sullen then.

That's not what it's like, Alexis went on. That can't be our life. You'd hate it.

How do you know?

I'd hate it.

Why the fuck would he want to stay here though? That's what Simon couldn't figure out. And he was suddenly furious about it all, about the interview and the forms and those fucking boats patrolling all the time, couldn't even look out to sea these days without spotting them, slug-like, on the horizon. There was so much here to get away from, why not leave? And it wasn't for him, wasn't for Simon that Alexis was staying, because Simon had already offered to leave with him. It must have been something else keeping him here. What was it? Who was it?

He closes his eyes tight against it all, wraps his arms around his body and imagines it's Alexis he's holding on to. But Alexis is gone and he's nearly at the police station and suddenly it's like he doesn't remember how to move. He just stands there as a pair of blackbirds squabble over by the fence, as Bobby drives past in his cab, as the water collects in the corners of his eyes and runs down his face. He stands there and waits for someone to see him. He thinks about his breathing. He thinks about Alexis. He remembers kneeling on the rocks by the sea. He remembers Georgie's gloved hand touching his. He thinks about falling to his knees again, and then someone is tapping on his elbow.

'Excuse me,' the voice says.

He turns.

It's Pamali. From the Spar. He looks at her like he's searching through fog, like she's someone from another life.

'I've got to report a crime,' she says.

He stares at her.

'Is there something wrong with you?' she says.

He doesn't know what to say. He swallows.

'What is it?' he manages.

The sound of his own voice wakes him up.

'I've decided, I'm not having this any more,' she says.

He blinks. He becomes aware of the rain on his face, of the wind streaming off the coast.

'I've been keeping a record, and now I'm reporting the lot. Come on!'

Pamali strides towards the front door of the police station, and finally Simon remembers how to move.

LOW TIDE

I need to understand where I am. Get to know this cave. I have walked the beach all my life and never found it before. Can't stay here, cowering by the entrance, staring out at the sea. Below the wind there is almost a whisper. Can you hear it? Must be the wind through the rocks. Hairline cracks, for it's not so stale, at least not here at the front. The wind is finding its way in. The voices.

I take a step back without turning and feel for a foothold, for somewhere safe to stand. The floor is not pebbled, not in here. It is a flat sheet of rock with shallow dips and troughs like footprints. I take another step back, deeper into the cave, but in the distance something catches my eye, deep green and bundled, near the dark stretch of wet rocks where the sea is edging forwards. Lapping. It's not supposed to be there. But the water is going to take it. When I look again it will be gone. That's the way looking works, sometimes.

There were people down on the beach today, despite the storm. Police, I think, walking with deliberate steps, watching the ground as though they'd be able to find anything between those rocks. They stared at the water's edge – it must have been a search. Whatever is down there, though, they didn't find it. Perhaps it was hidden from them. On my next step back my left palm touches rock, cold, a slimy feel to it. The air gets closer around me, like a response. I turn.

It is different, facing inwards. No more sea. No more horizon. Just rock, deep brown and veined with shadow, fitting tightly around me. My eyes move slowly from the floor to the crossed twigs tied

43

with red ribbons, balanced on every ledge. Why have people done it? The shadows intensify and I take another step and see a white stag gouged into stone, bright against the grey. My hand moves up of its own accord, following the curves as the cave draws me deeper. I pass a rusted metal figure, its limbs awkward and broken in places like snapped bones, its hands tapering to sharp points. The floor slopes down and I'm pulled further and there it is: a tiny, decaying doll wrapped in cling film. She must be suffocating. A worry doll. I remember them from when I was little. Whisper your worries to the worry doll before you sleep.

The smell back here is the smell of something rotten, worse than the blood on my clothes. The walls narrow as they rise, close in against the air, and the height of them crushes my chest as my eyes strain to see through the dark. Then something shifts and there are shapes pulsing in the rock. I try to turn. I can't. My legs are paralysed. A scratch against my skin. I'd scream if I could but my voice catches in my throat. I stumble back and the shapes follow me, stretching high above me and I fall, my ankle twisting, my arms grabbing on to nothing and above me there's only the height and the stone as my head smashes onto the floor.

13:25

Wet footprints lead into the police station. Georgie quietly looks around, walks in slowly, takes her time. There's been nothing from the door-to-door but folk are asking questions, trying to push their way in. She can hear voices down the hall.

Burrowhead police station is the size of a small bungalow, with its front room a reception area in desperate need of a fresh coat of paint and its kitchen equipped for the staff with a cheap plastic kettle, a second-hand fridge, a square wooden table and four out-of-place dining-room chairs. There are two single bedroom-sized offices, one used by Georgie and the other shared by Simon and Trish, a small interview room opposite and a cell at the back with a low bench and a basin in the corner. The box room beside it currently houses a mop, disinfectant spray, broken furniture and some old, damp toilet roll but could be used as a second makeshift cell if such a thing were ever required – though it's been years since anyone was locked in it. Cal and the forensics team are based up at Crackenbridge, where they have a modern open-plan office for their half-dozen staff, a small but reasonably well-equipped lab and a mortuary. That's where Dr Cosse will be now. But Georgie and the Burrowhead police are left to work here, in a station that hasn't had funding for replacement light panels let alone computers for years, and the worst of it is that Georgie's afraid to ask for the money. Some part of her thinks they're only still running because everyone else has forgotten about them.

Down the corridor, towards the back office with the two desks, following the voices and the wet footprints glistening in the harsh fluorescent light, the door to the office is open. Inside, Georgie sees her friend Pamali sitting on the swivel chair and Simon beside her on his own, lower chair, leaning forwards like he's trying to offer comfort. A mug of tea is on the desk.

'What's happened?' she asks, something familiar twisting in her stomach. 'What's happened now?'

Simon stands up, offers Georgie his seat.

'I'll get another from the kitchen,' he says, pausing, turning back. 'The Spar's been attacked.'

Georgie sits on the seat, falls into the same pose as Simon had a few seconds before and reaches for her hand but Pamali pulls away, her back rigid.

'What's happened, Pami?'

'It's not so bad as he says.' Pamali smiles, though it's a little forced. 'They've been at it for a few months now.'

'Who?'

Pamali shrugs. She looks restless, impatient maybe; Georgie wonders what she's feeling underneath. She thinks about Trish, back at Dr Cosse's office with the forensics team. About Dr Cosse lying under the swings this morning. And now this.

'Tell me what's been happening.'

Pamali nods. 'I thought it would go away at first. I thought if I ignored it...' Reaching into her bag, which is on the floor by her feet, she pulls out a notebook.

'Look. I've been keeping a record,' she says. 'For the past few months. It's little things, mostly. But...'

Georgie looks down at the notebook with a feeling of dread.

'Oh, Pami,' she says.

She almost doesn't want to open it. Her hands run over the home-made tie-dye cover, swirls of yellow and orange, with a pale green ribbon as a page marker. It's lovely. She glances up at Pamali then

46

opens the notebook. Each page has a date and a time, followed by a description of the incident. It starts last November.

'That wasn't the beginning,' says Pamali. 'Just when I thought to start keeping the record. There had been a few things before. Today was the second time, with the eggs. It's disgusting. I've had enough. I've decided...'

Georgie looks at the words. At the description.

Arrived at work 7.45 to open shop at 8 a.m. Raw eggs smashed against front window. Still runny. Cleaned windows with soapy water. Didn't see anyone on street. Bit of yolk visible on pavement, shell between the stones – nothing I could do about that. Opened late, 8.10 a.m. No one noticed.

'Oh, Pamali,' says Georgie. She has a slow way of speaking, Georgie, slower than most of the folk in the village. Her words have a weight to them, a slight twang that marks them out as something different. 'This is...' She shakes her head, like the way Walt Mackie shook his head earlier today. 'I'm so sorry, Pamali.'

Pamali is sitting tall.

'I'm fairly sure it wasn't you,' she says.

Simon carries in a chair from the kitchen, sits down opposite them. She glances at him then continues looking through the notebook. It's been regular, the harassment. Every few weeks something new. She must have been afraid, going into work of a morning, wondering what she would find. A green bag of dog poo pushed through the letter box. Drawing pins and chewing gum dropped in front of the door. Things that had been happening to her friend for months and Georgie had missed it all. She feels that surge again, in her belly, that nausea, but she pushes it down; she wants to do her job well. Georgie is someone who believes, deeply, in doing her job well. Best way to do that is by staying calm.

'Did you see who's been doing it, Pamali?' she says.

'I thought I saw someone running away once. They were wearing a hood. Fairly tall. Probably a man, but could have been a tall woman. Running like they knew how to run, you know? But I don't know who it was. Could have been anyone really.'

'And you cleaned it all up this morning?'

'There were raw eggs smashed on the window, of course I—'

Georgie reaches for her hand, and Pamali lets her take it at last.

'I'm just asking because of the evidence.'

'I know,' Pami whispers, and for a fleeting moment Georgie thinks she's going to cry. She doesn't, though. She pulls her hand away instead.

'I don't suppose you got a photo, on your phone or…?'

Pamali shakes her head, goes back to looking determined.

'I wanted it cleaned,' she says. 'I wanted…'

'It's okay.'

'I thought I could fix it myself,' she says, quieter now. 'I didn't want everyone knowing.'

It's not like her, though, Georgie knows that – Pami always smiles and waves at people from the shop, always has a friendly word, is always chatting to folk. She stands out, of course, same as Georgie herself. There have always been comments. But that's all it used to be, in Burrowhead at least. Wasn't it?

'Thank you, Pami,' she says. 'That's helpful, what you've remembered there.'

'Really?'

'Yes, really helpful.'

Pamali looks unconvinced and Georgie can't blame her. She decides to email the super, right after this. Follow up on the voicemails she's already left. Whatever it is that's going on, it feels bigger than her and too big for them to ignore.

'Well,' Pamali says, standing up suddenly. 'My lunch break's over. I'm going back to work.'

She looks around like she's forgotten something, then her eyes fall on the notebook and she looks away.

'Shop gets busy in the afternoons, with the schools out. They'll be wanting their cans of pop.'

'You can stay here a while,' says Georgie. 'Another cup of tea. Stay for a chat?'

Pamali shakes her head, already pulling on her coat. 'You've got everything written up in there.'

'Pami … we need an official statement. And we need to send someone round to check for any evidence. CCTV. See if we can't find out who's doing this.'

Pamali hesitates for a second. Georgie wants to give her a hug but something holds her back, something in the way Pamali's avoiding eye contact.

'They'll miss you, but those kids can live without you for one afternoon.' Georgie smiles.

'I want to keep going,' she says. 'I need to keep—'

'I know.'

'But it is happening, isn't it?'

Georgie nods.

'I'll make an official statement now then,' she says, straightening up again.

'Thanks, Pami. That'll really help us—'

'But the important thing is that I'm not frightened, Georgie,' she says. 'I want you to know that. I'm not frightened of them at all.'

SOME THINGS CAN LAST TEN
THOUSAND YEARS

Fergus feels pretty pleased with his photos as he looks over them on their home computer. He and Georgie, they share the computer now, seeing as how he sold his laptop last year so he could afford to upgrade his bike. Georgie would have given him the money, of course, but he didn't like to ask. Didn't like to raid the joint account – the cycling was *his* hobby, nothing to do with her and anyway, it's good to have a decent-sized screen. Fergus feels it's important to recognise a silver lining when you've got one. He's got plenty to be positive about. Though sometimes there are whispers in the village.

There was a group standing about on Church Street as he cycled home, right enough. He's not sure who they were. Collars high, dark scarves pulled up. They must have been cold. Fergus rarely feels the cold himself – in fact he's finding it quite clement today – but that group on Church Street, he could hardly see their faces at all. Just heard the laughter, low and bitter, when they saw him. Well, no matter, they moved on soon enough and Fergus continued through the village, stopping outside Walt's, who was watching the street from his armchair by the window. Good to see a friendly face. He waved, but Walt looked startled. Then overhead he saw what he suspected was the largest bird he'd ever seen, in the wild at least. He can picture it now, just can't identify it. He knows his birds quite well; he can tell a kite from an osprey, he's comfortable enough with buzzards. But whatever it was circling high over the village, it wasn't anything he could recognise. Then it swooped down viciously and disappeared above Church Street. Everyone was disappearing down Church Street today. But not Fergus; he rode home with his mind focused on the work ahead, made a quick cuppa, then uploaded his photos to the computer, where he is now studying them one by one. It's a shame he doesn't have a proper camera – a powerful zoom is what he needs – but what he's got is a smartphone and some software and a place like this to photograph.

You can see all the way up to Warphill in a couple of them. It looks small, grey and blocky, and on the southern edge there's the field with the single standing stone. He clicks on the oval icon and draws a ring around where the stone must be. Admittedly, he can't actually make out the stone itself, but he'll go there in person tomorrow, get some close-ups of the markings; get a sense of the size and shadow of it. The stories say the menhir was part of a series of ancient standing stones, leading to the site of a sacred henge. It kept the rains true, they say, kept the harvest full and the birds at bay. No one knows where the henge is though, or where it was. No one knows which way the menhir is supposed to point. To the south there's the cup and ring stone buried in the woods, and further on lies Burrowhead itself. To the north, there's Warphill and the road to Crackenbridge, the border – this is the photo he has. In the foreground there are the old council flats, which he thought would add a modern perspective, but actually, looking at it now, he decides to crop them out for the website. Warphill's got more atmosphere surrounded by soggy brown fields and the laden sky. It's a brooding place, there's no hiding that; might as well make the most of it.

To capture a proper bird's-eye view of the whole place, the standing stone leaving its deep shadow in amongst the lines of the land, the clearing of the cup and ring, the fractured curves of the coast, that'd be quite something. Like those pictures you see of crop circles, where up close they're nothing but trampled corn and then from high above: the eerie magic of vast shapes that seem to belong to the land even though they shouldn't.

He stops, leans his elbows on the desk and presses his fingers into his forehead. This headache he's had for weeks, he can't shift it. It's settled in deep behind the eyes. He's not sure how long he sits there for, time seems to change on him, but after a while – minutes, he hopes, not hours – he straightens his back and pulls himself together, opens his eyes wide and tells himself to get to work. It's worth doing. He says that out loud. Just 'cause he's not getting paid doesn't mean it's not a thing of value. A website like this might attract visitors to the villages, or archaeologists even. That'd be a thing, to get a fresh excavation going. Maybe the school will be interested. He could show kids around the sites. He'd be good with the kids.

His panoramic shot came out pretty well too: the sea and cliffs starting on the far left, thrashing greys melting into the soggy brown of earth before resolving into the blocks of Warphill, then the insistent streak of the road leading past the motte to Burrowhead, following the whole circle of the village to the splash of colour at the playground and finally joining the sea and cliffs again on the far right.

The Archaeological Society of Burrowhead and Warphill – that's the name. He types it in bold, dark green Copperplate Gothic. Then he tries to imagine it, back through wars and starvation, back to the standing of the stone and the people once buried in the Iron Age tomb inside the motte. It was surveyed, back in the 1980s. They even dug a trench on one side, found some Celtic artefacts. They're in the local museum in Crackenbridge – that's where he'll go in the morning, before visiting the standing stone. Though now he thinks of it, he's sure the menhir is older than anything they found. The layers of history around here, nothing stands alone; everything is laid on top of everything else. He alters the colour balance of his photo, increases the contrast to make it look more dramatic.

The villagers need something like this archaeological society to remind them of their shared history. There was such a sense of community when they first moved here, him and Georgie, the kind of community that went back through the generations, tying folk together. Now there's graffiti spreading across the closed shopfronts of Warphill, encroaching on the school walls and bus stops, edging closer to Burrowhead; now he gets angry glances from the men smoking outside the pub in the afternoons. But he doesn't want to think about that. Better to make plans instead. There's the spring fair this weekend – that's the place to recruit folk. He'll choose the best photos and print them out big to attract people over. Hand out flyers and membership forms, get people to sign up to his newsletter. He's not sure yet what the archaeological society is going to do exactly, but it's a new project and Fergus loves to get started on a project. A sense of purpose, that's what it is. He could give free membership for the first twenty sign-ups. He's quite excited about it actually. Then he remembers poor Alexis. He's ashamed of himself now, getting carried away when such a thing has happened here, in this village, in his home. And poor Simon, too. He'd been meaning to invite them both over, for a Sunday roast or something, a woodland walk. Somehow he'd never got round to it. Now he'll never be able to.

Fergus stares at the photos he took looking over to Burrowhead playground. There's something yellow, a smudge, nothing that could be recognised, except that he's realised it must be police tape: the crime scene. He zooms in, the screen becoming a mosaic of tiny coloured squares. Georgie could be in there somewhere. And Alexis. The grey of the sky isn't grey any more, it's… Suddenly he can't take his eyes off the screen. There's that huge bird again, an eagle, he's sure of it. The same one he saw over the village. It's swooping low in the sky above the dead body hidden in the pixels of his photograph.

SHOULD HAVE BEEN TIME FOR TEA

Georgie knows it's time to take Simon's statement. What with him a PC and first on the scene, in a relationship with the victim, possibly the last to see him alive as well, it's not good. She'd be a friend to him now, if she could, she'd talk to him off the record, maybe invite him round for some home-made stew with her and Fergus tonight. Instead, she's got to put him on the spot and catch him off guard if she can, like she would with any other suspect. He might not even be expecting it. He's been crying at his desk this afternoon, though he said he'd been doing last week's paperwork – when she glanced in his office door, pretending to be passing down the corridor, she saw his body slumped forward, keyboard pushed away, shoulders shaking. And there he's sat, waiting for her to knock. He doesn't know she knows about the Kingfisher yet. He's probably expecting her kindness. Georgie hopes that her officers think of her as kind.

She knocks on his door, pushes it open without waiting for a response.

'Time for a chat, Si...' She leaves it hanging, part request, part question.

He pushes his chair back and stands.

'Of course,' he says. His eyes are dry, though the skin around them looks raw. 'I've been trying to piece together his movements—'

'Next door,' she says, shaking her head. 'We're all set up.'

She steps out of the room backwards, keeping her eyes on him, but suddenly there's someone behind her, taller than her, and she spins round fast, barely keeping her balance.

'Andy!'

'Sorry, boss,' he's saying, 'I thought you were going in, I mean, didn't think you were walking back—'

'What are you doing here, Andy? I told you to stay home.'

His face falls from hopeful to rejected in an instant.

'I want to help, boss.'

'Help with what?'

He's folded in on himself, all long gangly limbs and awkwardness.

'With the' – he looks over his shoulder; Trish has heard the commotion – 'with the, you know...'

'No, Andy. I don't know, and you shouldn't be here.'

'With the murder!' he says, suddenly stroppy. 'Everyone's talking about it.'

'Everyone who?'

Georgie steps forward and Andy steps back; she's keeping Simon and the office out of reach, and her own door is shut.

'Well, boss,' he says, recovering himself and trying to look official, like he has important information for her, 'my friend Lee told me, and he heard it from his brother who works in the butcher's and he starts early, right, and he saw that van, the forensics van from Crackenbridge driving along High Street like it was coming from the playground—'

As he talks Georgie is edging him back along the corridor to the reception area, Trish helping her do it – she must have realised what Georgie's up to, can't have a work experience kid back here, not now.

'—we all know the forensics van, see, from what happened last year, with Pauly and Rachel, and he was like, what's happened now? So on his fag break he walked up the cliffs and Suze was there, in her uniform and that – she was the one who gave me the idea I could be a policeman – and there was yellow tape and no one was allowed in. And on his way home Mrs Smyth and Mrs Dover were talking by the fountain and Mrs Dover was saying she'd seen the police car heading through the village and she'd followed, because she's a right to know what's happening in her village, and she thought it might've been the vandals but when she got to the top of the lane she saw several policemen kneeling next to a body under the swings, and one of them was taking photos and there was the van and you were there and she didn't want to interfere or nothing so she went round to her neighbours' for tea and toast. I think all those old ladies like to have breakfast together.'

Georgie exhales slowly, through pursed lips, and pulls the hall door closed behind her. The three of them are standing in reception now.

'But then also Gav Bennett from Warphill popped by the farm and he said he'd heard from Bobby who hears everything in his cab that someone had been killed down in Burrowhead and that's why the police were out asking questions and it's all anyone's talking about today, and that was when I decided I'd better come in, you know, to help. So can I help with the investigation?'

'No,' says Georgie. 'You can't be here today, Andy. I've told you that already.'

'But... Please, boss?'

That smile he has. It makes her hear another voice, from another time, another teenager saying, 'Come on, sis?' with his disarming grin. She softens, a little.

'Head on home now, Andy. Help your dad with the farm, eh?'

Trish is looking at her, and though Georgie can see she doesn't want to overstep the mark, her expression reminds her of what Trish told her that morning, about Andy's dad beating him up, and he's a good kid, she knows that. Still, he can't be anywhere near this investigation.

'Maybe...'

'You got an idea, Trish? 'Cause we've got to do this right.'

'I know. I was just thinking maybe he could answer the phone, out here in reception. If folk are talking already—'

Georgie closes her eyes, shakes her head. 'No.'

'What about cleaning out the store cupboard then—'

'*Trish*—'

But there's Andy, looking hopeful. It's been a rough day for Georgie. For all of them. This violence, it doesn't belong here, in their village. Taking Pamali's statement this afternoon, she kept thinking, what is happening to this place? Georgie loves her job when it involves helping folk. Out here, that's what she gets to do sometimes. Finding Walt Mackie when he goes walkabout, talking to the high school about responsible drinking and the dangers of drugs – she'll get through to some of those kids, one of these days. Setting up the 20 mph zone to keep the village safe when the Burrowhead community council came to her and asked if she could No money for speed cameras, she was told, so she got Trish to set up fake ones; should be good enough to fool the tourists. Though she feels a stab of anger thinking about that – they'd have actually had some road camera footage to help them now if there was ever money available for Burrowhead, instead of these constant cuts. It's been a rough day and it's making her sick, but here maybe there's a chance for her to show a bit of kindness after all.

'Okay,' she sighs, and Trish beams at her. 'Only when one of us is here to supervise. Got it?'

Andy's face lights up, arms rising in excitement as he almost jumps on the spot, his long legs bending and stretching. 'I can do it, boss,' he says. 'You can trust me.'

'Listen carefully now. If people ask you what's going on, folk from the village or anyone else, you tell them no comment, alright? It's important.'

He's nodding like he's lost control of his head.

'Good lad. Trish here will help you get set up. Okay?'

She turns to get on with the interview, but Trish catches her arm before she leaves reception.

'Thank you, Georgie,' she says, under her breath.

'No more favours, alright?'

Trish lets go of her arm, steps back.

'And if anyone comes into the station, keep them here in reception. No one gets through that door.' She points to the internal door leading back to the offices, to where Simon's waiting. 'We follow the rules. Do you understand?'

BEFORE GEORGIE CAME OF AGE

Georgie glances behind her, checking they've not been followed, pulling him along as she sprints her way down the sidewalk. She's got his hand clasped tight but he's wriggling his way free – course he is, he's her little brother. They're both fast. The teachers probably haven't even noticed they're missing yet. Another foot down, check, leap. Sun's blistering today, roads runny like tar. He slips his hand out of hers. Her knapsack's clinging to her back, stuck with sweat and excitement.

'Errol!'

S'not easy looking after a ten-year-old, leading him astray.

'Stay with me!'

But Errol has spotted a Labrador pup along the road and he's running for it, arms outstretched. It's okay, so long as no one finds them and sends them back to that school – she's not having that. She wasn't the one who started the fight, and they deserved it anyway. Calling her names was one thing, but she wasn't going to take what they said about her mom. Only reason *they* didn't get in trouble was 'cause Troy's the mayor's son and Georgie knows that's wrong and if the teachers aren't going to do anything about it then she'll have to do something herself.

Up ahead, Errol has reached the puppy and knelt down to stroke its head, to smoosh his face into its coat. Then around the corner come the pup's owners, old Jess and Margaret – the new pup a replacement for their old collie who was hit by that truck last

59

month that drove on through town without even stopping – and the alarm in their eyes when they see Errol and then look up and see Georgie is enough to make her ball her hands into fists; she's had one fight today already, she's not afraid of another. This town never did forgive her dad for leaving the way he did, and far less for coming home again with an Algerian wife, even if he was from one of the oldest families hereabouts – that only made the fall further, her mom gets that just fine and Georgie gets it too. Jess and Margaret put on their polite faces though, call the pup away. He's an obedient little thing. Georgie's going to leave this town one day, and she's taking Errol with her. But first they've got to get beyond the graveyard.

He's slowing down already, her little brother. He's still afraid. Even Georgie can hear her mom's voice, *hold your breath as you pass*, but she laughs it off – there's not a spirit in the world going to make its way inside her body.

'Come on!'

She grabs his hand, runs with him ten, twenty, thirty paces till they're past the dead, and then they're catching their breath, creeping along beside dirt yards and low wooden fences until they see the mayor's house. It's taller and whiter than the rest, the roof rising over the next block up ahead. Georgie leads them the long way round to the back of the house, because out front the mayor's mother sits on her rocking chair and watches all day long. The white porch circles the house and there's a big full garden with bright green grass and trees and plants she doesn't recognise. Georgie picks a few stones from the gravel path that they're avoiding and puts them in Errol's outstretched hands. Holds her finger to her lips and crouches low, crawls her way to the shrubs where the redbirds are pecking at seeds scattered from the feeder. She moves slow, so slow and careful and silent she can hear Errol's breath behind her, she can hear the creaking of the rocking chair out front and the beat of the sun's rays on the back of her neck. She moves a hand closer, then a knee. Her bare skin on the grass, the prickle of it. They're arrogant, the redbirds, sure of their place – they're not afraid. She edges closer. Bright red feathers, black eyes, red beak. They even look like the devil. *Peck peck* at the ground. She reaches out her hand and stretches her arm and at the last second moves fast as a whip and grabs the nearest bird, the rest in the air with a scratch of wings and the shrill *chip chip chip* of warning but it doesn't matter: she's got one. Its wings try to lash out against her palm, her fingers are clenched tight. She's on her feet. Its claws scratch.

'Go!' she mouths silently at Errol and he hesitates – they're not supposed to throw stones, and he doesn't like being in trouble, her little brother. '*Go on!*'

With her other hand Georgie grabs a fistful of stones and hurls them at the back window: the shout comes from the front porch, the creak of the rocking chair emptied, footsteps on wood. Georgie moves fast, Errol beside her. They race round to the front and she's up three steps with a single leap, in the open door and her arm high and the bird released with its angry cry and desperate flight to the ceiling, the wall, the closed window, a bright red feather floating through the air. Georgie turns, sees Errol waiting on the steps, grabs his wrist and they run, Georgie thumping her fist on the rocking chair on the way past, and they're round the corner and no one saw them and she feels a laugh rising up her throat and flying out into the world as they keep sprinting, round another bend, through the trees, until her legs slow and she stops, leans back against a trunk, gasps for breath. Errol is staring up at her. Eyes big and black and scared.

'That'll teach them!' she says, gasping for breath.

Errol is still clasping his stones in his hand.

She opens his palm, grins at him.

'You can drop them now,' she says. 'We did it.'

He turns his hand upside down and his stones fall to the dust by his feet and he looks up with wide eyes.

'Now we're free for the whole afternoon,' she says. 'What shall we do?'

She brushes the dirt off his palm, only then noticing that her own hand is all scratched and bleeding from where she held the bird captive. But Georgie's not afraid of a bit of blood. She wipes her hand down her skirt and puts her arm gently round Errol's shoulders.

'You did well,' she says.

He grins up at her at last.

'I'm proud of you, you know that.'

She leads him through the trees and down to the river, where they can get their feet wet and sit in the shade of the willows till it's time to go home and pretend like they've been sat in school following the stupid rules all day.

AN INTERVIEW WITH
PC SIMON HUNTER

Staring out the window. Dense cloud and low light, not a patch of blue in sight, just that stormy grey blowing through the sky and sinking deeper all the while.

'Where do you want me to start?' Simon says. His voice is different to how it used to be. Flatter, somehow. The recorder is on. He looks anxious.

'Where were you yesterday evening?' Georgie says.

He closes his eyes, and without them his whole face looks drained of colour. She can tell he hasn't eaten all day. She wishes she could put her arm around him, offer a smile, but the best she can do now is wait and listen.

'Yesterday,' he says. And he takes a deep breath, lets it out. 'After work I walked straight home, not paying much attention to the street, got a change of clothes. I didn't have that much time seeing as I was getting the bus up to Crackenbridge and there's only the one an hour, you know? Well, course you know. I was getting the bus, 'cause Alexis was supposed to be driving there to meet me so...'

Georgie nods at him to keep going.

'So I got the bus, fairly empty, took about forty-five minutes, like normal. You know how it goes through all the villages and that. Through Warphill. I got to the Kingfisher about quarter to eight. Alexis...'

Simon looks at her, his pale eyes still red around the edges, in the cracks at the corners. The salt wind wouldn't have helped. It bites down by the coast, but even through the dim light it's obvious how much he's been crying. At least he's told her about the Kingfisher without her needing to ask. He's not hiding anything. Well, not anything she already knows about.

'Alexis had booked a table for eight. It was, er…'

He breathes a few times, swallows.

'It was going to be our celebration, see. He'd got his citizenship and I'd thought, well we'd both said it could be a new start. Things had been…'

Georgie knows better than to finish his sentences, and he's taken enough of these statements to know how it works.

'Things had been a bit strained, what with the interview coming up and that. I thought we should leave. Well, I don't know if we'd really have left, but it's what I'd been saying. Alexis wouldn't go, though. He'd not leave until he had no other choice.'

'Why do you think he wanted to stay so much?'

He shakes his head. Hand through his hair.

'It wasn't for me,' he says. 'That was the problem. I thought there was someone else. I mean, I thought he was seeing someone else. I thought they were the reason he was set on staying here.'

'Why'd you think that?'

'I could just tell. You can, when someone's lying to you. He'd be late coming round… We'd make plans and he'd show up late to the pub. It wasn't like him – he always used to be on time. Then he never wanted to say where he'd been. He claimed to have a client he had to visit at home, who wanted things kept confidential. He was seeing someone away from the office, that's for sure, but I doubted it was a client… Oh Christ, I don't know what he was mixed up in. We'd had some fights about it, but I thought…'

The silence hangs between them for a minute.

'So what happened in the Kingfisher?' she asks.

'Well' – Simon purses his lips, like an acknowledgement of something, a kind of helplessness – 'he never turned up. I waited. At first I thought, you know, I was a few minutes early, but then…' He rubs his hand over his face, forehead to mouth. 'Anyway, he never turned up. I texted – no reply. Tried calling. I think he had his phone switched off. It kept going straight to voicemail. I waited an hour then left. I put a fiver on the table for my drink and walked out. I think I knocked a chair over on my way. Trish saw me outside, from over the road. She tried to wave, but I stormed off. I was angry. With Alexis, I mean – I was angry with him. I'll not deny that.'

The way he sighs then, it's enough to make Georgie want to cry. Just twenty-six and some part of him destroyed.

'I'd to wait for ages at the stop for the next bus, and it was bloody raining and, well, that's partly why I was pissed off. He was meant to be driving us home, see, but instead he left me there to get the bus. Stood me up. Sounds stupid now.'

'No,' Georgie says. 'Doesn't sound stupid at all.'

She'll track some people down from the bus. The driver too. Should be able to get proof that Simon left Crackenbridge alone. That's assuming he's telling the truth, of course, and he doesn't look like a man who could lie, not in this state.

'What time did the bus arrive, d'you remember?'

'Just after half nine. I checked at the stop. So I could yell at him about it.'

'That would have got you back to Burrowhead after ten then?'

He nods. It's close, the timing of it. But if Cal's right about the time of death, that would place Simon in Crackenbridge, or on the bus, when Alexis was killed.

'Got home about quarter past ten, drank a couple of beers, went to bed. But I couldn't sleep. Kept running through it all in my head and imagining the worst case… It wasn't, of course, I just mean…

Eventually I decided to go and find him. Have it out. I went to his house, but there was no answer. I went right inside, because the front door's never locked, but his flat door was and there were no lights on. I knocked. I shouted. He wasn't there. So I went outside and started walking around. I don't know, trying to walk it off.

'It was quite light out, I remember that – the moon was bright. The sky had a blue glow to it, even though it was the middle of the night. I sat by the fountain for a bit. No one was around. Started walking up High Street. I don't even know why, just started walking to the coast. But then I got to the playground. There was... He was... I called it in. Guess it was about seven by then.'

'It was,' says Georgie.

'I keep thinking, why'd I not go looking for him immediately, you know? Maybe I could have... If I'd got there sooner or if I'd realised something was wrong.'

'I doubt there was anything you could have done, Si,' says Georgie, but she knows it sounds hollow. There's never anything anyone could have done, and yet there's always something they could have done differently. That's the thing about the world. What happens has happened, but that doesn't mean it was inevitable.

'But whoever it was that Alexis was seeing,' Simon says, leaning forwards now, his face paler than ever, 'well, they could have done this. They could have killed him.'

'Hold on there,' Georgie says, though she's glad to see some energy from him. Still, no use jumping to conclusions.

'Or they'll know something,' he says, desperation in his voice. 'They might know something. They were the last person to see him alive.'

'That's for us to look into,' she says. 'Unless there's anything else you can tell us about Alexis's movements that evening?'

He shakes his head. 'That's everything.'

She can see it in his face though, what he's thinking. That it should have been him. That the last person to see Alexis should have been him, and then all this could have been different. She pauses for a minute, waits for him to lean back a touch; to decide the interview is over.

'When *was* the last time you saw him?'

'What?'

'When was the last time you saw Alexis alive?'

There, the tension in his jaw – he's defensive now, a little angry.

'Sunday,' he says. 'He was preparing for the interview Monday morning.'

'Interview?'

'This citizenship crap.'

'So you saw him Monday morning as well?'

'No.'

'Didn't stay the night?'

'I...' Simon shakes his head. She can see him taking a deep breath. 'I saw him Sunday afternoon and we got into an argument. I wanted us to move to Greece, he wanted to stay. I thought he was seeing someone else, like I said.' His eyes, staring at hers. 'I left his place before dinner. Didn't know when I'd next see him. He left a message Monday lunchtime to tell me he'd passed the interview, invited me to the Kingfisher. That explain everything?'

'That's all for now. Thank you, Simon.'

She terminates the interview, switches off the recording. Simon's lips are pursed tight, but she doubts that'll last more than a few seconds.

'What about Alexis's phone records?' he blurts. 'Incoming calls on Monday?'

Georgie shakes her head. She's already checked, and the calls were all from Simon.

'Forensics? Did you find something pointing to me, is that it?'

He stands, then sits back down again.

'There could be, of course.' As quickly as it flared up, his anger is gone. In the silence between them a car revs its engine outside and the gulls that must have been on the ground by the window suddenly rise, the noise of them setting Georgie's teeth stinging.

'Get some rest, Si,' she says once the birds have gone, her voice soft again. 'Trust me, okay? I will find whoever did this.'

Georgie hates making promises she's doesn't know for sure she'll be able to keep. But he needs to go home, and she needs to confirm his alibi. That's all either of them can do right now.

LATE AFTERNOON, GETTING ON

Trish has been pacing back and forth between her office and the interview room. *Kevin Taylor.* There, in the day planner this morning – she knew she'd recognised his name. Didn't want to say something stupid, not when it was just a hunch, but now, well, now she's got something. The kid has a record, doesn't he. Georgie's going to be pleased.

He was at the same school as her, good few years behind, and God knows some of the boys at that school were no good, fair number of bullies among them. Trish hated that school, couldn't wait to get away – never thought she'd choose to come back here, but here she is. Uncle Walt, maybe. The way home seems different, once you're away from it. The city just didn't fit. They didn't get it, those cops, what life was like out here. Or, if they did get it, they certainly didn't care. It's not the drink, it's the boredom that leads to it – like kids have decided it's hopeless before they've even reached their teens. One time, when Trish was at school, they were all called to assembly to have their bags searched. Cigarettes, of course. Weed. Speed. Knives – Christ, the number of penknives. She'd put money on it being worse now. What did Kevin Taylor carry round in his rucksack, besides what he'd stolen on the way to school that morning?

That was part of the reason she'd wanted to help Andy. He was a good kid; there was something gentle about him. He didn't deserve that school and he sure as hell didn't deserve that father. Trish knows what it can be like, too, growing up without a mum. Not much kindness around. She had Uncle Walt, at least, but Andy Barr has no one. Maybe, with a bit of work experience and a good reference from her, he might be able to get into the force, start his training – give him a sense of purpose. She's been keeping a close eye on him. He's doing well, too, going through the store cupboard. He's pulled out the broken chairs and mop and the old blackboard (Jesus, when did they last use that?) and found an old jar of instant coffee and a pack of red biros that might actually come in handy. She's set him to cleaning the floor in there now, and he agreed more readily than most teenage boys would have. Trish has been deflecting phone calls all afternoon – folk wanting to know what happened at the playground, including a local journalist Trish managed to get rid of despite her threat of coming round to the station in person – and when Andy was taking a fag break outside Trish saw him watching the front door as protectively as any guard dog, bless him.

Cal had called as well, with a message for Georgie – they'd found nothing on the beach. Trish isn't too surprised. She'd seen nothing down there herself, and if you were fleeing a murder in the middle of the night in a storm like that, you'd be a fool to risk a broken ankle in a rockslide, with nowhere to hide and miles of stone visible from all along the cliffs. It's possible of course, and they all know Georgie's got instincts, but with no evidence and the tide on its way up again the beach is looking like a dead end, like that door-to-door. Not so the body, though. That's the other reason he called. They'd found a hair.

She hears the door to the interview room open and is on her feet, meeting Georgie at the door to her office with the news:

'Kevin Taylor. Name in the day planner.'

Georgie raises her eyebrows in that infuriatingly calm way she has.

'I've got something.' Trish gestures to her computer, trying to stay patient. 'See? Right there on the database. Seems our Kevin has a record,' she says.

Georgie leans forward to read what Trish already knows by heart. Shoplifting, drunk and disorderly.

'He was underage.'

'Not any more though,' says Trish. 'He's eighteen now. Maybe he's graduated.'

Georgie nods. 'The question is, why would a kid like that be going to see Alexis?'

'I don't know, but I want to find out. I've got an address. Can I take the first interview, see what we have?'

Trish finds the wait interminable, but she sits on her hands while Georgie stares at the screen with a frown on her face. Then she remembers.

'Cal called too. More good news. They've found a hair on Alexis's shirt.'

'Colour?'

'Blonde.'

Georgie looks away.

'And long.'

'What exactly did he say?'

'Just that. A long blonde hair, pulled out by the root too – he's sent it off for DNA and emailed you what he knows so far.'

'Right. This is good, Trish. Well done. Pass me the phone, would you?'

Trish pulls the phone across the desk, watches while Georgie hits the speed dial for headquarters. She can tell it's the answerphone, though it's out of character the way Georgie slams the receiver down without leaving a message.

'I'm coming with you,' she says suddenly.

Trish stands, though Georgie is staring at the screen like there's something there waiting for her.

'What is it?'

Georgie pulls up the internet browser and types in a search, and suddenly they are both staring at the news. No wonder they're not answering the phone. It's the chief superintendent standing in front of headquarters with the city skyline behind her, and a rolling feed along the bottom of the screen: TWENTY-NINE DEAD IN LATEST TERROR ATTACKS. POLICE ON THE SCENE IN MINUTES.

STAYING PUT VS GETTING OUT

The light's already low outside when Pamali hears the familiar jangle of the bell above the Spar door and looks up from her sketch. She's chosen a scene from the village, in late autumn when everything feels quiet and still and the sun through the tree canopies over Church Street turns the air golden. When she left the police station Georgie told her to head home, get some rest, but she came straight back here instead, opened up the shop, even had the door open wide for a bit so the quartet they were playing on the radio danced out onto the street. When folk passed by she smiled, she waved, called them in for tea. No one had stopped yet, though; the shop had been empty since she got back. Until now.

It's young Andy Barr, wandering in looking a bit lost even though he's lived here his whole life. He always looks a bit lost, that kid. Pamali likes him though, and she's pleased to have someone to talk to.

'How are you, Andy?' she calls over from the till.

Andy grunts what she thinks is 'alright' and wanders his way over to the cans of pop she's got in the fridge.

'Georgie tells me you're doing a work placement at the station.'

He looks up and grins at that.

'I've been sorting things out for them,' he says, making his way up the aisle now with his drink and a bag of pickled onion Monster Munch. 'And keeping watch. Not letting anyone in, not telling anyone anything.'

'Then I'll not ask you anything about it, Andy,' she says with a laugh, then regrets it as his face falls a bit and he thrusts a fiver at her. She tries again, though, as she gives him his change. 'What're you thinking of doing after school then?'

He shrugs.

'Police work?'

'Anything to get away from here.'

She's surprised by the sudden force of his voice. Still, there's not much here for young people, not much work. What would he do in Burrowhead?

'University then, maybe?'

He snorts.

'You know, I remember that exhibition they held at the school with all the work from the art class a few years back – do you remember it?'

'No.'

'You had a couple of pieces up on the wall, big paintings. They were really good, I thought.'

He's noticed her picture now, he's staring at it where she put it down there on the counter when he came in.

'That's what I did, you see. I went to art school in London.'

The symphony that was playing has stopped, the radio's switched to voices, someone phoning in, the line distorted. Sometimes it seems like everything beyond Burrowhead is so distant it crackles.

'Then why're you here?' he says.

'You mean running the Spar?'

Another shrug.

'This was my uncle's shop, before he died.'

She knows she's not really answering his question. Her grand-parents had moved here from Sri Lanka when they were young. Her dad grew up in the village, met her mum through friends in London and settled there a few years later. Family holidays in Burrowhead when she was a girl, playing on the beach with a bucket and net, catching tiny transparent fish and pink crabs, always throwing them back into the rock pools so they could go on living. Then the feeling of being crammed onto the Tube two hours a day for a job that didn't pay what she needed, student loans, impossible rent, priced out of London, no one able to help. Except her uncle, offering her work in the shop. The air up here. The sea.

'Okay, so there's not much money in art. No jobs. Not for me anyway.'

'But you could leave,' he says. 'You could...'

'I like it here,' she smiles. 'This is my home.' She wonders how many generations it would take to make you a local in Burrowhead. 'And working in the Spar's not bad. I get to see lots of people, I like that.'

'Can I have a job here then? For the summer?'

Her heart sinks a little bit when he asks. He's not the first.

'I'm sorry, Andy, but we can't afford to take on someone else, even part-time... It's a struggle to keep the shop going, that's the truth of it.' She'd have thought he would be working on his dad's farm for the summer anyway. That's how it usually goes, round here. He looks like he knew what she'd say.

'That's good though,' he says, nodding at her drawing.

It's nice of him, changing the subject so she won't feel awkward. 'Where is it?'

'It's here,' she says, surprised. 'It's the village. Look, it's the view out from the square towards the old ruin.'

He stares at it like he can't recognise Church Street, can't recognise the conker trees or the hills in the distance or the light.

'I'm thinking of setting up a stall at the spring fair this weekend, you can come with me if you like. Maybe you've got some paintings you could sell?'

He gives a half-smile at that and shakes his head and she feels suddenly, deeply sorry for him.

'It *is* possible, you know, Andy. Uni, art school, a job in the city maybe. If you really want to leave.'

He opens his can and tips his head back to drink: three, four big gulps like he's not had a sip in a week.

'Got to get home,' he says. Then he turns and heads for the door.

For a minute Pamali imagines it, selling up, leaving Burrowhead behind, going back to London. But no. She'd miss the coast too much, the wild beach, the huge expanse of sky. And if she left now then she'd always feel like she was pushed away. She's not having that.

'Leave it open, Andy,' she calls as the bell jangles his departure.

The Spar is open for business. And he's right; her picture of the village is beautiful.

Kevin's mother answers the door, which is unsurprising really, given that it's her house. Not many eighteen-year-olds round here able to rent their own flat, far less a semi, even if it is bang in the middle of Warphill. Georgie holds out her hand.

'Burrowhead police,' she says, shifting a foot forward to stop the door that's already closing in her face. 'Mind if I have a chat with Kevin, Mrs Taylor? Is he around today at all?'

A teenage girl's face appears from a door down the hall then disappears again, but the sound of the door creaking is enough to make Mrs Taylor turn and Georgie step through the threshold, Trish following close behind her. Mrs Taylor gives a sigh and heads for the kitchen.

'You'll be wanting a cup a tea then?'

'Aye, ta,' says Trish.

'Kevin!' Mrs Taylor's voice, when raised, has a slight rattle to the back of it.

There's a pounding of footsteps from upstairs, another girl's voice shouting 'Arse!' before Kevin himself appears at the top of the steps.

'The fuck is it now?'

'Kevin.'

He drags his feet down the stairs and Georgie gestures for him to follow his mum into the kitchen. 'Let's have a sit down together, shall we?'

'Aye, whatever you say.'

Georgie's familiar enough with what the teenagers round here think of the police. It's an ongoing project of hers to get through to them, show them a bit of help and support. Though Kevin's guard has shot right up; he's got something to be defensive about, that's for sure.

'Here we go.' She pulls back a chair, sits down at the table. It's large, pale wood, with an orange-and-white-striped runner across the centre. Crumbs under her elbow where she's leaned on it. She wants to seem approachable, non-threatening. 'We were just wondering if you could tell us where you were last night, Kevin.'

'Right here.'

'Here in the house, that's good. And you stayed in all night, did you?'

'Course all bloody night.'

Georgie nods and takes the custard cream Mrs Taylor is offering, shares a glance with Trish over the table. Trish was a teenager here once, same as Kevin and his sisters. Georgie might have thought that would make Trish more sympathetic, rather than less so, but she knows Trish better than that.

'Can anyone verify you were here?' Trish's tone, unlike Georgie's, makes her suspicion perfectly clear. Kevin stretches his legs out under the table.

'Her.' He points at his mother. 'Penny-Ann' – he gestures back to the hall – 'and Esme. My sisters.' He pushes his chair back onto two legs, arms crossed like he's in the clear, smug look on his face. Over by the kettle Mrs Taylor is picking teabags out of a Tupperware pot and dropping them into ornate blue-and-white-patterned teacups. There are feathered dreamcatchers hanging in the window, five of them in a row.

'Good,' says Georgie. 'Thanks very much. I'm glad we got that out of the way.' She smiles. 'Now, the reason I'm really here is to ask you about Dr Alexis Cosse...' She pauses; she needs to get this right. 'Did you know him at all, Kevin?'

The kettle squeals and Kevin's expression changes to that of a child on the verge of a tantrum.

'I didn't fucking want to, did I. It were you lot made me go to his stupid therapy.'

Georgie waits, but Kevin doesn't elaborate. It's the unlikeliness of a kid like Kevin having counselling that Georgie was curious about.

'It was a condition of his sentence,' his mum explains. 'Just the community service and a round of psychotherapy.' She hands Georgie and Trish their cups of tea, precariously balanced on saucers. 'Four sessions.'

'And what did you learn, Kevin?' Georgie asks. She'd genuinely like to know, too. There was a time when she'd been offered that kind of help and had turned her back instead, and she regrets that sometimes. Eighteen-year-old Georgie had problems enough to rival any kid in Warphill.

'Anger management.' Kevin grins.

Georgie doesn't. She can't press him to talk about it, of course, but the truth is Kevin has an alibi for last night and a perfectly valid reason for seeing Alexis. Attitude aside, there's no reason to consider him a suspect.

'And how's that working out for you?' Trish says.

'Look, I've done nothing, alright. Why you here?'

'He's not been in any more trouble,' his mum says. 'I can vouch for that. I'm watching him.'

Kevin scoffs.

Georgie's eyes have fallen on the lumps of pale pink quartz on the windowsill.

'You've seen my crystals,' his mum says, standing up proudly like she's going to bring them over.

'God, Mum,' Kevin groans. 'Don't.'

She sits back down and smiles apologetically at Georgie. Across the table, Trish picks up her tea, doesn't drink from it, and puts it down again. She's had an idea, Georgie can see it. She gives her a nod.

'You been over at the Spar in Burrowhead recently, Kevin?' Trish asks.

'Aye, the Paki—'

'Kev!'

'It's what Dad always said.'

'Well, your dad's gone.'

'Aye, and now we're no allowed to speak—'

'You speak plenty.'

Kevin's mum looks at Georgie and rolls her eyes. 'He's just trying to provoke, he doesn't mean…' she begins.

But Georgie's sitting up now, alert, and she knows how to make herself heard when she needs to.

'When were you last there, Kevin?' Her voice has the kind of authority that works best when used sparingly.

'I dunno,' Kevin shrugs. He looks younger now. 'Couple a weeks back.'

'There's more choice there,' his mum starts in. 'Pamali has a better selection of cheeses, that not right, *Kevin*?'

'Tobacco, you mean. *Mum*.'

'You both know Pamali, then?'

'Aye,' says Kevin. 'Pamali's alright.'

Georgie raises her eyebrows.

'So?' he says.

The attitude seems to switch on and off quicker than a blink.

'So I need to know where you were this morning between the hours of 6 a.m. and 8 a.m.'

'I was here, wasn't I. Where else am I going to be?'

'Here alone?'

'No. With all of them.' He waves around the kitchen furiously. 'Like bloody always.'

Georgie looks at Mrs Taylor, who nods.

'Like he's going to be out of bed before eight in the morning. Unless he's been up all night – and I'd of heard the racket if he was.'

A glare passes between them, like this is part of a recurring argument.

'Will the girls be able to confirm that?'

'Aye,' says one of them from the kitchen door. Blonde hair scooped high. 'He was snoring. And we've none of us left the house today. We're out a milk, too.'

'You could go to the shops yourself, Esme,' her mum shouts, but the girl has already disappeared again.

'Well,' Georgie says, standing up now. 'We've got your fingerprints on file. If anything comes up, we'll be back for another chat. Do you understand, Kevin?'

He's looking at Trish, not her.

'Someone robbed the *Spar* then?'

'Know anything about that?' Trish says, staring him down.

'Course not.'

'Right then,' Georgie says. 'We'll show ourselves out. Thank you for the tea and biscuits, Mrs Taylor.'

'You're welcome,' she says. 'And you know, if there's anything we can do to help with the investigation...'

Georgie stops. They've heard about the murder already then. Trish is standing behind her, Mrs Taylor behind Trish, and at the end of the hall there's Kevin. She can see him, the way he suddenly looks interested, and more than that too; there's an intelligence there that she'd almost missed. But then he's gone and Georgie realises she's causing a bottleneck in the narrow hall. She moves again, opens the door, shudders at the way the sky has descended.

On the drive back to Burrowhead, Trish is quiet. Very quiet, for Trish.

There's a dark line of cloud clinging low.

'You okay, Trish?' she asks. Though of course none of them are okay; Alexis was part of their village.

'This place,' Trish says. 'It's my home, you know. It's a part of me, but my God. The stuff that goes on.'

They're approaching Burrowhead. Spitting rain sharp as gravel on the windscreen. The street lights look garish in the dull dark of evening – they leave everything else in shadows of black.

'Penny for your thoughts, Trish?'

'It's just… I'm going to fix this place.' Her voice sounds angry, and Georgie wonders if she's been hurt in ways she doesn't know about. 'I'm going to sort it out, even if I have to arrest half the inhabitants myself and lock them all up.'

The Spar stands out soon as they reach High Street, pale green like a fresh shoot surrounded by old leaf mulch. Pamali was hoping the residents would be inspired, paint their own house fronts blue and pink and yellow – they wanted none of it, though. Burrowhead is chipped white turning grey, and stubborn with it too. There's a cluster of birds, black birds, bright orange beaks, right outside the shop, and suddenly Georgie slams on the brakes.

'What?'

'I saw—'

She saw something, out in the alley beside Alexis's flat, a shadow, something more – she felt it, crawling over her skin, the back of her neck. Something slick and wrong. She gets out of the car; looks around. Trish is behind her. But the alley is empty. Slowly, she retraces her steps, finds herself standing at the door to Alexis's flat. The crime scene tape looks garish in this light. Cal's team have finished their work, padlocked the front.

For a moment Georgie stares out into the gloom. There's nothing here. No one except them.

END OF THE WORKING DAY

Walt Mackie likes a walk on the beach, end of the day, see off the sun and show the moon she's welcome, and the truth is Walt likes the night better than the days, some of the time. He likes the peace that comes with night, at least out here on the beach. It's a solitary sort of time, this, and Walt's okay with that. He's a solitary sort of man, these days, just his Trish he cares for really. Everyone else left long ago, but not him. He's stayed put, waiting for them to come back for him. Waiting for the land to recognise him and show him the way, like in the days before. He can see it as it was fifty years back, him and Arthur and Big Jack, the dawn sun striking the menhir just so, their voices rising to meet the birds' chorus. But where are they now? One dead and one dead to the world, everything worse now they've gone. One man alone isn't enough for the old ways. Still, he's rooted in this place, in the ancient soil and stone of it, like the pebbles on this beach, battered by the sea so long their edges are smooth as feathers. And they will come for him, that's something he knows; the Others will come for him. He needs to be patient, show he's one of them, untouched by time, or by the times. No one by the fountain tonight at least, the village square was empty when he passed, the footpath out to the beach silent. He didn't go via the playground, couldn't manage the track down the cliffs, hasn't tried for years, no, he took the footpath out of the village and walked the long way down to the shore. From where he is now he can't even see the cliffs; the coast curves round, north of Burrowhead, to this sheltered bay of rounded pebbles and unexpected grasses grown up through the stone.

His legs are getting sore, though; old legs, old body. He's tired of it, wants to be lighter than this, to move like a young man again. Sitting down, the pebbles nudge against each other, refuse to settle into any one position – they're too old to rest comfortably, just like him. He pushes his hands down between them, unafraid of the damp or the seaweed that clings in layers below the surface, and looks out to the gentle peaks and dips of the beach that have been left behind by retreating waves. It is beautifully empty. Not a thing that doesn't belong, just the pebbles, the rock pools, the silver of the sea where the clouds thin out and let the moonlight through, and he closes his eyes. The rain was still drizzling when he arrived, but not any more. With his eyes closed the air feels suddenly clear, freshened by the day's storm and sweet where once there had been salt. When he opens them again, there is something down by the lapping tide. He watches it for a while, the way it rises and falls with the waves, the way it half floats and half sinks, and the colour of it almost translucent; he has no idea what it can be. It is for him, though. The beach is making that clear.

He stands, steady on his feet now, and walks calmly to the tideline, his dressing gown dipping into the water and his feet so numb they're oblivious to the cold. Actually, he feels like he is floating, hovering over the stones, and when he bends down to pick up the waterlogged holdall it seems lighter to him than paper. It must be for the pebbles; they are beautiful, shimmering below the waves. He bends down and starts to collect them, placing them one by one inside the bag until it feels like a real thing, with substance and weight, and then he knows his work is done. He begins the slow walk back towards the land, follows the footpath round to the village, and no one sees him as he passes except Simon, who has been out walking the hills alone, trying to empty his mind so he can sleep despite knowing he will not be able to.

Having circled through the fields and trees and up along the coast path, avoiding the stretch near the playground, Simon's heading back into the village when two things catch his attention. One, of course, is old Walt dripping wet, dressing gown hanging loose over waterproof walking trousers, the belt leaving ripples through the puddles along the pavement. He would have waved at Walt, had Walt noticed him, but Walt seems fixated on the sky, his neck craning upwards and his eyes blind to the street level entirely. Simon follows his gaze, and that's when he sees the bird circling above him. It's huge, dark, can't tell whether it's black or brown in the night, though it's so dark it's almost a shadow against the sky behind it, an omission of what should be there, and it seems to Simon that there's something evil about it, though he pushes the thought away – it's people who do evil things, that's all, and he knows it. Still, the size of it, and it's swooping lower now, Christ, he can't shake the feeling that it's seen him, that he's the centre of its orbit as it circles lower, threatening to dive. Then the growl of the car driving down High Street, they're like predators converging and he's acting on instinct as he darts behind the hedge, only real-ising at the last minute that it's Georgie driving past, and before he has time to think, she's gone, heading out of the village behind him to follow the single-track road that leads out to her and Fergus's place. It's one of the oldest cottages hereabouts, and far enough out of the village for them to have remained apart from it in a way that he suspects Georgie and Fergus don't realise – or at least would never comment on.

Meanwhile Fergus has become so engrossed in his research that he's clean forgotten to do the dinner, even though he'd said he would. The rituals associated with menhir and henge sites across

Europe, with the boglands and the places where water meets earth; there's something ancient and awesome that he can't seem to stop reading about. He needs to get better images, an aerial survey of the whole area – imagine if there were structures under the soil, under the fields, that he could discover – and he's found the perfect thing online. Georgie will understand, he's sure, about the cost of it. Though as he hears her car pulling up outside he thinks maybe he'll wait till morning to ask her. She's opening the front door and he's trying to pull himself away from what he's writing when she calls out:

'What's for dinner, love?'

He doesn't answer. Soon she's standing behind him, and he's showing her what he's created – the homepage with the photos, the landscape and local sites of interest, the old church ruin, then the people of the motte and the myths of the menhir.

'Do you want to read it?' he says, and even though she shudders he doesn't stop. 'I've been working on this all day,' he tells her. She replies that she is going to heat up yesterday's stew. She's had a rough day. The truth is that he barely hears her. *The old ways*, he's written, *have been passed down the centuries through stories whispered in the deepest phase of the night. The gathering at the menhir to choose the purest among them. The sacrifice made by three deaths on one body: a slit throat, a neck tied, a soul cast into the sea.* He doesn't join Georgie for dinner – he's not interested in food. He stays downstairs reading even though he hears Georgie heading to bed. He doesn't know where the time goes, he can't have fallen that deeply asleep, not with his head on the desk and his arm dangling down to the carpet, but by the time he wakes and makes his way upstairs it's beyond late at night; it is early morning. Too early for light, too early for the birds, too early for a cup of tea, though he has plans to bring Georgie breakfast, make up for forgetting about dinner. He knows how hard she works, knows what an awful day it must have been – can't remember how he could have let himself become so absorbed in those stories of carved stone and human sacrifice. He has to stop. He reaches the landing and listens for the sound of breathing. Georgie, his Georgie, is dealing with death in the real world, and the least he can do is be here to support her through it. But when he pushes open the door to their room he finds the bed empty and Georgie already gone.

WEDNESDAY

SHEPHERD'S WARNING

'This is a bad thing,' says Georgie, standing at the doorway and pulling the SOCO-suit hood over her hat. She's brought a beanie with her today, in the hope it'll last out the wind. More streamline to the head. Not exactly standard issue, but what does that matter. 'A bad, bad start to a Wednesday.'

Cal's face is masked in shadow, but from what she can see it looks like he's not slept either. With a sigh he turns the body over. It is stiff with rigor mortis.

'Oh, Bobby,' she says.

Her twang is strong this morning. Not a drawl, that'd be the wrong expression. It's just that her words come slowly, each letter accentuated, as though every syllable is formed deliberately in her mouth before being spoken.

'Aye, you knew him too then,' says Cal. 'I thought maybe, what with him being new to Warphill...'

Outside the sirens are still going, and the light from the police cars takes turns to fill the room with a harsh blue glow then sink it back into darkness. No street lights out here. No sign of the sun but that deep red spill on the horizon.

'Recent times he's been the only cabby who'd come to Burrowhead out of peak season.'

Georgie turns away from the body but it's hard to know where else to look, there's that much blood. It's on the walls, splatters of it on the window. He must have been standing up, running maybe, running from the blade. No blood out here in the hall though, so the stabbing must have started and finished in the room there. The slashes are clear enough across his torso, his back too, one right down his face. There's a bit of nostril hanging off, where the knife sliced clean through. She looks down at the carpet, tries to focus on that for a minute while she absorbs the shock of it. It's making her feel quite nauseous, which is not what you want in her job, not what you want at all.

It is dark, the carpet. Dark purple against the white of her shoe covers, and threadbare in places, though that's disguised by the blood that must have seeped into it. And there's a pattern on it, like ornate flowers or something. Dated. But then it would be, in these flats. No one's lived here for that many years. They were supposed to be demolished once, but somehow it never happened – they were left to this slow crumbling decay instead. Empty, but haunted. Maybe the council will finally deal with them now. That helps her pull herself together a bit. She makes note of the cracked window, the mould crawling up one wall, the fag ends and broken bottles dropped over years of teenagers sneaking in here.

'A commuter saw the knife, on his way up to the city for work. Called it in.'

'Long way to travel,' Georgie says.

'Aye, good hour and a half. Don't know why folks do it, myself.'

'But it had been dropped there?' she says. 'The knife. After all this, just dropped outside?'

Cal nods.

It strikes her as a different sort of crime to yesterday's. Stabbing, yes, but more erratic movements, with some surface slashing, hesitation maybe, and chasing too. Dr Cosse didn't seem to have been chased at all. It was like it caught him by surprise. Not Bobby; Bobby had been afraid. Bobby had tried to escape.

'Is there anything…'

Cal turns back to her. He's been thinking it too, of course, he's shaking his head in response already.

'No note,' he says. 'No paper at all, and nothing in the pockets. Nails bitten down, meaning we're unlikely to get any DNA even if he did manage to scratch. But I'll try, Georgie. I'll try.'

Georgie nods her thanks and pads over to the window across the hall. There are a few more cars about now, for sure. A few more lights. People will be driving up to Crackenbridge, or out to the fields, some of them. Not so much farming hereabouts as there used to be, but still a fair bit; got the cows, the sheep, potato fields in season and the abattoir the other side of Warphill. You can smell it. Still, Burrowhead's got the salt. Always going to be something in the air that you'd prefer not to be there; trick is to accept it, when you can. The salt, Georgie decided a long time ago, was something she could live with. So she stayed in Burrowhead. She didn't have to, but she did.

'Cal?'

'Aye?'

'Where are we with Alexis's flat?'

'We've pulled his phone records, for a start. There was a landline in the office, though he didn't use it much. Dinner reservations now and then. The garage. A call to the council – that was the day the water went off a few weeks back. Guess he was reporting the problem.'

'Him and the rest of Burrowhead.'

'And Walt Mackie once a week. The day before his appointments, just a reminder, I would imagine. Kevin Taylor's mum, few months back.'

Georgie nods. It all makes sense. None of it helps.

'Records from the missing mobile too… Mostly calls to your Simon.' He holds her gaze then, until she turns away. 'No surprises there.'

'But he must have had more than two clients.'

Cal shrugs. 'I've got someone going through his computer and files. I'll let you know if we find anything of interest.'

Georgie turns back to the window. 'Thanks,' she says, her breath misting the pane for a second before vanishing again. She imagines Fergus sleeping through the morning and feels an unexpected surge of irritation. Surely not here in the village, he'd said. Why not here in the village? That's what Georgie should have replied. But another car's pulling up outside and soon as it's arrived the engine's off and Trish is out, slamming the door, locking up and running towards the flats. She's not one to waste time with walking, not Trish. As Georgie hears her climb the stairs, she pushes the window open and leans out into the dawn. There's a space down there, between the two blocks of flats. Dark, gloomy. There might be something. Perhaps the old wheelie bins? But the council would have had them back, surely. She straightens her shoulders and looks into the window of the flat opposite, lit up once a second by the spinning blue beam of the police car. There's old furniture in there. A cupboard, with the door hanging wide. A metal bed frame. Old wallpaper that looks like it's from the 1970s. It's like a ghost town here, but worse. A ghost town would imply some historic tragedy; a ghost town would be emptied of everything but spirits, not drenched in blood. Georgie can feel a drop of sweat running down her back; she hates these suits, but she swallows down the creeping unease, pushes her shoulders back, takes a deep breath and plants her feet firmly onto the floor. There's death here right now, in the present, that she needs to deal with, and there's no reason to expect the violence has run its course.

A DIFFERENT KIND OF SKY

Georgie turns to Trish, pulls the window closed behind her.

'I'm glad you're here.'

The two women look at each other for a moment. They both know, without needing to say it, that a second murder means something and there's no going back now.

Trish takes in a large gulp of air then blows it out slowly through her pursed lips. 'Fuck.' She holds her arms around her body for a second. 'Never thought I'd have to see anything like this.'

She's so petite, Trish, she looks like a kid to Georgie sometimes – she has to repress the urge to give her a hug.

'Feels different, doesn't it? To the other...' Trish clears her throat. 'To Pauly and Rachel last year, I mean.'

They are the only other dead bodies they've investigated together.

'That was...' Georgie shakes her head. 'I still feel it now.' And they were just sixteen. She can't understand it, why they did it, why like that.

'They've planted two trees, at the school. Apple trees out by the sports field.'

'That's nice,' Georgie says. 'Thoughtful. But you're right, this violence is something else. There's hate here.' Georgie feels it like a pressure against her skin. Every time she pushes it away it seems to come back more insistently.

'I was at school with Bobby Helmsteading,' Trish says. 'Primary school, for a while. In Warphill.'

'He was raised here?'

'Before he disappeared off to that boarding school, aye.'

The longer Georgie stands here, the more the humidity is getting to her – it's like all the blood is saturating the air, generating a heat she can't explain. She sees the flash of blue sky through a coach window, her brother's long legs stretching out under the seat in front, arms folded behind his head. Please, not here. She forces her mind back to Bobby, tries to picture him instead. That short brown hair, shaved close, the stubble, those broad shoulders on him, black jeans and a maroon shirt pulling tight around his back, like he was about ready to burst out of it – she'd noticed that when she was in his cab, the sheen of his shirt where the fabric stretched.

'What was he like?'

'He was just a boy.' Trish sort of shrugs. 'I didn't like him much 'cause he always used to grab the football at break time, to play with his mates. Who didn't include me.'

'He had friends?'

'That he did. He was popular actually. It was like he had a following.'

'I thought he was new to the area.'

Trish shakes her head. 'He liked to pretend so, recently I mean, but he's as local as I am.'

Couple of months back Georgie took a taxi ride home from Crackenbridge, the car left overnight with a flat tyre and Bobby talking all the way home about the years he'd spent in Australia. She'd wondered if it was all lies, even at the time. He never mentioned having grown up round the corner.

'What brought him back, then, d'you think?'

'Family's my guess. His mum lives up the road.'

Georgie opens her mouth to speak, then changes her mind. Poor woman. No one's called her yet. She doesn't know.

'We'd better go and talk to her,' Georgie says. 'It'll be hard.' What an awful thing, to have to tell a parent their child is dead. Georgie's glad she and Fergus never had kids; she doesn't think she could have taken the worry about it, knowing what she knows about the world.

'It will,' says Trish. 'It will. She might remember me, though I'm not sure of that. Don't know if it will help either way.'

'I don't think there's much that helps, with something like this.'

'Honesty, I guess.'

Georgie likes that about Trish. Now and then, when you least expect it, she comes out with a truth like that.

They make their way down the stairs together, letting Cal know they'll be off – he's by the main door, checking the entrance. No lock on it these days. He promises to call later, with the fingerprints and ink comparisons.

'There were fingerprints, then? On the paper from the two notes?'

Of course; Trish hasn't heard about that yet.

'Aye, there's a couple of partials for sure,' he says. 'The notes look to be written by different people, but on the same paper. I'll know more around two when I get the results back. And there was no note found here at the scene.'

'Nothing?'

'Nothing,' says Georgie. 'No note, no prior threat we know of. No words anywhere so as we can find.'

'Then there's not necessarily a connection between the crimes,' Trish says. 'Is that what you're thinking? Could be two separate killers? Similar weapon, maybe, but different approach. No note. I didn't see that coming. I was sure… But of course he's not foreign, is he. He's from right here.'

'He's from right here,' Georgie says.

'And there was nothing with the eyes this time?' She pauses. 'The lack of note seems important, right? And I don't know of any particular connection between the men themselves. Lived in different villages. I don't think they were friends, though they'd probably have met one way or another.'

'Probably…'

'And the murders took place in different locations,' Trish continues. 'One indoors, one outdoors…'

'That's all true,' says Georgie. 'All very true. There is one thing though.'

'What's that?'

'There's a car, parked down the side alleyway. Away from the main road. It took me a minute to notice it, tell you the truth. Could hardly see it from upstairs. It's right in the shadow between the flats, there. See?'

'Oh my God,' says Cal.

'My thoughts exactly. And we'll need to confirm it, of course, but now I've got a better view of it I'm fairly certain the car parked right there opposite the flat where Bobby Helmsteading was murdered belongs to Dr Cosse.'

Trish has her restless energy again, Georgie can see it in the way she straightens up, bends and stretches each arm.

'We have a connection,' Trish is saying. 'We. Have. A. Connection.'

Cal's already calling to his team, and Georgie's as eager to see what they find in the car as Trish, of course she is, it's just that she can't shake the feeling there's something she's not seeing yet, something bigger. And then there's this itching in her legs. She'd been running away a long time before she found Fergus, and together they found this sleepy stretch of coast, and for the first time in a long time she wonders if maybe she needs to be moving on again. She's not sure why or what that would mean, exactly, but the thought makes her insides twist. That's when she sees them, though. Way over by the horizon, like yesterday.

'Do you see, over there, Trish?'

Trish looks at her, confused.

'You're pointing at the sky, Georgie.'

'Yes, but look at those lenticular clouds, over there to the north. Don't they look special to you? So smooth and almost… well, I don't know. Ethereal, don't you think? They were up there yesterday too. They're some of the most beautiful clouds I've ever seen.'

'They're just clouds,' Trish says with a shrug.

Georgie forces a smile. They're more than just clouds, though. She knows that. They're something rare and transient, and they needed to be seen.

OPENING TIME

Fergus gets to Crackenbridge Museum at nine o'clock on the dot, only to discover that it doesn't open until half past – there's a note on the door saying the school run comes first. It's probably staffed by volunteers. Next door is one of the old charity shops, he remembers it 'cause they used to have a great assortment of army coats, but now it's all closed up and there's a sign in the window saying RETAIL UNIT AVAILABLE FOR RENT. He goes for a walk around the block, past the Morrisons, past the row of B & Bs with vacancies, through the new estate, round past the old cinema that was abandoned halfway through being converted into a restaurant, graffiti on the plasterboarded windows, and eventually turning back to the museum, where he is still fifteen minutes early but he tries the doorbell anyway. Can't tell if it actually rang inside, but no one comes to the door, so after a few minutes of standing there he sits down on the step and rests his head back. He's just letting his eyes close over when he's startled awake – feels like a right numpty as the woman, hands full of bags and a buggy containing a sleeping toddler, nods at him with the words, 'We've got a keen one, eh?'

'I'm sorry, I thought...'

He rises awkwardly to his feet. Doesn't quite know what to do with himself as she searches for her keys, though pretty soon he finds himself holding several of her bags and peering at the toddler in the buggy. Georgie tells him that sometimes he apologises for himself too much. She's probably right too, but it's a hard habit to break. Still, he didn't apologise for forgetting dinner last night. Maybe he should have.

The woman has unlocked the door now, and he helps her up the step with the buggy, waits patiently as she seats herself behind the front desk and pulls out the postcards (50p each), leaflets (free to a good home) and a battered paperback. 'Three pound for adults,' she tells him, and he fishes out some coins from the side pouch of his cycling rucksack. He's in his Lycras again, so no pockets. The sweat he'd worked up on the cycle over is cooling fast – no heating on in here overnight, that's for sure. Could be there's no heating at all. It's closed all winter. Not enough folk coming to justify even a volunteer's time. They've got a postcard of the standing stone though, there on its own in the field, slightly lopsided, grey with smudges of white, looking rough and weather-worn against a pristine blue sky. And there's another of the large bowl he remembered, the size of a casserole dish but taller, with handles either side and figures carved into the metal, their faces upturned and mouths open to the sky.

'Time to see the original,' he says to the attendant. He recognises her now, he's sure of it. 'I run the local archaeological society.'

She smiles politely and he can't decide whether she already knows who he is or simply doesn't care.

'And you know' – he picks up the postcard of the standing stone – 'I'm thinking of getting some aerial footage of this. Maybe you'd be interested...'

But she's started reading her book already. There's an image on the front, a twisted knot of red rope, with silver and night blue behind it. The toddler is fast asleep, clutching onto a floppy purple doll with orange wool for hair and well-chewed teething rings dangling where its hands should be. The book and the doll seem like the only colour in here – the lights are dim, the walls a grubby off-white, the floor brown carpet. Fergus leaves her to her reading and follows the arrow pointing through a door to his left.

Crackenbridge Museum is a single room. He doesn't know what's on the top floor of the building – from outside it was clear there must be a top floor – but in here, what would originally have been a residential home, presumably, has been converted into an entrance hall and a single, open-plan room housing four tall glass cabinets and about a dozen information posters along the walls. The windows look out onto the street but are clad in thick curtains. Maybe it's to protect the exhibits, though it's probably more that no one could be bothered to open them. Overhead, two energy-saving light bulbs fail to fill the room with light.

He reads the posters first. It's mostly modern history: Crackenbridge during the First and Second World War, pictures of gas masks, the locals going to fight, the monument built when they didn't return; an artist's rendition of a typical family home in Victorian times, with a description of four generations living in a single room; a series of posters entitled THE INDUSTRIAL REVOLUTION ARRIVES. It's not till he's round on the far wall that he finds the poster with the photo of the excavation at the motte. Archaeologists crouch beside a trench and a series of close-ups show the artefacts they found: fragments of a dagger that might have had ceremonial use, and the bowl he had remembered – behind him, it's the centrepiece of the exhibit. The poster says it has similarities to the Gundestrup cauldron, though it's made from iron and copper alloy. The imagery is Celtic, ritualistic; they date it from between 300 and 100 BC. *Note the large man with stag's antlers*, the write-up says. *The true meaning of the engravings may never be known.*

It is in the central display case in the middle of the room, to allow you to walk around and see its full circumference. In the dim room, it seems to reflect the light with a copper-tinged glow. The engravings are accentuated by shadows, and a spotlight illuminates the stag-man. He is twice the height of the figures around him, with large antlers sprouting from his head. His followers wear cloaks and tall, conical hats, and they reach up towards him with pointed fingers;

they strike Fergus as desperate, pleading. The stag-man holds a figure by the ankles, their head and torso disappearing into a cauldron. It seems, to Fergus, that they are surely being boiled alive. Circling the rest of the bowl is a procession of naked men and women, all wearing torcs around their necks and conical hats and they have the same pointed fingers – except they are not fingers, he suddenly realises, they have been carved with birds' beaks instead of hands.

Next to the central display case is a small white block on the floor. A typed and laminated sheet of paper resting on it says the replica of the standing stone has been temporarily removed due to inaccuracies. Fergus frowns. Turning over the sheet of paper, he sees a photo of the stone itself, the original, except that something is wrong – it's not as he remembers it. This stone is unmarked. Lichen-covered. Where are the carvings, the strange curves and shapes in the stone that he once felt with his own hands? He has to see it, in person. He has to get detailed, professional photos, and he needs the kit to do it. Georgie will understand. He cycles fast to the retail park outside of Crackenbridge – he knows exactly what to get, he even checked they had it in stock last night – and then it's in his hands, smartphone-compatible, compact and portable, expensive: his very own drone. He pays from the joint account. She probably won't even notice, and anyway it's important he does this. The standing stone is calling him.

HALF TEN OR THEREABOUTS

Mrs Helmsteading looks beyond Georgie's shoulder, her eyes drifting side to side as if distracted by the nothingness she sees there. Trish opens her mouth, then closes it again. To Georgie, it's one of those houses that seem more silent than is natural. There's always noise at home, with her and Fergus. There's always something. Music playing or Fergus humming to himself. The two of them, talking together. Though they haven't done enough of that recently. She shouldn't have felt annoyed about him earlier, doesn't really understand why she did. The comforting noise of him is something she's been taking for granted but there's not so much as a clock in here, not even the clicking of radiators warming up, the morning stretching of the pipes.

But then a small dog scurries in, a terrier, and suddenly it's all *yap yap yap* and skidding to and fro. Trish tucks her feet beneath her chair, trying to keep them out of harm's way. Georgie understands that – from all the manic barking it sounds like a dog that would take a quick bite just to say hello, just to get the feel of something solid in its mouth. Must be desperate for some attention, the poor thing. Actually, it seems hyperactive the way it's darting about between them. He. It's a He. If he would slow down for a minute, she'd give him a pat, soothe him a bit.

'Oh,' she says, her hand moving unconsciously to her neck.

What with all the sudden noise and scampering, it's taken Georgie a minute to notice he only has three legs. No wonder he's all over the place.

He slides under the low coffee table, there's more scratching of claws on laminate flooring, then he barks at Trish, who's now pressed back into her chair as far as she can get, before leaping towards Mrs Helmsteading's ankles. Mid-jump, though, Mrs Helmsteading reaches down – the fastest movement Georgie's seen her make – and scoops the dog up, where he sits, calmer at last, on her lap, his stump curled underneath his body.

Georgie wants to ask what happened to the dog, but she doesn't.

Mrs Helmsteading's eyes return to their searching for something behind Georgie's shoulder.

This time Georgie turns to see what it might be back there, hidden in thin air. And actually, there is something there. There's a window, facing out onto the street. The sun's broken through the cloud for a second and it's coming in low, casting the figure in front of the window in silhouette, but she's fairly sure – yes, she's quite certain now that through the faded, dirty-looking net curtains she can see the gawky shape of Andy Barr peering inside.

'Trish, you didn't—'

Trish is up like a shot, opening the door.

'What are you doing here, Andy?' she says. 'You're not supposed to be here. And it's rude, you know' – this spoken under her breath to him alone, though of course everyone in the room can hear her – 'it's rude, looking in someone's window like that.'

Georgie's on her feet too. She shouldn't have been so soft the other day. Trish is trying to teach him, trying to help him, she gets that – and she remembers what Trish said about his dad, it's been haunting her – but this is totally inappropriate. Then she hears Mrs Helmsteading's voice.

'Bobby's gone,' she's saying. 'Bobby's gone.'

She's pushed past Georgie and she's pulling Andy down into a hug and Andy, dwarfing her at his six-foot-six and thin as a coat stand, looks baffled, totally baffled.

Suddenly Georgie understands. Mrs Helmsteading doesn't remember Trish, but she knows Andy. She's seen Andy recently; he's been around in her life. He didn't come here to be work-shadowing her or Trish, he came here to see Bobby. They knew each other – though she hadn't known that before. They must have been friends. That's what it looks like, as Mrs Helmsteading's words and the police's involvement gradually sink in. For a second it looks like his knees might collapse under him, but they don't. That's not what happens at all. Andy goes the other way.

'Who did this?' he demands of Georgie. 'What the fuck happened and who did it? Who the—'

Georgie doesn't even have to speak; Trish knows what to do. She's putting an arm around Andy's waist, leading him gently back to the door.

'Let's sit outside,' she's saying, 'you and me, pal. This is a nasty shock for us all. Such a sad thing to have happened. Let's have a sit down outside, in the fresh air, okay?' And Andy is following her, his shoulders lowering with her words, the anger falling out of him already. He's not a naturally angry boy. Georgie knows that; they all do. 'Okay,' Trish says, 'you come and sit with me outside now, pet.'

Georgie doesn't think she's ever heard Trish call anyone 'pet' before. It's worked though, Andy is quiet and there's been nothing bad said, just some honest upset. With what Mrs Helmsteading's going through, probably Andy cursing a bit makes no difference either way. She looks back to the three-legged dog, cowering underneath Mrs Helmsteading's chair, but there's something she's thinking, something about how Mrs Helmsteading doesn't quite seem… Well, she's upset, certainly, distant and vague, but not in shock, that's the thing. Not the way Andy was.

The door clicks shut behind Andy and Trish, and Georgie is left alone with Mrs Helmsteading and the dog. On the far wall there's an ornately tiled mantelpiece over a flame-effect gas fire. She steps closer to it and her eyes run over the crammed row of chipped vases filled with feathers, half-used candles – from the smell in here she'd say they've been lit recently – old wedding photos, painted china horses and a curved metal figure of a woman and a child. She turns and says to Mrs Helmsteading, 'I need to ask you a few questions, I'm afraid. Would it be okay if I asked them now?'

Mrs Helmsteading nods, and the two women face each other across the room.

'Why did Bobby come back to Warphill?'

'It's his home,' says Mrs Helmsteading. 'Was his home. Of course he came back. Why would he not have come back?'

'Of course,' says Georgie. 'Of course. It's just... Why didn't he come back straight after school, then? What's he been doing these last few years?'

'Man's got to make his way in the world,' says Mrs Helmsteading, sadly.

There's no surprise, that's the problem. She's grieving, but she's not been surprised by anything Georgie has asked.

'Why did you decide to send him away to school?'

'He was gifted.'

Georgie waits a beat.

'My late husband thought it was a good idea.'

'And who is this, in the photo here?' Georgie asks. She picks up the frame, carefully, from its dust-edged position on the mantelpiece.

'Oh,' says Mrs Helmsteading.

That's when she takes a step forward, and Georgie notices the shake in her legs.

She reaches up and takes the photo from Georgie, then strokes a finger, very carefully, over the girl's cheek. Except that the photo is quite small, and her finger quite padded, so what she really does is smoosh her finger over the girl's entire face. 'That's my daughter,' she says, 'that's my little girl. That's my Dawn.'

'Is Dawn here now?'

Mrs Helmsteading shakes her head.

'Was Dawn sent away to school too?'

'No, Dawn stayed here. Dawn always stayed with us.'

'I'd like to talk to her.'

Mrs Helmsteading looks up at Georgie, and the frame falls from her grasp.

'Where is she?' asks Georgie. 'Where can I find Dawn now?'

Mrs Helmsteading leans her weight down on the corner of the coffee table, which almost topples but doesn't.

'I'd rather—'

'Can you give me her number? I need to ask her a few questions—'

'You'll not upset her, will you?'

'I'll be sympathetic, Mrs Helmsteading. I promise you that.'

Mrs Helmsteading nods slowly, and writes a number on the pad of paper lying on the coffee table. Rips it out and offers it to Georgie, who thanks her for it. Then she bends her way slowly to the floor, where she sits down like a little girl. She just sits there cross-legged on the floor. There's a slight stoop to her back, more pronounced now she's down there. Her hair's thinning a bit on top. She picks up the frame, and strokes at the photograph again, and then she looks up to Georgie and says, 'She's sensitive, my Dawny. You'll not go getting her upset?'

Georgie's phone vibrates in her pocket. About time too. It's police headquarters. They might not care much about what happens in Burrowhead but she knew, after this morning, they'd have to step up.

DS Frazer will be with you by the afternoon, but you're the SIO. Uniforms from Crackenbridge at your disposal. Sorry we can't spare more people.

Trish is back, striding across the room.

'What is it?'

Georgie shakes her head. She's never heard of this DS Frazer. Suddenly the dog, with a crash of claws and paws, is sliding across the floor to where Trish stands frozen until, with the slightest movement and at the very last minute, she turns her foot to the side, catching the dog off balance and sending him hurtling into the leg of the coffee table.

Mrs Helmsteading looks up at them both from the floor. There are tears in her eyes, and a deep sadness that catches Georgie in the back of her throat.

'I'm—' Trish begins, but Mrs Helmsteading just shakes her head.

'I think I'd like yous all to go away now.'

11:55

Trish is kicking herself on the way home. Just as Georgie was developing a bit of trust there, she had to go and trip up that dog. The scene keeps playing out in her mind, the way she turned her foot without thinking, Georgie's stern look at her, Mrs Helmsteading throwing them out. What she should have done was to kneel down, catch the dog in her arms. Maybe ruffle his fur a bit. That's how you set a dog lover at ease; show them you love their dog. She knows that *now*, of course. Too late. She wishes she had more poise, like Georgie does, and didn't keep putting her foot in it, but it doesn't come natural. Hopefully it's about learning self-control, rather than having to work around the personality you're born with. A light flashes to her left – the Slow Down sign she had installed last year. The speedometer says she's doing thirty-six. She presses the brake a little too firmly; if Georgie hadn't noticed she was speeding, she will have now. Her eyes flick to the passenger seat. Actually, Georgie's staring out of the window and she seems unaware. Trish relaxes a bit. She'd love to know what it is Georgie's thinking, staring intently out of the window like that. It's a strange sort of morning, right enough. Dense cloud pierced by low light, blinding when it streams in through the windscreen there but not a patch of blue in sight. Just that stormy grey blowing through the sky, sinking deeper all the while.

This is the biggest case they've had round here, since she's been back at least. She left a PC but came home a detective – got plenty of comments about what a waste it was too, newly qualified and returning to a rural station like this. No chance of promotion. No guarantee the station was even going to survive the next round of cuts, let alone the round after. Stuck on drug abuse and traffic violations, having to do the work of a uniform, any case that calls. Community policing, most of the time. But she knew it could be more than that, and this week, this proves it. There's work to do here.

She pulls into the station car park, switches off the engine and opens the door in one swift movement. No one loitering on the corner today – folk must have got bored and gone home; that, or the storm cloud's keeping them in this morning. Good. The station feels eerily quiet though, what with Simon at home and Andy off for lunch before they interview him about Bobby later. Georgie's unlocking her office door and Trish is standing there awkwardly beside her.

'I'm sorry...' she starts, and Georgie looks at her, startled. 'Sorry about the dog. I didn't mean to...'

Georgie's door swings open.

'It's okay,' she says. 'Interesting, how protective she was. Let's have a coffee and talk this all through.'

Trish grins. 'I'll get the kettle on.' It gives her a chance to straighten her thoughts out too. They have leads, and she has ideas. Time to prove it. Some chocolate digestives on a plate – Georgie likes chocolate digestives, as does Trish. Carrying it all through to Georgie's office. She flicks the lights on – God, it's dark in here today. Clasps the marker for the whiteboard. Right. Let's do this.

'People we know,' says Georgie.

'With any connection to either crime?'

'All four crimes. Two murders, the racist notes, and the vandalism at the Spar.'

'Right you are. People we know...' Trish glances up and Georgie nods. 'Uncle Walt. Think we can rule him out?'

'Leave him on for now.'

'PC Simon Hunter. Connected to Alexis, but got an alibi.'

'Leave them all on, Trish.'

'Right. Aye. Kevin Taylor.'

'We need to check his prints against whatever we find on the notes.'

'And could be he's involved in the vandalism at the Spar?'

'Could be,' says Georgie. 'Well done on that, by the way.'

Trish keeps her smile to herself. They're a long way from anywhere right now.

'Mrs Helmsteading?'

'Add her on. Connected to Bobby, obviously. No known connection to Alexis. Seems unlikely she'd be sending racist notes.'

'And then we've got whoever did write the racist notes,' says Trish. 'They've got the hate, they've got the motive – could be they were responsible for Alexis's murder too.'

'That's all true, about the hate. They could have seen him as an enemy. Lots of that going round. But we don't know who they are. And they'd have had no reason to kill Bobby.'

'And what about those initials?' says Trish. 'N.P.'

Georgie's frowning.

'Pencilled into the day planner. Carelessly rubbed out,' she continues. 'Did Alexis have a new patient? Someone he decided not to see?'

'And then,' says Georgie, 'there's Dawn Helmsteading.'

Trish stares at her.

Shit, of course, that's right. Bobby had a sister. She was younger, quite a few years behind her and Bobby at school.

'Now, Dawn is Bobby's sister. You probably know her a bit yourself, being raised near Warphill – and she seems to be missing. At least, her mum couldn't tell me where she is.'

'Missing?'

'Could be. Her phone's going straight to voicemail. So, could she be a witness? Could she be involved?'

'Could she be in danger?'

'That's a good question, Trish.'

They both go quiet for a second. A body a day so far, that's how this case has been working out.

'I never really knew her,' Trish says, as though it's an explanation. 'Different generation.'

'What does that make me?' Georgie says.

'Different generation in the other direction?' She smiles.

But Georgie is staring out of the window, staring and staring out there. Trish follows her gaze, sees a large hawk or something circling high, above the houses, above the mist.

'Okay, Trish,' Georgie says, her eyes returning to the room. 'I want everything you can find on Dawn Helmsteading. History and present-day. Probable locations – home, work, friends.'

'Absolutely.'

'It'll be good to have that in place when DS Frazer arrives.'

'Who?'

'He's coming from the city to help.'

Trish doesn't know what to say to that, but Georgie doesn't seem to want a reply anyway.

'Where's Andy?' She looks at her watch.

'I sent him off to go meet his pals for lunch,' Trish says. 'And break the news about Bobby, I imagine. He's right cut up about things. Seems they all used to hang around a bit. We'll not be able to keep this one quiet.'

'We've not managed to keep much quiet so far.'

'But he'll be in this afternoon.'

Georgie looks alarmed.

'For an interview, I mean. He knows it's important.'

'Okay, yes. Good. That's fine,' Georgie says, but she seems distracted, keeps staring out of the window. Trish doesn't get it. 'And Cal's calling at two—'

'With the fingerprint and ink analysis from the notes,' Trish completes the sentence for her. 'And whatever they've found in the files at Alexis's house. Paper and electronic.'

Georgie doesn't reply.

'So…'

'So now, we get our lunch.'

'What?'

Trish has absolutely no interest in taking a lunch break, but Georgie is heading for the door, and Trish is left alone in the station with her cold cup of coffee and a vague sense she's missing something.

LEAVING BEHIND

DS Frazer likes to drive with no music playing and the windows down, so he can hear the engine, feel the connection of the tyres to the tarmac. The city is a smudge of motorway in his rear-view mirror already and it's easier to make a big splash in a small pond – so he tells himself, at any rate. This is an opportunity. There are rumours about the villages, of course, the drugs flowing through them, the isolation keeping things hidden that would be noticed in the city. He's never heard of this one though, this Burrowhead. It's the smallest station in the force apparently, and they're one of the smallest forces in the country. He did a bit of research before setting off, likes to know who he's dealing with, who and what. Not that there was much information to find. Rain starts pelting his car out of nowhere and he taps the button to close the windows. The sky looks wild out over the coast, and there are fewer cars now too. It's been a bad couple of days in the city, bad time to be leaving – not his choice. But it's an opportunity. A truck carrying a static caravan sways past in the other direction and he turns the air conditioning up and the headlights on, the sky suddenly dark and muggy and heavy, a sign for the next exit looming up faster than he was expecting. This is where he turns off. He indicates. Leaves the motorway. The calm, reassuring female voice of his satnav tells him to turn left about twenty seconds after he's done so.

He'd thought about calling his wife's mobile before he left, leaving an answerphone message, but he didn't in the end. It would have been good to hear her voice, though. He wishes he had now. The noise of the car seems different off the motorway, the drive of it too: rougher, more growling, and there's an inexplicable drift to the edge of the road when he releases his grip on the steering wheel. A sign saying 20 mph and a picture of loose gravel makes no sense at all; there is no gravel. A few minutes later all road markings disappear and the rain is replaced by a fine haze of drizzle that seems to float above the road. Forty miles to Warphill, it says. That's his way. Out to the coast. He hasn't seen another vehicle since turning onto this single-track road. He taps the button to open the windows again.

The air's different here; it carries the taste of fish. Is he imagining that? Can't see the sea yet, just brown fields and the overgrown hedge either side of the road. He swerves to avoid a branch and glances down at his mobile, which shows no signal, no Wi-Fi connection. The satnav hasn't spoken to him in a while. Every now and then there's a small rectangular white sign pointing down tracks on the left or right to villages he's never heard of, and he scans them dutifully for any mention of Burrowhead but sees none. He keeps following the road, glances at his phone. Swerves to avoid another branch.

Burrowhead village. Burrowhead police station. What with all the closures and mergers these days he doesn't know how it's survived, a country station way out here with three mismatched staff. It's like someone forgot it was there. Like the villages themselves maybe, Burrowhead and Warphill, the one coming with the other. There were blank faces all round when they were told about the murders this morning. Not an officer in the building had been there, nor wanted to go. And then he was picked out, and here he is already nearing Warphill, must have been in some kind of a daze and honestly he couldn't even describe that last bit of the journey or how long it's taken him, how long he's been following the winding curves of this little road, but that sign there, Burrowhead straight on. He sits up a little taller, this must be right, the hedge up ahead showing a steep turn to come and the waves, he can hear them now, crashing down on the rocks and the sea will be just around this bend but it happens so fast he doesn't know how it happens or what happens only that he's skidding and he's lost control and the collision forces him forwards and he feels like he's been punched in the lungs and the stomach and the ribs all at the same time and his breath, when it comes, is rasping and thick and then he sees it. Straight ahead, between the trees. Towering over his car, facing him down with eyes like his father's, round and black and bright, but its coat is the smoothest white he's ever seen on an animal, any animal, and its antlers are huge and intricate and gleaming and strong and impossible – he closes his eyes. Opens them again. There is a stag standing between the trees beside the road, untouched and commanding. The front passenger corner of his car has hit a tree. He's okay. The car's okay. Just a dent. But that creature. He looks again, this time seeing brown flecks among the white. Its breath misting in the air. It is achingly beautiful. He blinks. There's mud on its legs and now he looks again the antlers are no larger than normal. It is an ordinary stag. Of course it is. He hears his own laugh, timid and unconvinced, then clears his throat. He starts the engine, reverses away from the tree, and when he glances up the stag is gone and his engine is idling and his car is back on the road. He turns the engine off again. He needs a minute. His hands are shaking. There, to his right, so obvious he doesn't know how he didn't seem them before, are the tall jagged cliffs of the Burrowhead coastline and beyond that, disappearing into the grey of the sky at the horizon, lies the sea.

FAILING LIGHT

I'm not sure how long I've been unconscious. The cave is in darkness, but I know where I am. We used to whisper about this place.

I sit up, my ankle screeching its pain, my back, my hair wet from the puddles in the dips of the floor. It's strangely warm, like there's heat somewhere within these rocks. When I stare at the back of the cave there's nothing but stone. Rough, yes. Shadowed and sharp, but only rock.

Stay calm and start at the beginning, you say.

I wish you were here with me. I wish I hadn't had to see what I saw. But there's no rewinding time, you taught me that, even though it wasn't the lesson you intended. You taught me there's more than looking, too, so maybe I can find some truth in the messages that have been scratched and buried deep in the rock. Low down and etched into limestone it says PLEASE HELP MY MAMMY. I start at the base with my index finger, following the curve of the letters around to the right. How did she get here, this little girl – did someone bring her, to scratch her pleading where it would never be read? Will it be submerged, eroded by salt and clawed at by crabs until it is nothing? But there are scratches that look old, from years ago, so perhaps the pleading has some staying power.

Please help my Mammy, she whispers.

Higher up, PD and RT have carved their initials inside a heart. It is fragile. It makes me sink and I don't know why. There's the smell of cheap perfume. My fingers follow the scratch of their heart and I hear them, teenagers; whispers of love, low and distant. Something is wrong. I move further along the cave's wall, my hands following the contours of stone. It is dim back here. My shadow combines with the darkness of the rock until we are the same, and there is something ancient, more threatening about the scratches on the walls here, something that tugs at the back of my mind. Here is the stick figure, carved out of iron and wedged, standing, into the rock. Its head is pointed and it has long, vicious hands that taper into the sharp tips of beaks, the mouths open, ready to bite. As my fingers move over it I feel a jab of pain, snatch my hand away and stumble backwards into something soft. I freeze. I need to turn, see who it is, but my limbs won't move. Words disturb the air. Shapes I can't grasp but can't deny. Turn round. *Turn round.*

Finally, my legs obey.

Her skin is so dark she melts into the rock, more shadow than substance; tatters, a wisp of lace. For a second I feel her hand reaching out to me, but then she is gone and in the rock behind where she was standing I see it – the worry doll hidden deep in a crevice. I reach in for her, clasping damp, stringy cling film between my fingers, and my mouth fills with saliva, pooling under my tongue. I'm going to be sick. I lean down, glimpse swirling carpet. Something grabs my ankle. I feel his fingers. Old skin, cracked like rice paper. I force the doll back into the rock, but it's too late for that. From where he lies on the floor I hear the croak of my name.

THE IMPORTANCE OF LUNCHTIME

When Georgie gets out to her car, she notices that the cloud cover has dropped down even lower than it was this morning. She can almost feel it, glistening, on her skin. Gives an eerie feel to the village, to the countryside, no doubts about that. Like there's something unpleasant they're going to find soon, and there's not a thing Georgie can do to change it. These murders, they're seeping deep into her mind while overhead the clouds are clinging onto the trees, easing their way in between the branches. The mist is shrouding the slopes of the hills beyond the village like dread, the hilltops above surreal in their clarity, separated from the ground beneath. The world is divided. She turns on her headlights, the heater too – there's such a chill in the car. She'll be driving right through the cloud mist, soon as she's out of the village, soon as she's heading for home.

She doesn't get that far, though, has to slam on the brakes as she gets to the village square. Nearly hits poor Walt, not that he notices she's even there. He's in his dressing gown and walking boots, unlaced, wandering across the road towards the fountain. She reverses back to the kerb, parks up and opens the door. Steps out into air that feels heavy. Walt has made it to the fountain and by the time she's reached the grass he's climbed his way in. The stone of it glitters in this weather – must be the water droplets in the air, bringing out something crystalline. Beyond the village square, the houses fade into murk.

'You alright there now, Walt?'

He looks startled when he sees her, like he wasn't expecting anyone to be out here, even though he's in the busiest part of the village in the middle of the day. Even though he's just narrowly missed being knocked over by oncoming traffic.

That said, Georgie has to admit there's no one else around. It does have a deserted feel to it today.

'What are you doing there in the fountain?'

'That you, Georgie?'

'Yes, course it's me, Walt, course it is.'

'Good,' he says. 'Good. I was wanting a word, see.'

'What can I do for you, Walt?'

'Shh.' He puts his finger to his lips. 'It's only you I want to talk to. Off the record.'

'Right you are, Walt,' she whispers, though she's careful to articulate clearly – Trish says he's going deaf, along with the rest of it.

'In you come.'

'What?'

'In you come, Georgie.'

In the mist she realises what he means.

It's about waist height, the fountain, so she pushes herself up backwards with her arms, sits for a moment on the edge of the fountain's pool before shuffling down into it to sit beside him, feet tucked round to the side. There are stones in it, tiny round pebbles and shells she pushes away from under her legs. It's not comfortable. She couldn't say it was comfortable. But he seems happier now she's in. Less anxious.

'I knew you'd come,' he says, hand on her arm. 'I knew you understood.'

She nods to him, waits for more.

'They're ancient, you know.'

He keeps his voice low, and it does feel strangely private now, sitting in the empty fountain in the mist, barely able to see the length of the village square. Not another soul in sight, nor a sound either.

'Are they?'

'Oh yes, yes. They've been here for thousands of years. Visiting us for thousands and thousands of years. Tens of thousands, probably.'

'How do you know?' whispers Georgie.

'You can see it, in the rocks,' he says. 'In the ancient rocks and stones of the land. You're sensitive, aren't you Georgie? The village needs someone like you. I think you're someone who can be trusted with fragile things.'

Her fingers are straying around the pebbles that have been left in the fountain, sanded smooth over years of the rough tide.

'Do you mean the cup and ring, Walt? The stone etchings buried in the woods out past the motte?'

'That's what they call it. But it wasn't no cup they were carving, Georgie. You can feel the connection when you press your hand against the stone. Ten thousand years is a long time, but you can still feel it.'

His arms reach out in front of him, drawing circles within circles in the air.

'That's nice, Walt. I think that's a nice idea.'

'It's not going to be the same when they come back next time, though.'

Her hand catches on something sharp.

'When are they coming back?

He puts his finger to his lips.

'I'm glad I can talk to you, Georgie,' he says. 'You can stay in the fountain for a while, if you like.'

She's holding that sharp shell now, her fingers running along the edges of it, but she doesn't break eye contact.

'Where are you going, Walt?'

'Following the birds,' he says.

She watches as he slowly lowers his legs over the fountain's rim, his shaking wrists barely able to support his weight. She watches in case he needs her help, but he manages on his own. As his feet reach the ground, he picks up his big holdall, his eyes glancing furtively round the empty square. Looking for all the world like he thinks someone might be following him. She glances down to her hand and gasps. There is a tiny human tooth nestled in her palm. A prickle crawls up her neck but Walt leans closer, nods his head a few times.

'A good offering,' he says. 'Generous, to give the milk teeth. They'll like that.'

Georgie stares at him. He stares back, waiting, as she slowly tips her hand until the tooth falls back into the fountain. The skin on her palm is tingling, cold.

'Don't know about you, Georgie, but I feel better now.'

Her mouth is too dry for her to reply; he doesn't notice her silence, though, he's drifting away already.

'Well then. So long, Georgie,' he says, turning and heading towards Church Street, leaving her alone with the contents of the fountain. She feels nauseous, swallows it down, is conscious of her own breath as she watches him go.

'So long, Walt,' she whispers, once he's disappeared into the mist that has obscured each street of the village from the next. Pushing down from the fountain, she takes a moment to brush her clothes clean, to make sure there are no remnants on her hands, her skin. It's the middle of the day but it feels like night's descending, and when she gets back to the car she notices she's left her headlights on. In their beams she can see tiny specks, and she thinks at first they might be the first drops of the rain that's coming. But then she realises they are tiny insects, moths, fluttering low to the ground and drawn to the light. She gets into the car and shuts the door hurriedly. She wants to get home now, to see Fergus, to heat up some of her chicken and vegetable soup. To get away from all of this. But when she gets home he's not there.

She puts the soup in the microwave. It's frozen. Then she calls his name. When there's no answer, she finds herself looking through every room in the house, though quite what she's searching for she can't say. He's left the computer on. She pushes the mouse a fraction and the screen comes alive. All his photos are there, and the notes he's been taking for his website. *The Archaeological Society of Burrowhead and Warphill.* Georgie closes her eyes for a second, listens to the soft ticking of the clock in the hall, the occasional creak of the radiators, the pulse of her home. Then she sits down and pulls the chair closer to the desk. There's no sign in the browser history of any job searches, just pages and pages of Iron Age archaeology, carvings and artefacts, burial sites, articles on Lindow Man, and a gruesome story about the skeletons of a pregnant woman and a young man found in an underground shaft in East Yorkshire, a wooden stake pinning their arms together. Georgie feels sick. He has a Word document entitled 'The Threefold Death' on his desktop, but when she opens it the document is empty.

The desktop background is a photo of them, Georgie and Fergus, from ten years ago. She'd just made inspector back then and he was project manager at the BAE nuclear site down the coast. They look so hopeful, in that photo. Standing together in a garden alive with the yellows and purples of spring bulbs. She's hit by a wave of exhaustion at always being the one to worry, about the future, about money, about keeping them afloat and paying for the Wi-Fi he's using not to look for work but to research, what, ancient human sacrifice. In the kitchen, the microwave pings. Exhaustion doesn't cover it. She moves to the table and eats her soup in silence.

TIME SLIPPING BY

Fergus finds himself standing before the menhir, in the shadow it casts on the ground. It rises above his head, wider at its top than its base. The sky is heavy again; that storm from yesterday's not finished yet. But as he reaches out his hand, ready to touch it, something like static repels him and he can't bring himself to make contact with the curves and dips in the stone. Stepping back, he carefully places his bag on the ground and pulls out the box that contains his new drone, finally fully charged. It took some patience, sitting at home with it plugged in, waiting, waiting; increasingly irritated by all the clingy plastic packaging it had come in. He wishes everything in this world could be recycled. But then the red light turned to green and here he is, the drone in his hands, ready to fly. It is a beautiful creation, the round central body of it gleaming black in the storm light, the four winged arms slender and perfectly balanced, the propeller blades themselves so delicate they become almost transparent as he switches it on and they start to spin. Holding it out gently in front of him, he lets go and, miraculously, it stays airborne, hovering before him.

He pulls out his phone, opens the app, makes the connection. His own face appears on the screen, pale-skinned and freckled, with the remnants of a flush in the cheeks from the cycle over here. He tries a smile, then presses 'Capture'. What a remarkable thing. He touches the controls and the drone flies up and to the right, looking down at him, insignificant beside the standing stone to his left, his shadow lost within it. He brings the drone in lower, to the blades of grass around the stone's base, to the way some have been flattened while others seem to be reaching towards it. Then something changes and he's not sure how it happens but he's drawn upwards, high over the standing stone, soaring, weightless, and the grass seems to blur, to become a swathe of greens and browns that blend into the background, undulating and indistinct. The drone rises again and his gaze follows it up to where the clouds, the greys and purples of the storm are swirling, and they too have lost their edges, become an impression of depth and danger so the only thing between the ground and the sky, the only thing that matters, is the menhir.

The drone's automatic focus kicks in, the image on the screen resolving and enlarging in a way that makes Fergus sway. He'd fall if he kept looking up, but he can't bring himself to look down; all he can see is the top of the stone, the deep concentric rings etched there, drawing him closer to something lodged within. He can't make out what it is at first, he just stares at his phone as the image resolves, magnifies, blurs, enlarges, resolves; it looks like a shiny marble has been placed there, glinting wet with dew or rain. Right there, on top of the standing stone. It enlarges again and he stumbles backwards, his wrist turning, his phone dropped suddenly into the mud. It's an eye. He's sure, it's… God, please not human, but he saw it, he can still see it, staring up at him from his phone's screen in the dirt, staring up from the carved rings of the standing stone to the gusting clouds overhead. His legs won't move. His feet are sinking into the ground, the soil itself pulling him deeper. He closes his eyes, breaks contact, takes a breath and stumbles backwards, picks up his phone. Closes the app, fast. Calls the police. Stay where you are, they tell him. Some officers are on their way.

So he stays put. Forces himself to look straight ahead – and there in front of him is the standing stone, tall and, suddenly, astoundingly beautiful. The moss and lichen covering it make the most extraordinary colours, purples and maroon and a vivid, glowing gold, and between them the stone's contours are undeniably man-made. At last he can reach out a hand; he needs to understand their shape, the curves and patterns that disappear into the stone like footprints in wet sand, but under his palm he can feel them. He'd expected the stone to be roughened by rain and erosion, coated in guano, but he is wrong: the texture is even, almost sleek, and the shapes and ridges that his fingertips locate are precise. There's a heat to it, as though it's been storing up the sun's energy. He's searching for letters, for something he can make sense of in the shapes etched flawlessly into the stone. There are curves and rings, horizontal lines that seem to lead somewhere until they thin and vanish, and at one point he imagines an animal, a horse or a deer, but then it is gone. There's a curved dip he presses into with his thumb, and lines reaching out from a central ring, branching like the veins of a leaf. How can they not have a whole display dedicated to this in the museum; why is this stone left out here as though no one cares? It should be studied. It's extraordinary. But then, he wouldn't move it. It belongs here more than him, more than any of them. These markings, they cover the whole surface. He needs both hands to follow their shapes as one minute he is kneeling, pressing into a hollow in the stone with his curved fist, and the next he is reaching up, searching for figures near the slant of the stone's head and he finds himself leaning against the stone with his whole body, pressing his forehead into it and he's getting another of his migraines, it's hard to think when he feels like this, the pain behind his eyes is so severe he can't focus on the world around him, needs to close his eyes and block everything out, except for the stone, the menhir, the warmth of it against his skin and for a second, the slightest of moments, he thinks it has grown, it stretches up ten feet, twelve, into the sky and the next thing he knows Suze is there, Suze from the Crackenbridge police, touching him on the shoulder.

'Fergus,' she's saying. 'You called us out, remember?'

127

He blinks. Pulls himself away from the stone, even though he can still feel it, connected to him, and points up towards where the eye is still lodged on the top.

'You haven't moved it, have you?'

It's not exactly suspicion in her voice, more a kind of assumption that he might have done something daft.

'I couldn't even reach it,' he says. Even he can hear that he sounds defensive. It's not often he misses wearing a suit and tie, or having authority over his staff. 'I haven't done anything to it.'

The drone, he notices, is lying placid on the grass.

'Okay,' she's saying. 'Calm down now—'

'I'm perfectly calm.' Though his head is splitting, this is one of the worst migraines he's had, he can hardly keep focus on anything, what with the piercing light in the sky and the way she's talking to him.

'Of course you are, Fergus,' she's saying, and she's holding him by the arm now, taking slow steps back from the stone as though he needs to be talked down from some kind of stand-off, as though it could explode any minute and he's the one holding the trigger. 'I'm going to call this in, okay, get some help on the way if we can. We're a bit short-staffed today, you know how it is' – the truth is he's been assuming something bad was going on since he found the bedroom empty this morning and Georgie gone without so much as a note – 'and then you can tell me exactly what happened.'

'Of course,' he says, straightening up now and pulling his arm free. 'I'm glad I'm the one who found it. Not kids playing or... I'm here for research.'

'That so?' she says, phone to her ear, eyes sticking to his.

He feels himself being pulled back to it. The height of the stone, the heat of it, all those carvings, but at the same time he knows not to turn away.

'I'm setting up an archaeological society,' he says. 'For the local area.'

She sort of half-laughs at that.

'We had to study that in school. The Celts and the Druids.' She pulls a face and does jazz hands. Whispers 'human sacrifice' in a spooky voice.

Fergus frowns, covers it with a smile. If she wants to think he's daft, then he's going to let her think it.

'Well, I guess this might get folk more interested in the history round here,' she says. 'That's something. We're a gruesome lot, aren't we?'

'Who?'

'Human beings,' she says, with a shake of her head. 'Folk'll be round here looking for the other eye, soon as word gets out.'

'I'm not going to tell anyone.'

He blinks again and there it is: the standing stone.

'Of course not, Fergus. I know we can trust you. It's just that people are already talking and you know what it's like round here, if you're not careful...'

But he's not listening any more; he can't hear a word she's saying. There's a high-pitched ringing in his ears that tells him the migraine isn't gone, it's intensifying, and the menhir is smaller than he'd thought, not much taller than him, grey and white and eroded and rough and speckled with guano, and the worst of it is that from back here where she's pulled him, he can't even see the markings any more.

TWO O'CLOCK ON THE DOT

It is uncanny, the way Cal likes to have his timing so precise, and the rest of the world seems to fall into line. Results. Fingerprints. Autopsy. The whole mechanism of forensics work. He said two o'clock, that's what he said.

Georgie answers the phone on its first ring with his name, because, after all, who else could it possibly be.

'Give me some good news, Cal.'

'I can give you some news, Georgie. Don't know whether it's good or no, that's for you to decide.'

'Let's have it.'

'Well, we got back the fingerprint comparisons on the two notes. One found under the body of Dr Cosse, the other found by you and Trish in his office. We've got three different prints in total, including the two partials, and one of the sets is on both notes. But whoever they are, they're not on the system. No match to Kevin Taylor. Oh, and they used the same pen for both notes, too.'

'Same pen?'

'Might have been written at the same time. Or in the same place but at a different time.'

'And the paper?'

'Ripped from the same pad.'

'So they weren't careful. I mean, doesn't seem professional, does it?'

'Not particularly, no.'

'Best guess?'

'Not making any guesses here, Georgie. But I can tell you, they left prints all over the notes, and they ripped these pages out of a notepad. Find the pad, and you've found the culprits.'

'Think they've got murder in them?'

'Maybe, maybe no. It'd be a rash business, from whoever wrote these notes. They're not that smart, if you know what I mean.'

'So a messy stabbing would just about fit, then? Chucking the knife away like no one's going to notice?'

'Not sure about that.'

Georgie finds herself thinking about Pamali. She hasn't received any notes, but then maybe the notes are a new thing ... maybe they're working their way up to more personal attacks. Well, the vandalism felt personal, of course, with the eggs, awful. But in a way it was more distant than actual writing. It would be a big jump, though, from that to murder.

'Do you think it could have been a mistake, the first killing? Could they have just wanted to scare Dr Cosse, but things got out of hand?'

'They stabbed him five times.'

'Yes.'

'I'd say they might not have intended to start it, but they certainly intended to finish it.'

'I need a favour, Cal.'

'Name it.'

'Can you drive down here and call into the Spar? I think we need to dust for prints in there. I think there might be something ... because of the harassment.'

'Spar? The whole village'll show up, see. Everyone shops in there, time to time. We'll get your prints. Mine. Trish's. Everyone's. No way to distinguish from who was in there to smash some eggs from who was in there to buy them.'

'I know, I know. But indulge me? I've got a hunch, that's all.'

'Alright, Georgie. I'll have a gander this afternoon.'

'Thanks, Cal,' she says, though she wishes he sounded a bit more serious about it.

'There's one last thing,' he says. 'We've, er, we've found one of the eyes. Or rather, your Fergus found it.'

'Fergus?'

'Out by the standing stone, on the outskirts of Warphill. From the body, there's no reason to think it was plucked out by anything other than birds. But...'

'What is it?'

'Well, he was behaving pretty weirdly, Georgie. It's like he was … hugging the stone.'

The pause is beyond uncomfortable.

'Just thought I'd better mention it. The team's there now.'

'He's setting up an archaeological society,' she says, cringing as she hears the words from her own mouth. 'That'll be why he was there. At the standing stone, I mean.'

'His latest project, eh?' says Cal, laughing.

Georgie feels that nausea sweep over her again. Pushes it down. Swallows, leans back in her chair. And right there, out of the window, circling high, black wings swooping from between the clouds, then up again and out of view.

'A bird of prey, you mean? Could have taken the eye?'

'More likely gulls, I'd say. They're nasty, gulls.'

She has a sudden image of them, the local gulls, picking through a carcass at the shoreline, a dead crab, the way they squabbled over the bits of it. The limbs. Pulling the legs between their beaks. She can hear the noise of them now, the croak of their call. Like they're here, trying to get inside.

'Anyway,' he says. 'I'll be in touch when I've something new to report 'bout the second killing. We're still dusting the scene for prints. Not that I'm expecting to find much in that tip. Plenty of dust, course, but plenty of prints to get lost among.' Then he hangs up the phone, but Georgie stays sitting in the same position, holding the receiver to her ear long after the line's gone dead. She needs to talk to Fergus. It's been hard for him these past few years, course it has. She understands why he got depressed after he lost his job, how hard it's been for him to claw back a bit of motivation, the frustration and everything, but this...

'Erm...?'

It's Trish, standing behind her, clearing her throat like she's got something new to report.

'Some of the locals,' she says, 'they're posting tributes on Bobby's Facebook page. Might be worth taking a look through?'

'Is it not private?'

Georgie's never understood the appeal of Facebook. Or the existence of it, to be honest. Maybe it's about time she learned.

'They're all going up as public posts.'

She shifts her chair over to the side so Trish can pull the spare in front of the computer. As the page loads up, she can see she's right – it's a catalogue of his friends and acquaintances, most of them lads, Andy fairly prominent among them. A few of the other kids from the school too.

Someone's put up a video of Bobby playing the guitar. It's sad, watching it – the way his eyes avoid the camera and look down to the frets, like he was really concentrating. Like he really wanted to play well. There's a message from Terry who runs the garage, a few names she doesn't recognise – friends he had from boarding school? A picture of a sports car – he was into his cars, he'd told Georgie on that cab ride. And there are photos too, photos of Bobby in the pub in Warphill, drinking a pint, looking a bit flushed. A bit drunk. One of him outside, half turned away, mid-stride. Georgie leans forward.

'What is he...?'

'Just having a bevvy.' Trish sighs. 'With Ricky Barr, by the looks of it.'

'No, I mean in the photo below.'

Trish clicks on the image to make it bigger. Yep, it's a photo of Bobby walking away from being in a photo, a dark day, grey sky and dull stone in that wall he's walking towards. Georgie knows where that is. Is it a coincidence?

'There was something your Uncle Walt said,' she says to Trish, to herself, to anyone who'll listen. 'As he headed down towards the old church.' Her eyes dart from the window to Trish's face. 'He said he was following the birds.'

Georgie is starting to wonder if there's something out there. Something that needs checking out. Something wrong.

'Following the birds?'

'To the old church,' she says. 'The old ruin. Right where Bobby Helmsteading is standing in this photo. Can you tell me everything you know about it, everything you've heard?'

Trish shrugs, shakes her head. 'Old wives' tales and ghosts stories is all,' she says. 'They were made up. Stuff about how the graves were rising through the earth. Then there was the hanging girl. The ghost of the hanging girl. Haven't heard that story since I was at school, mind.'

'Tell me.'

'They said, the other kids, you know, older kids when they were trying to scare us? They said if you went right inside, on your own, on the darkest hour of the night, and looked back out then you could see her hanging from the tree in the graveyard. No one ever did see her, course.'

'What did they see?'

'Nothing, Georgie. I mean, it was always a place to go, you know? Kids, teenagers meet up there, have done for years. To smoke, you know. Smoke a bit a hash. Drink. Get frisky.' She sort of laughs. 'It's where you'd go for anything you need to get away from village eyes for.'

'I think it might be a place worth us visiting.'

'For the case?'

'Yes.'

'Well, could be, I guess. Because of the photo?'

'And because of the birds,' she says.

Trish looks unconvinced.

'They're circling out there, Trish. Like there's something they're attracted to on the ground. Something rotting maybe. Like…'

Like the kind of thing that could attract the scavengers. Like gulls. She doesn't want to think it, as though thinking it would make it more likely someone else was going to turn up dead, picked at, eyes stolen like Alexis's and blood congealed in the ruins of the old church. In that graveyard with coffins rising through the ground. She's heard the story herself, knows where it comes from and all. She's seen the mounds in the churchyard. She's never liked it there, never felt right there. And then there are the rumours. The stories about why it was abandoned, the crimes left unspoken and unpunished.

'Maybe I'm…' Georgie presses her hand across her forehead, trying to rub away the sharp pain that's appeared there.

'I'll go check it out then, shall I?' Trish says. 'We'll see what I can find. Shall I go now or after I finish looking into Dawn Helmsteading? I've got her education and career history, addresses past and present, the family tree—'

And that's when the phone starts ringing again. They both stare at it for a minute, as though its ringing is more unexpected than it should be.

'Hello?' says Georgie.

'PC Susan White here.'

'Suze?'

'Georgie, aye.'

'What is it?'

'Well,' she says. 'Someone just came up to me… A friend of mine actually, so it's a bit… I'd got back to the flats after talking to your Fergus—'

'What's happened, Suze?'

Georgie doesn't mean to snap.

'She was just passing, she said, but then she saw the tape and everything, the crime scene, and seeing as she knows me—'

'Who is it?'

'Elise Robertson. We were at school together, see, and she's wanting to talk to us about Alexis Cosse.'

'What does she know?'

'Well… Everyone's talking about it, about the murder—'

'Get rid of her, Suze.'

'But she says she knows something, and I thought—'

'What?'

'Well, apparently he was acting as her hypnotherapist.'

Georgie gives herself a second to take it in, to think it through. Then there's a knock at the office door. An unfamiliar face. Young, serious, smart, black, newly arrived from the city. Good. She knows what to do. 'Bring her in,' she says down the phone, as she gestures for the man waiting patiently outside to come in. 'We'll be ready.' She hangs up the phone, stands.

'DS Frazer, presumably,' she says, glancing at him then turning away. 'About time too. I've been needing some reinforcements. Trish, give him a quick tour of the station, will you?' She doesn't wait for a response. 'You're up to speed I take it, Frazer?'

'Yes, ma'am.'

'Trish here will get you a desk, so you can drop your bag and your coat and be back here in three minutes. And Trish, when Andy turns up, get him outside washing the cars, okay? Or send him home if he prefers. We'll get to his interview when we can.'

Trish opens her mouth to protest, but for once she's too slow.

'No arguments now,' Georgie commands. 'Frazer, I'm going to need you with me in the interview room.'

A BAD TIME FOR NEW
ACQUAINTANCES

Trish is mighty pissed off. It's not bloody fair, that's what gets her. He's practically still a kid, straight out of uni and fast-tracked into outranking her, ticking all the equal opportunity boxes as he goes. What does he know about anything that's happening round here? Not as much as seven years' experience in the police and a lifetime in Burrowhead has taught her.

'This way,' she says, opening the door for him. 'Sir.'

He's holding his shoulders too straight, trying to act the part. Probably got his mother to iron his suit for him. She tries to catch Georgie's eye as she leaves the room, but she's giving nothing away. Elise Robertson will be on the way with Suze by now, and Trish is sent to show this DS Frazer around the station when she should be preparing the interview. She knows Elise too, from way back, they were all at school together – she could have helped in the interview. Though the knowledge that a stranger will be of more help than a friendly face is shoved to the back of her mind.

'That was the DI's office,' she barks, striding down the corridor and gesturing into the rooms she passes. 'Interview room there, me and Si—'

'I'm going to need somewhere to do my paperwork.'

'And here we are.'

Trish stops in front of the door to the room at the end of the hall.

'This is a cell,' he says.

'Aye, well...'

'I want a desk, in an office.'

She turns to face him. Is met by two stern brown eyes and a frown that doesn't so much wrinkle his forehead as ... wait, is he suppressing a laugh?

'Here,' she says, marching off again. 'Have mine. I'm only a constable.' Grabbing notes and pens and files, sending a stapler crashing to the floor. 'Don't touch that.' Dumping all her stuff in the box room with the mop – at least Andy's cleaned it up a bit, good lad – then rushing back to log out of her computer. 'This we'll have to share. You log on as Guest.'

'Right you are, DC Mackie.'

Sarcasm too.

'I've got work to be doing.'

Which is true, actually. She's still got to narrow down Dawn Helmsteading's last known whereabouts. Maybe it's good she's not needed in the interview; she might find the next lead on her own instead. A bit of investigating she can get her teeth into. Find them a proper suspect.

'I was hoping you could bring me up to speed.'

'I thought you already were up to speed.'

'After that tour we've got two minutes to spare, I reckon.'

She breathes deep to give a sigh then thinks better of it. Mind you, he looks like he knew it was coming.

'Start with the first murder,' he says. 'If you don't mind.'

So she does it – never let it be said Trish is not a team player – and two minutes later he's got copies of every entry in Dr Cosse's day planner, Cal's phone number, the fingerprint analysis from the notes, scans of the notes themselves, Trish's notes from Kevin Taylor's interview (which she hasn't formally written up yet, much to Frazer's consternation) and both crime scene reports.

'Now, Dawn Helmsteading,' she says. 'She's Bobby's sister, right?'

'So?'

'What?'

'Have you got prints from the knife yet?'

'Erm...'

'The one found at the second crime scene. Phone Cal to check on that, will I?'

'Aye.'

'But this,' he says, tapping at a page from the day planner, '*this* is interesting.'

Trish leans down, trying to see what he's found.

'N.P.' he says. 'Looks like someone's tried to rub it out, too. Any idea what that's about?'

'New patient,' Trish snaps.

'Or it could be initials.'

'Either way, we don't know who—'

'Small community round here though, wouldn't you say?'

Trish bristles a bit but doesn't quite feel she can deny it. Who is he to start casting judgements on a place he only set foot in ten minutes ago?

'You could start with Burrowhead,' he says. The way he pronounces it is like... like you can hear too many of the vowels. She's suddenly irritated by the shape of his mouth. 'Everyone living in the village. Go through house by house if you need to, and make a list of anyone it could be. First name and surname, or first name and middle name. Or any other kind of abbreviation.'

'I've got other research to do.'

'But this could be a lead, this. Based on some actual evidence. How long has it been sitting here?'

Trish doesn't reply.

'I assume someone's already gone through all the police records?'

They lock eyes, and Trish is damned if she's going to be the one to break it first, this stand-off of theirs.

Down the hall, the front door opens. She can hear Suze chatting away, Elise too, and Georgie going to meet them.

'Look, you didn't have to give me your desk,' Frazer says quietly, though he's already standing up and straightening out his suit jacket. Suddenly it is piercingly clear how hard he wants to make a good impression. 'I'll check the timing to see if New Patient could be referring to Elise. But, while we're doing this interview, couldn't you check the department's records for anyone with a name that could be shortened to N.P.? I'd really appreciate it.'

Well. What was she supposed to say to that?

Elise is still talking outside, and as Frazer goes out to join them Trish catches the tail end of her boast: '... I've been thinking about it since I heard, see, and there's lots I've got to tell yous about that Dr Alexis Cosse...' before the door to the interview room is closed.

WHAT WEDNESDAYS
WERE LIKE BEFORE

Simon's staring out the window of his bedroom, his back to the village, his view out over the disused field and the community shed that sits alone and derelict in the middle of it. They made it entirely from fallen trees, thirty years back now, the whole village had helped out – or so they say. Families used to meet there for play days, Adventure Wednesdays they were called. Simon went himself as a kid, though it's hard to imagine local children running round in the field today. Overgrown with willow herb and gorse and nettles, weeds lodging in the timber walls of the shed, the roof rotten with damp. How or when it fell into such decay he can't say, only that it slipped by while he was looking elsewhere. The families stopped going first of all, maybe there was an issue with safety; he thinks there was a story once about a man sleeping in there, folk arriving to find excrement in the grass by the back wall and a pile of mouldy blankets in the corner. Then it was relaunched as a 'man shed' for the old folks of the village, to help address the loneliness of the ageing male population, but the woman who'd been managing it moved away to the city and the old men stopped dropping in and then one day a padlock appeared on the door and no one was quite sure who had the key. It had just become a part of his view, like a tumbledown stable or the disused boat shed by the coast, until he woke up once in the middle of the night to find Alexis staring out at it.

We have to fix it up, he'd said. Maybe we could get a grant from the council. Imagine what it could be.

They'd stayed up talking about it, how it could be a centre for the whole community, with vegetable patches outside, an allotment for the village, and maybe fruit trees further out in the field. They had made a lot of plans that night. Never got round to applying for the grant, though. Simon doubted the council would have given them anything, but he didn't want to say that to Alexis – didn't want to ruin the hope he still had for building a home out here.

They'd meet after work sometimes, after Simon had finished at the station. Alexis didn't usually work Wednesdays, said it was good to give yourself a break midweek. He was a big believer in giving people a break, was Alexis. Often he'd have put a fresh loaf on, maybe made some hummus or got in some cheeses from the farm down the coast. Especially in the summer, when the light could linger all the way to midnight and the evening felt like the start of something.

If the wind were calm, they'd walk along the coast path, take the binoculars and see if they could spot any oystercatchers. There are some good seabirds hereabouts, if you know when and where to look, and there's more overhead than those cursed grey gulls that are dominating the skies this year. When it's warmer, when it's migration season, they get swifts and house martins, the terns that can be so territorial they dive-bomb your head, and sometimes ospreys too – they once saw one sitting majestic on a fence post. Didn't even startle as they walked past. Alexis got a photo of it, on his phone.

He liked taking photos, Alexis. Simon didn't usually bother – and besides, the pictures Alexis got were better than any he'd take himself. He did the crime scene photos sometimes, for local stuff, but that was about it. Alexis though, he liked to get the big sky, all the shades of grey. Maybe it was from growing up in Greece, having always seen the same blue sky, that somehow the billowing grey over here struck him as beautiful. He was one of the only ones – most folk in the village complained non-stop about the weather. But Alexis could take photos of the sky for hours, he really could. Trees, too. Alexis was quite into trees. So that's what they'd do, walk along the coast in the shimmering light of the late evening, take photos of sky and trees, find a rock to sit on for their picnic. It could be damn cold too, even in the middle of summer. Stunning though, really. No denying that.

And they'd hold hands. It was good to be able to do that, and not something Simon took for granted. In Crackenbridge, even in Warphill, they'd have been a bit more cautious. Not that either of them ever said they were doing it, but generally, walking down the street in Crackenbridge, they'd not hold hands. Alexis said it was better here than in Greece. Simon was never sure if it was really the whole culture made him feel that, or just his family within it. Still, his family were probably formed by the culture they were in – it's a thin line for the external to become internalised. Can't really judge an individual without putting them in their context.

There had been a moment, late on Monday night but not so late that his world had already shattered, when Simon had thought to himself that he just needed to get through the next two days. Because then it would be a Wednesday again. They could go on a walk despite the wind – and it was spring already, supposedly, so maybe they'd get a warm spell – just the two of them out on the cliffs with a flask of tea. Then whatever it was Alexis was doing, whatever he was keeping secret and whoever he was seeing behind Simon's back, wouldn't exist any more. It would all go away, and the world could be Alexis and Simon and the sky and the trees. One shared moment of that, Simon was sure, and they'd have found a way to fix everything.

15:54

Elise Robertson is standing just inside the statement room of Burrowhead police station, chatting away to Suze. Well, gossiping would be the word. It's making Georgie bristle, and she's not normally like that. They're both about the same age, Suze and Elise, not that young but not that old either. Georgie's trying to work out if the apparent friendship between them is genuine, or if there's something else going on. Last week she'd have given them the benefit of the doubt, but now?

'Afternoon, ma'am,' Suze says with a casual smile.

Georgie nods, but doesn't speak. Beside her, Frazer is staring at the pair of them, standing tall, though truth is he's a few inches smaller than Georgie. Still, he's bringing a bit of formality to the proceedings – when Suze notices him the smile slips away and she adjusts her uniform before moving back to let them inside.

'I'll take it from here,' Georgie says, and within seconds Suze is gone and it's Georgie and Frazer sitting on one side of the table, and Elise at the other. It's important to change the atmosphere, Georgie knows, if you want truth out of people that they might not want to give. Not that she has any reason to suspect Elise has come here to lie. There was something about their laughter, though, something about the easy way they were chatting to each other that put her guard up, and she can't explain it by anything other than instinct.

'I've to head in a minute,' Elise begins, before Georgie has even spoken. 'I left my neighbour to keep an eye on Da, see, before heading out for a bit – I need a break, now and then, like anyone – but then I saw the police tape by the flats and I'd already been thinking maybe I should call, though you don't want to waste police time without reason, do you, and Ricky was coming up the lane there and even he said maybe I should report it like and so when I saw Suze I figured I'd have a quiet word, and she thought it would be a good idea to come in. But I'll have to get back to my da soon enough, he's not well, he's no doing well. Though it's been good to get a break from it if I'm honest with yous.'

Georgie waits for the silence to settle, but is not given the time.

'So like I was telling Suze, on the drive down here, and I'm going to need a lift back by the way but she said she'd drop me right home, so that'll be good, it's just that he'd been getting a bit weird, see, and to be honest I'd been thinking of stopping altogether anyway, then in our last appointment—'

'When?' says Frazer.

Elise looks as startled as Georgie feels. Perhaps it's the change in pitch that makes it sound so sudden, so unexpected in the room. Frazer's voice is deep and hard, whereas Elise's is high-pitched and tinkling.

'When what?' she says.

Frazer softens his voice for the next bit, or maybe he'd been surprised by the force of the word too. Georgie reckons maybe he's nervous.

'When was the appointment?'

'Oh, I see.' Elise looks at Georgie, then to the door by which her friend left the room, then back at Frazer. 'Well, it was at two. Two o'clock I mean, in the afternoon.'

'Which afternoon?'

'The day he…' Her voice trails off and Georgie knows she's looking at Frazer. Not often you see an unfamiliar face round here. 'Erm, Monday,' she says.

'Thanks, Elise,' says Georgie. 'But could you start by telling us how long you'd been seeing Dr Cosse?'

There had been no mention of Elise on the computer, as far as Cal's team had found, and Simon seemed so sure Alexis had been meeting someone in secret. He'd thought it was a man though, the secret client. Or fake client. Whoever it was Alexis had been meeting behind his back.

'Oh yes, well, see, it all started last year with my da, who's not well as I mentioned before and I've been caring for him, I mean of course I have, who wouldn't, you know? You would, of course, you do, even though it's difficult with my job and everything...'

Her words come fast and flutter through the air; they need to be caught before they're gone.

'... but he'd started talking about all these things I can't even remember, and it made me wonder if there was something had happened years ago that he was wanting to talk about. So there was that. Then at the same time, see, I was finding it hard, I mean it is hard, watching someone you love... He's fading away, see. More every day, though when the doctors come round he always puts on a good show for them. Frustrating, when I can see he's putting it on for the doctors, like it's some kind of exam he needs to bluff his way through. But he's dying, that's the truth of it. I just wanted someone to talk to about it all, yous'll know what I mean, and Alexis...'

When she uses his first name Georgie feels the air gives a shudder at the familiarity of it, how personal it sounds, but Elise doesn't stop.

'... had been helping me come to terms with it over the past five, six months, see. With losing him but also realising there's this big chunk of his life I never knew about. Maybe that always happens with our parents. I don't know though, I always felt I knew my mum really well, like I knew myself really, and when she passed a few years ago I was younger and the feelings were simpler somehow, just loss, just emptiness but without the sort of confusion I'm feeling with Da, because I'm angry about something and I don't know exactly what it is. Alexis was helping me come to terms with it, see, all of it really, with the stuff it was bringing up, you know? Stuff from the past. That's what Alexis did.'

'What do you mean?'

'He helped people to remember.'

She looks at Georgie then as if she's wondering whether or not to say more.

'That's what he kept saying, see? That he wanted to help me remember. That's why he started trying the hypnotherapy with me, a few weeks ago. I wasn't sure about it myself, all sounded a bit dodgy, tell you the truth, but he was … well, he was a bit insistent actually. And I thought, where's the harm? I didn't believe it would work anyway, 'cause of how I'm very strong-willed really, everyone says, and I'm not prone to suggestion or anything like that. But Alexis, he thought he could help me remember more about my relationship with my da when I was really young, see. He thought that might be why we'd never really got along, why I was so angry at him for dying…'

Georgie is leaning forward.

'But Dr Cosse wasn't a hypnotherapist,' she says 'Not as far as I know.'

'Well, he didn't have the qualifications, that's the thing. So he asked me to keep it quiet, what we were trying. He kept calling it a new procedure, like it were something special. And I trusted him. Maybe I shouldn't have but I did, at first anyway… He had such a gentle way about him, I felt like I could tell him anything really. But I never remembered anything much, with the hypnotherapy. It was soothing, though, at first. That's why he came round to the house, because it helps to be somewhere you feel at home. I could lie on my own bed, see—'

'On your bed?'

'Oh yes, it's much better to be somewhere comfortable, somewhere personal. He told me that whole therapist's couch thing is nonsense, much better to lay down on your own bed. I mean, that's what he said.'

Georgie pushes her seat back, Frazer clears his throat. Elise seems to get it at last.

'Oh no, no… It was nothing like that,' she says, with a slight laugh. 'I mean, nothing like what you're thinking. He was' – she looks around the room, for confirmation – 'I mean, he was so camp, it's obvious, isn't it? Everyone knew he was…'

'Homosexual?' Frazer's voice has a hint of accusation in it.

'I'm not saying anything bad—'

'No need to get defensive.'

'I'm not! Look, he was different to most blokes round here, that's all I'm saying, and I'd never care about something like that.'

'Do other people?'

Georgie's watching their back-and-forth; he's doing well, Frazer. Elise doesn't know how to take him.

'My da would make comments like, well, you know, that was his generation, wasn't it? But the point is, there was nothing going on between us. Not like that.'

'But he used to visit you at home?' asks Georgie, softly now. 'For this hypnotherapy?' It seems out of character for Alexis to have been doing something like that, unqualified too. He was always so professional.

'Aye, he used to drive over and meet me at home, in Crackenbridge. My da's been living with me for quite a few months now, which is better really, 'cause he wasn't right for looking after himself, and I couldn't stand the thought of… Well, I'm my father's carer, and I can't leave him alone too long, so Alexis would come round. He was good like that. Actually I had to call on my neighbour, to keep an eye, while I came in here. I'm a bit worried now though, I do need to be getting back soon, but the thing is, once I'd heard about what had happened to him, I really felt I had to tell you about how weird he'd got, the last couple of appointments.'

Elise pauses, looks between them, Georgie leaning forwards over the desk and Frazer leaning back, and all three of them sit in the silence.

'When we started the hypnosis sessions,' she says eventually, quieter now, more controlled in the way she's speaking, 'I didn't think anything was happening at all, to be honest. We'd talk about my life, you know, what I remember from when I was a kid, memories of my da and my family and that. Afterwards I just felt like we'd had a good chat, that's all. Like I say, I'm not very suggestible. Maybe I was resisting it. I've read somewhere you have to be open to hypnosis for it to work. Anyway, last week, at the appointment before the last one, something changed. It was a full hour we had, but honest to God I can't remember where the time went. Alexis said it was like being in a trance state, and he was really pleased about it. Said we were making great progress. But I didn't like it.'

She looks up from her hands.

'I didn't like the way he told me not to tell anyone, either. Just seemed ... I don't know. Not how a therapist is supposed to behave. Maybe that was why it didn't work the next week. Last Monday. He did it all the same, but I didn't go into that trance state again – I knew exactly what he was asking me. And it was ... weird. He was asking me about my da's friends, if they used to visit the house when I was little. Then he said, "Tell me about your friend who went missing," but I never had a friend who went missing. He asked some of the normal stuff too, like how I was feeling and what I'd say to my dad if I wasn't worried about hurting his feelings or anything, but then right towards the end he says to me, "Describe the time when you were most scared as a child." And I couldn't do it – I don't remember when it was, even. But for a second there, I don't know, something in the way he said it, all keen like that, it felt like he wanted me to have been scared. Like he was hoping for it.'

THE INACCURATE TIMEKEEPING
OF THE CUCKOO CLOCK

Mrs Helmsteading is standing by the worktop in her kitchen trying to open a can of dog food. But she can't get a grip on it. Can't get the tin opener to latch on right. Can't shake the feeling she's about to get dragged right through the floor, either. Used to be bright, this kitchen, not this dim space of under-counter shadows and threads of dust. The overhead light is one of those energy-saving ones they got free from the power company but it never seems to get bright, just lets out a sickly yellow that leaves everything not in its path darker than it was before. And there's no other lights in here left working.

She had a mouse issue a while ago, seems to her like maybe they're still nibbling away through the wires, or maybe they always have been, though Bobby put down all that poison when he first moved in, a few months back. She's been finding dead mice ever since. In the corners, in the crevices. And now she doesn't want to climb up the stairs to the room he was staying in – doesn't want to go up there at all. Not that he was spending much time there, really, but the stairs with their dark-brown carpet lead up to the darker landing that turns a corner and she can't bring herself to climb up there, doesn't even want to look. Drops of liquid fall onto the worktop as she stands there, though she doesn't make the connection between them and her tears.

The can of dog food drops right out of her fingers – her hands have been shaking all day – and it topples and rolls along and then right off the counter to fall onto the floor. Rattle is down there waiting, poor dog. Not his fault, is it. She won't bend down to the floor to get it, though; doesn't know what she'll see under the cupboards. So she gets some biscuits from the shelf instead, tips them into his bowl till it's full, then drags her feet through to the living room where the photo of Dawn is lying on the coffee table. She lets herself drop down to the rug. Sits with her legs out in front of her, disappearing under the table.

There is a cuckoo clock on the wall that has been stuck on the same time for over four years. Its hands stopped moving back when her husband got ill and she's never fixed it. Never will. It is, in fact, the exact same model of cuckoo clock Walt Mackie has in his sweltering living room, though neither Mrs Helmsteading nor Walt himself are aware of that fact. They were being sold thirty years back in the gifts and hardware store in Warphill, shelved between the varied assortment of multicoloured Rawlplugs and the large bags of bird feed. Perhaps it was this bird theme that prompted their positioning in the shop, though they would have been better housed among the cheap mugs with cows on them. Even so, both Walt Mackie and Mr Helmsteading bought a cuckoo clock while they were in stock, Walt for himself and Jack Helmsteading as a gift, and Walt's is still going, just about, while Mrs Helmsteading's has given up.

Dawn used to love that clock. Mrs Helmsteading remembers it like it was yesterday, though it was decades ago, when Dawn would sit cross-legged on the floor and wait for the cuckoo to pop out of its box. She would laugh and laugh and laugh when she saw it, point at the wall like it was total magic. Mrs Helmsteading stares at the cuckoo clock now, willing the time to change, the hands to move, the little door to open so the cuckoo can appear, but of course it's no use. She drops the photo into her lap and stares down at it through the silence, one corner of the old wooden frame tugging at the fabric of her skirt.

She is still wearing the slippers she was wearing when the police came round this morning, and young Andy too. She didn't much like Bobby's friends – didn't much know them to like them, at least – but Andy seemed like a sweet kid. He always called her 'ma'am'. She suspected Bobby used to buy them cans, what with him being older and the rest of them underage. He enjoyed having a following. Boys who'd do what he told them to, kids who owed him something. She didn't much like that either, but she didn't want to interfere. Best to keep out of it, was what she told herself at the time. Just look the other way.

She turns the photo frame over and undoes the back clips and lifts the photo out so she can hold it properly, feel it with her hands. The glass tips out, without the back of the frame keeping it in place, and she can feel an odd sort of pressure from it lying there on her thighs. It's got sharp corners, though, they prick at her skin through her skirt, so she puts it back on the coffee table, along with the disassembled pieces of frame. It catches the light in a weird way, makes it look like there are half-visible shapes moving on the glass. But she doesn't want Rattle to cut himself on that, getting overexcited the way he does sometimes. Or is it that he gets frightened? She's not sure now. But it's like the dog knows when she's thinking of him, 'cause just that second he comes scampering out of the kitchen – almost hysterical, like he's being followed – sliding desperately over the lino and pushing his nose in under Mrs Helmsteading's elbow. She lifts her arm up, to give him room, and he scrambles his way onto her lap. Mrs Helmsteading runs her hands through his fur and readjusts his position, helping him tuck the stump of his bad leg under his body the way she knows he is most comfy. Rocking him like she would a baby. She leans over and lets herself smell his fur, rest her face against that soft back of his. Just for a few minutes, she tells herself. Take a bit of comfort now, just for a few minutes. Then get back up and do what you've got to do.

But as she's leaning there, her eyes closed and her face rubbing the soft bristly hair on Rattle's back, she feels something. A draught. Could be from the kitchen, did she leave the window open a crack? She cuddles Rattle closer, can't bring herself to open her eyes. Breathes in the warm dog smell of him, cradles his stump while with her other hand she reaches up to touch the goosebumps on the back of her neck. There's a high whining noise coming from the back of her own throat. Open your eyes, she tells herself. Open your eyes. She doesn't need to, though. She can already see them: the shapes that peer out from the dimmest corners of her home. Less than knee-high, suddenly leering above her, then down by the floor again. Facing the wall, trembling. Tiny hands, open then closed, fingers spread, fists curled. Sitting, cross legged, faces hidden in the dark. Just eyes that glisten and heads angled up unnaturally to stare at the cuckoo clock high on the wall.

AFTER THE INTERVIEW

As Georgie walks out towards Simon's house, the mist that has been rising and sinking all day thickens around her and the road seems to disappear. She sways, places a foot carefully, pauses to regain her balance. To the left, a decrepit barbed-wire fence suddenly appears, its rain-strung cobwebs marking the field's edge. To the right, tree branches loom over the road to form a canopy hanging low over her head, and there's a flock of gulls pecking at the ground. They look ghostly white in the dying light. Unnatural. Georgie wonders what's down there, summoning them, and she feels herself falling downwards, backwards, into a version of herself she doesn't want to remember. The pressure of other bodies against hers, hundreds of them, anger simmering, the shout of slogans, nausea creeping up over her like sweat. Even Simon's house seems to arrive uninvited, summoned from the gloom with its bright red door, its one lit window on the top floor, its dark squares of rooms below. She doesn't ring the bell at first, thinks maybe he's sleeping, and he needs that, God knows, but within seconds she hears steps from inside, a light comes on, and he opens the door as though he'd been expecting her.

'Si,' she says.

After a second he nods, invites her in by stepping aside.

She walks past the small side table in the hall, a couple of unopened letters that look like bills or bank statements, a 'Sorry we missed you' card from the Royal Mail, the kind they put through the door when they haven't delivered your parcel. The living room is at the end of the corridor. It feels empty to her; the whole house feels empty. Like it's given up. They sit with the coffee table between them, him on a chair, her on the sofa, facing each other as they had in the interview room.

'I'm sorry, Si,' she says. 'But I need to ask you about Alexis.'

She can feel him stiffen, withdraw even further.

There's a half-drunk cup of black coffee on the table and she wonders if it's warm or if it has been sitting there for two days, the last remnant of what Simon was doing before he left the house that night. Before he found the body.

'Of course,' he says eventually. 'Whatever you need.' But his voice is flat. 'I'd have come in to the station.'

'It's just a chat,' she says. 'I thought you'd be… Maybe I needed the walk.'

'Has something else happened?'

She wonders if he's heard about Bobby Helmsteading. Maybe not, if he hasn't left the house today.

'Well, I need to know if Alexis was practising hypnosis.'

'What?'

'Hypnotherapy. Did he use it, professionally?'

'No.'

He sounds surprised, almost as though Alexis would have been offended by the question.

'Or was he learning, maybe?'

'No. Not that I know of. He was a psychotherapist, he wasn't interested in anything else. And he would never have practised hypnotherapy without being qualified. He just wouldn't have.'

'Are you sure he'd have told you if he had?'

Simon looks over to the dark mist of the window. His lips are cracked. He shrugs.

'I think so,' he says, his eyes suddenly on hers, their blue even more intense against the lack of colour in his cheeks. 'I'd always have thought so, before. But I can't be sure, can I?'

'I don't think he was seeing anyone else, Si,' she says. 'Not like that, I mean … not so far as I've been able to find out. Whatever he was hiding, I don't think it was about being unfaithful.'

Simon averts his eyes.

'His career was important to him. He did everything right, took it all seriously, from accounts to patient confidentiality. I don't think he'd have done anything to risk that.'

Georgie nods. 'Thanks, Si.' She wonders if he's eaten anything. Thinks about suggesting he have a good home-cooked dinner, but then Georgie doesn't like to tell others what to do, especially not others she respects as much as she does Simon. He's a good policeman. Always gives people a fair chance, a good hearing-out. She is worried about him, though. He's got an edge to his voice, an anger under it that wasn't there before. She tries to remember the stages of grief. Anger is in there, after the shock, after the first wave of loss. She remembers the anger.

'Will I… Would you like me to fix you some soup, Si?'

He shakes his head. 'Is that all, then?' he says, standing.

But it's not all, and Georgie doesn't want to leave yet.

'You and Trish went to the same secondary school, didn't you?'

'Aye,' he says. 'Everyone from round here went to that school.'

'Did you know a girl called Dawn Helmsteading too?'

'Not much,' he says. 'I know the family, but that's mostly 'cause Bobby was in the rugby team with me.'

'You were friends with Bobby?'

'No. I thought he was an arse.'

Georgie smiles.

'Besides, that was years ago.'

'And Dawn?'

'She's quite a bit younger. And I left for sixth form so I think I was gone by the time she started at Warphill… Don't think I'd recognise her if I saw her, to be honest with you.' He looks right at her then. 'Why?'

'No reason.'

'I want to help.'

'You have.'

It's a warm house, this, actually. Not draughty and cold like half the old cottages in the village. There's a modern feel to the furniture. Comfy sofa, too. Maybe she was wrong to think of it as empty, to imagine Simon was giving up.

'How is Dawn involved?'

Georgie doesn't reply to that. It's time for her to go, though she wishes she could stay. She can see the questions behind his eyes.

'For God's sake, Georgie.'

She's on her feet.

'Try to get some rest,' she says.

'When are you going to let me back in?'

'Try to have some food.'

'I'll stay away from the case,' he says, following her down the hall. 'Put me on desk duty. I'll do some admin.'

She opens the front door. The blue mist is ready for her.

'Please.'

'We'll see,' she says, turning back round to him, the gloom from outside clawing at her back. 'Maybe tomorrow. I'm … I'm sorry, Si. I'll be in touch.'

Then she's out, on her own again. She hopes the slam of the door behind her is just the noise it makes when it accidentally swings closed. Either way, she needs to keep moving forwards. She doesn't know what's got into her with this quiet, creeping fear of the dark; stepping down from his porch, she feels like the ground is unstable beneath her feet. Nonsense. Moving from light to dark, that's all it is, her senses playing tricks on her. This case, all this violence. The fear of more to come. That, and the continuous effort of staying in the present when the past keeps trying to pull her back.

HIGH TIDE

I'm caught between the dark world of the cave behind me and the familiar thrashing of the waves beyond the pebbles at my toes. Outside I'll be found, but in here he waits, at the back, whispering my name. Please, he says, look at me.

But I cannot.

I stare out to where they will come from, if they come, to the grey beach with its sea all churned up and stinking, seaweed clinging to the land like something half alive. The waves edging closer. Whispers behind me. Soon it will be high tide and I will be trapped, but I won't look back into the cave, despite this tugging at my shirt, a fingertip gently stroking my palm—

I spin round and glimpse what almost looks like a mess of pale hair, feel the comfort of a small hand clasping my thumb, guiding me into the cave. There are shallow pools on the floor, rainwater in the dips of the worn-down rock, and a little boy is lying on his back, hands clawing the air. He is tiny, a year old if that. I stumble, filled with pity, but there's nothing here except whispering and a trickle of water running down through the rock. I scoop some up, splash my face, drink, and when I look up there is light shining from black skin like flickering candlelight and then teenagers, curled together on grass, waving as though they know me. I taste blueberries, the tang of juice on my tongue turning sour as my hand turns suddenly cold, and I know they are afraid. They vanish as a low grating chant emerges from the rocks; a scratching against stone, stretching shadows looming over me, sharp pinches at my skin – they are everywhere, all around me – a flash of shattered teeth, rancid breath and I fall, curl on the floor, knees clasped to my chest, my scream lodged in the back of my throat.

They were here all along, waiting to finish what they started.

I thrash; my feet slip against stone, my head hits rock but they follow, their lips splitting and peeling back into darkness. But no. I remember eyes: human eyes, deep with hate. The way he reached out, like he was trying to tame me. I remember the smell; I remember what I have in my pocket: the lucky charms I carried with me to the cave. My fingers curl round them and feel their heat, their strength. Quick as a bite I lash out, scratch, scream—

A voice. Please, he says. Please. Look at me.

I can't!

Then the shadows are gone, and my worry doll is lying on the floor beside me.

THE SHAPES OF THE EVENING

Simon waits until Georgie has disappeared up the road before stepping out into the cold. He doesn't bother locking his front door. He's wearing black jeans and a dark winter coat, collar up. Trainers on, to keep his footsteps nice and quiet.

God but he wishes Georgie would stop telling him to eat. He's a grown man and he's trying to get through the week the only damn way he knows how. There's a twitch at the blinds of Mrs Dover's house, but he's keeping back to the shadows. He ducks off the road soon as he can and takes the lane between the fields heading out of the village. Burrowhead Hill rises gently to his left, a dark lump in the land this time of day without the green of its slopes. At its peak a row of oak trees, each one taller than the next, leading out to the coast. Not got their new leaves on yet, still bare-branched, all knuckles and twisted bark. The lane doesn't take him up the hill, though, just skirts along its lower slope then follows the laurel hedge beside High Street all the way out to the playground. The swings are nothing but dark diagonal lines in front of the glittering black sea that's been calling him. He doesn't let his steps falter. Keeps walking the way he does, hands stuffed in pockets, rucksack on his back, straight past them without looking at the ground, only stopping when he gets to the bench that looks out over the cliffs.

That's where he sits, though the wood slats are wet from the salt spray and the wind is angry as it gets, up here, straight from the sea with no respite to be found. No matter. He reaches into his bag and pulls out the flask of hot tea he's brought with him, followed by a plastic cup. For himself, he'll use the lid of the flask, like he always does. Like he always did.

He watches the waves for a while, cradling his flask-top of tea in his hands. The rhythm helps. Beside him, steam rises from the cup of tea sitting next to him on the bench. Maybe Alexis was right, he'd never have been able to leave Burrowhead; the sea would never have let him. He won't turn around to the swings, he refuses to do that, but he can hear the creak of the roundabout as it slowly rotates and the groan of the springs from the horse and donkey getting buffeted back and forth. They'll be headbutting the ground if this wind gets much worse. He watches the horizon, looking for any boats out there tonight, but it's too misty to see far; a smudge of light, perhaps, to the south, but he can't be sure. The moon caught in the mist or haze – could be sheets of rain out beyond the coast. He pulls his hat lower down, zips his coat up to his chin. Watches the dark mass of stones on the beach. Feels the prick on the back of his hands that tells him someone is watching him.

He's up on his feet. No one in the playground. No one on the road. The dark of the hedge, solid. Movement: up on the hill, by the trees, a figure, no, a branch. He can't tell. Fuck. There's someone there, in the dark, by the trees, his flask-top is dropped, tea splatters the ground, his shoes, but he's running, three steps to the edge of the playground, three more but there's no one there. Just the twisted black trees in the wind. Gnarled branches like broken arms silhouetted against the sky. The human croak of the roundabout as it turns. The ache of it.

He reaches down, picks up the lid from where it fell on the ground. Slumps back on the bench and pours himself some more tea. After a moment or two he tops up the other cup, which is untouched but turning cold. Do you see? he says, to Alexis, to the empty shape that is no one sitting beside him. Do you see what you've done to me?

LOCKING-UP TIME

Trish, sitting at Georgie's desk, has been through *all* their departmental records. Arrests, witnesses, interviewees, victims, even members of staff – and she's been through addresses and the phone book too, and not just in Burrowhead either. She's done the whole area, up to and including Warphill.

Alexis Cosse's mysterious N.P. is nowhere to be found.

She goes striding into her office to where Frazer is sitting at *her* desk, staring at *her* computer. She glares at the wobbly chair leg, willing it to collapse under him, but no such luck.

'Well, if he exists at all, he's not local,' she announces to the back of his head. His hair has formed a little tuft there, from where it's been squashed under his hat.

'What makes you think he's a he?'

Oh, bugger off, she thinks.

'He. Or she. Is not local.'

That is when he swivels round in his chair to face her.

'I'm telling you, go look for yourself.'

'No need for that. I believe you.' He speaks quietly – probably trying to make a point.

'About time.'

'So we're looking for someone who's not from around here.'

'Yes.'

'Okay.'

He looks over at Simon's chair then, and Trish grabs it, sits down herself like that was what she'd meant to do all along.

'What have you been doing?'

'Making a proper report of everything we have.'

Trish rolls her eyes. Subconsciously, of course, she doesn't mean to or anything, but...

'Look, I know it sounds boring, but it has to be done, doesn't it? Nothing had been filed when I got here, nothing written up, evidence spread across different people's computers. With that kind of sloppy—'

'You can stop right there,' she snaps, fair fuming. 'You think we don't know you lot'd love a chance to close us down?'

'It's not me—'

'Pissed off that you've got cuts to deal with too and we're still here, still going, doing the bloody best we can with half the staff we need and these ancient—' She waves a hand angrily at the computer on the desk.

'Okay, okay. My apologies.' He's leaning back; he looks almost scared of her actually, and that's when she hears Georgie getting back to the station. God but she looks tired – like things are getting to her too, wearing her down. Trish doesn't know what's got into the pair of them. At least Andy's out there scrubbing the cars, putting his back into it – sure he had a bit of a moan when she sent him out there, but she could hardly blame him for that. This isn't the work I was expecting, he'd said, and frankly there are times when Trish feels the same, but at least he's got some energy to him, she likes that – she likes a bit of fight.

'Let's talk this through together,' Georgie says, sitting down heavily. 'Where are we tonight?'

'Evidence-wise, we've got the two prints from the note in Dr Cosse's office, and the one different set from the note under the body.' Trish talks fast, making sure to get in before DS Frazer –

though he doesn't seem too keen to speak just now. 'But no prints on the bodies themselves, nothing on the knife, and an overload of prints from the surrounding areas.'

'Lots of folk go on the swings,' Georgie says after a pause.

'Exactly. And lots of people have been in the old flats over the years. Prints in the dust, the dirt...'

Trish waits impatiently as Georgie nods, sighs, twists her wedding ring round and round on her finger.

'So other than the notes themselves,' she says eventually, 'is there anything to suggest Dr Cosse's murder was racially motivated, or even committed by the same people who wrote the racist notes?'

Trish shakes her head. Frazer's hand is over his mouth. She can't have upset him that much; he'd not last long here, that's for sure.

'I'm starting to think the murders aren't connected to the notes,' Georgie says. 'There's something else going on here, something we've missed. Could the motivation be financial? Homophobic?'

Frazer is rubbing his head like he's in pain.

'Something wrong?' Trish asks.

He looks at her in such a searching kind of way that Trish drops the attitude without even noticing it's gone.

'Just ... those notes,' he says. 'The attack on the newsagents ... all this racism everywhere. It's deep, here. Ingrained.' He swallows. 'I'm sorry, I ... How can you live with it?'

Trish doesn't know what to say. Wants to defend herself, but doesn't know how.

'But it's not...' she begins. 'I mean, folk here, they... This is my home.'

'It's been a long day,' Georgie says. 'Maybe we all... Have you got a place to stay?'

'Hotel in Crackenbridge.'

She nods.

'We'll start fresh in the morning.'

His smile is almost kind, when he gives it.

'What's this you've written?' Georgie's noticed his report, currently open at a timeline for Elise Robertson's association with Alexis Cosse.

'She'd been seeing him for four and a half months, so she doesn't explain the N.P. in his day planner. She wasn't his new patient, I mean, so...'

Georgie's shaking her head.

'But look,' she says. 'He suggested they try hypnosis on the fourth. That's the same week. He wrote N.P. on the Monday, like a reminder for himself.'

'But...'

'Not about a new patient,' she says. 'A new procedure. That's when he started the hypnosis, with Elise at least. Could have meant professional disgrace for him too.'

Trish leans back in her chair and doesn't need to say another word. Frazer glances at her, looks away, looks at Georgie.

'Of course.' He clears his throat. 'That's, er ... of course.' He looks so embarrassed Trish could almost feel sorry for him. 'Sorry.' He glances at her again.

She shakes her head. 'It was worth checking anyway.'

None of them seems to know what to say now.

'Let's call it a day,' Georgie says. 'I'll send Andy home – we can do his interview tomorrow. Get some rest, both of you.'

Frazer scoops up his coat with a nod and a 'ma'am' and is gone.

'You head too, Trish,' Georgie says, but Trish isn't going anywhere.

'Let me keep at it,' she says. 'I'll lock up and that.'

And so it is late, and dark, by the time she's finally able to get round to researching Dawn Helmsteading. Still, she has time to make a few calls, start to piece her history together. Turns out Dawn has been living in rented accommodation outside Warphill, in one of the old cottages, and been working as a nurse at the GP's in Crackenbridge for the past few years. She went to Warphill

Primary, just like Bobby, just like Trish herself, though Dawn was eight years younger, but unlike Bobby she was never sent away to boarding school, and unlike Trish she never left the area at all, but lived at home while training in the city and took the first job she could find in the local community. A real homebody, far as Trish can tell. Tends not to go out very much. Never really stayed in touch with anyone from school. In fact, she seems not to have any friends at all.

Her father, Mrs Helmsteading's late husband, was originally admitted to Crackenbridge Hospital with stomach pain over four years ago, then transferred to the city for surgery after the cancer was diagnosed. In recovery, he was sent home in Dawn's care – unsurprising given her nurse's training and the infamous lack of bed space in the hospital. He was expected to have a decent quality of life for a few years, though he would need to be fed primarily on fluids because three-quarters of his stomach had been cut away. On the patient release form the doctors gave him three to five years. They were wrong: he didn't last five months. He was cremated, his ashes scattered.

Dawn was last seen in the Crackenbridge surgery the previous Friday, when she worked her full shift and 'appeared to be on good form'. (Unlike the doctor Trish speaks to, after hours.) The receptionist at the surgery – who is far more willing to have a chat – describes her as being punctual, polite and efficient, if a little stand-offish. Finally, on Monday, Dawn didn't turn up for work.

Trish writes it all up, gets everything in order – Georgie will appreciate that, and it'll show *the DS* who the professional one is and all. Moving fast now, she locks the office, turns the lights out, sets the alarm, locks the front door and strides past Mrs Smyth and Mrs Dover, huddled under their umbrellas on the corner across from the station. Looks like they've been watching for any goings-on. Typical. People are talking. Trish is having none of that though, she'll not give them so much as a word to pass around the village. She breaks into a run, feels good doing it, races her way home through the darkness, and once there she pelts the boxer's punchbag she has hanging from her living-room ceiling. She finds it very therapeutic.

HIBERNATION

When Georgie gets home she finds that Fergus is not alone. The front porch light is on – though he might have put that on especially for her, he often does – and she can hear their voices drifting towards the door from the living room.

'What's all this then?' she says.

'Georgie,' Walt exclaims, bit by bit standing himself upright. He's changed out of his dressing gown. It's been replaced by golfing trousers, a shirt and a striped sports jacket. 'Georgie, am I glad to see you again. Wasn't sure when you'd be back, so I figured I'd wait. And Fergus here…'

'Been a pleasure having you, Walt,' says Fergus. 'Good to spend time with a fellow enthusiast.'

Behind them, on the floor, is some kind of robotic toy, but Walt is up now – he can be sprightly for someone who seems to have trouble moving from his chair – and he's taken Georgie by the arm in a conspiratorial way and is guiding her back out towards the hall, where a large cardboard box is sitting behind the staircase.

She frowns a little as she looks at it, or more precisely, as she listens to it.

'I expect you know what I'm going to ask of you, Georgie,' says Walt.

In truth she has absolutely no idea.

'They need someone who understands,' he says.

'They?'

'I'm not going to be here for much longer—'

'Oh, Walt, don't say—'

'It's not what you think.' He presses his finger to his lips, and then points up at the ceiling. 'They'll be coming soon, I'm sure of it, so I need to make my preparations.'

Georgie presses her hand to his arm, just gently. She's not sure if she's trying to soothe his fear or offering sympathy for his mind, his old age, the decline he's unable to face head-on. And who can?

'What's in the shoebox, Walt?'

'My bees,' he grins.

'My God, all of them?'

'Course not, Georgie,' Walt chuckles. 'Just a cup full, and their new queen.'

Georgie doesn't want to make any sudden movements, but she does find herself taking a step back. She glances over to the living room, where Fergus is standing in the doorway blocking her view of whatever he's got on the floor.

'Should they not be outside, Walt?'

'It's not warm enough yet,' he says. 'I bring them in for the winter, see, to live with me, keep them cosy till they're ready for their new hive. It's important. We're family.'

'I've never heard of—'

'It's my way, Georgie, and the bees appreciate it. They hardly ever sting me these days.'

She raises her eyebrows.

'I'm a part of their community, see?'

Fergus steps out into the hall and kneels by the box.

'It's wonderful, Walt,' he's saying. 'It's magical.' Glancing up at Georgie for confirmation. 'We keep the box closed, do we?'

'Aye.'

'And keep them somewhere warm, out of the way?'

'I keep them in the cupboard under the stairs.'

'We have a cupboard under the stairs too, don't we Georgie?'

'They'll need a cleansing flight every couple of weeks, when you get a warm day.'

Fergus nods, seriously. 'A warm day. Alright.'

'And I've brought you the inverted sugar. They can eat that without processing it, see. They don't need much, my bees.'

'I'm not sure if this is the best idea,' Georgie says.

'It'll be okay, hon. I already said we could look after them...'

She feels another flash of irritation.

'You can give us instructions, can't you, Walt?' he says.

'Is that a *drone*?'

'I've brought you my bee book.'

He holds it out to Georgie and she takes it instinctively, turns it over in her hands, notices the pages are worn, the book well used. The front cover is a photograph of a beehive with bees flying around it, on a white background. On the back is a picture of Walt. He looks younger, sturdy, though he has his stick, country cap on his head. Tweeds. Standing in a field, arm on a post. In fact, that's the field just outside Burrowhead, behind Simon's place.

'You wrote this, Walt?'

'It's my bee book,' he says. 'Now, Georgie...'

He pulls her away from Fergus, as though wanting her all to himself, and Fergus tactfully retreats into the living room as Georgie steers Walt towards the front door.

'I need to tell you about them, Georgie.'

'The bees?'

'No, no.' His finger pointing up again, urgently. 'They're ancient, Georgie,' he says. 'They've been coming here for thousands of years. I want you to understand.'

She doesn't have the heart to remind him he told her this already.

'You can see the signs of them in the stones,' he says. 'In the rocks.'

'Okay, Walt,' she says. 'It's going to be okay.'

He nods, slowly, and keeps nodding for a while, chewing the inside of his mouth. The bee book is still in her hand; she flicks through the pages, notices a photo of Walt and two other men, dressed head to toe in protective white suits.

'Who's this?' she says, and Walt looks up at her confused.

'Why, that's Jack there, the big one. And there's Arthur. They were my friends, see. And they understood the bees, that they did.'

Something about one of the men in the picture is nagging at her, but she can't put her finger on what it is.

'They're gone now, though,' he says. 'So that's why I brought the bees to you. Normally they live inside with me, all through winter, see, but I've got to be leaving, and I'm terrible concerned about them.'

'I understand, Walt,' she says.

'Will you take care of them for me?'

'Of course I will. We will.'

His hand is on the door latch, but he hesitates before opening it.

'They need someone who appreciates them.'

'It's going to be okay, Walt. You can go home. Get some rest.'

The evening air is cold, sharp. She feels a stab of guilt, though she's not sure what for.

'They're sensitive, Georgie.'

'Yes,' she says. 'I'll take good care of them for you. I promise, Walt. I promise.'

Even as she says it, her skin is crawling. Then Walt is gone and the door is closed, and she can feel Fergus standing behind her, sort of hovering there as if he's afraid to be the one to speak first.

'I hear you were at the standing stone today,' she says, turning to face him.

'It was for the society,' he says. 'I wanted to—'

'And that?' She gestures to the drone squatting beetle-like in her living room.

'I needed aerial photos to put on my ... for the society's website.'

There's a buzzing, she's sure of it. Is that the drone or the bees, the collective noise of them? She doesn't need any of this.

'Maybe I shouldn't have...'

Georgie swallows.

'I wouldn't have even seen it if it wasn't for the drone though, truly. And I called the police out as soon as I realised what it was. That … that eye.'

She doesn't want a fight, not tonight. But the tone in Suze's voice, the way Cal left the silence hanging.

'They said you were hugging the stone.'

'What?'

'They told me, Fergus. The police found you hugging the standing stone. What were you thinking?'

'I wasn't hugging it, Georgie, I was examining it. I'm a scientist – you know that. There are markings… I'm going to show you.' He takes her arm, leads her through to the computer. 'It's amazing actually, I never knew the markings were so complex, so clear.'

He seems oblivious, actually oblivious to the fact that her job relies on being respected, that what he does reflects on her and the people round here, they talk. If she loses her job, if the station's closed down, what then, what'll they do?

'Look at this,' he says, opening his photos on the screen. 'It's beautifully…'

But to Georgie the computer is showing a photograph of a pale threatening stone surrounded by dirty white gulls and a dark grey sky; she can hear the squawking noise of them as they pecked at Alexis's face, feel the stone reaching deep underground to something cold and wet and rotten.

'It's beautifully intricate,' he's saying, 'though I admit it's hard to see it in the photo, I mean you can hardly see the carvings at all, but up close, when I put my hand on it, I could feel the shapes and the markings…'

That eye belonged to Alexis.

'You have to be there, Georgie. You have to experience it. It's like there's some ancient meaning there, trying to get through to us. Something from where we all came from.'

'Can't you just leave this alone?' she says.

He looks hurt and confused, and also like he's not going to leave anything alone.

'Is the case going badly?'

Georgie doesn't reply, but there was something Frazer said that has sunk deep under her skin and she can't seem to shake the nausea it's left her with.

'Well, this stone is part of our heritage, isn't it?'

Not mine, she thinks, but she doesn't say. It is part of *their* heritage, though. Not hers, or Alexis's, or Pamali's, but it is undeniably part of this land, solid and ancient and immovable, deep and ingrained.

THURSDAY

TWO HUNDRED AND FIFTY YEARS BEFORE THE SLAUGHTER OF DR ALEXIS COSSE

The story of the church that stands on the outskirts of the village of Burrowhead is a story that tends not to be told by the villagers of Burrowhead, and that, of course, is how things come to fester. But the truth is that no one quite knew where she came from or who had brought her here, the young black girl with old eyes who unnerved them all so much. The local boys who'd gone to work on the ships were away again soon as they'd docked, soon as they'd passed on their cargo. It reminded some of the smuggling, but it was legal of course; no other way the minister would have got himself involved the way he did.

There must have been a night, they whispered, when the slave ships docked further up the coast, though they didn't usually, wasn't the norm around here; but there must have been a night when the minister travelled to the harbour by moonlight and bought himself what he thought he needed. His mother had died, you see. Less than a year back she'd withered away and they'd noticed how the minister became withered himself, spindly like willowherb but without the flower. Until he bought himself what he thought he needed. Her arrival marked a change in him, they were sure. They just didn't quite know what it meant.

It was on a Sunday he first showed her off in public. In his church. On a Sunday morning in his church, it was. All the village there, waiting for their sermon, shivering on the stone pews and watching how the winter sunlight came through the arches and made her skin shine. There were plenty of whispers that Sunday morning in church, but the minister carried on regardless, and the girl stayed right where she was, her eyes fixed upon him. After, he walked over to her and offered his arm. This they all remember seeing – how he'd offered his arm like he was courting her. And he walked her like that down between the pews and out into the churchyard, where he stood by the beautiful old cherry tree to shake the hand of all the villagers as they left. It was a strange Sunday, they all agreed later. None of them shook her hand, as they might have done a minister's wife, but they all stared long and hard. He'd dressed her up in his mother's deep green gown and petticoat, with pale lace up to her neck. It was very peculiar, they all agreed, though probably best not to pass judgement one way or the other.

And so the villagers continued on with their lives, they ploughed their fields and cooked their broth and attended their church on Sunday, they dealt with the new sheep and the rising rent of the land and they worked hard – they worked very hard, make no mistake about that – and they watched as the minister became fuller again, his face bearded, his eyes bright, his belly bulging from his black jacket as he strolled from his church to the village and out again to the coast.

He spent a lot of time at the coast, they whispered to one another. They both did, him and the girl. They went on long walks, like he used to take with his mother. She'd been a silent sort of woman, they knew but didn't say; she'd always followed him, always stayed a fraction of a step behind. Or maybe he'd always stayed a fraction of a step in front. And yet, remember how he had withered when she was gone? Perhaps he got his strength from knowing she was behind him, they thought, and now there was the black girl, following his steps, and it did seem to be agreeing with him.

Her name, they learned, was Mary. Oh, they said, surprised, that's a good name. Wasn't that the minister's mother's name, after all?

What a coincidence, they said. What a happy coincidence. Or perhaps it was something to do with God. But then again... They hushed their voices, and soon enough they'd all developed the habit of turning the other way when they saw them out walking together, along the coast track on the cliffs. Though it was more to do with the changing crops, they said, the turnip and the cabbage, with the work needed on the land, increased demand from the city, preparing the sheep for the market. A time of change, no doubt about that. A time of new landlords and new laws from the city. Some folk left. Some folk stayed. The village slipped through another summer barely noticing it had arrived and greeted autumn with a bitter shudder.

Mary never spoke, though she would nod if ever they stared long enough to be caught staring. Her eyes never seemed less wide than the day they first saw her; she wore the petticoats and gowns but she did not lift them out of the mud. Then one day it happened that she wasn't there in church on Sunday. He came out on his own to give the sermon, they all thought, but he didn't preach to them that day. I need your help, he said to the people of the village. Mary has disappeared. We need to form a search party. We need to bring her back home safe. His eyes, they noted later, were darkened; they had lost their light. It seemed portentous, after the event. No one really wondered why Mary would have gone missing, and no one questioned the need to bring her back.

So it was that the villagers of Burrowhead found themselves scouring the fields and hedgerows, on a bleak Sunday morning almost a year after she had arrived, the sky fallen low to the ground and the frost nipping at their toes. She was not in the village, she would not have been given a place to hide in any of the village houses, that much was understood. They searched the woods inland, looked for fallen trunks that could provide shelter, and when the woodlands turned up nothing but fungus and weasels, they turned to the coast, to the long clifftop walks they used to take together. Maybe, they whispered, she fell.

Climbing down, down the cliffs by the path which had no rope, no chiselled step back then, the villagers scrambled to the stone beach that offered neither shelter nor harbour nor safe passage for a boat with any kind of cargo. It was a wild, desolate place the villagers preferred to ignore; no good to be found down there, they knew, just rotting weed and the crash of salt waves onto rock. But he led them across the beach, nonetheless, striding high over stones, cursing when he almost fell but refusing to slow, ignoring the creep of the tide. Looking back, they would wonder if he knew, all along, where he was going. If he wanted them to see. But down there on the beach, with the sting of salt in their eyes and the wind screeching as it was, all they could do was follow him along the dark crust of high tide until he found the cave.

The entrance was a slit in the cliff, nothing more, like a slanted eye cut up the sleeping rock face, and the ground smoothed out before it, from slimy pebbles to sheets of stone, a dark platform leading the way inside. She was in there, of course. They kept their distance but they could hear her wordless cries, the pleading of them: the villagers had formed a wide semicircle around the cave's mouth but the minister had gone right inside, to get her. One by one they took their steps back but made the decision not to leave. They could taste the salt on their lips, like destiny. They wondered if it had something to do with God.

She went quiet, after a while, and the minister came out with her on his arm, looking almost like she did after his sermons, except for how everything was wrong. Her clothes were drenched, clinging to her body, her very bones, her eyes bloody and swollen and the pale lace at her neck stained, and he stopped in the middle of them all and said, Mary would like to apologise now.

That's what he said.

They talked about it, afterwards, about why he said it, why he felt the need to say it. They wouldn't have said that, they'll tell each other. If they talk about it at all. But that was the moment Mary pushed him, pushed him away hard and he stumbled on the rocks and she ran, she ran to the circle of the villagers, around and around inside the circle of villagers who were watching her until the minister was on his feet again and he grabbed her arm and knelt on her back where she fell and he held her face down into the water. It was a rock pool. A finger's worth of water, no more. Salted, like they could taste on their lips. Like the air that was stinging their eyes. Her feet kicked up for a little while, but pretty soon they stopped.

Over the winter, one by one, the villagers stopped going to the church on the outskirts of Burrowhead, and by the spring they had all joined the congregation at Warphill, despite the hour's walk on a Sunday. It made them feel better, not to have to listen to his sermons, but they still saw him, taking his walks, withered again, out along the cliffs. Their whispers were replaced by looks; the questions of children were left unanswered. After all, they were not the ones who had done anything wrong. Why should they carry the burden of explanation? But occasionally they would think to themselves that Mary couldn't have been her real name; that of course they never knew her real name. Even more reason not to speak about her, then.

That year, potatoes came out of the ground shrunken and rotted black with blight, and bloated brown slugs could be seen gorging themselves on crops from beside the churchyard all the way out to the woods beyond the motte. Every time the people of Burrowhead saw the minister out walking through their village, the gnawing hunger in their stomachs reminded them of what he had done; they felt sickened by him, and by the relentless taste of salt in the air. And although no one is quite sure exactly when it happened or exactly who it was that tied the rope, by the following winter they had hung him up from the cherry tree in his own graveyard and slit his throat for good measure. He didn't protest, that much they all understood. His feet kicked out for a bit, but soon enough they stopped.

They buried him then, in the flooded ground next to the grave he had made for Mary, that he had marked with a headstone engraved with angels, like he had done for his mother. They buried him, as the villagers of Burrowhead tend to do with all their shame. It is the way of the village of Burrowhead. But shame has a way of its own, too. The scientists say it is something to do with the soil, but no one in Burrowhead believes that, not in their bones, not where the salt can reach them. What they do know is that the graves in the old churchyard of Burrowhead inch their way, year by year, back to the surface of the land in grassy mounds marked by sunken, weathered gravestones. You can see the shapes of the coffins in the ground itself. If you look, that is. Some people, even now, prefer not to look.

And so it is that, two hundred and fifty years after the congregation deserted the old church of Burrowhead and buried what they did not want to see, young Andy Barr finds himself tripping over a mound of earth in the old graveyard that he could have sworn wasn't there before. He lands, hands in the mud, then springs up before anyone could have had time to notice, hurriedly wiping his palms down his trousers and pulling his hood up against the rain. Looking over his shoulder once, twice, he shakes his head and gives the ground a quick kick where it tripped him. Then he enters the roofless ruin of the old church that sits simultaneously on the outskirts and deep within the heart of the village of Burrowhead.

A FRESH START

'Dawn Helmsteading,' says Trish, slapping a folder down on Georgie's desk. Inside, there seem to be medical records of some kind. 'I've found plenty, plenty information about our missing Dawn Helmsteading.'

Georgie has not yet had her coffee, and it was a sleepless night for her, what with the noise of the bees scrambling blindly around their box, and then tripping over that damned drone when she went down for a glass of water. There was Fergus too, the noise of him all the time beside her, and the way her memories kept creeping up from where she usually kept them locked down. Yes, it was a scratchy, sleepless night for Georgie.

'Ready?'

Trish is marching up and down the cramped office, all restless energy and impatience.

'Sit down, Trish, please,' Georgie says. 'Take your time.'

With two dead people and another missing, they all need to stay calm.

Trish pauses, running her fingers repeatedly through her fringe in that way she does when the world's not moving fast enough for her – and the world rarely moves fast enough for Trish – before eventually sitting down. 'Where's DS Frazer this morning, anyway?'

'Called me first thing,' Georgie says. 'Apparently he's stuck behind some sheep on the B4762.'

Trish snorts.

'Right then.' And without waiting any longer, she starts at the beginning, with Dawn's average school reports. Her nurse's training. Her job at the GP's.

'Nothing unusual there? When she was at the school, I mean?'

Trish shakes her head. 'Bobby got sent off to some boarding school when he was thirteen, Dawn was left at the local primary and continued on where she was. But he was the eldest, and he was the boy. So that's not unusual really.'

'Hmmm.'

'I mean, infuriating. Sexist. But not unusual.'

Georgie nods.

'And the surgery know to call me if they hear anything.'

'Good.'

'Things get interesting when Mr Helmsteading, Dawn's father, gets admitted to hospital.'

'Interesting?'

'Or rather, when he's discharged from hospital. Cancer. Dawn was the one to take him home, sign all the release papers. She even moved back in with her parents so she could be there, see, to look after him. Needed a lot of care, he did. Feeding, bathing and so on. Even still, they expected him to live for a few years.'

Trish pauses here, to make sure Georgie is with her. Which she is.

'He was dead within a few months.'

'Months?'

'Now her brother's dead too,' says Trish. 'Murdered.'

Georgie is taking it all in, and Trish keeps on going.

'I checked out the cottage before coming into work, couldn't find much of interest there – other than the fact that there was no sign of our Dawn. The door had been locked behind her when she left. Found the key under a stone in the front garden. Inside it was bare, characterless. Not so much as an ornament, no pictures on the walls. Clothes all neatly hanging in the cupboard. Kitchen that looks rarely used. No wallet, no money, no phone. Beige everywhere—'

'We should send Cal over—'

'Already left him a message.'

'Good. And arrange a uniform to watch the house, in case she comes home.'

'Will do,' Trish says. 'Though in my opinion, no one has been in there for quite a few days. Got that deserted feel about it. There was a letter postmarked Tuesday sitting on the front mat. Opened it – junk mail. But still, that tells us she's not been there since Monday at least. Monday, see?'

Georgie nods again.

'Now look what else we've got. I've been saving the best bits for last, you know.'

Trish actually seems to be enjoying this.

'Cal phoned first thing with some very, very good news. They found something in Alexis's paperwork after all, buried in among a load of council tax reminders apparently, and they've just couriered it over. Our Dawn,' she announces, 'was a patient of Dr Alexis Cosse.'

Georgie takes the patient registration slip Trish is holding out for her. It's handwritten. She reads it slowly, from top to bottom, shaking her head. Then she reads it again. 'This means she's connected to both bodies,' she says.

'That she is.'

'Her brother and her therapist.'

'Yep. Turns out there was a file hidden in his cabinet, for his extracurricular patients, so to speak. See, his records for folk in for the usual therapy – like Uncle Walt – were all kept on his computer, electronically. Nothing suspicious there. Appointments were put in his day planner, like we found. Nothing hidden. All above board.'

'Right.'

'And then there were a couple of others. Their admittance files in the back of the cabinet, handwritten, hard copy only. No sign of them on the computer. No records of the sessions that we've been able to find.'

'What do you mean, extracurricular...?'

'Well, there were only two of them, see. One, dated over four years ago, was for Dawn Helmsteading. The other, admittance dated just a few months ago, was for one Elise Robertson.'

Georgie says nothing. What does it mean? Why was he seeing them both off the record – if that's even what was happening? And what was it Elise said, that he was trying to get her to remember something about her dad...

'Do you see?'

'I'm thinking, Trish.'

'She's connected to both bodies. One was her brother. The other was her therapist. She's gone missing. She has to be our suspect.'

'Maybe.'

'She has to be our number one suspect. Look at this: reason for admittance,' Trish reads from Dawn's patient registration form that Georgie is still holding in her hand. 'Childhood trauma. You know what that means, right?'

Georgie nods, slowly. Blows her breath out through pursed lips. Not as rare hereabouts as it should be. Like some other things.

'Abuse,' says Trish. 'Got to be.'

Georgie could swear she can hear those bees, even here.

'So, let's say Dawn's dad was abusive,' Trish continues. 'She goes to Alexis because she's trying to come to terms with it. To face up to it, right? But her Dad's in the hospital, frail and sick... Now *he's* the one who's helpless.'

'You're jumping to conclusions, Trish.'

'I'm talking through an idea.'

'Then why would Dawn hurt Alexis?'

Trish shakes her head. 'To keep him quiet? Maybe he wanted to tell the police. Or he was trying to force her to confess. Blackmail, even?'

'Seems unlikely.'

'Aye.'

Trish looks deflated. But there, on the death certificate for Mr Helmsteading. His full name. Mr Jack Ernest Helmsteading. That's who he was, the man in Walt's bee book. Georgie knew she'd recognised him.

'He was a friend of your uncle?'

'Don't know about friend, but he kept bees too. A few of the old folks did. You know what it's like round here, everyone knows everyone. Why?'

Georgie shakes her head. That nagging feeling is back.

'Look here, it says nothing unusual,' Trish says. 'It says he died of natural causes, but...'

Georgie's thinking about Mrs Helmsteading, and about the photos on her mantelpiece. Her husband. Their wedding day. Then that old picture of Dawn she'd looked at with such tenderness right before asking Georgie to leave. The way she shut down, Georgie knew she was keeping something hidden.

'There was no autopsy,' she says. 'They just assumed.'

Trish nods. 'With the cancer and everything, there would have been no reason to suspect anything else.'

'Well we've got reason to suspect now.'

'But with the body cremated, no way of proving it either way—'

'Unless we can find Dawn,' Georgie says. 'We need to find Dawn.'

WASTED TIME

DS Frazer slams his fist into the steering wheel to give another, sustained blast on the horn. The sheep don't even startle, that's the thing. Don't even *move*. They just stand there, chewing. Is someone doing this on purpose? He could have sworn the woman who runs the B & B was laughing at his suit, though quite what was funny about it he has no idea. And she kept trying to get him to talk about the case. Had to give her a stern talking-to in the end. Unbelievable. And now he's late. Very late. It looks unprofessional – well, the whole place seems to be unprofessional, but *he's* not, that's the important thing. His suit looks good. And he hates the idea of being late. He counts five, four, three, two, one, like his wife used to. Head, shoulders ... whatever. What is the use? He doesn't like this place. Especially not this morning. It's falling apart around their shoulders – that police station, clinging on to life by a thread, the council flats, the vandalised bus stops and empty shops and that hideous old nuclear site – and good riddance to it.

Still, plenty to think about while he sits here, there's the silver lining. He'd called into Crackenbridge to see Cal first thing, before getting stuck in this nightmare, and he's glad he did – got two important new pieces of information to take over to Burrowhead with him. First, there's the knife.

No prints, but lots of blood. Messy, like the crime scene itself. And the blood – which everyone here had assumed all belonged to the victim – is now on its way to the main forensics lab in the city,

188

where they can do a decent professional analysis. It could have slipped during the stabbing, that's his thinking, especially during such an erratic crime; slipped back and the blade caught the killer where they held it clenched in their hand. He's seen it before. In amongst the victim's blood there could just be a speck of blood from the assailant too. Now wouldn't that make his trip worth the price of the petrol out here.

He read up about Burrowhead last night, after he got home. He's got this feeling he needs to understand something more than the crimes themselves, though he's not found out what that is yet. The station used to be where the local policeman lived, family and all – feels like a world away now, if only a generation or two. Most of the old country stations worked that way, once, before they all got consolidated. He didn't know any of them had survived till he got sent out here. Doesn't know why this one has. If it had been his call he'd have had the whole enquiry taken over. She's got a reputation though, DI Strachan, could have had quite the career if she'd been prepared to leave. But she was adamant she wanted to stay, according to the chief super, and with her being here, the station just seems to keep standing. Heaven knows why.

Movement over in the field beside the road catches his attention – yes, it's the farmer, driving along the ridge on what looks like a quad bike. He blasts the horn again. Surely he's going to do something. Doesn't appear to be stopping though. Frazer is not having that. The door's open, he's pushing sheep out the way with sheer force, eventually stepping out next to one with what he hopes is not a large smear of excrement hanging all down the back of its fleece.

'Hello there,' he calls. 'Excuse me...'

The quad bike is nearing the end of the field.

'Hey! I could do with some help over here. You up there!'

At last the man seems to hear him, turns round and raises his arm in a friendly wave before disappearing over the hill and out of view.

Back in the car. Five, four, three... He edges forwards. They're starting to move at least. Some of them. He squirts the windscreen wiper fluid, then has a better idea. He's got a litre bottle of water in the boot. Out, round, a nice loud slam and spray them. Well, he gets a few of them, at least. Then he revs the engine, keeps on inching forwards...

It's working. Progress.

And there's that other thing he's found, too. Yes, he should focus on that for a bit – he's very pleased with it. Especially now he's made it to seven miles an hour. This morning, he's been listening to the recording from yesterday's interview with Elise Robertson, and there's one particular line he keeps coming back to. No one in the room seemed to react to it. Not even the DI. It was fleeting, he'll admit to that, but he heard it. Goes to show, all the paperwork he did yesterday wasn't for nothing – he knows the names of everyone involved in this case now, no matter how tangentially, and there are a lot of them. Everyone seems to know someone who's involved in something, round here, and there's this sense of them watching him. Is he imagining it? Something watching him from behind the hedgerows, over the cusp of the hills.

He skips back to the start, to listen over. Not to that nonsense about hypnosis. Honestly, what kind of susceptible fool would fall for rubbish like that? No, what he's picked up on is something altogether more promising. He reaches ten miles an hour and as he turns the corner he thinks he can see an end to the sheep – he thinks he can see some actual tarmac. Here it is; this is the bit. Yes, it's a real lead this time. DI Strachan has to be impressed with this. And that Trish is going to be spitting feathers when he plays it to her.

EARLY ELEVENSES

Andy Barr comes ambling into the station all gangly, throat clearing with the words, 'How's the case going, boss?' and his wonky smile, like he knows he's not even supposed to ask. 'I'm here to help.'

'Thanks for coming in,' Georgie says, her back blocking the door to the office. 'I've got the interview room set up and ready.' She can see his hope turn to inevitable disappointment – she's not called him in today to help with the investigation in any way other than as a witness.

'But I've proved myself, haven't I?' His voice is rising, getting a bit stroppy. 'I mopped the floor, I washed your old car…'

He must have thought it was going to be like on TV, doing his work experience here. Instead all he's really had a chance to experience is cleaning and making the tea. That and losing his friend. Poor kid. Still, he and Bobby were good mates, and she needs to know what was going on in his life.

'You might know something really important,' she says. 'That's why we need to interview you.'

That clears his temper faster than the flick of a switch.

'Ah,' he says, keen again. 'But see I don't understand what could've… Doesn't make sense it would happen to Bobby. No one would've… You know he even got in a fight with my dad once, did you know that? Punched him and everything. It were…' He slows himself down a bit. 'Sorry. It were good to see, that's all.'

He's swaying from one foot to the other now, like he wants to go and start, right now, no more chat. But he's got something in his hand, and he seems to have just remembered it.

'I found this by the front door, boss. It's like' – he shrugs – 'like a letter or something.'

Sure enough, he is holding a white envelope with, presumably, a letter inside. Only the envelope has no stamp, and no address. It's been hand-delivered, slipped through the letter box while they were in here discussing the case. Trish has appeared, halted mid-stride by the sight. Even Andy stops moving about in the silence. Georgie already suspects what it might be.

She pulls on some gloves and holds out her hand.

'Well, it's got my name on the front,' she says to Trish, who's beside her now and holding her arm back as though she thinks she shouldn't open it herself. 'It's not going to be a bomb, is it?'

'It's not … wait … what …they're not here, are they?' Andy bumps into Trish, and she puts a hand on his arm to steady him.

Georgie has no idea really why he chose the police for his work experience. He's hardly got the right character for it – even if it was as exciting as they show it on telly. Especially if it was like that. He said on his application he wanted to see what it felt like, though he didn't say what 'it' was. Policing, she supposed at the time, but maybe he meant being in charge, in a way. Being in control. Not that Georgie has ever seen her job like that; it's not about power. Not for her.

'Everything is okay,' Georgie says, opening the envelope – it isn't sealed.

She pulls out the note, and recognises the paper, and reads the words silently to herself. *Foreign Bitch*.

She closes her eyes. She needs to shut it all out, just for a second. It's like being back there, though; this whole week has been like being back there. The non-stop violence of it. It had seemed like such a different kind of place, Burrowhead, with its sleepy white winters and colourful summers, with its smell of manure from the fields that reminded her of the earth, the slow chugging of old tractors on single-track lanes, the ice-cream van that parked by the playground and sold those old-fashioned cones. Did any of that even exist?

'It seems,' she says with a sigh, 'they have added misogyny to racism.'

Andy makes a snatch for it, but Trish holds him back. 'Wait, no,' he's saying, 'No, but this is wrong, this—'

'Christ, Andy,' says Trish. 'What are you doing?'

'Nowt—'

'Calm down! Calm down, pet, it's okay.'

Andy looks mortified; Georgie actually wonders if he's going to cry.

'You okay, boss?' he's saying now. 'It's not fair, it's no' – his words a jumble – 'it's no right.'

He takes everything to heart, Andy, he feels things, and when this is all over Georgie is going to pay a visit to Ricky Barr's farm, see if there is anything going on there that someone needs to take a look at. She's wondering if she should call child protection, though given the size of him now it's probably too late for that. But he's jittery, that's the thing. As though he's afraid all the time.

'It's alright now, Andy,' Trish says. 'No harm done. But this... *This...*'

She looks at Georgie.

Right then, the front door opens and the brisk footsteps of DS Frazer start marching down the hall towards them.

'I've been wondering when they'd get round to me,' Georgie says quietly, slipping into the office to place the note safely on the desk.

Trish is shaking her head, fists clenched now. 'I feel sick. This is repulsive.'

'And simplistic,' Georgie says. 'Still, it's another clue. Let's look at it that way. Maybe this time we'll be able to trace them.'

'There's been another note? Does seem to be a group then,' Frazer says, standing next to her.

'Good morning,' Georgie says.

'Not particularly, ma'am.'

'No, I suppose not.'

Georgie looks around for Andy, not wanting to talk in front of him, but he's disappeared off somewhere.

'We have at least three different sets of prints so far.'

Georgie feels a wave of fatigue that's becoming all too familiar. She's not sure, but she might be swaying on her feet.

'Do you want a cup of tea, Georgie? Maybe a sit-down?' Trish is pacing from side to side across the hall now. 'Fuck! Sorry. It's awful this is happening. We have to find them, we've got to... Sorry. Cup of tea?'

'I'm okay,' Georgie says, though she appreciates the compassion. 'I'm not even surprised really.' Maybe she's been expecting it, on some level. Waiting for everything to go wrong. It was strange for them not to be targeting her, now she thinks about it – she's such an obvious target. Maybe she's never belonged here at all. But then there's Simon and Trish, Pami, those delicate red butterflies with the purple and yellow wing tips that flutter through her garden every July, and the sky. The sky.

There's a noise coming from the kitchen, and Georgie looks up to see Andy wheeling a chair towards her, with a cup of tea and a plate of biscuits carefully balanced on the seat. When he gets to where she's standing, he picks up the mug and the plate.

'Maybe you should have a sit-down, boss. For me, aye?'

Georgie can't help but smile – or do as he asks. Though she feels a little silly sitting on a swivel chair in the middle of the corridor. He passes her the tea, which she accepts, and offers her a biscuit. She takes a chocolate digestive.

'That better, boss?'

'Yes,' she says, and takes a sip of her tea. 'Yes, Andy, it is better.'

Trish grabs another two chairs from the kitchen so they can all sit together in the hall and take a moment. Except for DS Frazer, who clearly wants to get on with solving the case. Georgie swivels around on her chair and looks down the corridor to the reception and the front door. It all feels strangely peaceful now.

'Andy,' she says after a minute, on an impulse really, but the idea's been lurking in her mind since Walt mentioned it, and now she's noticed the mud Andy's walked into the station. 'Do you ever go out to the old church ruin?'

'What, boss? What d'you mean, boss?'

He looks at Trish, at Georgie, at Trish, at Georgie, at Trish. Georgie fights back the urge to pat him on the head.

'It's nothing bad, Andy. Nothing bad at all, don't you worry. It's just that I thought young adults like yourself might hang out there sometimes. Heaven knows there's not much for you to do in the village.'

'No,' he says, 'No, boss. Not me. No way.'

Georgie's a little surprised by the desperation of his denial. It's fairly clear he's been there.

'Look, we need to get that note over to the lab. I'll arrange a courier,' says Frazer. 'If that's alright?'

'Thanks,' Georgie says. 'Please, go ahead.'

'And Andy,' Trish adds, 'we'll call you when we're ready for the interview. Till then, can you keep an eye on the front door for us?'

'Yes, I'll do that, absolutely, that's a *useful* thing.' He edges awkwardly past them then dashes down the hall and nearly walks head first into the door to the reception before opening it and wandering through.

Trish is shaking her head, grinning. 'There are only two reasons a kid his age would be out at the old church, Georgie, and that's to meet a girl or to smoke a spliff. Either way, he's not likely to go confessing to you.'

'I suppose not, Trish,' Georgie smiles. 'I wondered, that's all.'

'He's a good kid, our Andy,' Trish laughs. 'But he's a teenager like any other.'

It's good to have a smile. She bets Trish was a terror when she was a teenager. Still, it won't go away, her inkling about the old church ruin, her sense that there's something out there, something dark; she'll head up there at lunch, take a look around. Get a feel for the place again. She's not been there for years, had no reason to, but it's a place, out of the village, where people could go unseen, or hide, or worse. And she finds herself worrying about Dawn Helmsteading, Trish's number one suspect. In a strange way, Georgie hopes she is a suspect. She hopes that she's a killer. The alternative is that she's a victim for whom they've done nothing so far to help.

LOST IN THE MIST

I am standing ankle-deep in the biting waves, holding the worry doll in my palm. Her eyes are made of tiny blue beads and she has red crosses of stitching for a mouth.

Please look at me, he begs from behind me.

I tighten my hand until her face is hidden and all I can see are her green stripy legs, the little red shoes she wears.

No.

I raise my arm high over my head, channel all my strength and throw her to the desperate sea. She arcs through the air, through wind gasping like nightmares and down into the waves to sink, to drown, and for a moment I am free of it all. In the distance I can see the orange lights of the harbour up the coast.

Then he croaks my name.

Overhead is the sick green of the day. But I cannot keep staring at the sky. Looking down, I see that he is dying on the floor; his skin thin as rice paper, drool collecting in the corners of his mouth. His eyes are pleading for me to help. I gaze deep into the cave, but the rock is solid and still, and between us the worry doll has washed up right back at my feet.

It is time to face him.

WHAT SOME FOLK ARE LIKE

Andy's doing well, Trish thinks. He was adamant he didn't want his dad called in. She gives him a reassuring smile each time he looks up at her before answering Georgie's questions. He's worried he'll get in trouble for underage drinking, the daft kid. All those school visits of Georgie's, all that emphasis on education and information and support, and still he's a bit afraid. Not of her, as such – not of Georgie – but of the police, maybe. Of getting in trouble. Of something.

So Bobby's the one been buying them cans of cheap lager. When Trish was at school there was someone similar, course, the older brother of a girl in her year; there's always someone.

'Anything stronger than lager?' Georgie asks.

Andy looks at her; Trish nods her head.

'Just cans,' he says.

'And cigarettes, when you were younger?'

'Aye.'

Georgie raises her eyebrows.

Andy looks at Trish.

'My da'd kill me if I took anything else.'

'Did Bobby offer you anything else?'

'No.'

'You sure about that?'

Andy looks at Trish. She can remember it clearly, but at the same time it's a lifetime away, her years spent at that school. She was taking a lot more than lager and fags, so she'd bet Andy is too. She'll let it go though, for now. He's doing well, all things considered – and he'll be scared of dropping his mates in it too. She'd never have done that, always took the blame if she was caught, drove Uncle Walt to distraction at times. He never lost his temper though. Probably let her get away with too much, after her mum died, after that summer of watching her struggle, but then she had to do something to get through it, and it meant he could stay on her side. That's what she always had, when she was growing up: Uncle Walt on her side. Sure, she grew up angry, but she was never lost. It's different, for Andy. His mum's gone and there's no one on his side.

'He was on Facebook too, aye. His other mates'll be on there and all. Bobby had lots of mates.'

'Any of them had a falling-out with him recently?'

The Helmsteadings, though, it seems to be all about their family. Trish doesn't think this was a debt unpaid or a fight that got out of control, she thinks it's about family. Deep, personal. Georgie would tell her to stop jumping to conclusions. Slow it down, Trish, she'd say. Benefit of the doubt all round. Georgie is always on an even keel. That's her talent, maybe – makes it hard to be her friend though. Trish prefers a bit of fight. She wishes she could give that to Andy, too. Teach him how to stand up to his dad. Is that the answer? Not sure what would happen if Andy stood up to his father, hard to imagine it ever happening. He'll have to though, one day, one way or another. Maybe this'll help, this week of policing. Give him a bit of confidence, bit of strength. He's jiggling his legs under the table now – could be he's anxious, though Trish reckons it's more likely he needs the loo.

'It was for me,' he says. Georgie was asking about the pub fight with his dad. 'Bobby was standing up for me. He was good like that.'

Trish tries to picture it. Bobby Helmsteading always seemed more like a bully to her, but that was years ago now. And to take Andy under his wing, even if they were just drinking and getting high, maybe he'd changed.

'Why did he need to stand up for you, Andy?'

Andy looks at Trish.

'It's okay,' she says. 'It's confidential. We'll not tell anyone.'

'He said I was... My da, he was calling me weak. Laughing at me. Like normal. It wasn't anything ... but Bobby told him to shut it and then Dad called him a cunt and then Bobby hit him right on the jaw. It was good.'

Now *that* Trish can imagine. Bobby got into plenty of fights at school, even as a kid. Especially if he lost a race, lost a bet, lost a football match. He didn't like to lose. Looking back now, she'd say it was because he was jealous of just about everyone. Maybe he grew up.

'Anything else, Andy?'

He shakes his head.

'Anything you saw?'

A shrug.

Thinking of Uncle Walt, though, she'd not been able to get hold of him earlier. Thought he'd just been asleep. It was early, right enough. She hadn't worried at the time.

'If you can think of anyone who might've done this...'

'I'd tell you,' he says. 'He was my mate. I don't understand.'

'Thanks, Andy,' Georgie says. 'You've been very helpful, having this chat with us.'

'Have I?'

Andy looks a bit pleased then, pleased and young and genuine.

'You have,' says Georgie.

And it was kind of him to get the tea and biscuits for Georgie like that earlier on. She'll try and think of something a bit more interesting for him to do – something better than cleaning – that Georgie will let him near. She's guarding the case from him something fierce, even if she is all steady and cautious. Still, cleaning out the store cupboard, mopping the floors, there's no confidence-building in that. Maybe he could have a go at fixing up some of the broken chairs or organising the office supplies, he could work out in reception – at least he'd be out of the cupboard. His heart's in the right place, that's the thing about Andy Barr. His limbs seem to have a life of their own, but his heart's good and solid. Just like Uncle Walt.

She's grateful for Uncle Walt. Maybe she's been too hard on him recently. It's frustrating, sometimes, all the stuff about the Others coming to get him and the wandering off and refusing to wear his hearing aid and refusing to get dressed half the time. She's not got the patience she should have. But she's grateful to have Uncle Walt, grateful to have had him all her life. She needs to go and see him, soon as possible. She misses him, suddenly and acutely. It's like a punch to the chest.

THE DARKNESS SURROUNDING
MRS HELMSTEADING

Mrs Helmsteading's been out and she's in no rush to get home – she's not even sure why she'd ever want to go home again. But home seems to be where her feet are headed. Besides, she can't see any other way to go, so. Back to the darkness then.

She can see Dawn's face more clearly than she can see the ground she's walking on, her Dawn, her baby, and it's almost enough to block out the other things, almost but not. The storm clouds are dark smoke out over the hills. Her hands clasp in front of her, reaching out to grab at nothing at all, arms move like she's defending herself, like something invisible is trying to pierce her skin, blood spotting her blouse, red rings of it like pinpricks. Her feet start to carry her faster but she feels lopsided, three-legged like poor Rattle. That's why she's going home then.

No one sees her. No one's here. Not even a huddle at the bus stop, not even a face at a window or a car screeching by. The sky splits again but the water's not fresh, it's warm and slick like syrup and she didn't bring her rain hat. Turn at the corner, stop trying to see your way in this blackness. A mound of pigeon by the bin, scoffing on rotting litter. Away! Her hands swipe at nothing in front of her, she topples, falls into a hedge. Twigs catch in her hair. Scrape at her neck. But she knows where she is again now. She straightens herself, walks with more confidence through the gate on the broken hinge and up the path to her house. She'd left the door unlocked.

Rattle comes scampering up to her; he'd been hiding out by the back porch. Dog's scared of everything these days. Desperate scratching on the lino as he slips this way and that into her arms. She never did find out for sure what had happened to his leg, but then she knew, didn't she, like she knew so many other things she didn't want to know. She'd found her son once, when he was a kid, collecting worms so he could chop them up, a red bucket of the writhing things he had. Came with it into the kitchen, looking for lemon juice and salt. She told him to put them back into the ground, tried not to think about why the lemon juice, why the salt. And then the whining noise Rattle had made, the day of his accident. Before the car drove by. The car that Bobby claimed had hit him before speeding off, never to be heard of again.

The vets have always said that if his leg is causing him too much pain, putting him to sleep is the kindest way. She doesn't have the injection they would have used, but she can help him. It'll be good to know he's getting some rest. She sets him down on the sofa and chooses his favourite cushion, places it firmly over his head. He's a small dog but she's not much strength in her arms these days, has to sit on it till he's stopped scrabbling with his legs. Stopped trying to survive. He looks so small when she finally stands up, small and still and innocent. She'll make a nice grave for him, bury him in the earth the way she was never able to bury her husband. No fire and ashes, not for her Rattle.

But then she hears a noise. Upstairs. It's from upstairs. She knew he was going to come. She jumps as something crashes to the floor. He came as a little boy this morning, standing at the end of her bed with his chest all bloody and his face hanging off, but he's here as a man now, sure as he's dead and gone. Oh but it's dark up there. Footsteps without even a shadow, striding back and forth above her head, the stairs themselves disappearing up into the dark, just the shape of the light fitting with no bulb in it, hanging down over the stairs like that, swaying, the carpet all red and brown and stinking.

She's holding Rattle in her arms again, still warm, his fur soft against her cheek. She breathes in the smell of him, and breathes out again.

The footsteps are moving across the ceiling. He's in his room, of course – well, it was never really his room till he came back and needed a place to stay, but it was always his in her mind, while he was off at that school or away down south or wherever it was he went. She always wanted to think she'd provide a home for her son, when he needed it. She'd tried.

'I'm down here, Bobby,' she says, stepping closer to the shadow of the stairs, her head back and Rattle cradled in her arms. Her right thigh is shaking something awful. But her words have worked; the footsteps are gone. Was it too much to hope that he understood? No more of this fear. No more Rattle to look after either. It was the kindest thing she could do for him. Sweet Rattle; at least he understood.

REPLAY

Right. Chairs arranged ready, recording paused ten seconds before the vital clue. Soon as they've finished with the kid, it's time. Frazer clears his throat, straightens his tie, stands outside the main office until DI Strachan and DC Mackie appear and Andy Barr's been sent out to reception to fix some furniture they can't afford to replace. He heard him grumbling about it under his breath, Trish telling him it was important work since they mustn't ask HQ for any money – then she saw him listening and dropped her voice. Anyone would think he was the enemy. Fat chance he'd get consulted on a budget. Still, there's the DI now. Right. Here we go.

'That's the note arrived in Crackenbridge,' he says, before they've even taken their seats. 'They're checking it for prints.' He pauses for a beat.

'That's very help—' DI Strachan begins.

'Cal said they've analysed the eye too. Sorry. Ma'am. Didn't mean to—'

'On you go.'

'It belonged to Dr Cosse, as you thought. He thinks the birds must have taken it, dropped it on top of the standing stone. Still no sign of the other one – could be anywhere.'

DI Strachan looks edgy. Well, less relaxed than usual. DC Mackie hasn't said a word, she's just sitting there on her swivel chair.

'And, erm…' he continues, 'all they've found is some fibres belonging to the jacket of Fergus Strachan, who called it in. He's your…?'

He's her husband; he checked that with Cal. Scottish bloke apparently. Strange couple to find around here, where everyone else seems to be born and bred. You couldn't exactly call the place diverse. Other than the DI and Pamali, everyone he's seen since leaving the city is white; his own face is the blackest out here by a long way.

'Nothing useful then?' she says.

'Footprints, near the stone. Again belonging to Fergus Strachan.'

The DI just nods. Now's his time.

'And I've got more.'

At that DC Mackie stands up. Must have been something in his tone.

'I've been listening through the interview we did yesterday, got something to play you both. I've got it set up next door...'

So they follow him silently down the hall and into the second office, where the recording is ready to go.

'Have a seat, both of you, please.' He closes the door, deliberately, and turns the lock on the handle. 'Are you ready?' Without waiting for an answer he lets Elise Robertson's voice fill the room.

I saw the police tape by the flats and I'd already been thinking maybe I should call, though you don't want to waste police time without reason, do you, and Ricky was coming up the lane there and even he said maybe I should report it like—

He pauses. 'D'you hear it?' Plays the passage again: *—don't want to waste police time without reason, do you, and Ricky was coming up the lane there—* and stops.

'Ricky,' says the DI. Finally, she looks impressed.

'Someone you know?'

'Ricky Barr,' says DC Mackie quietly, looking at the DI. 'He was there.'

'Well done!' Frazer says before he can stop himself, but the way DC Mackie looks at him then, he suddenly feels ashamed. 'I mean, that's what I'm thinking, yes.'

'Ricky Barr,' she says, her eyes pointing straight ahead and her voice flat. 'Hanging around down the back lane of the abandoned flats where Bobby Helmsteading was murdered—'

'Andy just told us something,' DI Strachan explains. 'Bobby got into a fight with Ricky Barr down the pub a couple of weeks ago. He had a bit of a temper on him, sounds like, could take care of himself with his fists. Would have taken something to overpower him.'

'Then the fight's a good place to start,' says Frazer.

'Exactly what I was thinking,' says the DI. 'This is excellent police work, really, this is so—'

'No need for compliments, ma'am,' he interrupts. 'Just need your permission to go ahead.'

'You want to do the interview?'

'And bring him in for prints and DNA. See if we can get a match to the knife. I'm a stranger here – he won't know me and he won't be expecting me, that should put him off guard.'

'Not a bad idea,' she says.

DC Mackie is staring at him, making him feel awkward when all he wants is to do the job well.

'And you know,' DI Strachan says, 'Trish here suspected Ricky Barr, didn't you, Trish?' She's trying to be kind. Maybe he's stepping on toes.

'Couple days ago, maybe,' DC Mackie mumbles.

'You're still focused on Dawn Helmsteading?' says Frazer.

'Dawn's our strongest lead.'

'Messed-up girl like that, capable of this carnage?' He tries to say it gently.

'She was seeing Dr Cosse,' she snaps.

'Four years ago.'

DC Mackie goes silent. There's a buzzing coming from the fluorescent squares in the ceiling that suddenly strikes him as unbearable.

'Well,' says Frazer, sitting down – he hadn't meant to be standing all the while. 'Looks to me like we've got two separate crimes.' He glances at the DI and she gives him a nod. 'The first murder could be racially motivated – and if we find the owner of the prints on the notes, we might find our killer. Or it could have been a homophobic attack. For the second, we're waiting on blood analysis from the knife – could tell us a lot – and following this lead from Elise Robertson, I need to go speak to Ricky Barr.'

Still no word from the others. The silence is ringing in his ears. This isn't exactly the reaction he was expecting. He'd thought they'd be pleased, at least once they realised what a good lead it was. Heaven's sake, it's not like he asked to be sent to this backwater. He's even wondered if someone wanted him out of the city. They wouldn't have done, though. Would they?

'Okay.' DI Strachan steps in. 'We've got two strands to our approach, then. Trish, you're on Dawn Helmsteading. We need to find her, soon as possible. Frazer, you can go talk to Ricky Barr. How does that sound?'

'Good. Thanks, ma'am,' says Frazer.

'And for heaven's sake, call me Georgie,' says DI Strachan. 'You okay, Trish?'

'Fine,' she says.

'And I was thinking of checking out the church ruin. Make sure no one's been hiding out there. Cause of the… Well, just a hunch really. But worth a look, once I've called in on Pamali for lunch.'

DC Mackie nods. 'I've got to check on Uncle Walt too.'

Frazer raises his eyebrows then brings them back down before anyone notices. Quite what Uncle Walt and the church ruin have to do with the case, he doesn't know.

'Right, you do that,' DI Strachan says, though what Frazer thinks she should be saying is something rather different. 'And see if he can tell us anything about Jack Helmsteading while you're there. Then we'll meet at the Spar and head to the church together. Frazer, you keep us updated on Ricky Barr. Keep it informal for now. Any issues, you call me. Got it?'

'Yes, ma'am.'

'And it's Georgie, for God's sake, call me Georgie.'

'Yes, ma'am.'

He thinks he sees DC Mackie smirking at him out the corner of his eye, but when he glances over at her she's stony-faced as usual and her gaze is straight through the wall, beyond which he can hear Andy Barr hammering a nail into a wooden chair leg.

MISSING AT MIDDAY

Trish rings the bell, then bangs the door knocker several times, then calls out hello, and then – all this happens fairly quickly, what with Trish being Trish – peers into the window of his front room and raps her knuckles against the glass.

'Uncle Walt?' she calls. 'You in there?'

She goes back over to the door, rings the bell again.

Maybe it's everything that's been going on that's got her feeling so anxious, but she can't deny the sinking feeling in her stomach, or the panic that seems to be rising up in her throat.

'Uncle Walt?'

He wasn't sitting in the fountain when she passed; she's already checked. No sign of him out and about in the village. And he's not sitting in his favourite chair in his front room. So where else could he possibly be? It was early when she checked this morning, with no sign of him – God, he could have been gone a whole night already. She has this terrible vision of him fallen somewhere, lying wounded on the kitchen tiles, slipping in the bathroom, blood pooling around his bumped head. Or dead in bed.

'Uncle Walt!'

She's got the spare keys in her hand already, no sense shouting when she can look for herself. If he's inside and perfectly fine he'll have a moan about her not waiting for him to answer the door, but she'll be so relieved she won't care. Plus it would be a good excuse to remind him to use his damn hearing aid. He probably didn't even hear the door. That's what this will be. Wouldn't be the first time. She takes a deep breath and lets herself in, but as soon as she steps through the door she feels them brushing against her head: the fingered tips of long, smooth feathers. God's sake, Uncle Walt. He's strung them up over the door frame, must have collected them from the beach; they're grey and brown and sleek, strung high enough that they're above eye level but low enough to graze the head of anyone walking in. He does it to ward off evil, but she'd got him out of the habit after last year – that's what she'd thought.

'Uncle Walt?'

It means he's scared – the feathers mean he's scared, and so do the bowls of shells and pebbles lining the edges of the floor. He's not in the front room, as she saw from the window. He's not in the kitchen either, making his lunch or lying incapacitated on the tiles. She takes the stairs two at a time, checks the bathroom, checks the bedroom. His bed has been neatly made. Back down the stairs to the front porch – his walking stick is gone. His slippers are in front of his comfy chair. Walt is nowhere in the house.

She leans back against the wall for a second.

'Uncle Walt,' she says.

But she knows he's gone again. Gone wandering. Gone missing. Gone God knows where.

Last year he kept going on and on about seeing lights up over the clouds at night, wouldn't believe they were the black helicopters from the military base up the coast. During the day, sometimes, there were jets doing their practice runs out of sight, the sonic boom of them reaching the village once a month. It wasn't that she liked the sound, or the base – she'd signed a petition to get it moved, though heaven knows where they could have moved it to – but she didn't understand why Uncle Walt got so freaked out by them he decided it had to be the Others dropping by. Strange lights out at sea as well, he said. They were just patrol boats, she told him. More every year, replacing the fishing ships, replacing the cruise liners that one by one are changing their routes to tour the Mediterranean instead. They're keeping track of the seas, she told him. The borders. It's just the navy out there. But he's never been willing to accept that.

When he went missing before, though, last year, she'd had the feeling he could look after himself, more or less. True, he'd started forgetting things, but most of the time he was fairly lucid. Stubborn as always. Never wanting her to fuss. He'd disappeared out into Mungrid Woods for two days. There's nothing out there at all, just the ancient oaks. Some of the oldest trees in the country, so they say, and you can believe it too, the bark more lined than old skin, their branches twisting through the centuries. She still doesn't know what made him go there – he'd refused to even talk about it when he got back. He had this distant, peaceful look in his eyes, like he knew something profound that she didn't. The doctors said that sometimes, when this kind of thing happens, they'd be looking for a childhood home, but there's no houses near there at all. Uncle Walt has spent his whole life in Burrowhead. There was nowhere else for him to go looking for his memories. Didn't make sense. What had he wandered off to find?

There's a buzzing, though, she's sure she can hear a quiet buzzing coming from somewhere, and she storms down the hallway towards the sound, suddenly realising what's wrong. Opening the door to the cupboard under the stairs, a single bee flies out towards her, fast and desperate, like it's been shut up too long and will do anything it has to for freedom, and that's when she sees her uncle's small indoor hive has been moved. It's gone. That's not good. That can't mean anything good at all. Uncle Walt wouldn't move it, he wouldn't get rid of it, not unless things had got very bad indeed.

She was the one who helped him make it. It was their project, just the two of them, back in the autumn when they decided to start the new colony. It was something to keep his mind occupied. Something they both loved doing. She's been helping him feed the bees all winter with inverted sugar and it's nearly the new season, their queen is safe and they've kept her warm and comfortable in the box all through the winter, but now they've gone. The queen and her workers. The bees and Uncle Walt. They've gone.

LUNCH BREAK AND ALL

Georgie knocks gently on the door to the Spar before pushing it open and letting the bell jangle her arrival. The last thing Pami needs is for Georgie to be giving her a fright, what with everything going on. Though Pamali doesn't seem jittery today – she looks rather glamorous, actually. Georgie stands back and opens her arms.

'That dress is stunning on you, Pami,' she says. 'What's the special occasion?'

'No occasion,' smiles Pamali as she steps round from behind the till and gives a twirl. 'Just felt like making an effort this morning.'

'Gorgeous colours.'

'Made it myself.'

'You did not.'

'Did too!' Pamali laughs and stops swirling to give Georgie a hug. 'I feel like the most popular woman in town at the moment. Yesterday I had Walt and Andy popping in for a chat, and today it's you. You're not orchestrating this, are you?'

Georgie holds up her hands. 'Honestly I'm not. Though I wish I'd thought of it!'

'Well, you're here now,' Pamali smiles. 'Come on through. What lunch can I get you and what news can you tell me?'

It's amazing how thirty seconds with a friend make Georgie feel better; she should have called in earlier. That darkness, it's retreating again, she can feel it slipping away as she follows Pamali round to the back room and sits herself down, nodding at the offer of a cup of tea and starting to fill Pami in on the case. Not her case, not the racist notes, but the other one. The murders. Without the specifics, of course.

'We were hoping to keep things quiet, but since Bobby was found yesterday…'

'Everyone knows there's something going on, Georgie. Folk have been in here asking what I know – not that I told them anything. Telling me all their theories. Ricky Barr's pretty high on their list of suspects. Most people think it must be an outsider, though. Mrs Dover's counting the cars coming into the village and keeping a list of number plates. And folk are talking about the new constable you've got helping out.'

'Detective Sergeant,' Georgie says. 'From the city.'

'And I think… I think there's some whispering about Simon, too.'

'That sounds likely.'

'How is he?'

Georgie shakes her head. 'Staying home today, at least. He needs to get some rest. He's been trying to hold it together, you know, but…'

'It's worse for him than anyone.' Pamali gives the tea a stir. She turns back suddenly, though. 'Oh, and there was someone in with a camera, asking about the playground.'

'Well, they'll not find anything there now.'

'What about the derelict flats?'

Georgie looks up: the smell, thick as it was this morning.

'I heard some of the school kids daring each other to go in… They've decided it must be haunted.'

'That's all we need.'

Pamali passes a mug of tea to Georgie and sits back down next to her.

'But at least they all seem to be a few steps behind us. I'm planning to head out to the old church after this,' she says.

'Why the old church?'

'I'm not totally sure, to be honest. I've got this feeling...' She shakes her head. 'We've got a missing person...'

'The sister, Dawn.'

Everyone knows, then.

'Yes, exactly. And it seems like the old church might be a place to hide, I guess. The birds keep circling out that way, like there might be something out there. Food or... It's just a hunch.'

The image of birds pecking at something on the ground; she pushes it away.

'I'm not sure, Georgie. If I wanted to hide somewhere it's not the old church I'd go to. Talk about creepy.'

Georgie tries to laugh, but it comes out more as a shudder. 'We've got no shortage of haunted places round here.'

'My mum used to call this a thin place.'

'Thin?'

Georgie stops, mug held halfway between the table and her lips.

'She thought the boundaries of the world were thin here. The boundaries between the Earth and the skies. The living and the dead.'

'And between the past and the present?'

The front door jangles, but neither Pamali nor Georgie move.

'The ghosts and the living,' Pamali says. 'There is something ancient about this landscape. So many people have lived here before us.'

Trish, standing by the door to the back room, snorts.

'This is not about ghosts, you two,' she says. 'That's the kind of talk that has DS Frazer sneering at us. It's about bad people who need locking up.' She glances at Georgie. 'And I'm not afraid of Ricky Barr either. Now I know it's lunch break and all, but I've got a problem.'

'What is it?'

'Uncle Walt's gone missing.'

'When?' Pamali asks.

'Today. I think. Maybe late last night.'

Georgie shivers.

'He was in here yesterday,' Pamali says. Well, he's in most days really. I think he likes to check in on me, have a chat, you know?'

'Aye, sounds like Uncle Walt.'

'But he kept saying yesterday they were coming for him.'

'He's said that to me too,' says Georgie. 'He said the Others were coming.'

He said a child's tooth were a good offering, too.

'He's gone a wander,' says Trish. 'He's done it before. And we need to find him before he becomes a danger to himself. Gets run over or catches hypothermia or...'

Georgie suddenly realises Trish is upset.

'Of course we'll help,' she says.

'I've checked his house, and I've checked the fountain.'

'I'm going to call Fergus. Walt likes to pop round and see him sometimes.'

'Okay, thanks.'

'And then... Well, maybe we should try the old church, just in case. He mentioned it the other day to me as well.'

'He did?'

'Yes. No, not exactly. He said he was going to follow the birds. And then he went wandering up Church Street. We were planning to check it out anyway.'

'That sounds like the place to start then,' says Pamali. 'And I'm closing the shop for lunch and coming with you.'

Georgie opens her mouth to protest, but she doesn't get very far.

'I know I can't interfere with the case,' Pamali says. 'But at least this is something I can help with. Georgie, you phone Fergus. I'll get some sandwiches. Let's see if we can find Uncle Walt.'

12:45, BARR FARM, BURROWHEAD

DS Frazer arrives at the Barr farm and leaves the engine running as he gets out to open the gate – he's not walking along that mud track to the house, he doesn't have the appropriate footwear with him. Next time he's sent somewhere like this, he's going to be better prepared at least. And now it's raining again. Of course it is. Silver lining: maybe it'll dampen down the smell of fertiliser coming off the fields. No sign of a tractor out, though. No sign of anyone, in fact.

He's got an uncomfortable feeling in his stomach, had it there since he played the recording in the police station, like he's blundering in on something he shouldn't have. He's got friends in HQ, maybe that's the difference, he feels part of a team at work in the city, makes the violence of the job bearable. Easier to face a fight if you know someone's got your back. Feels more like a battle up here just to get through the day, and he could swear there's some kind of tiny insect forming swarms around his head, biting him in all kinds of places they shouldn't be able to reach.

The track is muddy and potholed but gravelled enough to prevent his car from getting stuck, so that's something. After a bumpy five-minute drive at another tedious five miles an hour, he notes the lack of any other vehicles – except for the wheel-less car bodies dumped alongside a corrugated-iron shack – and parks in front of the main door to the house. No lights on inside, despite the darkness of the afternoon. He's pretty sure the place is empty before he even rings the bell.

Hard to tell, having rung it though, if it actually made any kind of noise. There was nothing audible from out here, that's for sure. He tries again, knocks a few times. Even pushes the letterbox and calls through. The place seems deserted. Wherever Ricky Barr is, he must have his car with him – so he could be some way away. They could alert all police forces in the area, keep an eye out for that vehicle. He pulls out his phone to call DI Strachan then decides to be a bit more thorough in his inspection of the farm first, while he has the time and space to do it.

He walks a circuit of the house, stepping carefully around the mud and the puddles and what looks like a splat of slurry. A flutter of a net curtain in one of the first-floor windows: he freezes, stares up, waits. No one's there. The window has been left wide open – no wonder there's a draught blowing through. Leaving windows open in this weather, the carpet inside will be soaked by the time the rain's finished. Still, that's not his problem. It makes up his mind that the place is empty anyway – if there were anyone in, they'd have closed the window from the chill. Must be bitter, living out here all through the winter. The pang of sympathy catches him by surprise; they chose this life, after all. Well, some of them. He's thinking of putting a word in at HQ for that work experience kid. Help him get some real experience, and maybe a way out. It feels to him like there's something off here, something he can't put his finger on, whether it's just the relaxed attitudes of country police, the grating familiarity between them all, or something worse altogether.

He's following a muddy track out towards the field to the side of the house now, where there's a large outbuilding. Looks derelict to him at first, but the door's locked and he finds buckets stacked up against the far wall that make him think maybe it's being used for something after all. He's not sure what. Truth be told, he couldn't say what any barns are used for on farms – hay? There's a window. High up. He upturns a bucket, climbs on so he can look inside. The shed houses the tractor, a bunch of rakes and spades and farming equipment. It looks legitimate enough to him, despite the sense of unease he's getting. Thick wooden beams run the length of the room inside, with ropes and hoses dangling over them. The tractor itself is caked in mud, the huge wheels, the dark red body of it. He's clasping onto the wooden sill of the window, shifts his hand to get a better grip and feels the sharp prick of a splinter lodge itself in the crease of his finger. He lifts his hand, steps back with the pain of it and falls backwards off the bucket, landing awkwardly on his ankle and grabbing on to the sill again to regain his balance. Damn, that stings. He tries to pull out the splinter but can't get a grip with his nails, tries with his teeth. No good. He's going to need tweezers, it's in so deep. Keeping his fingers as still as possible, he continues on the path, peers into the field – muddy, brown, parallel lines of soil leading to the fence at the back, leading on to more brown fields – before retracing his steps and returning to the farmhouse. His ankle's aching; he pauses, gives it a flex. Round the back there's a garden, or what was a garden, overgrown with nettles and weeds, and what was once a wooden trellised archway now cracked and rotten, its climbing rose all thorns and twisted wood. What a place to live. That poor kid.

Back in the car, he thinks about calling the DI to see if she wants him to arrange that alert on Ricky Barr's vehicle. But instead he pulls up another number and makes a call. Gets the answerphone.

'It's me, love. Wanted to hear the sound of your voice…' He pauses, his head leaning against the steering wheel. The sting of his finger. Pain in his ankle. He feels a bit nauseous too, but maybe that's just hunger. 'I'll speak to you later.'

With a sigh, he phones the DI. Her number's engaged. He starts the engine. He'll head back to Burrowhead, type up a report. Andy's in the village, after all – at the police station, no less – and his farm is a working farm; Ricky Barr will be back.

HIGH GROUND

Fergus stands at the foot of the motte and looks up. It is steep right enough. It's a steep motte. That's what mottes are. The mound, now entirely grass-covered with no sign of the burial site below except the shape of the land itself, is over ten metres high. But this is the spot – and he's got this unshakable feeling there's more here to be found. Hence the metal detector. Heavy thing to bring all this way on his bike, the handle sticking out the top of his rucksack, but he managed it.

The path is a muddy track running up the side, with a rope strung between posts in the ground for people to pull themselves up with. There'd be no getting up without the rope, that's for sure – it's too steep to climb by quite some way. He's even got his climbing boots, for grip, and for the ankle support they offer. And that's where he is, standing at the foot of the track next to the soggy rope, when his mobile rings again. Someone's been trying to call him – he couldn't answer when he was on his bike.

'Georgie, how's it all going? I wasn't expecting to hear from you, love. Everything okay?'

'We're looking for Walt,' she says, a slight note of impatience in her voice. No, maybe not, that's unfair.

'I've not seen him since last night,' he says. 'But I'm not at home just now. I was cycling when—'

'So he could have popped round to the house?'

Fergus swallows.

'It's possible, I guess.' And then he keeps on going, filling the silence and talking it through. Can't help himself. 'Seems unlikely, though. A long walk, for a man his age. And we said we'd drive him over at the weekend for visiting anyway—'

'That's true.'

'Aye.'

Silence again. This time he lets it linger.

'Where are you?' There is something in her voice now, for sure. He doesn't want it to be suspicion, but what else can he call it?

'Just preparing to climb the motte.'

'What for?'

'See if I can find any artefacts. Coins, figurines. They only dug the one trench when they excavated. Could be much more out here. I'll be getting photos too, a full aerial survey of the area...'

Georgie is quiet for a minute.

'I thought it was worth a try, that's all. Be great to find some actual archaeological evidence left by the people who lived here before – I could bring it to the fair to show folk. But I know it's a long shot, don't you worry about me,' he says. And maybe that's all it is – concern. She's looking out for him. Doesn't want him to be disappointed.

'I'm not worried about you,' Georgie says eventually. Then she's quiet for another breath.

'Well, I'll keep a look out for Walt, from up here. And later, maybe with the drone...'

Fergus is getting worried about all her pauses – maybe he is the one who's worried about her – but perhaps he's overthinking it. He can do that sometimes. After all, she's out on police business and there could be things happening on the other end of the line that he doesn't know about.

'I love you, Georgie.'

He hears movement behind him and turns to see a blackbird picking at something on the ground beside his bike.

'I know you do,' she says.

'And you'll find him,' he starts saying. 'You're good at finding people, love. Have faith in yourself—'

But she's hung up the phone already, and he realises he's offering encouragement to an empty line. Still, she's probably busy. Well, of course she's busy. She's on a murder enquiry and here he is, able to follow his own interests and no need to report to anyone; he's very lucky really, he knows that, and he couldn't say the same for most of the men who lost their jobs with him when the site was decommissioned. He's got Georgie to thank, that's the truth of it. Not her fault if she's run off her feet. So he sends her a wee text of encouragement, the least he can do really, before turning his full attention back to the motte, the history, the ruins hidden deep under the land, and clasping the soggy rope to begin his climb to the top.

A LITTLE AFTER 1 P.M.

With every step Georgie takes towards the church ruin she feels it more – the dread, the creeping darkness, a knowledge deep within her that she's been trying to push down but which keeps forcing its way back up. Trish drove them here, parked some way from the gates so they could walk in slowly, keep their eyes open. The track leading to the small stone wall that surrounds the churchyard is muddy and trampled. Something's been along here, though whether it's sheep or cows or people is hard to tell. Pamali shivers, and Georgie slips an arm through hers. It helps.

They've been friends for years, since they were both young and new to Burrowhead; there's not many young people choose to arrive, so they felt a kinship. Pami had come to take over the Spar from her uncle who was ill and Georgie, well, Georgie just found it to be the most peaceful place she'd ever visited. She'd needed some peace. Where better to be a cop than somewhere that makes you feel the world can be beautiful, and with a man who sees it the same way? Fergus always reminded her of Errol, too – they were neither of them fighters. And he's good at seeing the best in people, her Fergus. She hopes no one notices him out with the metal detector, scrambling up on the motte; hates the thought of folk laughing at him, like he's the local crackpot, when he doesn't have a bad word to say about any of them. Or her. That's good, focus on Fergus, on the kindness of him; keep yourself rooted in that.

'Hold on,' Pamali says, and she pauses to wrap her skirt hem around her belt to keep it out of the mud. 'Don't want it to trail along the ground.'

They all look down to where Pami's standing, and they're clear in the mud – footprints. Multiple sets. All leading through the graveyard. Trish nods and opens the low metal gate that's hinged against the stone wall. It's a modern addition, relatively speaking, though no one is quite sure when it was put in, or why. Probably to keep the animals from the churchyard. It doesn't even lock. It's kept joined to the post by a loop of old rope. They all walk through and out of habit – or perhaps more respect – Georgie turns and closes the gate, looping the rope back over the post.

'Kids,' Trish says.

It's what Georgie expected, in a way – Simon had told her kids came here. And the evidence is mounting: beer cans dumped beside the larger stone coffins, a crisp packet lodged between the cellophane from a bunch of long-dead flowers and the headstone they were propped against. There are stones by the stems. Probably put there to stop the flowers blowing away in the wind. Some of the villagers must have relatives buried here, even today. When she forces herself to look past the litter, past the cigarette butts and the weeds, it is possible to see what it once was: a large, sweeping graveyard circling the church, with views over the fields to the sea in one direction, and back towards the village through an arch of oak and birch in the other; stone gravestones lovingly engraved, some with gold lettering, some with carved wings, that avoid the regimented lines of more modern graveyards and instead seem to wander amongst fruit trees, once tended but now grown wild. Under the largest cherry tree lie the oldest graves, their messages faded to curves in stone and obscured by lichen. She walks hesitantly over to them and kneels down, running her fingers over them, trying to decipher the lives beneath. It sends a cold breath down the back of her neck. Damp seeps through to her knees. She stands and backs away, keeping her eyes down. The rumours about this place, the reason it was abandoned, they must have started with something true.

Trish stops still, presses her finger to her lips. Sure enough, there is a noise, something coming from the ruin itself. Sounds like nail scratching rock. Nail, or perhaps claw.

Georgie nods. God, it's hard to turn her back on that cherry tree – she doesn't want to leave it unobserved – but she forces herself to follow Trish and Pamali, keeping her steps as light as she can, towards the ruin. The sight of it, the imposing shapes and shadows of it make it difficult to speak, even to breathe. As the roof crumbled, it left vast triangles of stone to rise at either side, and between them pillars reach up to the sky, unadorned but for the two gargoyles at the corners facing the churchyard, their features blurred and stretched by weather and age. It was a building that was added to over the years, over the centuries; it is not one thing, but many things. Shapes of light and dark move between the pillars, through the arched gaps in the stones that remain. It's the kind of place that can creep right under your skin.

Trish steps inside, and Georgie can tell from the way her back relaxes that it is nothing to be afraid of; that whatever is making the scratching sound is no threat to them. But still she holds her breath until she has stepped inside the ruin herself, until she can see past the crumbled stone wall and into the corner of what would have been the pulpit.

Chips. Takeaway chips, dumped half-eaten and left to the gulls in their damp yellowing container. Red smeared all over the place.

'It's ketchup,' Trish says, though her certainty is from visual inspection only – they all seem to be keeping their distance.

A dozen gulls are pecking at the floor, squabbling over the chip wrapper with its smears of grease and tomato sauce. They look greedy. Entitled. Like a gang of thugs. Georgie realises that the white sauce next to the red is not mayonnaise but bird shit. It doesn't stop the gulls from eating. Neither does their presence; these birds are not afraid of people, not in the slightest. It's Georgie who's edging away from them and suddenly she hears the noise again, shouts, slogans, all around her the push of bodies and anger and panic; they're just birds, she tells herself, God's sake, just gulls.

'Look over here,' Pamali says. She's walked over to the far side, past the stone pews that still stand where they once did, though spongy moss has found its way onto the seats, a green cushion which looks more luminous than it should in the diffuse light. It is a strange sort of sky, with a lack of colour, no sign of the sun up there. What Pamali has found, though, that is a sign. There are stones, dragged from the walls or perhaps the graveyard itself, positioned roughly around one of the broken pews.

'Someone's been sitting here,' she says.

'And using this as a table.'

All three women stand around the pew in silence, and none of them sit down on the makeshift seats. None of them want to, though not one of them could quite explain why either, if asked. But there's a wrong feeling here, and they all know it. Even Trish. She's subdued now, introspective. This place, Georgie thinks. I don't like this place. As a gust of wind howls through the open side of the building, the chemical smell of vinegar lingering on the air is replaced, for a moment, by the salt smell of the sea.

'I don't think Uncle Walt is here,' says Trish. 'I don't think he'd come here.'

'I think you're right.' Georgie looks around and thrusts her hands into her pockets. She's forgotten her good gloves today. 'It's nearly two...' But then she sees it. Or rather she feels it. A shadow, something dark, large, swinging beyond the thin arched space that was once a window in the far wall. Hunched over. 'There's...'

She can't make it stop. She can see a body, hanging beyond the ruins, long dead and blowing in the breeze, the colour of rotting skin, and she can see it everywhere, the deep red brown of old blood seeping up from the ground, bathing the village, the playground, the swings, seeping beyond to the derelict flats and on, to the standing stone, even to Fergus, reaching his feet, clawing its way up into his body. She scrunches her eyes shut against it and instead she feels something moving in the ground beneath her feet—

'Georgie.' Trish puts a hand on her arm, steadying her. 'We'll go together.'

From the sound of her voice, Georgie knows Trish has seen it too, the swaying shadow. It won't be Walt. It can't be. She's scratching between her fingers, trying to wipe them clean, but in her mind she can see rope hanging from a tree branch, a body left limp; no, he wouldn't have. But Dawn? She's got to stop thinking like this.

Trish clasps Georgie's wrist as they approach the collapsed part of the wall together, pausing before stepping over the rubble to see what's on the other side.

The wind breathes.

The shadows twist away.

'Oh, thank God,' Georgie says.

Trish is still grasping her wrist, tight.

The tree behind the wall is half out of the ground, its root ball strikingly flat and circular, almost obscene, sticking up from the soil at an angle and crawling with worms and woodlice. There's no body here. There's no one at all, just a tree felled, storm damage. She feels her eyes being drawn up to the white upon white of a featureless expanse of sunless sky.

'Must have...' Trish clears her throat. 'Must have come down in the storms these last few days. Or half down.'

The trunk's creaking every time the wind gusts, under the sound of the air itself; it reminds Georgie of Alexis's wrist, caught in the swing chains, the way they groaned. She takes a step forward, feels something slip under her shoe, sees blood. No, it's a slug, its insides burst.

God but it's cold on this side of the church. Colder. Like night's falling at two in the afternoon. But that's the shadow alright, the shadow she saw from inside the ruin – just the swaying of an uprooted tree. That's all it is. Trish slowly releases her hold on Georgie's wrist and forces a smile.

'Sorry.'

Georgie shakes her head.

'Don't know what I expected more, Dawn's murdered body or Uncle Walt having done something … something stupid…'

'I'm sure he's safe somewhere,' Georgie says, though she doesn't know if that's true.

'Oh,' says Pamali, climbing up over the stones behind them. 'Someone's left their bag over here. You two okay?'

'What bag?'

'Holdall there by the bushes.'

She's right – a dark green holdall, straps Velcroed together, looking empty rather than full. Looking waterlogged. Snagging a bit on the gorse.

'But that's…' Georgie moves towards it. 'It can't be.'

'What?'

'I recognise this bag.'

As she steps forward a flutter of tiny birds rises from the bushes, scattering into the air then gone.

'I've never seen it before,' says Trish.

'It was on the beach. On Tuesday morning. I think… It was washed back out to sea, or something, it vanished…'

Georgie kneels by the bag, puts on some gloves and carefully pulls the zip open towards her. Its grating sound is the loudest noise in the churchyard. Trish is kneeling beside her on one side, Pamali on the other.

'Pebbles? What the…'

Georgie lifts them out, round and grey and yellow, warm in her palm until—

'Is that a toy rabbit?' Pamali says.

'What?'

'There, underneath...'

Pami's right. Georgie doesn't touch, but she looks: a pink rabbit, water-stained. Off-white fluffy ears. Well loved, by the looks of it.

'And that,' says Trish, voice back to sounding like Trish again, '*that* is a mobile phone.'

Georgie's on her feet. 'Alexis's mobile hasn't turned up. Come on, both of you. Back up and don't touch. Trish, get Cal down here right now. We need to get a perimeter set up straight away – there's evidence here.' And something else too, though she doesn't say so out loud, something deeper and older than the ruin itself, something faceless and insidious. She felt it, seeping through the soil beneath her feet, and she feels it shrink away as she raises her voice and takes control of the scene. There is evil under the ground here. She's not going to be denying that any more. But she's also got work to do, and whatever ghosts haunt this graveyard, they're somewhere else for now.

SECOND CHANCES

The woman is sitting where I would be sitting, if I'd had the courage to admit what I've done: his head is cradled in her lap, her black hand wiping the sweat from his desperately pale head. His skin like cracked rice paper. Drool in the corner of his mouth. Her clothes are from another time; her dress is old and ripped and tattered, there's faded lace at her neck. We used to whisper about this place. The cave where the minister's slave hid, centuries ago, where she was killed, murdered in front of the village folk; where the dead of the village gather, hidden from the living – or so the stories go. I don't know how I ended up here, but this is where I am, and maybe there is a reason.

'I'm here,' I say, kneeling at his side. His eyes swivel to mine and I struggle to read their emotion: anger, blame, regret. I didn't think I'd ever have to face them again. I watched as they were burned, scattered his ashes over the cliffs and to the sea. I close my eyes to remember, to force it up and out. I close my eyes so I can picture his; the way they seemed to dry out when he died. They had been weeping, you see. They were watery before. I used to dab them for him, when the tears gathered in the corners and he'd not strength enough to blink them out. I had a special hanky for that, an extra-soft one so it wouldn't chafe – I think it was designed for a baby's skin, but it did the job. There is something similar about the skin of a baby just born and the skin of someone already half slipped into death.

I remember making soup. The starchy water-skin from potatoes, onion tears, the bubble of a simmering pan. Leek and potato and ham; he liked the meat chunky and the veg blended smooth. I knew which was the right spoon for spooning, which was the easiest bowl to carry in on the tray. He was frail and silver-grey when he came back from the hospital, hair an animal fuzz above watery eyes. Chemo kills everything, but the surprising thing was that it hadn't quite killed him. He was a survivor. We are a family of survivors.

Keep him warm, they say, keep him well hydrated, his strength will return. He has the both of you, they say. He is lucky to have the both of you. I am the one who makes the soup, though, and all the while I am filling in the blanks. The flat where we grew up, the bird getting in, its shit spilled down the curtains, a wardrobe that never closed right. Me, but smaller. Groggy and afraid. Moonlight; faces hidden. My tiny neck.

My Dawny, he says. Please, my Dawny.

EXCAVATIONS IN THE AFTERNOON

The old church ruin is no longer deserted. Cal's whole team are here, Karen setting up the tent – rain's looking like a sure thing – and everything from the rotten old gate and the overgrown graves to the stones that once framed the church hall are enclosed in the stinging yellow tape of a modern crime scene. Not so atmospheric now, not so easy to get lost in superstitions and ghost stories. Then again, it's the crime scene that feels out of place; the police are the ones who don't belong here. They're intruding, and it feels to Georgie like the ruin is barely tolerating them.

Suze is standing beside her, hand on hip and eyes out to the road; she's here to keep the scene secure, keep onlookers away – and they've got a few of them already. Must have seen the cavalry arriving, wondered if there was another body; folk are drawn to crime scenes like to car crashes and ancient tombs. Suze looks uncomfortable. It's not like her. She leans a little closer to Georgie and lowers her voice. 'I'm sorry about yesterday. If I seemed too … well, familiar, with Elise. Since old Art's been ill I've been helping her out, you know, bringing her shopping and that, popping round to give her some company. Didn't occur to me she might be… I should've kept things formal.'

'We've all done it,' Georgie says, surprised at the apology – and pleased with it too. Suze's confidence seems a little blinkered at times, and it's good to know she's got a sensitive side. 'Think no more about it.'

'Alright then.'

Mind you, that's a fast recovery.

'Let's get this scene secure, eh?'

Whatever Georgie senses here, Suze feels none of it. Probably for the best. June and Whelan have arrived, they're tying a strip of white cloth around a branch of the old oak by the gate as if they've come to honour the dead, but soon as Suze starts towards them they're asking all their questions, what's happened here then and is there another *incident* and what about poor Alexis why would anyone have done that and have they got any leads yet? Georgie closes her eyes against it all. They're just back from their caravan, apparently, and all this going on in the village – well. June helps Pami out in the Spar at weekends, runs the post office counter on Saturday morning. Suze is good at deflecting them, she'll give her that. Asking about their holidays and if they've seen anyone unexpected around; enquiring as to who took care of their dogs while they were away; talking news from the city, Tuesday's bombing. Georgie hears the word *Muslims* and feels her spine tighten. She does wish people would mind their own business, keep their ignorance to themselves. And she's starting to hate this feeling of being watched, all the time, everywhere she goes. She's not imagining that, is she?

Inside the old church the stone pews are darkened by the way the light's shining low behind them, and in the strange glow the team look like hunched shapes growing out of the ground, something monstrous about them, something primitive. She finds it hard to tell what they're doing at all until Karen straightens her back and Cal comes striding out to where she's waiting and the hunched figures on the ground resolve into people she knows, crouching down to get footprint casts, carefully uplifting the discarded chip wrapper after checking it for prints; doing their jobs. She notices a shading that has appeared in the sky, in the distance, a darker grey which carries an underside of gold. Every time the darkness gets too much, the sky seems to pull her back, reminds her to keep doing her job one step at a time.

'Georgie,' says Cal. 'I want to get this bag back to the lab. See what we can find on the mobile.'

'Absolutely.'

A brisk nod and he's off, she appreciates that about Cal – he's not a man to waste time, that's for sure. She watches him duck under the tape and stroll purposefully out to where he's parked and drive up the lane and out of view towards the road to Crackenbridge, which is a road that takes him north out of Burrowhead and directly past the distinctive mound of the motte where Fergus is manoeuvring his metal detector over one particular spot on the steep side of the motte's peak. He doesn't see Cal driving past, doesn't see any of the cars making their way between the villages, because he is entirely focused on the ground beneath the detector and the beeping noise it makes every time he sweeps it over this particular area. There's something down there. Under the ground. There must be.

He tries not to get too excited, because it could be anything – an old coin, a modern coin, cans dropped by folk up here for a picnic years ago and rapidly consumed by grass and mud. Then again, they only dug the one trench when they were here, the professional team of archaeologists, and look what they found: the cauldron, fragments of animal bones, the charred signs of a fire. There must be more underneath the ground, and why couldn't he be the one to find it? Especially if there's something that's been pushed up near the surface, something he can get to with his bare hands. He kneels down on the steep edge – no rope on that side, so he'll need to be careful not to stumble – and pulls up some of the grass right where the metal detector was beeping. The rain comes on, but it's just a drizzle and besides a bit of rain doesn't bother Fergus, because with each handful of mud scooped up from the motte he feels himself delve back in time and he can think of nowhere he'd rather be.

'Saw your Fergus on the way down,' says Suze, after June and Whelan have left and Cal's long gone. All trace of humility has vanished from her face and been replaced by something that looks like a smirk to Georgie, but she must be reading Suze wrong. She's getting touchy, and there's no good going to come of that.

'Oh yeah?' she says, noncommittal and hoping that'll be the end of it.

'He was standing on top of the motte,' joins in Karen, standing back to supervise now most of the work's been done, letting the junior members of the team finish combing the ground, checking the bushes behind the ruins, under the stones. 'Looked like, er...'

Georgie feels suddenly conscious of the weight of her heart.

'Was he playing with a metal detector?' Karen continues, sounding more baffled than amused at his expense.

'He's interested in history,' she says quietly.

They're both staring at her now.

'He's setting up an archaeological society. For the villages.'

'Like Indiana Jones?' says Suze. 'You could get him one of those hats...' and Karen starts to chuckle. Then she stops, and it gets worse.

'He's still not having any luck at the job centre then?' she says. 'Shame, with all his experience and everything. You'd think an engineer would be able to find something worth doing.'

Georgie has her eyes closed again. She just closed them without even realising she was doing it and now she's keeping them closed.

'We have a pen,' shouts one of the boys from inside the church. 'Looks like it was wedged beneath the upturned pew.'

'Careful,' Georgie says, back in charge – the racist notes. This could link it all together. She takes a step away from Karen and Suze; the ground's uneven and she stumbles, catching her balance but jarring her ankle on something solid. She doesn't want to look down. She already knows what she's done. She takes another step, this time off the sunken gravestone and onto the grass beside it.

That's no good either. The shape of the ground, the way it rises and falls either side of where she's placed her foot – looking behind, another gravestone, this time upright, low, old and worn and crumbling. The graves here, they are pushing their way out of the ground. She believes it, no matter what anyone says. Centuries-old coffins are creeping, slowly, up through soil, making themselves known by body-length mounds in the ground. She can't help but know it deep within her own skin; there's something under there they shouldn't allow to surface, that was always supposed to remain buried. Then there's Fergus, trying to dig it all up.

Her mobile rings.

'What?' she says, with an uncharacteristic urgency, even rudeness, as she answers the phone. The very noise of it, in this silent graveyard, suddenly strikes her as obscene.

'It's me, Georgie,' Cal says. 'You need to get back to the station.'

'What is it?'

'We've got into the phone.'

'That was quick.'

'Well, it's his. Dr Cosse's,' he replies. 'Seems he was using it to record his sessions with Dawn Helmsteading. You need to get yourself to a computer to listen to this recording.'

She ends the call and quickly writes a text message. *I think this has to stop, Fergus.* Then she hits Send.

Fergus, though, is elbow-deep in mud at the top of the motte and he neither hears his phone beep nor checks his messages because he's onto something important and fascinating and this, *this*, is what he is meant to be doing. There's something here for him to discover, something ancient and vital and it's almost as though it's been waiting for him, rising up through the soil to be ready for him. He pauses for a second though, 'cause his back's killing him, and he straightens up and looks out to the rolling countryside beyond the motte, the gentle hills and fields that layer into the distance without the jagged edges of the cliffs or the hunched mountains beyond the horizon.

God, he loves this place. Always has. Since he and Georgie first found it, that holiday they had before they were married, when the fields were a tapestry of gold and the stones of the cliffs shone maroon and terracotta and the beach glittered with quartz; he'd known then he'd found somewhere special. True, he didn't imagine what it would be like through winter, didn't imagine the site closing or the stench of the seaweed – good for the garden though, like Walt says, and the man makes an excellent point – but it's his home now. Maybe he lost his job for a reason; after all, he wouldn't be here if he were at work. Probably shouldn't say that to Georgie. But money's not everything, to Fergus, earning money doesn't make your life worthwhile, and there's something solid by his foot, where he stretched his ankle, is it another stone? He's found lots of stone. But no, it's in exactly the right place, where his metal detector told him it would be, and the edge of it catches the light, reflects it despite the mud and the dirt.

He kneels and carefully brushes away more of the soil around the find, using his hands, not minding the mud under his fingernails. He gently scrapes back the earth and from it emerges a metal sculpture, simple but recognisable for what it is: a man. Legs like a stick figure, a cloak of some kind, all shaped in iron. The head pointed. Or perhaps it's a hood. With the lack of a face, it's hard to tell. The feet are strange: three-toed and curved like claws. The arms protrude horizontally and the hands – there's something wrong with the hands. He's read about these figurines. They were used as offerings, buried with prayers to cure illness and injury. The wrists look broken, snapped upward, and the fingers are forced together so tightly they can't be distinguished at all, instead there's just an upper and lower edge, thin triangles sticking out from the arms, sharp and filed to a point. Almost like the beaks of birds, wide open in greed and ready to snap.

WHEN TO WALK AWAY

She's rung his bell twice already, Shona from the *Courier*. Simon remembers her from when she was a kid, knees always grazed and her hair in that short bob, racing about the village on her own – having too much fun going places to wait for the other kids, at least that was how she'd made it look. Not long out of school now, straight to work at the local paper. Internship maybe, or part-time, he's not sure. She wrote that article about the climbing tree getting blown down in the autumn storms, and he liked it actually, thought it was beautiful and sad the way she described it. She's after a different kind of story now though. He can feel it in the way she's pressing the bell and knocking with her knuckles, like she's not going to go away until she's spoken to him. He's watching from the landing window and she knows he's there; she's stepping back from the door now and staring straight up at him.

'Si,' she calls. Her hand held up in a stationary wave, her eyes … kind. If she'd been all stubborn determination it would have been easy to tell her to fuck off.

He steps back from the window and slumps down on the carpet, legs stretching down the stairs. He wishes Georgie would let him get back to work. Nothing worse than sitting round here, thinking. There's a clank – she's pushed the letter box in again.

'Simon,' she says. 'I thought you could use a friend, is all. Cup a coffee?'

It's more than emptiness he feels. He might even be willing to talk to her, if it didn't involve the energy of having to walk downstairs. Had to force himself out of bed this morning to have a shower, get dressed, when the only thing that would make being awake less futile was the one thing he couldn't do – work on the case. Find who did it.

'Will I try the back door?' she calls.

Might even be open. He can't remember.

'I wasn't sure if you'd have heard yet…'

'Heard what?'

'About Elise. What she told the police.'

It's not that he doesn't see through what she's doing. But Georgie was round last night. With those questions. Asking about hypnosis. Asking about Alexis. And Dawn Helmsteading.

'Might be open,' he says, almost under his breath – kidding himself that she might not even hear. She does though, of course. Seconds later, he hears the back door open, Shona walking in through the kitchen, calling out to him, 'I'm coming upstairs, Si.'

She sees him slumped on the top stair, climbs up and sits down by his knees.

'How you holding up?' she says, her voice quiet and gentle and when he doesn't reply she waits, quietly sitting by his knees and watching him, offering a hand on his knee when he starts to cry.

'Sorry,' he says.

'You've got nothing to be sorry for.'

'It's just, I'm better if I can get angry or something, but when people are nice…'

'Tips you over the edge?'

'Aye.'

He almost laughs then, pushing a fist over his eyes. Notices Shona's hair is wet, her blue hoody too, becomes aware of the sound of rain hitting the slant of the window.

'How about I put the kettle on,' she says.

'Wouldn't say no.'

So he makes it down to the kitchen for the first time today, locates a packet of ginger nuts while Shona boils the kettle, and even feels a bit better. She's got what she wanted already – he's going to talk to her now. Find out what Elise is saying for starters. Find a way in. Do something.

'Good coffee,' she says, heaped scoops landing in the cafetière.

'No milk.'

'Tastes better black.'

'Come on then,' he says. 'Why are you really here?'

'It's not like that. I mean, I can write an article if you want? Interview maybe, a call for information?'

'What did you mean about Elise?'

Shona takes a bite of ginger nut and a crumb gets stuck on her lip. Makes her look innocent.

'She came to me after speaking to the police. You know how she talks... I don't know how much she'd thought it through. Guess it made her feel important or something, the fact that she knew Alexis, and she had been seeing him just before—'

'What's she saying about him?'

Shona looks at him like she's not sure she wants to say it now, even though she was the one who brought it up in the first place. She pours the coffee, hands him a cup.

'Come on,' he says. 'There's nothing you can say that's going to make me feel worse than I already do.'

She nods at the chair, takes a seat and waits for Simon to sit down opposite her.

'She said he was being ... unprofessional.'

He feels a flash of anger rise up his throat, then swallows it back down again.

'Unprofessional how?'

'Said he was pushing her to be hypnotised so he could ask her all these weird questions.'

It's what Georgie was on about last night. Not that Georgie was able to tell him anything. But if Elise is gossiping to everyone she speaks to, no reason for him not to know as well. He'd been expecting some remarks about their relationship maybe, the usual homophobic crap, some delving into his past or assumptions being spread around, but not this stuff about hypnosis. It was the kind of thing Alexis would always argue against – not at all the way he saw his practice. No evidence for it even working, he'd said once, though Simon had heard plenty folk talk about how it helped them stop smoking and the like.

'What kind of questions?'

'Apparently he was asking if any of her friends had gone missing when she was a kid. And asking about her dad, who his friends were, what he was like.'

She could be lying. But then why would Elise lie? 'It doesn't make sense.'

'Maybe she's trying to discredit him?'

'Why would she want to do that?'

'I don't know.'

'And why wait till now, anyway? It's too late, isn't it? Why try to discredit him or blackmail him or whatever, after—'

'I don't know. But I was wondering...'

'What?'

'Do you know of any kids who went missing, say fifteen or twenty years ago?'

Simon shakes his head. He could find out though. If he could get back to the station.

'Or did Alexis keep recordings of his sessions? Maybe if we could listen...'

'All that stuff's at his office. Or with the police.'

'Could you check his office? Maybe they missed something.'

Georgie would kill him. She'd be right to and all. Simon takes a swig of his coffee. Shona's not ready to stop though.

'It just seems to me that Alexis might have found something out,' she says. 'Something he thought his clients wouldn't talk about if they knew what they were saying. Something people round here didn't want him to know.'

Simon feels something shift in him.

'Like what?'

Shona shrugs. 'But you've heard about Bobby Helmsteading? The way he was killed over in the derelict flats? And from what I've been able to find out, seems Dawn is missing and all.'

Suddenly his legs want to move. He stands.

'So that's got me wondering, did they know each other?'

'Who?'

'Alexis. And Dawn.'

BACK A FOUR

'Are you sure you want to do this, Dawn?' Alexis says. 'We don't have to do anything you don't want to do.'

He sounds kind. Hesitant. Thoughtful. Just like Georgie remembers him.

'I need to know who it was,' Dawn replies. 'Otherwise they'll get away with it, won't they. And it will happen again.'

'You'll need to relive it.'

'I relive it every day,' she says.

It's strange, the way gloom can pervade a room even when the fluorescent lights overhead are so bright they are almost blinding.

Trish is pacing. Frazer's standing over by the window, has been since the first time they played it – he hasn't said so much as a word.

The voices they can hear sound alive; Georgie can feel the pulse and breath of them, rescued from the static of data on a mobile phone, transmitted through air as the rise and fall of waves from Crackenbridge to Burrowhead. As real as having Dr Cosse standing here, talking to them, in this room. His hair styled, his shirt buttoned up to the collar. He had such a handsome, gentle sort of face. Petite, but not sharp-edged. Full dark eyebrows over intelligent eyes. And his voice – a rich tone to it, almost melodic, as she hears the words: 'Describe for me the room you are in, Dawn. Describe for me what you see.'

245

Again Georgie is catapulted back to the derelict flat, standing in it the way she was standing in it yesterday morning, but now instead of the body on the floor there is a table with a young girl sitting underneath, on a deep red carpet with blue and green swirls of leaves and flowers, dulled through years of use and prickling her knees, prickly tickly. She is clutching a soft pink rabbit with floppy white ears. Her voice is the voice of a child with the vocabulary of an adult, Mummy is cooking dinner, she says, mince and potatoes, she says, the smell of onions frying. And the light in Georgie's mind darkens from morning to dusk, she imagines a woman, a younger version of Mrs Helmsteading, pulling the curtains closed, telling her daughter to sit on the sofa, to get up off the floor.

Is Daddy coming home?

And he is coming home, he's here with his thick beard and his wide arms and child Dawn is scrambling up from under the table and running towards him, running toppling like toddlers do, calling *Daddy, Daddy* as he sweeps her up and lifts her high in his arms and he smells of the cigarette smell and she giggles.

How is my number one girl?

I laugh because of his funny scratchy beard, his smiling green eyes.

Georgie feels something pushing through her veins, forcing its way to the surface.

What can you see now, Dawn? Just describe what you see, what you smell.

I don't know.

Just try.

There's meat and onions, in the kitchen.

That's good. Focus on what you can smell.

Mummy's cooking dinner.

You've eaten your dinner now, Dawn. What do you remember next?

I don't want to. I don't remember going to bed. I don't know how I got here. It's dark...'

Just go with that.

I can see the moon.

Tell me about the moon.

The moon is… We learn about the moon in school, big and round, that's the moon, and the colour is silver not white, that's what the teacher said. I thought it was white but I was wrong. I'm too cold! It's so cold here…

Where are you?

At the playground.

Tell me about the playground, Dawn.

Daddy brings me here to play on the swings.

Are you on the swings now?

It's too cold, I'm so cold and I don't have my shoes. Where are my new shoes? I want to hold my feet, I want to hold my feet because it's so cold but I can't…

Why can't you reach your feet, Dawn?

Someone's holding me down.

Who?

They're kneeling on my wrists … there's a knife.

Who is it?

They've put my rabbit on my chest, my rabbit…

Who is it?

I don't know, they're all covered.

What's covered?

His face, all their faces.

Georgie doesn't move but her hand is clasped tight around the table edge. She can see them, out of the corner of her eye. Where she doesn't want to look.

How did you get here, Dawn?

I was in my bed … someone took me out of my bed… Cold hands at the back of my neck, I can't move, can't kick my legs…

Who was it?

I don't know. There are eyes, dark eye shapes cut out of the face and I'm scared, I'm trying to kick him away but more people come.

How many people are there?

I don't know.

What can you hear?

I can't breathe...

What do you feel?

It's getting tighter, it's—

Dawn, adult Dawn, is gasping for breath, choking as if being strangled, but Alexis still doesn't stop.

What can you smell? he says. *Focus on what you can smell.*

Dawn is spluttering and Georgie can imagine her, hands clasped round her neck, kicking out in defence. A masked man kneeling on the wrists of a terrified child.

There's more of them, Dawn sobs, screams out. *No, let me go I can't breathe let me—*

Her voice dissolves into coughs.

What can you smell, Dawn?

Cigarettes...

What else?

Meat, meat and onions—

On his breath?

Their eyes...

Describe their eyes?

Blank circles, rips—

Focus on his eyes, Dawn.

Their hoods—

His eyes?

Green and red— I can't breathe, it's too tight— No! — Please help me, it hurts, it's sharp—My neck— Help me, HELP ME!

This last a rasp, as though Dawn is blacking out, strangled into unconsciousness.

'You're safe, Dawn,' Alexis says at last, 'breathe with me,' and Georgie feels her stomach start to relax as Alexis talks her back down, helps her into the present where she is alive and safe. Except that it's not this present. Because somewhere Dawn is hidden and in danger, or hiding and dangerous. There was a group of them, she'd said. How many? Kidnapping, torture, attempted murder – if that's what they were trying to do. Here, in the village. To a little girl. In the playground. The feel of blood between Georgie's fingers is so vivid for a second she has to force herself to look. Nothing. She's here.

'You did really well,' Alexis says.

'Did we get more detail this time?'

Cigarettes, meat, onions, green eyes, red – as though they had been crying, perhaps, or sore, infected, old – more than two people, a group. Georgie was listening for the details, too. Someone placed her rabbit on her body, someone knew her, these were not strangers. She was drugged, probably, drugged then taken to the playground overlooking the beach. Strangled. Possibly cut with a knife.

The fluorescent lights buzz above them in squares in the ceiling and the buzzing won't stop.

Whoever did this, they were never caught. Nothing was ever reported. Dawn escaped, or was released; she doesn't say, and perhaps she doesn't even know. It sounds like she passed out, from fear or lack of oxygen. She went back to school, grew up, was afraid, had nightmares of men in masks and hoods surrounding her, strangling her, and no one ever knew and there are those terrible final words, seconds before the recording is stopped and the air returns to the heavy moisture of this week, to the weight of the sea and the violence seeping through the village.

'Oh God, it was him,' she says, and it sounds to Georgie as though she has sat up, fully aware of where she is and who she is speaking to, of the danger he might be in, prophetic of what is to come.

'You mustn't tell anyone.'

Her voice a whisper, and then it's over.

'Well, it sounds like...' Trish says, looking from Georgie to the computer that is now silent. 'It sounds like one of them, the ring-leader maybe, was her dad. The green eyes. The meat and onion smell, from their dinner. The cigarettes. Plus he'd have had access, been able to drug her.'

'We can't know it was him for sure,' says Frazer.

'I know that,' snaps Trish.

Georgie is thinking, trying to think, trying to stay calm.

'But there's what happened to her father as well.'

'Which is another thing we have no evidence for.'

Georgie closes her eyes to block it out. That noise, the relentless buzzing, it doesn't belong here.

'Come *on*,' says Trish.

'You're jumping to conclusions.'

'She got him released from hospital so she could do what she needed to. She killed him for what he'd done to her.'

'But why would she kill Alexis?' says Georgie.

'Maybe he worked out what she'd done. He confronted her or something—'

'And now what, you think she's gone on the run?' says Frazer.

'She could be scared,' says Trish. 'She might not have *meant* to do it—'

'Or she didn't do it at all.' Even Frazer is pacing the room now. 'I still think it's more likely to be the racists.'

'Which ones?'

'Well, *that*,' says Frazer, 'is the question we should be asking.'

Georgie doesn't speak. There are layers of fear here, layers of violence, layers of guilt running through the village. It's not just one thing, that's the problem. It's not entirely about racism – if it were, she'd have more idea how to fight it.

'Look, we've got to find Dawn, Georgie. I'm not saying … not necessarily… But she needs help. Obviously. Would you say something, please? We've got to act.'

Georgie waits for silence. Then says:

'Call in Mrs Helmsteading.'

Trish has finally run out of words.

'I want her here,' Georgie says. 'I want her listening to this, with us.'

'But the poor woman—'

'That poor woman was living with Dawn while this' – Georgie gestures at the phone – 'was happening. Get her in here. Now.'

UNDER COVER OF STORM CLOUDS

Burrowhead has turned a deep sinking grey by the time Simon leaves his flat and heads towards the centre of the village. It's not just that the street lights have failed to come on – though not a one of them is lit – or that the sky is so filled with swirling cloud it's hard to imagine any light ever getting through again. But the paving stones, cracked and weed-filled as they are, have lost that sheen they have when the sun catches them. The buildings themselves have not a hint of life about them left; nothing but brown stalks in the gardens, spindly-looking rose thorns desperately trying to reach a window's edge and the crawling woody stalks of dying geraniums. Was it always this bad? He can't even remember. Maybe he never saw the truth of it until right now, in the spitting mist of another dusk that's come too soon. There are narrow alleyways leading between the buildings, dead ends where bins are stored and broken bikes and the air smells of dog piss, and in every one there are shadows. The feeble light can't make it through the cracks between the homes.

'I need to help,' he'd said to Georgie. 'I *can* help. Let me back in.'

'Stay at home, Si,' she'd said, not so kindly as he'd expected either. 'This has got to stop.'

It wasn't as though he'd been calling in every hour, but he knew Alexis better than anyone round here.

'You *know* the damage you could do to the case.'

And he did, of course; he'd never forgive himself if the prosecution failed because of something he'd done.

But then Alexis wasn't just a case, was he.

What if they never find out who it was, not for sure? What if they do? Is that a part of it, of why Georgie won't even let him in the station; because she's not sure what he might be capable of? A dog barks furiously in the distance, and he can't shake this feeling of being followed, of being watched, the elongating shadows crawling right out of the alleyways and into his path. His head is splitting. He just needs something to help him sleep. Anything. That's why he left the house; what he told himself anyway. But if Shona's right, then that could mean his suspicions from before were wrong, that there's a different version of the story waiting to be found. Whatever Alexis was doing behind his back, he wasn't seeing someone else – there's another explanation for the secrets. Something he didn't trust Simon with. He pushes that thought away. Alexis's office is in darkness. He stares up at the blank windows, at the emptiness emanating from the flat. He needs to get inside. But something stops him. Pulls him away. Nausea, rising, swallowed down.

It's a deeper kind of silence he senses then, the smell within it like a room sealed and aching with damp. Threat. Rot. The alley beside the flat, sinking out of view, and something dark pressed low against the wall. For a second he can't breathe. The weight on his chest, like dread. What is that? *Who* is that?

It's nothing.

Litter, maybe. Smashed glass from the bins. A dog? Pile of linen, discarded clothes...

But his breath's coming ragged like he's been running, his mouth tastes bitter and his lips dry and his feet are refusing to move. How long has he been standing here? Whatever it is down there in the alley, it's not letting him walk away. It's dark and hunched and his legs are forced to move towards it. He's been here before. He's felt this fear, this horror. It's a body. He knows it's a body, dumped there by the bins like it's nothing, hidden in the centre of the village, broken and crushed under some old rags and left to rot.

Fuck, he can't bring himself to go down there, to kneel by the body and lift up the rags and face what he needs to face next; he can't do this any more. He could call someone. Georgie. No, he can't call her again. He can't move. Something flickers, the first of the street lights by the square, turning a septic yellow with a feeble buzz, but somehow it helps. He takes a cautious, silent step further into the dark. He swallows, calms his breathing some. Holds out his hand, palm open, as though it might be a dog, or a fox, a wild animal that could be soothed.

A fox wouldn't be staying still, though.

A fox would be scavenging, going through the bins; there'd be the sound of claws on the stone. He edges closer. One step at a time. Nothing moves. He reaches out to the pile of clothes, takes a corner between his fingers. Pulls. More clothes underneath. He straightens up, steps closer. It's just ... it's a pile of clothes, old sheets, torn and damp – he laughs, kneels down for a closer look: ripped sheets is all. And then he hears it. Behind him. Footsteps. He spins. Shouts out. It's a man, dark hood, dark jeans, balaclava, running from him now and Simon is on his feet, he's chasing, he's yelling *Stop! Police!* His chest is pounding with the cold gasps he needs to make himself move but it's instinct taking over now and this is where it's all been leading – he's faster and more desperate and he's nothing left to lose.

'Stop!'

The man darts across the road, Simon follows, down Church Street, into the dark, and he's catching up, he can feel the energy of it pounding round his body, through his muscle, through his skin and he can almost reach him – his shoulder, grab the hood, pull him round and swing. He catches him solid, on the jaw, and the man is holding up his hands and he stumbles back and Simon stumbles forwards, stands on his foot and the man falls and Simon falls with him. They hit the ground. Simon's hands on his shoulders, pinning him down.

'Who are you?' he demands. 'What's your name?'

'Please stop—'

'What were you doing outside that building?' His voice louder, shouting. 'Why were you trying to get in?'

Simon yanks the balaclava off his head. Sits back, startled.

'What are you doing here?'

'Please,' stammers Kevin Taylor, blinking repeatedly into Simon's stare. 'Please, I think my head is bleeding.'

A recording of four people listening to a recording of one woman describing how she was attacked as a child by a group of men while two dead bodies lie in the pathology lab; the layers of it. The terrible layers of it. And now she is a part of it too. Mrs Helmsteading is crying, and Georgie is there to watch.

They asked her a few questions, when she first arrived, brought in by a stony-faced Trish. They asked her if she'd heard from Dawn yet. If she knew where Dawn was. If she knew Dawn had been in therapy with Dr Cosse. Mrs Helmsteading answered no, no, no. The first two sounded despairing. The final one, afraid. And Georgie knew she was right to bring her in, that they had to do this.

But she could not be so cruel as to play her Dawn's words without an explanation. So they gave Mrs Helmsteading a seat and made her some tea and told her they'd found some new evidence relating to Dawn and the recent murders. That they knew this was going to be hard for her, that what she was going to hear was horrifying. It was about the possible abduction and attack on her daughter. They waited for a reaction, but Mrs Helmsteading gave none. Her eyes stared at them blankly. Georgie wondered if it was shock. If it was the numbness which can follow pain. If she had reached some kind of threshold.

'I'm sorry,' she said.

Mrs Helmsteading just kept looking at her as Trish waited for her nod.

Together they listened to the description of the flat, the exact carpet in the room where her son was found stabbed to death yesterday morning. The derelict flat that should have been demolished but instead was left to rot.

Trish paused the recording.

'Do you recognise the description of the room?' DS Frazer asked.

Mrs Helmsteading nodded, her eyes down. 'It was my home,' she said. 'A long time ago.'

They listened to the description of the dinner cooking in the kitchen, of Dawn running to her father when he arrived home, his scratchy beard, his eyes.

'Does this sound like your late husband?' Georgie asked.

That was when Mrs Helmsteading started to cry, as she nodded her response.

And now Alexis is guiding Dawn outside, talking to her about the moon, about the playground, and Mrs Helmsteading is making no attempt to wipe away the tears that are slipping down the side of her nose, pooling in the lined corners of her mouth, forming a drip on the underside of her chin. Now is the moment when they all have to listen together, when the truth is going to show. This time Georgie doesn't focus on the words. She watches.

I was in my bed … someone took me out of my bed… Cold hands at the back of my neck, I can't move, can't kick my legs…

Dawn's breath is loud on the recordings, urgent, desperate, as the men circle around her, faces hidden, masked – Georgie knows these costumes, the pointed hoods, the slits of eyeholes.

Who was it?

Mrs Helmsteading is turning away, like she wants it to stop, but also like she knows where it is going; she knows what will happen.

What can you smell, Dawn?

Meat, meat and onions—

Mrs Helmsteading makes a muffled noise, hands clasped over her mouth.

On his breath?

And Georgie sees them tying a rope around a child's neck, leering in close at her face; feels the knife at her throat, blood on her skin and she's back there, she can't help it, they're surrounded, the noise of panic and fear and the white robes and the hate.

I can't breathe, it's too tight— No!— Please help me, it hurts...

Mrs Helmsteading's eyes meeting Georgie's, pleading, and more, accusing, but Dawn's voice doesn't stop, not until she's choking and screaming and slowly brought back to Alexis's office and her own words, *Oh God, it was him—*

'No!'

Mrs Helmsteading stands up, suddenly, violently, her chair crashing to the ground behind her and Georgie is here, in this room, in control.

'Please calm down, Mrs Helmsteading,' Georgie says.

'No! This isn't—'

DS Frazer has lifted up her seat, offers it back to her.

'But he's gone,' she says. 'He's gone.'

'He's a suspected victim in an ongoing murder case.' Georgie's words are quiet and carefully paced and Mrs Helmsteading looks truly horrified then. Horrified and frail and desperate.

'It's too much,' she says. 'Please.'

'Please what?'

She's shaking her head, hands clutching at her throat like Georgie doesn't know what, but she recognises the fear. She does see that.

'Do you have something to tell us, Mrs—'

She stands, the chair falls again, desperation turns to determination.

'Let me go, right now.' Her voice thin but firm, her breath a stutter.

'We just want to talk.'

Georgie feels something in herself turning cold.

'I think it's time you told us the truth, Mrs—'

It's worse than cold. It's hard, it's angry.

'I want to leave!'

'You're not under arrest.'

'So I can go?'

'You can go,' Georgie says.

And with that, Mrs Helmsteading turns and leaves the room and Georgie stays sitting at the interview table. She might even look calm to someone who didn't know her, but her hands are clasped tight around the table's edge. Before she gets up she knows she has to see them, face on, the figures getting closer, surrounding her. They are masked and cloaked, with only their eyes glinting through rips in the fabric: familiar and cold and vicious.

HOW GEORGIE CAME OF AGE

She wakes Errol up at 5 a.m., their mom fast asleep and the dark's potential retreating fast – they have to go now if they're going to catch the first bus to the city and Georgie's not going to miss this protest, and she's not going to let her brother miss it either.

'Get up,' she whispers as loud as she dares, shaking his shoulder – his face is invisible, blankets scrunched over his head. He must be roasting. Or faking it. 'You're awake, aren't you. Very funny.'

The blankets wobble with his laughter.

'Why do we have to go…' His voice is muffled and amused.

She grabs the covers off him, throws him a T-shirt.

'To make our voices heard.'

'Stand up to the man?'

'They're fucking racists – and you should be taking this seriously.'

He pulls the T-shirt over his head, locates his jeans.

'I know, sis. I'm going, aren't I?'

'Bring your fake ID.'

'What for?'

'Just in case.'

They said you were supposed to be sixteen to join the protest, and since she went to the trouble of getting him the ID he might as well bring it along. Though he's so easy-going, her brother, he could probably charm his way into anything he wanted.

Full moon outside. Low and bright, watching her. Head down past the mayor's house, won't even look in. It's three years since she cursed them with the redbird, three years since his mother died in her sleep, two since the mayor had his heart attack, one since the mayor's son Troy got his gang to meet on a Saturday night and wait in the shadows till Jeff from the year below was heading home from his job at the diner. They surrounded him out back, five of them, one of him, took turns slapping him, laughing till he fought back and they piled on, kicking him to a broken nose and broken ribs and bloody eyes that would take a month to heal. *Stupid nigger*, they laughed about it after. Georgie overheard them. Cursing their homes with birds isn't enough any more.

They are the only two at the depot as the bus arrives. A scattering of passengers already on board, heads against windows, sleeping, gazing out at nothing. Georgie hands over their tickets, Errol chooses a seat at the back. Reads Georgie's leaflets over her shoulder as they weave through the last of the night. She's glad he's looking, angles them over so he can see. *Death to the Klan March*. They're starting in a housing project, marching through the town centre to end at City Hall. *Radical, violent opposition to the Klan*. There are going to be TV cameras there. They're going to make a difference. *Armed self-defense is the only defense*. And Georgie knows it, too. As they pull into the city, Errol looks at her with his big eyes and for a second he looks just like the little boy he used to be.

'You sure about this, sis?'

'Come on.'

They leave the bus. The light's ablaze. Georgie leads the way and he follows through streets already loud and throbbing. The dust and dirt of midsummer, the shove of strangers; this is what she's been waiting for. The road's rising and they climb. She's memorised the route, imagined walking it every day for weeks now, lying in bed with that restless anger pulsing through her, preparing her voice to shout. She's barely even taking in her surroundings until they reach the top and she stops, stunned. Below them, the crowds have gathered, men, women, banners and shouts and the beginnings of a chant that grows with each second that passes, the crowd buzzing like a swarm and she grabs her brother's hand and starts to run – she needs to be down there, needs to be a part of this. *Death to the Klan*, she can hear them shouting as her own voice builds up in her throat, she's never chanted, she's never been at a protest before, 'Death to the Klan!' she yells and they reach the edges of the crowd and suddenly they're engulfed in it. Errol's pulled his hand away, but there he is, beside her. He's the youngest here, easy. The crowd is pushing and pulsing and the energy sparks through her. 'I'm proud of you,' she shouts, but he doesn't even hear. *Fight violence with violence*, they're chanting now and they're right – they have to fight – and the crowds are pushing into her and she's finding it hard to breathe but her fist is punching the air and her voice is rough. 'Fight violence with violence!' She is here. This is everything.

Suddenly there are cars. She doesn't know where they came from. The growl of engines, darkened windows, dozens of them surrounding the crowd. They're taunting them. Threatening. But Georgie won't be scared. She feels a fresh surge of anger. This is just the beginning. She's deep in the rally and she's got her brother's hand. In her other, she holds a stone. Around her: picket sticks and slogans and rage. Now! Throw it! She does, high and hard over the crowd. It hits the hood of a car. She thinks. Can't see, can't hear. Again! A cascade of stones now and for a second, a second, they are powerful, they are fighting back. Then a car engine. More of them. Encircling the crowd. Something changing, something turning to panic, people surging forward and she has no choice, she moves with them, is one of them; she's pushed, she stumbles. Falls to her knees. Grazed, raw. It hurts. *Stand up!* someone says. They pass her another stone. The heat of the people and the sun. Her arm up, her back arching. Stones flying over the crowd. Sticks and signs launched at the van up front. It's them. Flashes of white, pointed, sharp, the slam of a door, so fast. It's them. White cloaks. Faces masked. It's them! Around her, people fall. Screaming. Shots, gunshots everywhere, her ears buzz. Can't hear words. Her arm pulled down. Her shoulder, stinging. Screams. Heat. His eyes rolling back. Her brother. Blood seeping from his neck. A scream coming from her throat. Blood on her shirt. Blood on her face. She doesn't understand. It was too fast. He didn't even want to be here. The screaming. Her screaming. There's blood between her fingers, slipping and wet and she's screaming, she's screaming; blood between her fingers and how could this happen and she's falling and she's alone and surrounded and the noise and screams and people and blood and

TOO LATE

The night gets darker. A deeper dark than it has been for many years, though some say it's been threatening for a while now. Black like the soil and the kind of wind that suffocates with too much force. Nights like this, in Burrowhead, seem hopeless, and so people tend not to talk about them. It's their way. Curtains are drawn all along the street, doors locked from the inside, though they can't put their finger on why. Aye, they say to themselves, pulling chairs closer to fires and turning their eyes inwards. A dark night.

Pamali is cashing up at the Spar when they come. Balaclavas over their faces, all fists and boots and hoods. 'Sit down,' one of them yells, 'hands in the air!' but she's already sitting on her stool behind the till so she puts her hands up and stays where she is until they change their minds.

The lights go off, the switch pummelled with a fist. Her eyes move to the panic button. She imagines reaching forward to press it, tries to will her arm to move, but it won't and it's too late.

'Stand up,' he shouts then. 'Bitch! Stand up!'

So Pamali stands, and he drags a chair to the middle of the shop, tells her to sit again. She doesn't think they have weapons. But they have fists, boots, anger.

'Fucking sit.'

She sits, palms out like she can calm them. Instinct is all it is. Doing what she's told to calm the situation.

The shorter one grabs a packet from the shelf, rips into it with his teeth. Nylon twine. She makes to stand but she's roughly pushed back down, hands forcing her shoulders. The one holding her on the chair is the angrier one, it's steaming off him – then there's the lanky one over by the till. She has this awful feeling she knows them. That she's served them and smiled.

They tie her up on the chair, using that twine she sells in the shop, around and around her body, her arms pinned to her sides, her ankles tied to the chair legs. Her eyes strain through the darkness, seeing the white flicker of the drinks fridge down the side of the shop, the strip of it reflected in the eyes that peer out from their woollen masks. The twine is sharp, thin, bites into her skin. It's happening too fast now, she's not reacting right. But how bad can this get, in Burrowhead? It's her home. A dark night, but still. She stays calm. They're probably just here to steal. She left the cash drawer open.

'If you want money—'

'Shut up!'

Then the smashing starts. Everything in the shop. It makes a racket, but no one comes. Down the aisles they grab and smash cans of lemonade and ginger, cereal packets burst, trampled, light bulbs hurled to the ground, disintegrating into glass specks and slivers. The tall one writes something with a spray can, indoor graffiti, she doesn't know what it says, she can just hear the hiss of it as they make their marks over the front of the counter where her till stands.

A kick, on her chair leg, and her whole body jolts. She needs to speak.

'What is it you want, boys?'

She tries to hide the shake of her voice, but it doesn't work.

'She knows us,' the little one growls.

'No she don't.'

A packet of yellow dusters is being ripped open now, she doesn't get why at first.

'Tell me what you need and you can have it. Cans? There's plenty behind—'

'Shut the fuck up.'

He's staring at her now, right into her eyes, the one who tied the twine too tight, staring and staring and she looks back, right into his eyes, the only bit of his face not hidden. The slap is such a shock she doesn't understand what's just happened.

She looks him in the eye. Looks at him and recognises him.

'She knows who we are!'

'So what?'

'She's a witness.'

'It's not a fucking movie.'

They're kicking at the shelves now, her neatly ordered shelves of shampoo and cotton thread, washing-up liquid, peaches in syrup, safety pins, batteries. It makes a crash when it hits the floor, everything falling, scattering, smashing. She's wriggled her arm loose, but he knows it. He's watching her. Surely someone's going to hear all this. He grabs her wrists – 'Like that, is it?' he spits – yanks her arm behind the chair to tie her up better, but she's resisting now, holding her arms tight round the front of her body – 'Fucking bitch' – and her wrist is grabbed and pulled so far back, so fast and the pain of it, shooting from her shoulder to her wrist, she can't even scream at first, her eyes are wide and filling and then she's screaming, and she's screaming and screaming and the pain of her arm is too much it's too much.

'What've you done?' the one with the spray can says, and still she's screaming until the yellow dust cloth is rammed into her mouth and she's struggling and crying and her screams muffled and desperate and he's laughing, the one who tied her up, all rage and spite. He's laughing. She can't breathe. The cloth is choking her and she's starting to retch and the feel of it in her mouth is dry and fibrous. She has to breathe. She has to get through this.

'That's shut you up some,' he says. 'Not that it makes much difference round here. There's no one listening.'

FRIDAY

BEFORE SUNRISE

Outside the night is deeper than oceans but here, in my cave, at last I can see: red ribbons tied lovingly around pebbles, prayers offered to the dead of the cave because the living have stopped listening. Twigs are tied into crosses, a reluctant farewell; a heart frames the initials of people who wanted to be remembered. PD & RT 4EVER: Pauly and Rachel, on the cliffs, eating berries, the day they died. They are happy to see me. The little girl too, with her dirty face and petticoat, her bare feet, her small hand slipping into mine as I dab the sweat from Dad's forehead.

Please help my mammy, she whispers.

We are near the front, the wide room inside the cliffs where we are welcome, where others have sheltered before me; we do not look to the back, where the shapes gouged into stone are older and vicious, where the stretching shadows reside, the violence that threatens our peace. My own violence is giving them strength, but I have to remember: the weeks that pass as I make my dad soup. I spoon it to him gently, my hand shaking when he says thank you, like he is grateful to me. Like he loves me. Until one day I realise who he is. I know the smell, I know his eyes, how they peered through holes cut in a mask as he held my wrists down and it is too easy to stop him breathing, to hold the cool flannel over his face instead of his forehead. He'd said thank you as though he loved me, but he never will again.

I'm here, I say, kneeling at his side. His eyes swivel to mine and I struggle to read their emotion: regret, sadness?

I have my worry doll clasped in my hand.

Love?

He reaches out for me. I drop the doll and our fingertips meet and then I feel them again: the sharp pinches at my skin, the hiss of rasping breath and I look up to see them, clinging to the rocks that edge the cave, watching us and waiting. I hold Dad's hand and glare at them, unafraid; I am not a child any more. They are fear that stretches and shrinks, that is all, they are rotting breath, the scratch of unseen claws. Vicious words seep from their mouths, but this morning they are weakened and gasping.

Don't look at them, Dad, I say, just look at me. I'm here, I'm safe.

The little boy looks up at me from inside his coffin. He is so young; the girl seems old and wise beside him. We will not leave him to suffocate alone. His hair is clumpy and uneven; I imagine scissors hacking at it, held by the same hand that forced him into this box. He is calm now, though, and when the girl sits cross-legged beside him his toothless smile is wide. Perhaps he is grateful to have the company. Perhaps Dad is too. His eyes are watery so I wipe them for him, gently, and the creatures writhe within the rock. There is a scratch at my skin, but I rub it away – the men who attacked me didn't have beaks for hands, they had fists that forced my chest onto stone, fingers tying rope around my neck, a knife pressing into my throat.

Is there something you need to tell me, Dad?

The breath is his alone, from the pain of his last days.

A sudden screech from the rock, then silence again.

We're too late for that now though, aren't we?

Mary's eyes are the same gold as the charms in my pocket; they both give me strength. I offer them to her but she shakes her head.

What can I do?

Rachel holds out a blueberry, glimmering in the sunlight, and pops it into Pauly's laughing mouth. Black curls frame his face and his eyes dance. Rachel is wearing his ring on a silver chain around her neck, a long dark skirt with gold flowers sewn through – it is what she was wearing when they died. This is the moment they die. It is happening again. Something shifts. Cold. Sickly. They're not alone. Hate melts out of rock and claws through the air, nails are dragging on stone, getting stronger with every step, with every scratch until Pauly and Rachel distort, their smiles turning to grimaces, their lips peeling back away from their jaws—

Leave them alone!

I push out towards them and fall through shadow, a gash along my arm where they stab at me, my face burning with sharp wounds, the rasping noise getting louder all around, and I feel Dad's fingers closing around my wrist; I'd only left him for a second. My Dawny, he croaks, but it is too late – his face is elongated, his eyes are gone, please no, I beg, he's not one of you, don't take him, please, but Mary is looking at us and even as the rest of her fades her eyes remain and they stare right into me and the girl has gone, the little boy has gone and I'm begging them to stay – don't leave me, please – but I am alone, my dad is gone and Alexis is gone. I am alone here in the cave in the cold with my guilt and the sky outside has turned blood red.

RED SKY

Georgie's wide awake, woken by Dawn's pleading voice, by images of violence and a little girl, helpless and terrified in the grit of salt wind at the playground by the coast. Five men in cloaks that hide their bodies, tall and looming over her, kneeling on her tiny wrists; masks made out of sheets hanging over their faces, looping rope around a child's neck – their eyes, she sees their eyes, the raw pink skin around their eyes leering out of slits of fabric. Alexis knew it too, and now he is gone, lost. The look on his face; blood pooling above his collarbone, washed from the ground under the swings to seep into the soil of the village. She has to get some answers.

But how much do the answers help? That's what Georgie's struggling with as the wind groans and she finds herself tiptoeing down the stairs. Were the answers going to help Dawn? Would they help Alexis? Or her; would the answers help her? People in Burrowhead dressing up like members of the Klan to attack a local child – it doesn't make sense. If it was all racism she'd know how to fight back, if it was all misogyny, if it was all from one person, even a group, but this – violence used against a local girl, a gay man, threats and vandalism, racism, murder – is it every kind of otherness they hate? And it's not just now, is it, it hasn't just started, it's historic, it's endemic. She's staring at Fergus's flyers, his membership forms:

The Archaeological Society of Burrowhead and Warphill

There are photos: the pockmarked standing stone against a threatening sky, the church ruin emerging from snow.

Learn more about our history

A Celtic carving of a bird: the beak wide open, vicious.

Celebrate our local heritage

And then she sees it, standing on the table, her coffee table: a small twisted metal figurine, a featureless face, sharp hands like beaks and that pointed head, ugly and rusted and threatening, mud still clinging to its robed torso – it's one of them, a carved figure of one of the men who attacked Dawn, right here in her house, and she's staring with something dangerously close to hatred.

'What is it?' Fergus says. He's followed her down. His voice is cautious, concerned.

'What is *that?*'

'Amazing, isn't it?' he says, kneeling down beside her. 'I found it in the motte yesterday, about a foot deep in the earth.'

She can feel the heat of him from here, the sleepy warmth of his body, and it makes her turn away.

'It's awful,' she says. 'It's—"

'It's ancient, Georgie.'

'Are you sure?'

'There have been similar figures found all over the Celtic world. They're offerings to the gods.'

'Offerings for what?'

Fergus shrugs. 'A better harvest. The cure for an illness. A child, maybe. Whatever they couldn't control...'

He's reaching out towards it, like he's drawn to it, like he needs the feel of it between his hands.

'I think you should get rid of it.'

'But that's—'

'There's something rotten in all this, Fergus.'

He swallows, looks at the figurine, drops his hands back to his knees. His bunting looks garish and inappropriate – maybe he's finally noticed.

'How is the ... how's it going?'

He doesn't say case, or investigation, or violence, or murder. For a second she wants to describe to him exactly what she's seen, make him witness it too. Would that change him, a brutal jolt like that?

'I don't know what could make people do such awful things,' he says. 'I don't understand it, Georgie.'

It's true, he doesn't. And she can't be the one to make him.

'Because there's none of that darkness in you,' she says.

'You mean us.' His face is gentle, those hopeful eyes again. 'There's none of that darkness in us.'

She leans forward and rests her head against his. Is it possible that the reason you start loving someone can be the very same reason you stop?

'Sometimes I want to leave this place,' she says, her voice low, like a confession.

'But why? Not everyone, not all… It's our home.'

Georgie leans back, away from him.

'I was down at the old church yesterday,' she says. 'The ground out there, all uneven from the graves.'

'The soil pushing back?'

'So they say. Soil or something worse maybe.'

'It's just the kind of earth we've got here. Always moving about.'

'Do you believe in that story, Fergus? The one about Mary and the murders… The villagers hanging the old minister.'

Fergus breathes. He's not really a sigher, but when his thoughts take a dark turn his breathing gets heavier, like he's trying to hold something back, or something in.

'I believe there's elements of truth in it,' he says. 'We might have the details wrong. But there were slave traders hereabouts, just like all over the country. Plenty for the old villagers to be ashamed of. To want to bury.'

'I think the school kids are hanging round out there again. Loads of litter. Cans and that, crisp packets.'

'That's no good,' Fergus says. 'I might swing by there later, get that rubbish up.'

But it's not enough. In fact, none of the things that used to be enough seem to be helping any more. Breakfast in bed, home-made soup, warm gloves, picking up other people's litter. None of it can make things okay. She closes her eyes for a second then looks at him, feels a wave of grief for something that hasn't even happened yet.

'What is the point in this,' she says.

His head shakes, just slightly.

But now the phone is ringing. Georgie has a terrible sinking feeling – it's been getting worse every morning this week. Fergus lifts the receiver; Georgie swallows down dread. Please don't let it be another death, she thinks to herself. Please no more of this. Please not Dawn. Please not Mrs Helmsteading. She sees a flash, an image of Fergus on top of the motte, arms spread and body hanging limp and she doesn't know where it's come from, only that her mind is telling her there's something very wrong and she can't shake it.

'Oh my God,' he says, and she looks up at him, into his eyes that for a second she doesn't recognise. 'Oh God, not Pamali.'

Pamali?

Georgie is up.

Georgie is running.

FIRST BIT A LIGHT

Simon's creeping around his own home. Lights off, just the sliver of dawn trickling in through the windows and the faint snoring coming from the living room. What the bloody hell has he done? Losing it on the street, pinning Kevin Taylor to the ground, grilling him about what he was doing sneaking into Alexis's flat and then what, the sudden realisation that he might report him, that he might have been caught on CCTV; thinking like he was the criminal. So he helped him up, made sure he was okay – didn't want to send him home so brought him back here instead, with the offer of a drink and all – cleaned up the grazes on his head and picked the gravel out of his hair. Gave him an ice pack for his jaw, another for the black eye. Jesus. A glass of whisky and an apology, then Kevin had crashed out on the sofa.

Bloody Shona, sending a kid like him to go breaking into Alexis's office – as if Kevin Taylor was going to find some vital piece of evidence the police had missed. He didn't know what Alexis had stumbled into, but he knew Georgie would have found anything there was to find there. Damn idiot in his balaclava. There he is, waking up now.

'Alright mate,' Kevin mumbles, sitting up and fluffing his hair in a failed attempt to make it look stylishly messy. 'S'the time?'

'Bout six.'

'Fuck...' He seems to have just remembered the eye. Holds his hand to it and winces, gingerly pats it again. 'Thanks for this.'

Simon raises an eyebrow. 'Breaking and entering. Attempted burglary.'

'Alright, alright. I'll no be telling anyone if you don't.' He touches his jaw, almost grins. 'Lucky for you I can take a punch better than you can deliver.'

'I was going easy.'

'Course you were.'

Simon shakes his head.

'What the bloody hell was Shona thinking?'

'Someone's got to find out what happened, don't they?'

A fox screeches in the distance, but Kevin doesn't even notice.

'And I know my way around his office, from my therapy—'

'So you just had to do what Shona told you to do?'

'I told you. She's my girlfriend…'

'Serious is it?'

'Aye.'

She seems about five years older than Kevin, but they'd have been in the same year at school right enough. What a girl like Shona would be doing with him is anyone's guess. She confirmed his story though.

'There's coffee there.' Simon nods to the side table, where he's left a mug of black.

'Ta.'

He picks up the mug, wincing again. He does look bruised.

'What exactly did she think you were going to find?'

'Files,' he says. 'Any connection between Dr Cosse and the Helmsteadings.'

'Because of Bobby?'

'Aye, and Dawn.'

'I take it she's still missing then.'

'Police have been calling round everyone, and no one's seen her – I heard folk talking about it on the bus on my way over. Everyone's looking for Dawn Helmsteading.'

Simon shakes his head. They're doing a good job of keeping things quiet, then. This connection with Dawn though, there might be something there.

They did know each other, in a way, Alexis and Dawn. It wasn't anything he'd have remembered really, or ever thought about again, except that now with her missing it was building up to something in his mind, something he was working out how to use. They'd been out on one of their walks – one of the first ones, in fact, several years back – out along the coast path one evening. Must have been late summer. The montbretia was flowering, swathes of orange. Coral sun and sea full of diamonds. When they got to the bench past the curve of the cliffs there was a woman there. Simon just saw her back at first, her pale hair twisted and clipped; he recognised her as Dawn a second or so before he realised what she was doing, with that urn in her hands and the dust on her fingertips, on her clothes. He was going to walk past without disturbing her, it was such a private moment, her standing there in the golden light scattering her dad's ashes out over the cliffs, but she must have heard them approach. She turned and Simon went to smile. She wasn't looking at him at all, though. She was looking straight at Alexis. Her expression was almost defiant – no tears, no sobbing, nothing like that. Alexis said her name. That's all it was.

'... And then I saw Trish driving back to the station with her mum in the back seat.'

'Wait, who?'

'Mrs Helmsteading. Yesterday afternoon.'

'They've arrested her?'

'Don't know about that. But she was taken into the station, so Shona's fair convinced the Helmsteadings are involved.'

'It was still a stupid thing to do, planning a break-in.'

Kevin grins.

'You could have been arrested.'

'Nah.'

'Still might be.'

'Not now I've been in your home and all. Bloke like you could've taken advantage…'

'Get out.'

He should never have brought the little shite back here. Kevin's grinning again though. 'Thanks for the whisky,' he says at the door. 'See you round.'

'No doubt.'

Then Simon is alone again and pacing and thinking, and he doesn't want Kevin Taylor to be right about anything but the thing is, Alexis did stand him up to meet *someone* on Monday night. Didn't tell him who or why, even though he must have known it would start a fight. It must have been important. He was trying to keep something hidden. Or someone. And when they saw her on the cliffs four years ago, it was intimate, the way he said her name, just once like that.

VISITING HOUR

The hospital smells of cabbage and there's a hole in the floor by reception. Georgie has been driving round for ten minutes just to find a bloody parking space. When are they going to sort out the car park here? Just cause they're in the country they don't all need to behave like total amateurs. Fergus touches her arm. She takes a deep breath. Asks the man on reception to direct her to Pamali's ward.

'Visiting hours start at two,' he says.

Her badge is out like a flash.

'She's been attacked. I'm the police. I need to see her. Now.'

She strides up the corridor, Fergus following behind – the corridor's not quite wide enough for two, at least not with the beds along the side there – to the shared ward where they've left Pamali to sleep a bit. She's not sleeping though.

'Oh, Pami.' Georgie rushes to her bedside.

She's lying propped on some pillows, her left arm in a sling. A bruise on her face.

'Pami, oh my God, I am so, so sorry.'

'I'm okay, Georgie.'

'I came as soon as we got the call. Where is everyone?'

'They've just left. The forensics people, I mean. Took my clothes, checked my hair, my nails—'

'I meant—'

'I don't think they've called anyone else yet. You're my in case of emergency person.' Pamali smiles.

'And I wasn't there to help.'

'You're here now, Georgie. And Fergus, thank you for coming.'

Fergus crouches down by her bedside and takes her hand – the one not in a sling. He pats her wrist, gently. Looks at her face, shakes his head. Georgie can see he doesn't know what to do.

'I think there are chairs round there.' Pamali nods to the end of the ward, by the window. There's an old woman sleeping in one of the other beds, her snores coming in waves, and an old man over in the corner staring vacantly at the TV screen over on the wall. Fergus stands, collects a couple of chairs, brings them back to Pamali's bedside. He sits in one while Georgie stares at the other.

'This is too awful, Pami,' she says.

'It's just a dislocated shoulder.'

'It's not just a dislocated shoulder.'

'No.'

Georgie sits on the edge of the bed and holds Pamali in a hug, her body lifting in a sob, but she pulls back from crying. She needs to do something more useful than that. Fergus reaches over, places a careful hand on each of their backs. Georgie shakes him away.

'I thought…' Pamali begins, then stops. Her breath is all jagged. 'I thought, at one point, they were going to kill me.'

Georgie holds her tight, holds her and rocks silently on the bed.

'But they didn't,' Pamali says eventually, pulling back and straightening up. 'I'm not sure they even meant to do this.' She looks down at her arm. 'At least, I don't think they both meant for it to happen.'

'Don't excuse them,' Georgie says. 'Not for a bloody second.'

Georgie doesn't think Pamali's ever seen her get angry, but if ever there was a time, now is it. She's not sure why Pamali seems so calm. Or why Fergus is hovering behind her.

There is a window in this ward, a square one, with the flimsy blue curtains pulled over to the side and a view over the disused field behind the hospital. Beyond the window there is a flock of seagulls, ugly and grey, pecking at the grass and sometimes at each other. Georgie's mind reels back to the old church, following connections that won't connect: Alexis's broken wrist, Pamali's shoulder, bodies pushing against hers, graves forcing their way up out of the earth.

'Can you tell me what happened, Pami?' she says. 'Only if you're ready. Just what you feel able to.'

'I can tell you everything, Georgie. I know exactly what I need to say.'

It dawns on Georgie that Pamali is angry too, but she's been carefully shaping it for this moment.

'There were two of them,' Pamali continues. 'Locals. They go to the high school.'

'They were kids?'

'Teenagers. Boys. And one of them...'

'What?'

Pamali swallows. Her eyes are clear now, her expression calm but certain, and Georgie feels a swell of admiration for her.

'One of them was Andy.'

Georgie blinks. She must have misheard.

There's silence between them for a beat, nothing but the click and pad of hospital noises and the gulls outside.

'Andy who?'

'Andy Barr,' she says quietly. 'Your Andy. It was him and his mate.'

Georgie is staring, just staring at what they've done, at Pami's arm and the bruise shading her left cheek.

'Not young Andy,' Fergus is saying. 'No, he can't have meant... I'm sure he wouldn't have...'

Shut up, thinks Georgie. Shut up, shut the hell up—

'He was spray-painting the racist stuff on the counter,' says Pamali firmly. 'His friend, Lee I think it is, he was the one who dislocated my shoulder. Andy didn't like that. He didn't stop it though.'

Georgie's skin has gone cold, there's a stinging pain behind her eyes.

'They tied me up and dislocated my shoulder, hit me, smashed up the shop, swore, called me names, and then they ran off and left me there, tied to the chair with my arm...' She's talking fast, determined, like she's got to say it all now. Like she'd been rehearsing it while she was tied up there. While she was terrified. 'There was a cloth in my mouth, so I couldn't scream. I passed out for a while. When I woke up, the string had been cut. The twine tying me to the chair. I was shaking like... The shock, I guess. I was sick soon as I stood up. Collapsed. Then I heard the ambulance arriving.'

'Who untied it?' Georgie's voice is distant, even she doesn't recognise it.

'I don't know. The ambulance brought me here. Sorted out my shoulder. Next thing I know it's light out and they're telling me police are on the way.'

She takes Georgie's hand, but Georgie can't stop staring out of the window, watching those wretched gulls.

'Georgie?'

Georgie shakes her head. Shakes her head and forces herself to speak. 'I'm so ashamed,' she says.

'None of this is your fault.'

'Some of it is. I've failed you, Pami.' Things have changed now. She is changed. 'Failed to see what was going on. But I'll bring them in,' she says. 'Lock them up for starters. They'll go to jail. They've ruined their own lives, that's what they've done. Oh, Pami.' Georgie wants to stop and lie down or stand and scream but instead she pulls up Trish's number on her phone. Then skips past it.

Simon's voice when he answers the phone is gruff. But he's been saying for days he wants to help, and now there's a way he can.

'Si,' she says, 'Si, we've got to make an arrest. They've attacked Pamali. There'll be interviews to do as well. Meet me by the gate to the Barr farm?'

09:45, CRACKENBRIDGE

That stag, that bloody stag he nearly hit on the way in, Frazer can still see its eyes – he's anthropomorphising of course, but by God they looked human. Like the way the birds screech every morning and for a split second he hears it as a scream, a child's scream at first light and then he pulls himself together, heads down for breakfast at his B & B and pretends not to notice all the pairs of eyes staring at him. He's the only person in the breakfast room, of course, but then there's the boar's head on the wall, those china figurines they've got lined up on the bizarrely elaborate shelf unit, the woman who brings the breakfast, the dog always loping around her ankles. All of them, watching him, just like all the people he passed on his way into the station – he's not imagining that. Everyone on the street looking at him, people peering out of car windows, the tell-tale flick of curtains in front rooms and all because he's *not from these parts*. Even here in the forensics lab he can't shake the feeling. There's work to do, though, and he's the one to do it. Maybe that's exactly why they're watching him. The fear of what he's going to see, with his eyes that know how to look at things differently. Sometimes it takes an outsider. The fact everyone claimed to have seen nothing on the first door-to-door only makes him more convinced they know plenty. Here's Cal though, here's some evidence; here's the bag which belonged to Dawn Helmsteading, and it smells of damp mildew and stale seaweed, a rotten fabric smell. Beside it, Cal has laid out the contents, each item labelled and a full analysis printed out for him. Finally, some professional work out here.

There's the mobile phone Cal managed to get into, where he found the hypnosis session recording. Next there's a wallet with Dawn's debit cards, ID from the GP's, about £35 in cash, and a thermos flask that was apparently filled with milky tea. And finally a soggy pink rabbit with floppy white ears, its fluffy fur worn away to bald patches in places.

'She kept it, all these years?' he says.

'Seems so.'

She must have brought it with her to meet Alexis, to help with her memory – it's very possibly the same one, the fluffy rabbit she talks about in the hypnosis recordings. Someone put it on her chest, out at the playground, one of the cloaked figures placed her favourite toy where she could see it while they wrapped a rope around her neck. She couldn't reach it, though – she had her arms pinned down. What was it then, a threat? Part of the torture? Or something to keep her calm, keep her occupied? It suggested the attack was personal, the attackers known to her, just like she thought. *Oh God, it was him.*

'The ID is genuine?'

'Yep, the surgery have confirmed.'

'And the cards?'

'Not been used since before the weekend. £40 taken out from the machine in Warphill, last Thursday. Nothing unusual.'

'But why did she dump the bag?'

Cal shrugs. 'Maybe she didn't on purpose. Maybe she dropped it. Maybe she was running from the crime and it was slowing her down. Or maybe someone took it from her.'

'You think she murdered Dr Cosse?'

'Not necessarily. People dump bags when they're running for their life, too.'

It's true enough.

'Well either way, it's time we find Dawn Helmsteading. I'm getting a fresh search going, leading it myself this time.'

'What makes you think she's still around here?'

'Purse in the bag. She couldn't have got that far with no money, and in a bad enough state she'd thrown this whole lot down the cliffs, whatever the reason. I'd say she might be in the local area. Could even be in the village.'

'You don't think someone's hiding her?'

Actually it wouldn't surprise him at all, but Frazer doesn't want to get into that right now – his suspicion of the villagers is something to keep to himself.

'I'll get her picture over to the train station,' he says. 'To local bus drivers—'

'Have you spoken to Georgie?'

Frazer takes a deep breath.

'I need to get over there now. Fill them all in. See what latest theory Trish has come up with, too.' He smiles, then regrets mentioning her when he sees Cal's raised eyebrows.

'Local girl, our Trish,' Cal says. 'We're all very fond of her around here.'

His gaze lingers on Frazer's wedding ring.

Frazer feels that familiar ache, the warmth of the gold band against his skin.

'I bet you'll be glad to be heading back to the city soon,' Cal continues.

Frazer straightens his shirt, stands taller again.

'Not till we've solved the case,' he says.

But as he leaves he could swear the staff in the communal office are watching him; he can feel all those pairs of eyes, following him out of the building.

RAIN, MORNING

Simon's standing at the top of the lane into the first field, and the sky has opened. It's not just a little bit of rain, this, no spitting or drizzle. No calling this the ocean spray, like Alexis used to do. This is vicious, cold, heavy rain pelting him. This is drenching. The kind of rain Alexis used to stay indoors for. That Simon used to tease him about.

Spot a rain never hurt anyone.

He thinks of pulling up his collar but he leaves it where it is, rain forcing its way down his neck as he looks up the lane for Georgie's car, but there's no sign of it yet. Then he's turning, looking at the gate, holding onto the post the way he held on to the swing's frame three mornings ago. Christ, feels like three months. Three minutes. It hits him in his chest like this when he's answering a phone call, when he's cleaning his teeth, when he's standing at a farm gate in the rain. He looks at his knuckles. Grazed, red from last night, a flap of skin just below his second finger. Such a stupid thing to do; unprofessional, brutish. He's going to make things right today though. He rocks on his feet.

Behind him, a car is pulling up the lane. That'll be Georgie. God knows what went down last night, bunch of kids raiding the Spar by the sound of it. What was that, boredom? Frustration? Something worse? The racism of these villages, fucking inexcusable. But then some of these kids have never left. It is all they know, this closed little bit of world. Look at Ricky Barr, born here, bred here, buried his wife here, beat his son here if the rumours have got it right, and yet it was a struggle for him. Hard life, running a farm, no denying that. Hard life and often futile – the weather, the soil, the grants, the shops, the tax, all out of your control – and the Barrs had been running this one for generations. What was being passed down then, from his father, his father before that? Scared of change, aye, fucking terrified of it. But something deeper too. A need to feel like you got some power. A need to pick on someone else so as you don't notice you've been handed nothing but struggle.

'Si.' Georgie stands beside him, the pair of them leaning on the gate in the rain. 'Bit damp out.'

'Aye.'

'The lads, they broke into the Spar. Hurt Pamali. Dislocated her shoulder, left her tied up.'

'Jesus.'

'It was Andy.'

'He was one of them?'

'Yep.'

Simon sees it all. Gangly Andy with his eager babbling and the way he cowers a bit every time someone shouts, the kids at the school, the bullying, the nastiness of them. He remembers it. Christ, he was one of them once. He wasn't picked on in that school, but he'd seen it happening, he'd laughed along. They all had. He'd say he kept quiet because he had something to hide, but that's a pathetic excuse. What's Andy's going to be?

'I've sent Suze to collect the other one, bring him back to the station. Pamali recognised them both, despite their stupid balaclavas. The other one's a kid called Lee.'

Simon nods. He knows the one. The mention of balaclavas brings back the image of Kevin Taylor though, creeping outside Alexis's flat in his black balaclava and hoody – where were all these kids getting outfitted?

'And Trish is at the hospital, getting Pamali's full statement.'

'It's not related to the murders, is it?' he says.

'Not likely. You wouldn't de-escalate from murder to vandalism and assault.'

'True enough.'

'But we'll make the arrests, see what they know. Forensics are checking the Spar too. I want to clean it up once they're done. Pami shouldn't have to...'

She looks down, shaking her head, rain dripping from her tight curls.

Simon sighs. 'How's she doing now?'

Georgie pushes her hair back out of her face. 'Seems okay. Determined. Might not have really hit her yet. Don't know if she'll want to be going back to the Spar...'

'They keeping her in the hospital?'

'For now.'

'That's good. Give her some time to rest. I'll pop by later.'

'She'd like that.'

Simon pauses.

'This'll be linked in with the racist notes though,' he says. 'Sent to Alexis. To you. Cal got prints off them, right? So good chance we can get forensic evidence to back up Pamali's statement.'

Georgie nods. 'They weren't even wearing gloves. And there's a CCTV camera in the Spar too. We'll have the idiots on film.'

Nausea sweeps over him – Kevin Taylor, yesterday evening, 'What time did they break in?'

'Just after ten. Pami was cashing up.'

Several hours after he was there. He might be okay. Christ, what a way to be thinking. He's going to make it up to them though. To Georgie, to Pami. To Alexis. He hated dishonesty, did Alexis. Must have taken quite something to lie to him, to keep whatever was going on with Dawn a secret. Today he's going to find out exactly what that was.

'Si?'

Georgie is reaching out for the gate but she's stopped before opening it, turning to look at him.

'What's wrong?' he says. Stupid thing to ask. Or maybe not. Georgie looks different. He's only just noticed but she does, something's changed – no smile in her eyes, a sharp edge to her jaw.

'They left Pami there on her own, with a dislocated shoulder,' she says. 'She was all on her own. For hours.'

NO GOOD TIME TO GO

Walt throws the last of his feathers into the fire. It kept him warm through the night, but now the flames are silver blue, telling him the time has come, and for that he is grateful. His eyes flick from the dead leaves under his feet, through the matted cover of branches and up to the sky, where the clouds are deep and the light turning a hazy purple: something bad is up there, spilling its way down here, and there's more to come. He doesn't know what, exactly, but he knows where he's going, through the dirt and the rotting ferns coating the ground, he does know that, at least – he's been there before. The bite of the wind through his cloak, reaching his bones even as a young man, the shimmer of a full moon on stone, their voices carrying the chant from one world to the next and a knife, sharpened and glinting, though he doesn't have his knife with him today. Doesn't have anything he should have, does he? But somehow none of that seems to matter any more.

He didn't say goodbye. No point really – it wouldn't make his going any easier, or the memories any better. His memories of Trish are as good as memories get, anyhow. Sweet girl that she is. So loving. Not many youngsters want to walk about with an old man, but Trish never grows tired of it. He feels bad, being all the family she has around – but then she's all of his family too. The both of them, everything each other has.

There was this one time, when she was about three or four, just a few years back – so clear is it – and she decided she wanted to go out camping. Surviving, she called it. A weekend away, surviving. Out in the wild, she meant, just the two of them out surviving in the wild. He never knew where she got the idea from, but he found his old tent in the attic and set it up in the garden, to make sure it was all there, all the necessary bits of it. Once he was sure it stayed up and kept the rain out, they went off for the weekend, out into the moors. Uncle Walt and Little Trisha, surviving together.

She'd been good at it, too. Good at climbing hills. All that energy. Good at finding berries and making the fire. She'd never much appreciated his camping stove, she wanted the real thing. Build a nest of twigs and leaves and light a flame in the middle of it; tend to it through the night. Roasting marshmallows on sticks. She wouldn't approve of him now, heading off without the tent, but she'd have appreciated the fire he made. Besides, he knew he wouldn't be needing to survive too long; that's not why he's out here this time.

Aye, he'd known it was coming. Not just the past few days either, he's known this was on the way for years. Some things you can't fight. The way it's been seeping up through the paving stones, getting right into folks' houses, right into their hearths. His foot sinks into a boggy bit between the clumps of bracken, sinks ankle-deep and some of the wet mud gets in over the top of his boots. He keeps trudging, though. It's a longish walk where he's going. Not too many flies about yet, too cold for that. At least his bees are taken care of.

Poor Fergus. He's still stuck at that place of trying. Walt knows that place – a place of trying to do something, of believing you are in control. Him and his archaeological society, reaching back to the past as though it can be touched, reclaimed, understood. No, Walt's the only one who gets it, the only one who stands a chance of getting through to them. He stops for a moment. Turns back around, looks at the path of his own footsteps through the undergrowth. He's wearing his dressing gown. Good thing too – chilly up here. Now where is he going? Overhead the sky is darkening where it should be getting lighter, but no matter; the pulling is back. Something is pulling at him, tugging hard on a string anchored somewhere deep in his stomach, and it doesn't matter that he's got no coat or torch or knife, no idea any more of the way home, he's got no choice but to follow it. Besides, he's been here before. He can feel it, he can smell it on the ground, in the peeling tree bark and the sodden grass and the low mist which hangs, out here, for whole seasons, for whole lifetimes – maybe just a sit-down, here on the log. The wind is brutal, it truly is, the way it bites at his bones, and his dressing gown keeps flapping open though he's tied the belt in a special knot, in one of his Celtic knots. Got to keep going though, that's a part of it, see, he's got to keep on going until they're ready. He stumbles and stops, walks on, circles back as the mist deepens and the trees thicken and the leaves whisper, and he follows their voices until the ground swells and the trees part and the clearing appears before him. The clouds descend and meet the low-lying mist as Walt lies back and lets the stone reach its ice-cold way through his pyjamas and to his skin, and the years dissolve and he's back there again, back here, exactly where they were: him and Art and Jack, they've all been here before.

ARREST AT 10 A.M.

Georgie and Simon find Andy in the kitchen hanging up the washing. The farmhouse door was closed but not locked when they arrived – there was no answer to their knocking, so they'd just come on in. No sign of Ricky Barr when they passed, though his tractor was parked out in the fields. Spreading slurry first thing is her best guess. The mud sprayed up all over it, thick and dark, even from a distance. The gulls are brown out here, not white, not even grey – brown and dirtied, flying low over the land like a threat.

'Where were you last night, Andy?' Georgie says, standing in the door to the kitchen, watching him carry an armful of clean clothes to the drying rack hanging over the table. She takes a step closer. Gives him a second to think.

Andy puts the clothes down. Keeps his eyes down, too. Shoulders hunched in that way of his, like he wants to shrink himself down a bit. Still at that age of being uncomfortable in his own skin. Mind you, Georgie's not sure if Andy's one to grow out of that. Some people never do.

'I was here,' he mumbles.

'You were not,' Simon fires at him, and for a second Andy's eyes are up and his face is hard and stubborn.

'I was here!'

'You're a shit liar.'

'Well you're a ... a...'

'Yes?' Simon's got his arms folded and his face set and he's twice the width of Andy, easy, and he's blocking his only exit too.

'Alright, Andy,' Georgie says in that kind drawl of hers, standing next to him now. 'Don't say anything you don't mean. I trust you, you know that.'

'Trust me to clean your floors for free.'

'I wouldn't have let you into the station at all if I didn't trust you, would I?'

Andy looks down again, his hand picking away at the splintered side of the table.

'And Trish, she cares about you a lot. You know that? But see, if you were here last night then we'll need your dad to corroborate.' She hears Simon shift his weight by the door. 'So we'll just wait till he gets back. Do you know where he is this morning? No? But he's going to support your version of events?'

Then she waits, the dim light barely picking out the colour of the clothes he's been hanging. She hears the relentless screaming of those gulls outside, watches the way Andy's opening and closing his mouth, pursing his lips, shaking his head; she was right not to bring Trish here.

'Andy?'

The rain battering the windows like that, the wind shaking the frames – there's no warmth here, that's for sure, but he's got to make his choice.

'It were…'

'Go on.'

'It were never supposed to happen like that.'

'Like what?'

'I thought we were going to paint the counter is all.'

Simon steps closer to him, watching his hands, his eyes, ready for any movement, but Andy's not running anywhere. After all, where's he got to go?

'Tell me what counter you were going to paint, Andy.'

'The counter in the Spar,' he says, his voice dragging like he's being forced to recite lines at detention. 'You know which one, boss.'

'I'm not your boss, Andy.'

He nods; he knows that. He wanted to try it out though, a bit of camaraderie, he was still hoping there was a chance he wasn't going to look guilty. But he is, and he does. Georgie has a sudden vision of him, standing huddled over the upturned pew out in the church ruin, writing racist spite on an old school notebook while gulls picked at his discarded chips, soggy with rain and vinegar. Her head throbs.

'We broke into the Spar, me and … just me.'

'We've got Lee too, you arse,' says Simon.

Andy's temper flares, though only his eyes show it.

Georgie holds up her hand, gives Andy the space to calm back down and finish his confession. He doesn't know what he's doing, that's what's getting her; he's got no control over himself. Doesn't know how to be a criminal. Doesn't even know how to lie, not really. But he's been storing up blame and anger, years of it, letting it fester, and she hasn't been paying enough attention to see the signs.

'Alright then,' Andy says. 'We broke into the Spar, just to paint our message on the counter and smash it up a bit. That's all. We'd said we'd do it, for Bobby. I…'

'What?'

'I just wanted her to leave.'

Georgie stares at him.

'It's our village. It should be our shop, for *us*—'

'What the bloody hell are you talking about?' Simon snaps, and Andy looks to Georgie, though whatever he's expecting to find there he doesn't get. She can see the battle in him, watches him weighing up his options.

'Look, I… I don't know how the other stuff happened.'

Georgie takes a deep breath.

'And before last night?'

'Boss – Ma'am?'

'Is there anything you'd like to tell us about your behaviour prior to last night? Been writing any other messages I should be aware of?' Her voice is getting harder.

'Oh. That.'

'Go on.'

'You mean the notes? We just… It's just there's no jobs or anything and … and there's nothing to do…'

An image of Fergus, collecting rubbish, reading about history, starting a community group; the kindness of the way he dealt with having no job. Violence doesn't have to be the response. It's a choice you make.

'We didn't mean anything by it…'

'The note places you at the scene of Dr Cosse's murder.'

'No! It were last week we sent it, it must've fallen out his pocket or something. And I never thought he'd send one to you—'

'Think that makes it okay?' Her words come fast and sharp, her pauses are gone.

'No, but … everything's going to shit, isn't it. What are we supposed to do?'

'Christ's sake,' Simon bumps into the table and Andy half jumps out of his skin.

'Alright,' says Georgie. 'That's enough for now. Andy, I'm taking you down to the station on suspicion of the assault of Pamali Silva.'

'No, but I—'

'You were there, Andy. You're a part of this. Now, where's your dad? We need to tell him we're taking you in.'

Andy startles, rubs his hand like she just scalded it with boiling water. 'Please don't tell him. He's at the market anyway, he's not here. We'll go to the station, just us.'

'Can't do that,' she says. 'You're a minor.'

'I'm seventeen! Please, Georgie, I'll come with you to the station, I'll not be any trouble or anything… But yous don't have to tell him, do you?'

'Of course we'll have to tell him,' she snaps. 'None of this is going away.'

Andy nods and holds his hands out for the cuffs.

'Let's go,' he says. 'Before he gets back. Please?'

She'd thought maybe she'd feel sorry for him, but something has switched in Georgie and it's not going back again.

'Just get in the car, Andy. We're parked out by the gate.'

She's not going to cuff him; what would be the point? He's too scared to run off.

'Okay, boss,' he says, weakly. Eyes down.

But before they leave, she writes a note for Ricky Barr. Says they need to interview him down the station. That they've taken Andy in for questioning. Leaves her card and tells him to phone.

Rain like needles now – less soggy, more sharp. A smell of rotting seaweed in the air. There are ghosts about.

Andy holds the gate open for her then climbs in the back of the car.

For a second, she misses Fergus like an ache.

Without another word she slams the door shut.

WHEN WALT WAS HERE BEFORE

The air was carrying something extra that night; Walt and Jack and Art felt the shudder of it through their clothes, just like the rustle of the dried leaves in the fountain and the clicking of the street lights that flickered then fell dead – the whole village, in fact, found themselves bolting their doors and closing their curtains over that last crack to make sure not a breath of the dark was getting in that night: harvest moon in a year with no harvest, farms forced to close and folk desperate and the smell of burned livestock clinging to the fabric of the land itself. A bad time for the village, and there are things which must be done to survive in a place so thin and old as this; that's understood by the villagers of Burrowhead, the ones who have heard the stories from their grandfathers by the flicker of candlelight, and it's not something that can be understood by the ones that haven't, so they keep it secret and they keep it close.

Walt felt he'd been walking for hours, through dense woodland and muddy bog, gravel crunching underfoot replaced by the slip of rotting leaves, and though he'd walked the tracks many times he knew the stone carvings didn't always appear when you went looking. The distant call of an owl, followed by the strange silence of no reply. The smell of damp vegetation mingled with the smell of the burned cattle, the way it caught at the back of his throat, until at last: a clearing, a fresh gust of wind, the long deep slabs of stone glowing against the night and the three of them forming a ring. They didn't speak, didn't greet each other, just pulled their hoods low over their eyes, kept their faces invisible and raised their voices in unison, ancient words chanted deep and strong, held by the air thickening around them.

So thick and heavy it was hard to breathe.

Collecting in his throat, the nausea, the fear, the awe. Walt's skin prickled with it. The hairs on the back of his neck, behind the ears; he felt it travel across his back, the knowledge that they were not alone. He closed his eyes and bid them closer, called them to join the circle, and three men became four, then five, then a dozen, faces obscured and cloaks billowing in the wind, their voices like whispers, like the hiss and breath of distant waves and he could feel them, pressing closer, the chill of their touch, their blood in his blood and his legs stretching and his head twisting back and he saw it: the stag behind the tall trunks of the silver birch, its eyes dark gold and its coat perfect white, and the rope looped through the air and the creature didn't even break its gaze; it stared at them as they did it, the knife catching the moonlight, slipping easily across its throat, the black of the blood spilling down its flawless chest as its front legs stumbled and it fell to kneeling on the stone carved with the ancient cup and ring. The wind whipped up the leaves and a branch creaked from the old oak and there was a noise, then, from behind the trees, a noise which shouldn't have been there, a scratching, a sneer.

Jack turned, quick as flame, and ran to the trees, grabbed his boy Bobby by the scruff of the neck – *sneaking after me, you don't belong* – and the air was thin and empty again, the stag limp and lost and Art's hood fell back and beneath it his eyes were deep and hollow and Walt knew he'd lost everything, Jack too, all of them, and Art spoke softly, barely a whisper: 'It's not enough, is it?'

'It's all we got,' Walt said. 'It's what we are.'

The stag's blood ran through the curves and lines of the carvings on the stone and was diluted by rain that rushed in to fill the air, turning rusty in the moonlight, and instead of cleansing the air the smell returned: the smell of the burning carcasses, the cattle and sheep they were forced to cull, the putrid black smoke rising from pyres all over the land, and the unspoken thoughts which came creeping in to the dark spaces left behind.

AFTER ELEVEN

Trish drives from the hospital straight back to Burrowhead police station, blaring her horn at every goddamn car in her way and screeching round corners like the road itself deserves to be locked up for life. She can't believe it. She cannot fucking believe it. What an idiot she is! Looking out for that boy, helping him with his bloody work-experience report, fixing his spelling, feeling *sorry* for him, for Chrissake. And all the while he was sending racist spite to her friends and trashing the village and hurting people – smashing and kicking and hurting. God, she is so furious she flies right over a pothole and winces at the clanking of her car – but the tyres hold and she keeps on going. Easing back from ninety, but still. Andy effing Barr, the little monster. She's going to kill him.

The sight of Pamali in that hospital was too much, it was the last straw for Trish, she isn't taking this crap any more. Everyone responsible for this whole bloody mess, everyone, is going to be taken down, if there's nothing else she achieves in this world. She slams on the brakes approaching the station car park and spins into her space, stopping an inch or two from the low concrete wall at the edge, and in she goes, slamming the door open and letting it ricochet back on its hinges, storming down the corridor. Lee is in the cell, Simon with him, and Andy is in the box room next door, which has been transformed into a second cell. The door's open. Georgie's in there. Everything's being recorded so Trish says her name, walks in, and Andy's looking straight at her, kind of pleading. Suddenly all she can do is stare back as he crumples up against the wall and slides down to the floor.

'Andy,' she says, surprising herself with how quiet she speaks, how sad she sounds. 'Andy…'

He's trying to look away.

'Look at me, Andy.'

'I can't.' Andy's lips are downturned, his hands clenching and unclenching. 'Yous all hate me.'

'You could have killed her,' Georgie says.

'I've not killed anyone—'

'What were you thinking?'

Fast, sharp, unforgiving; Trish has never seen Georgie like this. Andy's scared of her.

'I don't… You don't know what it's like.'

'So tell us,' Trish tries.

He takes a deep breath. Lets it out. Takes it in again.

'They're stealing our jobs,' he says, voice hard all of a sudden and unfamiliar. 'They're stealing all the jobs and houses and they—'

'You sound like an idiot,' Georgie snaps.

'No one is stealing anything from you, Andy. Who's been telling you that nonsense, eh?' Trish says, her voice gentle. He's going to cry. And what has he got, really, what's he got to look forward to?

Andy just shakes his head. He's stopped talking – he's back to looking down at the floor.

'Think about Pamali,' Georgie says. 'You know Pamali, you've known her all your life. She lives here, same as you. She's a human being and a friend and she's never taken a thing from you.'

'But my dad says—'

'Your dad, is it?' Georgie's almost shouting now, and Trish wants it to stop. 'You want to be like him, do you?'

'That's not what I said.'

'And Bobby Helmsteading?'

'He wanted us to make a stand.'

'By hurting others?'

'He was a mate.'

'You've got to think for yourself, Andy,' says Trish.

'All you're doing is picking on the people who've got less than you.' Georgie's standing, pacing. 'You're just a bully.'

Andy slumps on the floor.

'It's no good, you being like this,' Trish says, kneeling down. She wishes she could reach out to him, put an arm round his shoulders. 'It's no good, Andy.'

He's crying now, sobbing like a child.

'Don't cry,' she says. 'I know you must feel trapped here, sometimes—'

'You going to tell me to go to university and all?'

She shakes her head.

'Like I can go to fucking art school.'

'I understand,' Trish says. And she does.

'But whoever's been saying this stuff to you, they're lying,' interrupts Georgie. 'Your dad, and Bobby Helmsteading too. You think I was born with money? You think Pamali was? We're not the ones making life hard here, Andy! Try looking at the CEOs who moved all their work to the city, the politicians who decommissioned the nuclear site, did away with student grants...'

Andy sniffs.

'You've got everything the wrong way round.'

'I cut her loose,' he says, in a weak voice. 'I went back and I ... I called the ambulance, made sure she was okay—'

'You also let it happen in the first place,' Georgie says, her voice more forceful than Trish has ever heard it. 'So I want you to stop with your excuses, right now, and tell me exactly what you did.'

COMING UP LUNCHTIME

'I don't *need* a lawyer,' Lee spits out, head high. 'I told you, I did it. It was my idea an all.'

He's short and stocky and surprisingly pretty for such an angry little shite, not a hint of stubble on his chin yet, no spots of grease on his nose, but what really strikes Simon is the way he keeps repeating his confession, like he's proud of what he did to Pamali, like he's claiming it.

'We've called your mum in,' Simon says, and Lee snorts. 'She's had to take the day off work, sounded right upset—'

'She doesn't *work*. They don't even pay her.'

'Well, she said she'd have to close the museum.'

'So?'

Simon sighs and looks down at his notes. Everything he's said matches Pamali's statement. He's not lying to them. But God he's furious, all full of rage and hate and the way he's looking at Simon with no fear whatsoever.

'You people,' Lee says, leaning back in his chair with a smirk on his face. And there is something then in the way he's staring at him – not to do with the crime at all, maybe, but a sort of leering, a sort of challenge, like he knows it all and wouldn't think twice about leaving Simon bleeding on the kerbside. Like he can see right through his clothes.

'Right then,' Simon says, standing up. 'Interview terminated.' Locks the door behind him, down the hall, and it's not till he gets back to his office that he realises his knees are shaking. God, he feels sick. Acid rises up in his throat. He takes a swig of water from the bottle on his table. Rubs his hand across his forehead. Tries to focus on the job and not think about Alexis, not think about what else he could be investigating and what evidence there might be here in the station. Logs on to his computer. Opens up Facebook. He's going to check their pages, Lee, Andy, Bobby – Andy's already given them the password to get into his account along with his email and mobile phone. Messages between them, clear enough what they were planning, and there were a few other kids in on the racist notes too, a right gang of them it seems. Bobby had been collecting angry adolescent boys and grooming them into something, though quite what the endgame was he can't tell. There are all kinds of links on his Facebook page. Alt-right websites, racist forums. Simon doesn't think any of it is quite illegal, but there's plenty to show the kind of man he really was, and it's all the same shite Andy has been spouting too.

But then he hears it. The ringtone of a mobile he doesn't recognise, DS Frazer's voices answering, 'Cal?' and Simon can't help it, he has to know, have they found Dawn? Or something else? He's standing outside his own office, back pressed into the wall, staying as still and silent as he can, listening to DS Frazer sitting in Georgie's office talking into his mobile.

'It's definitely Dawn's then?' he says.

Cal's answer, presumably, is yes.

'The hair does more than place her at the scene. It was on his shirt. They were close….'

The blonde hair. The hair Georgie once thought could have been his. Suddenly Simon is hit with the image, again, of Alexis lying on the ground, his blood staining his shirt, his skin; the noise he would have made as he tried to speak, as his lungs filled with blood and it rose up his throat but now there's Dawn, standing at the playground with her back to the sea and something dark in her, something desperate. His head rocks back and hits the wall, a thud loud enough to bring him back to the station, to the phone call.

'So it was pulled out?'

Simon wishes he could hear both sides, but then this is more than he thought he'd get. Georgie wasn't going to let him anywhere near the case. And she shouldn't. He knows that. He's not going to do anything. He's not—

'And her father dead too, in suspicious circumstances... Well, she's a suspect in his possible murder, given what she said in her hypnosis sessions.'

Her dad? Alexis had realised Dawn killed her dad, was that it? He'd have tried persuading her to tell the truth, to confess it all – that's what he would have done. He was always advising the truth. He wouldn't have expected violence. He probably wouldn't even have fought back.

'I've sent her picture to the train stations and bus depot.'

She's here then, they think she's still here.

'... organising a team from Burrowhead and Crackenbridge to search for her.'

He's doing the job Simon should have been doing all along. Except Simon's not at home grieving any more, Simon's right here – and he needs to be a part of this, not pushed out and standing in a damn corridor. He needs to be right in the middle of it. His own statement, he can hear it, buzzing in his ears, what happened on Monday night, how he'd thought Alexis had stood him up, was with someone else, sleeping with someone else, but that wasn't it, and now he knows: Alexis went to meet Dawn that night. She was the one with him, at the playground. She was the one watching as he bled on the ground, as Simon searched the streets and drank and blamed. She was the one who killed him. And Simon needs to end this. Today.

SEARCHING

Frazer is arranging it all. A new and thorough search for Dawn Helmsteading: he's got people out combing the villages and the countryside between, asking about *any* sightings of Dawn, *any* information at all. He's getting into his stride now and Georgie's caught up with that racist kid in the back room, meaning he's free to catch a suspect. The Crackenbridge police force are heading out for a fresh door-to-door in Warphill, reporting directly to him, word for word – and by 'force' he knows it's only four PCs but still, they're out there doing something, instead of in here making endless cups of damn tea. Someone in these villages knows something, he's never been so sure of anything in his life. These people round here, they know something they're not saying, and he's going to get to it. Meanwhile, in the bus depot at Crackenbridge, a printer spews out posters with Dawn's face on and one by one the drivers, arriving to drop off and pick up, are told to keep an eye out.

'Aye,' they say, pulling their hats down and their collars up. 'Roads flooding today. Worse than ever.'

Posters plastered into the shelters, where they turn dark with rain cause the shelters don't shelter much; posters taped on bus windows where they're peeled down by passengers and read and passed back as the windscreen wipers screech and the glass fogs up with the heat of their breath. The stop at Warphill gets one too.

'That lass from the GP's,' they say, umbrellas inside out from the wind. 'I know her.' No one knows where she is, though. Best they can do to find out is head to the police station in Burrowhead and see what's going on down there.

And the PCs knock on the doors and the folk tell each other, 'They're down to old Bessie Wilkie's now,' then a bit later on, 'Saw them heading in to Colin Spence for a cuppa,' though no one gets interviewed who's actually seen Dawn these past five days. Even Kevin Taylor gets chatty once he realises it's Suze come to talk, and sure, Kevin knew Dawn back at school, a few years older than him but still. 'Didn't say much, though,' he says.

'What happened to your eye then?'

'Few too many down the pub, you know how it is.'

'You lads,' says Suze, shaking her head.

'Have a bicky?' says Kev.

'How's your Shona doing?'

'She's a peach.'

They move on, another house, another nothing, while the bus that left Warphill has arrived in Burrowhead full to bursting, with brakes screeching worse than the gulls round here. Folk from Warphill don't much like Burrowhead, but it's not every day you get the chance to take part in a murder investigation. Down past the fountain, turning off on the road that leads to the station and sure enough, there's Mrs Dover and Mrs Smyth on the corner, sharing a brolly, and there's big Fergus, and some of the kids too, aye, should be in school that lot, but who can blame them? This is not your usual day hereabouts.

So by the time Simon arrives in Warphill the streets are strangely quiet, and since the Crackenbridge search party are all in a police car it's easy enough to avoid them – they're in the wrong part of the village anyhow. Mrs Helmsteading's house seems calm enough, lights on – a good sign – and no one to see him park a few doors down and wait. He's got binoculars to watch for her, check the windows for any movement. Not that he has to wait long. The front door opens and out she steps, long mac wrapped round her and hair in one of those old-lady scarves. Making her way out of the village and heading for the coast road which takes you down past the old flats. Simon waits for her to turn, then gets out of the car. Shuts the door over nice and quiet. Pulls his hood over his head and follows her out of the village on foot.

ESCAPE AFTER MIDDAY

There is someone walking up the beach. I can't even stand so there's no way I'm running. I'll just let them take me. What else did I think was going to happen? At least I got the truth. The chance to look him in the eye. There is whispering on the wind.

'Dawn,' it calls. 'Dawny, are you here?'

I think I know the voice, but the wind can play such spiteful tricks, even as I feel hands on me, stroking my hair, helping me sit up.

'Dawn?'

My eyes search her face in the strange glow. I had forgotten.

'Dawn, my love, the police are coming.'

Of course, of course.

'They're looking for you. They've worked it out, sweetheart. Can you hear me?'

She looks over her shoulder, as though they're following, but I can't hear any more whisperings. I want to close my eyes and cuddle up now, with my mum stroking my hair. Maybe we can go back.

'They're investigating your dad's death. They're looking for you.'

But no, we can't go back. No one to go back to.

'Do you understand, Dawny?'

That's the trouble. Was the trouble. 'Do you?' I whisper. But she doesn't hear me. Or she doesn't want to hear me.

Look at me, Dawn, he whispers.

'I've brought you food and water. A flask of tea, just how you like it. Will we have some tea?'

I watch as she opens a flask and the steam rises and she pours me a little flask-lid of tea, places it carefully in my hands, closes my fingers around the warm sides of it.

'How did you know I was here?' I've made her look hopeful now.

'We found you here once before, remember? Well, not me. It was your father.'

And I remember him coming to find me and how cold I was with my bare feet and only my rabbit for company. He promised me everything was okay. That he was going to keep me safe. He gave me a worry doll and we whispered it all away and we left her here in the rock along with what I wanted to forget.

I curl up into a ball on the floor and I say sorry. I'm sorry, Dad, I'm sorry. I got it wrong.

'There's no time for this, baby. You have to run.'

'But where should I go?'

'Run along the coast. Today, you hear me? By this evening you'll get to the harbour at Lillfort.'

'You're sending me to sea?'

'Leave the country, my Dawny. My baby girl.'

She strokes my hair and her eyes are sad. I drink my tea because it is in my hands and I feel the heat of it moving through me. She looks over her shoulder again. She's shivering and I notice the cold, seeing it on her skin like that.

'Do you understand what I'm saying, Dawn? You have to go. Take this money. It's everything I have. Your passport, here.'

'You'll come with me, won't you?'

'No, my darling girl. I'm sorry.' She kisses my head, my hands. 'I'm so sorry.' Her eyes are wet. 'But you have to escape on your own.'

'I don't want to…'

Then I feel it, a cool pressure in my hand, his fingers clasping mine: my dad is back again, like he used to be, standing beside me.

'Run, Dawn.'

'Now?'

'Now.'

So I stand, pass my mum the teacup and squeeze my dad's hand tightly. It feels good. I am lighter and faster, I can fly over rocks and sand and waves and Dad feels it too – look, he is standing tall, he is strong and kind and his eyes shine with hope—

'Run, Dawn.'

I remember running, running is what I do. But I will not run alone, not this time. 'Come with me,' I say, 'come with me!' calling it out to the cave, to the little girl, to Pauly and Rachel, to the boy clawing the air and Mary who has retreated into stone, but one by one they turn away.

'I can't leave. I can't go.'

'You can,' Mum says. 'You must.'

You can, Dad says. *I'm with you.*

He takes my hand and together we start to run. We don't look back to the cave, we look out to the urgent waves and the beach of grey and gold and Mum calls out into the wind. I snatch her words from the air and I'll carry them with me, wherever I go: 'Forgive me,' she calls. 'Forgive me.'

EARLY AFTERNOON, GETTING ON

The sky bruised and darkening, the rings upon rings of stains on her desk, the dirty beige paint on the walls and the thin patchy brown carpet and rage seeping out from the cells down the hall; Georgie feels heavy with it all. It's like something's pulling her down, the connection of her feet to the ground intensifying against her will, and there's DS Frazer, wanting to get on with his speech, clapping his hands to gather their attention. She gives him a nod. He might be trying too hard, but at least he's trying.

'We're restarting the Burrowhead door-to-door,' he announces, then stops and clears his throat. 'I think … people round here have been watching. They've been talking, and they've been saying things behind our backs. They're hiding something. I know it.' He glances at Georgie – and the thing is, Georgie knows it too. 'So it's time to find out exactly what they're saying, and exactly what they've seen.'

Georgie glances over at Trish, who's crossing and uncrossing her legs, lips tight.

'We've got plenty of evidence to show that Bobby, Andy and Lee have been sending racist messages, vandalising the village and carrying out racist attacks,' Georgie says. She's not going to tone down her words, or Frazer's, to make anyone feel more comfortable.

'Well, Bobby was orchestrating it all, from what Andy's told us,' Trish says quietly. 'Leading some of the local kids astray, churning things up—'

'Got to be something there to churn up in the first place,' Georgie interrupts. 'But yes, he was forming a group of neo-Nazis. Lee as the ringleader, Andy too, with Bobby pulling the strings.'

'And the fingerprints on the notes—' Frazer says.

'Lee, Bobby, Andy.'

'Though Andy's prints were on the one that came to the station, so we all saw him grab at that one...' Trish's voice trails off.

'Trying to cover his tracks, presumably.'

Trish needs to stop bloody excusing him, that's what Georgie thinks.

'They're delinquents,' says DS Frazer. 'I get it. And the racism here, well... It's going to take more than the arrest of a couple of teenagers to change things. But Bobby's dead, and he didn't kill himself. Dawn has to be our primary suspect. Besides, we've got the hair placing her with Alexis on the night of *his* murder, so we need to find her. As far as we know she has no money with her, and there's a chance she's hiding out somewhere in or near Burrowhead.'

'And you think the villagers know where?'

He's in the middle of the room now, pacing between the desks.

'They know *something*,' he's saying. 'I'm sure of it. They've been watching...'

'They *are* watching,' says Trish, nodding her head to the window, where there are thirty or so locals gathered outside the station 'Doesn't mean they're hiding anything.'

Georgie wishes she'd stop trying to defend the village. Reminds her of Fergus: *surely not here in the village.* Yes, of course here in the village. Right here.

'What happened to Bobby, then? You tell me.'

'Well, that,' says Georgie, 'that is the question we need to be asking now.'

But just as she says it she hears this terrible beating of wings and looks out to see a flock of thirty or forty gulls rising up from the pavement outside the station to stare in through the window, judging her, pushing up against her, bodies and heat and voices, she can hear them, shouting, chanting with the beat of their wings and a scream rising up – is she going mad?

'The evidence for that crime is on the knife,' Frazer says. 'And Cal's going to text me soon as the results are in. Hopefully they'll get a blood sample, and that'll lead us straight to the killer. But for now—'

'That's the phone,' says Trish, already reaching to answer it. 'Suze... What? That's what she said, seriously?'

She turns to Georgie, still holding the phone up to her ear, but Georgie reaches for it, takes it herself.

'What's happened, Suze?'

'Mrs Helmsteading's just turned herself over to the police. She says she wants to confess.'

MIRAGE IN THE LATE SEA MIST

We're running down the beach over stones and pebbles, grit, sand
and all the crushed little shells. I gasp another breath and it makes
my teeth sting worse than drilling. Shoes slip on the slimy rocks but
I don't fall – I keep running like there's nothing else left. Because
there is nothing else left. Just us. Dad is beside me; he doesn't have
to breathe and he doesn't have shoes at all. We are moving fast.

I think I saw a person up on the cliffs, a big dark shape, but they
didn't see me. At least I hope not – I have to escape, like my mum
told me. I think maybe I am invisible now, invisible and invincible
racing along my beach, blending in with the twisted seaweed. Gasp
and breathe. My ankle gives way. Don't stop when it hurts. Whatever
you do, don't turn round. Look up! There's the clouds overhead
with their lights on, smooth like magic, and all the while we run. I
haven't seen clouds so alive before but it's good to see them now,
good to remember we are not alone. I hope those noises I can hear
behind me aren't footsteps and breath, just the sea getting angrier
with the storm winds and desperate birds helping us on our way.

The wind is singing a grit-song now, spitting the sand at my eyes.
Groaning high and low like it wants us to give up, but we mustn't
stop. I know where the harbour is. Where the boats come in full of
tourists in the summer – the harbour on the edge of Lillfort, further
up on the coast, a few miles yet but reachable before dark. I hope
the person on the cliffs wasn't real, because if he saw me he might
have run down and started chasing me; Mum said the police could

be coming. But block out the noises and you'll see it's no one but me and my dad and sometimes other bits of me, all running together in the same direction at last. Dawn the child and Dawn the victim and Dawn the killer.

I don't like to think of that word.

But Dad has let go of my hand and is floating out to sea, bobbing up and down like a fishing boat smashed by the waves. I'm sorry, Dad, I call out when I see him, I said I was sorry, but he doesn't reply. Maybe the wind's in the way. The wind and the waves crashing up as the tide rises. I took care of you, Dad, for a while, until the wrong faces started appearing in my dreams. And even then I cared for you with kindness. But you were innocent of it all, Dad. You are my innocent, my wrong face. I couldn't see it at first, but I see it now. I'm sorry. But not that sorry, because now I want to survive. The shape, that shape, is not on the cliffs any more. It's on the path higher up the beach. Racing towards us; getting closer. Run now! Everyone, faster along the rocks and don't stop. I look behind and see him, he's with us now, he's running too and I'm floating up and over the stones and we all hold hands, little girl Dawn and scared Dawn and strong Dawn, we hold hands and we rise up off the ground like we're angels.

INTERVIEW AT 14:30 HRS

The station is humming with badness, that's what Georgie thinks. Fluorescent lights flickering in the corridor, causing an instant headache to settle over her right eye. Even through the closed door she can feel it, the buzzing of sharp lights. She wonders what would happen if they just went out, if the whole station went dark with only the grey of the outside seeping in through the small square windows, the locks on the cell doors opening and Andy and Lee, all full of violence and rage, spilling back out into the world.

She tries to shake herself out of it. Mrs Helmsteading needs her help.

'We need to ask you about Dawn—' she begins, but Mrs Helmsteading is already shaking her head.

'I want to tell you the truth now. It's time.'

Yes, Mrs Helmsteading needs her help. It gives her focus. Makes her feel like Georgie again.

'We've been looking into your husband's death,' Georgie begins. 'Let's start there.'

'I killed him.' She almost interrupts, like she wants to be the one to say it first.

Georgie closes her eyes against it, just closes her eyes.

'How did you do it, Mrs Helmsteading?'

Georgie tries to imagine her smiling. She hasn't seen Mrs Helmsteading smile.

'I suffocated him,' she says. 'It was very easy. He was so weak by then. I held his wet flannel over his face… I'd been using it to cool his head down, you see. Maybe he was sleeping…'

Georgie opens her eyes. 'Maybe?'

'Trying to be accurate, that's all. He had his eyes closed. I didn't want him to realise what was happening.'

'But you wanted him dead?'

'I thought… We… I'd got it wrong. That's why I'm here now, telling you everything. He was innocent.'

Silence but for the nail-scratching click of the fluorescent squares on the ceiling. Georgie has to force herself not to put her hands over her ears.

'He was a kind man, my husband. Gentle and loving. I'd forgotten, but I know that now. He was a good man, and I should be judged for what I've done.'

'What made Dawn decide to kill him?' Trish says.

'No, no, aren't you listening to me?' Her voice louder, high-pitched. 'Dawn didn't kill him, or anyone else. Dawn couldn't. She wouldn't hurt a fly, my Dawny.'

No smile now, of course. Just a desperate, lined face and a longing to go back.

'What exactly is it you're trying to tell us?'

Her deep breath seems to rattle; at least that's how Georgie hears it.

'My Dawn, well, she was seeing a therapist. Alexis Cosse – you know this bit.'

Georgie nods. Trish leans forwards.

'He was using hypnotherapy, to help her remember more details of what happened to her. At first she didn't know who it was, you see. For years she'd lived with that. The shapes of those men surrounding her, their faces hidden behind sheets turned into masks, those awful slits for their eyes… Dawn told me everything, eventually. It wasn't easy for her, but she did.'

Georgie listens, scarcely breathing herself. She listens for every inflection, every waver in her voice, though quite what she is listening for she couldn't say. Truth, perhaps.

The details had come slowly at first. Four, nearly five years ago this was, while her dad was in hospital and Dawn started seeing Dr Cosse. She wanted to stop the nightmares – all her life she'd had them. Reliving what they'd done to her, waking up in the cold, in the dark, surrounded by faceless creatures, the knife at her throat, the rope around her neck. She just wanted peace from it. But Dr Cosse, he wanted to know who it was. So he persuaded her to try some hypnotherapy, said patients could sometimes remember vivid details they'd lost. He'd let her describe what she remembered, asking questions, is there any sound, is there any smell... And there was a smell. That's what she remembered first. The smell of mince and onions. The meal her mum had cooked that evening, before Dawn was taken from her bed.

'He kept trying,' Mrs Helmsteading says. 'Kept leading her to the playground, wanting her to describe what she saw, what it felt like. I asked Dawn why she kept going back, but she said she needed to know the truth.'

Georgie looks up, meets Mrs Helmsteading's gaze.

'But it wasn't until she recognised his eyes that she was certain. There was the smell – the meal we'd had that evening. There was the prickling she felt from his beard when he leaned close. And there were his eyes, peering out of the slashes cut in the mask. She'd seen her father's eyes.'

Georgie nods.

'And he wasn't home, you see,' she swallows. 'That night, I woke up. Must have been the middle of the night – it was pitch-black. He was gone. He wasn't in bed. I didn't even know Dawn was missing, didn't know anything was wrong and I just thought...'

'But then Dawn remembered?'

'The smell on his breath, the eyes. She thought it was her dad. The ringleader. The one who held the knife to her throat.'

'Yes, it was.'

'No, that's the thing. It didn't work right. The hypnotherapy, it was making her remember things that weren't true.'

'False memories?'

'She was... She remembered *what* happened, but it was the wrong man she was seeing. She believed it though, completely, and so I believed her.'

'You're saying you killed your husband in revenge for what you thought he did?' Georgie speaks quietly, slowly.

'Yes.'

'And now you think he was innocent after all?'

'Yes.'

Trish cuts in fast. 'And Dawn knew about your plan.'

'No!'

Georgie reaches for Trish's arm, giving Mrs Helmsteading a chance to lean back, to reach for her plastic cup of water. Though her hands aren't shaking.

'So what happened after your husband died? I mean, after you cremated him.'

'Nothing, for a few years. We were trying to move on. We thought we could put it behind us, once he'd paid for what...'

'Dawn stopped seeing Dr Cosse?'

Mrs Helmsteading nods.

'But then?'

'A few months ago...' She shakes her head. Looks down. Looks ashamed, truly ashamed, for the first time since the interview started.

'What happened a few months ago? Mrs Helmsteading?'

'A few months ago, Bobby came back.'

NO MORE OF THAT HERE

Simon walks the last few paces to where Dawn Helmsteading is lying crumpled on the rocks. His pulse is still pounding from how fast he ran down the cliffs, but he wasn't expecting her to turn and fall, her arms splayed out like that. Like something broken. He'd needed to catch her, accuse her, put every fucking thing he had left into how fast he could run; maybe he was expecting a fight. But whatever he was expecting, it wasn't this.

Her eyes are closed but she's singing something, humming to herself. She looks like she's been out in this weather for days, her hair knotted and plastered to her face, her clothes drenched and her skin, her hands, red raw from the wind, the salt. She's wearing a dress and her legs are bare beneath, prickled blue with goosebumps. It doesn't feel right to be towering over her like this, and so he sits down beside her instead. He can feel the bite of the sea on his face. The tide is on its way in again.

'I've come to arrest you,' he says, his breath ragged from the run. Even so, it is strange how difficult he finds it to speak.

And the way she sings, it's like it's coming from somewhere else, or maybe from everywhere, the sound being pulled from the rocks themselves. There's a sea mist out towards the horizon, a purple-grey haze separating the land from the sky. She sits up then, pulls her knees up to her chest and turns to face him with a question in her eyes.

'I know you,' she says.

He nods. 'We went to the same school.'

'No,' she says. 'I don't mean that.' Her eyes are searching for something, or someone. 'I heard you shouting to the wind. Do you remember? It was a long time ago. Years and years, I think. Or maybe days.'

Yes, Simon remembers. So she was there, watching him. Hiding behind him as he choked on everything he had lost. The awful violence of it. Falling to his knees in the sea. She was watching him.

'I wanted to help you,' she says. 'I wanted to reach out—'

'Fuck you.'

But she reaches out now, touches her frozen hand to his face. 'It sounded like you were all alone.'

He'd thought he was angry, at last, that he could stop with this pain, this aching. That he could place the blame where it belonged. He tries to say 'I'm arresting you' but he can't even finish the sentence, his throat's closed too tight around the words.

'It's good to cry,' she says. 'My mum says that.'

Simon forces a breath, presses a hand across his eyes. There's seaweed floating in with the tide. That's better. Black. Lumpy. Ugly, like it should be.

'You can't get away,' he says. 'I won't let you get away with it.'

She puts her head onto his shoulder and curls her legs up beside her. 'That's okay,' she says. The water from her hair seeps through his shirt, touches like ice. He can feel her shivering now.

'We can shout together, if you like,' she says. 'Shout it all away, then sit here and watch it go. The colours will change as it moves over the waves and this is a beautiful spot for watching, don't you think? The sea is coming closer now.'

'I'm arresting you,' he says, his voice stronger now. 'I'm arresting you for the murder of Alexis Cosse.'

She makes a noise like a breath, only slower, her arms stretching out to him as though she imagines him to be her father, or her friend, or her child. 'I was dreaming that he might have been okay,' she says. 'I wanted so much for him to be okay.'

'He's—'

Simon doesn't even know why he lets it happen, but Dawn has put her arms around him and is rocking back and forth. Maybe he could push her off, stand without falling, march her to the station, shout, blame, but he doesn't. Somehow he can't.

'I'm sorry, Alexis,' she says. 'They're whispering again, can you hear them on the wind? I'm so sorry.'

'Why did you kill him?'

She starts that singing again, like a lullaby.

'He was just trying to help you.'

'He did help me.'

'That's all he ever did, he tried to help people.'

'I know.'

'But then you … you blamed him and you' – he forces himself to say it – 'you stabbed him over and over again and left him to die. Why did you do it?'

At last her arms are gone from around him and she's looking at him with her transparent eyes and there are tears flowing down her cheeks but she doesn't make a sound, she doesn't sob or cry or even try to deny it.

'He gave me something special,' she says. 'And then he told me to run. Run, Dawn, run – that's what we've been doing. He gave me a present. But I think now that he should have given it to you. If you arrest me, can I take you back to the cave to get it?'

'What are you talking about?'

'I'd like to show you the cave, before we go back to the police station. To give you the present he gave to me. Just before he saved my life.'

SHOULD HAVE BEEN TEATIME

'You're saying you had no idea what had happened to Dawn until she told you?' Trish leans back and regards Mrs Helmsteading over the table.

Mrs Helmsteading shakes her head.

'But my husband...'

'What?'

'He knew. I mean, he must have known – that's what I've realised. He must have known Bobby was up to something and so he followed him, or found him out there, with Dawn. I still don't know exactly. Dawn knows she passed out at the playground, when they tied the rope around her neck, and next thing she's back in her own bed. Her dad must have found her and carried her home again. When I woke up in the morning, everything was normal except that Jack had decided Bobby had to be sent away to boarding school... He was adamant about it. He'd not even let him come home for holidays most of the time, always sending him off to camp or to stay with his uncle down south. Said it was for his education, but that wasn't true. I understand now. It was to keep him away from Dawny. To protect her. To protect me, too.'

She looks pleadingly at Georgie, but Georgie gets up and walks to the window: gathered in a flock right out there on the weedy grass in front of the police station, a reeking mass of grey-brown seagulls pecking at the floor, pecking in the bins, pecking at a small blue plastic bag of dog shit, turning the world into something revolting.

'Please, you have to believe me – I had no idea what had happened at the time…' Mrs Helmsteading shakes her head, scrunches her eyes shut. 'But I could always tell Jack was keeping something hidden from me. So when Dawn remembered, when she said her dad had taken her … it seemed to fit. He wasn't in bed that night. I'd always felt he'd had a secret. There was that group of them, him and Walt Mackie and Art Robertson, always meeting up without their wives, without their kids. It was a beekeeping society, they said… Bobby always wanted to go, but Jack wouldn't let him. He even followed him one time, came home all covered in mud and Jack was fair furious.'

Georgie glances at Trish, but she's staring straight ahead and her face is expressionless.

'Anyway, he *was* keeping something secret, just not any of the things I'd thought. He was hiding the fact that our thirteen-year-old son had drugged and kidnapped our daughter. If I'd known, I'd have gone to the police or… I'd have done something. Bobby was a bully, I'd always known that, but I never imagined … torturing a little girl, his own sister. I keep imagining it, poor little Dawn terrified out there on the cliffs and *Bobby*… He'd been jealous of Dawn since she was born. He'd always had this spite in him, I knew it even though I didn't want to see it.'

'Your husband didn't go to the police?'

She shakes her head. 'He wanted it buried, even from me. Don't know why. The shame, perhaps. I wondered if he thought it was his fault, not raising his son right…' She looks at Trish, then back at Georgie. 'Well, maybe it was. Maybe it was our fault.'

'But you didn't commit these murders,' Georgie says to Mrs Helmsteading. 'I don't believe you killed anyone.'

'I did.'

She's calm now, calm and sitting tall, and she's got a surprising authority to her.

'You're trying to protect Dawn,' Georgie says. 'Because you didn't protect her before. I understand. You're her mother. So you're trying to protect her now.'

Mrs Helmsteading takes a breath as though it's travelling all the way down through her body, burning as it goes. Her hair is turning grey. Wispy curls rise up from her head in all directions.

'I killed my husband.'

'There's no proof of that, Mrs Helmsteading.'

'There's my confession.'

'But Mrs—'

'I killed my husband. And I killed my son. I brought him in to the world, so I needed to be the one to take him out.'

'There's evidence, then? Your blood on the knife? Clothes covered in blood?'

'Yes!' she says, 'Yes, of course, they were all covered in blood. I put them through the wash so they'd not be smelly for you. I mean, they're all clean now but—'

'There's no reason for you to have killed Alexis Cosse.'

She glances up then with something that looks almost like triumph.

'Oh, I didn't hurt Alexis. And neither did Dawn.'

Georgie leans back, tries to block out some of the noise. It's no good, to be hearing those birds screaming all the time, seeing impossible clouds in the sky; giving in to the anger she's kept down for years.

'Then tell us what happened on Monday night, Mrs Helmsteading,' Trish says.

This is the question Mrs Helmsteading's been avoiding for the past half hour.

'Dawn was upset. She'd been having her nightmares again. Waking dreams, like she could see her memories playing out in front of her

330

eyes... Her and Bobby, they hardly knew each other, see. He'd been away all these years.'

'Go on.'

'It was like they didn't want to be in the same space together. I didn't push it. Had a family dinner to welcome him home, gave Bobby my spare room while he got on his feet. Only what any mother would have done. I couldn't turn him away, could I? But Dawn stopped coming round. Until that Monday night. I remember the way she stood there at the bottom of the stairs just as Bobby was coming down. Off to see Ricky, are you? she'd said, and he'd snapped back that at least he had friends to go see and then she spoke really carefully, I remember that, said that actually she was going to meet Dr Cosse. I looked up the stairs and saw Bobby there, and I knew. He had done it. I turned back to Dawn and she was gone. I haven't seen her since.'

'What did you do?'

Georgie doesn't move, not an inch, not a muscle.

'Didn't know what to do. Tried to keep Bobby in the house while I worked it all out. He scoffed his dinner I'd made him and all the time he was staring at me in this intense way. I had to say something, didn't I? I said, why did you do it, Bobby? His eyes, staring. His knife and fork clattering to the plate. Then he pushed right past my chair, next thing the front door's slammed and he's gone. I didn't know... I mean, I never believed he'd actually... I should've stopped him, I could have prevented...' Mrs Helmsteading is crying now. 'So I had to stop him from hurting anyone else. Didn't I?'

'Are you lying to us, Mrs Helmsteading?'

'I had to stop him.'

'Are you taking the blame to protect Dawn?'

She's shaking her head violently. 'It was me, I did this...'

'You won't mind giving us a sample of your DNA then?'

'Take whatever you want,' she says, and she is standing, the chair clattering to the ground and Trish's coffee spilled and something

331

has broken in her as she holds out her hands as though she wants them to cuff her. 'It was my fault,' she half-says, half-sobs. 'Please…' She backs into the corner where there's nothing but brown tiles and dust and she cowers on the floor, pulls her knees into her chest and whispers, 'It's all my fault.'

IN LOSTHAVEN CAVE

Simon waits at the entrance to the cave, Dawn's wrist clasped in his hand, the sky above a deep bruised purple and the sea close at his heels, froth from the waves gathering in the pockmarks of the rock. It's a creepy place, darker than shadow and damp like rot, a smell of something more than stale seaweed and crushed salt. The air changes as he steps inside, drops a few degrees and tastes different on his lips – rough and thick, refusing to be disturbed.

As they'd climbed over the rocks to get here, he'd seen the offerings left by desperate people over the years. A crucifix large as a man, made of branches, resting against the cliff face and tied with rope, stones piled into crosses that stayed standing even when they looked like they should collapse. Symbols and icons and prayers, warnings and totems, markings of death everywhere. Dawn is trying to pull her wrist free.

Looking down, he sees torn bits of cling film scattered on the cave floor, soggy and old, and a worry doll that looks like it has been thrown there, discarded in disgust, old and mouldy and damp. He kneels, picks it up. Cold on his skin and soggy with the sea, it had fallen into one of the dips in the rock in which water or rain or something else entirely has formed shallow, stagnant pools. Its eyes, once buttons or beads, are gone, and now it's just a cross of black thread each side that once held the eyes in place, and a similar line of red stitches for the mouth. It is ghastly.

'Did you do this?' he says, handing it to Dawn.

'She told me she didn't want to see any more.'

The crosses of its eye sockets are mirrored all around, on every face of the cave are crosses made of sticks and twigs, driftwood, scratched into pebbles lodged in the crevices of the cliff face. Etched into the walls over centuries. It is an ancient place, he remembers that from when they did local history at school, but he didn't know people were still coming to pray, to hide – didn't even know the cave was still here.

'I used to be so scared of that playground,' Dawn says. She's cross-legged on the floor now, stroking her blind worry doll's hair. 'Couldn't go near it. Even as a grown-up I was too scared, until that last night, when I had Alexis with me and I knew the truth.'

Simon feels his knees shaking – tells himself he should have eaten some lunch, drunk some water, but it's nothing to do with that. He leans against the wall, and his hands slip over the surface like through seaweed.

'Alexis kept saying sorry to me as we walked together. He was upset. I'd told him about Dad, see. About how I'd got everything confused. He said it was his fault, but it wasn't really. It wasn't anyone's fault except Bobby's. We met at the old flats. I wanted to explain everything, tell him the whole truth now I'd finally worked it out. It sort of made sense to follow it through, to end up at the playground so I could confront it one last time and finally move on. That's all I wanted to do, you know. Move on. They can't hurt you any more, he said. We were standing by the swings, looking out to sea. It was very beautiful out, on Monday night, before the storm arrived. Then he took off his gold cufflinks and said they were for me. For luck, he said. Told me he didn't need them any more, because he was already as lucky as a man can be.'

Simon has slid down the wall and is sitting beside her now, on the damp rocks. There is nothing left to do but listen; he has to listen.

'Then Bobby's there. It happens so fast. Car, screeching. He has a knife. Long, thin, sharp. He's lunging at me, grabbing at my hair and screaming, lies, you're telling lies about me, and I'm back there, a terrified girl staring into his eyes, so like my father's, except now Alexis is here, grabbing Bobby's arm and keeping himself between us, holding up the swing to block the knife. Run, Dawn, he says. Bobby stabbing at him, going crazy and there's blood everywhere and Alexis's voice, his gentle voice, telling me to run. Run, Dawn, it's okay. I'll be okay. Run.'

The worry doll falls from her fingers into the stale pool that Simon had rescued it from. Neither of them moves to pick it up again.

'That's what I wanted you to know,' Dawn says. 'I'm sorry I ran away. But that's how he saved my life.'

Simon finds himself kneeling on the rock, kneeling close to the wall, and his fingers are running along words that have been scratched into the cliff face, their lettering like a scar against the grey. PLEASE HELP MY MAMMY, says one. PLEASE HELP. RIP. That is common – REST IN PEACE. Who could rest in peace in a place like this? Who would want to come here at all? Though so many have, scrawling their initials all over the rock. And the smell, he can no longer deny, is urine. He keeps following the words. Further back into the cave they lead, figures with broken wrists, with broken legs, pointed heads, someone's daughter, someone's ribbons tied around thin sticks, a stag, a painted heart, and he feels himself stumble, his boot slipping against the slime on the rocks underfoot and there, scratched all over the wall, is something new and urgent, something for him, Dawn's words: BROTHER, BROTHER, BROTHER, and he knows it's true. He knows she scratched these rocks and lost herself to the horror of what she'd seen.

His phone flashes with an incoming message, casting a blue light over the rocks; ghostly shapes and faces squirm beneath his feet, fingers reach out from the cracks in the cliff and are gone again to darkness. He reads the message. Trish. They're coming for Dawn.

Except that she's innocent. She didn't hurt Alexis. She killed the man who did.

'You killed Bobby,' he says, quietly.

Dawn doesn't reply. She's staring down at the ground, her eyes flicking back and forth as though she's watching something moving down there, something Simon can't see. Her hand to her mouth. Her eyes filling with tears.

'I'm glad of it,' he says, and he falls away from the words, falls back towards the fresher air near the entrance, away from this stifling rotten breath, and he knows Alexis was caught in the mess of her family and her pain and he's gone and it's not fair or right and none of it should have happened but it has and it's high tide now. The sea almost reaching the cave's entrance. It is going to flood. The water, shimmering with light that shouldn't be there, that he can't explain, and everything he knows about the sea and the tide tells him it must be about to flood. But it doesn't. Something happens instead and he doesn't know what it is – something shifts in the sky, in the air, the light changes and there's a sudden stillness that is dark and beautiful and unlike anything he has ever known. The air is fresher now, serene but new and crisp, and the water has an endless deep turquoise within it that he almost falls into. Almost. He nearly loses his balance as he stares down into that water, stares down at the stars, but he doesn't fall and instead the silver glinting lights resolve into the two tiny blue buttons that had once belonged to the worry doll, and he rescues them from the waves.

Dawn is standing beside him.

'Do you remember Pauly and Rachel?' she says.

Simon doesn't understand. 'Last year, the suicide pact—'

'It wasn't suicide,' she says. 'They asked me to tell you.' And she's holding something out towards him. Two gold cufflinks, glinting like hope. Like love. He holds out his hand, and she carefully places them on his palm. They feel warm.

'He would have given them to you himself, if he knew what was coming,' she says, her arm still held out towards him. 'I'm certain of that.'

In her other hand dangles the worry doll. Simon looks at the two blue buttons he rescued from the sea, gives them to her and gently closes her fingers around them.

'But he didn't know what was coming,' he says.

'Neither of us knew.'

Simon understands, at last.

'I think he used everything he had left to tell me to run.'

'Then run,' he says. 'The police are coming.'

She looks at him, looks right into his eyes.

'It's okay,' he says. 'I'll be okay, Dawn. Run.'

DESPERATE HOUR

All the doors of Burrowhead are open, though many of the curtains remain closed; folk are collecting in the village square by the waterless fountain, except that today it is filled. Rainwater, people guess, storm rains, though it is fresh and clear like no kind of rain they get running through the streets; still, the sky makes up for that – it is beyond grey now, a deep churning brown that swirls into impossible shapes above the village, so they huddle close and pull their scarves closer and curse that black city policeman who refused their cups of tea and dragged them all out here.

There he is now, standing up and balancing on the edge of the fountain there, his smart suit fair drenched already, and they must admit they quite enjoy the mud stains going all the way up to his shins. He seems oblivious, though; all he cares about is one thing, so he tells them now: he is here to find Dawn Helmsteading, and they are going to help.

Groups of three then, and off they set down Church Street, High Street and Main Street, knocking on any doors that refuse to open, checking down alleys, scouring the gutters for anything that might have been dropped down the drains. All the bins are overflowing now, they think, but when did the council stop emptying them and mind that explains the birds, the gulls, the crows – the scavengers hereabouts, they'll move on once the litter's gone again. Or so they say.

DS Frazer his name is – with a Z, explains Trish – and he is marching up High Street with a group of villagers following at a bit of a distance, and good Lord the wind fair stings the way it's channelled along here from the coast. Coldest road in Burrowhead, they say, though not so gloomy as Church Street – they're all secretly glad they're not headed down there. Big Fergus is here with some contraption, a drone, or so it spreads through the group, and he's showing it to Frazer and Frazer's nodding and shaking his hand, and as the villagers pass Fergus he keeps mumbling, 'DS Frazer, what a decent bloke, am I right?' But then the bright red-and-yellow striped swing frame of the playground looms out of the rain and they stop their gossip and think about the blood that must have seeped right into the ground. He won't break his stride, though, and Trish is on her phone again and they're all standing at the top of the cliff path looking down the zigzagged track that once before led the collective villagers of Burrowhead down over the loose stones and sandy gravel to the stretch of rough rocks reaching to the sea. Searching for a girl again, they think but do not say, and they feel the salt biting their skin and their lips break in the wind, but they follow him down all the same. Rain so thick and wild down here it's hard to see the ground you're treading on, but along the beach they go, scrambling, tripping at times, a cry as someone twists their ankle, a gasp, and the crash of frothing yellow waves all the while. And from up on the cliff path, Simon watches the search party crawling its way along the shore, grey figures in the haze of rain and mist and sinking daylight, and the sight of it makes him sick.

A NEW WAY OF LOOKING

Fergus waits as the search party disappears down the rocky track to the beach, as the storm seems to follow them down, as the clouds thin – he's sure of it – just enough to let a promise of light through, and then it's time. His drone is not supposed to be used in high winds but these are extenuating circumstances and he has to try, doesn't he, so he holds it out in front of him and gently, cautiously, lets go. It hovers in the wind, holding its own; this could work. Fergus can feel it in his bones. And although the range isn't huge and its power won't last long before it needs recharging, especially battling against the weather, from where he's standing he'll be able to get a view of the village and surrounding fields, in and out of the hedgerows, a look at the disused shed by Simon's place – all the old cracks in his village where someone might be able to hide.

He takes a deep breath as the drone rises above head height, buffeted by the wind but staying true. His eyes follow it up and its camera looks back down at him. There's a speck of light in the middle of its lens, like the reflection in a pupil. He shakes off the feeling that it's blaming him for something. As he touches the controls, it turns from him to look instead at the patchwork of square, stained, matching grey-and-white houses of the village. That way first.

He follows the road until the markings appear and the houses nestle together, then rises above the thorned roses that twist around their front doors, flies up over their roofs. Old tiles, weather-worn, chimneys without smoke; a child's bike rusting in a back garden; slanted car windscreens catching the low sun and flaring in the lens, all transmitted back to Fergus's phone screen. A crumbling Lego village. He feels a tug at his chest and guides the drone past Walt's house – no sign of poor old Walt, either – and on to the village square. Colour at last, but it comes from litter and a fresh stab of graffiti, and the fountain itself: dirty, stained, filled with junk. Over to Simon's place. Down to street level – his windows are dark – then round to the field behind, over the gorse and nettles to see the shed, half rotten, empty and discarded by the same community it was built by, built for; he has to get out.

Higher then, up into the mist of cloud until the village is veiled and beautiful and he can let it go, to follow the thermals as they carry him north to the full expanse of the land, higher, higher again, he needs to be truly above. There: the river winding behind the fields, a silver thread from up here, serene and glistening; mud and weeds dissolving into swathes of green, the land pastel-coloured, like how it exists in his mind. Room to breathe again. It is so beautiful, this land of his. But, of course, he must keep searching.

He flies lower, sweeping under the clouds to follow the wide curve of the graveyard around the church ruin, in and out of the stone pillars, swaying, darkening, the lens spotted with raindrops, through the shadow of arches that once were, then along the jagged edge of the cliffs to glance down at the pebbled beach below, where the stones are shimmering wet. Something down there, of course: the beach is speckled with people moving like a swarm, drenched and desperate, and so he rises again, his finger forcing the controls, the lens covered with water and everything distorting but he keeps going, looping further inland and gazing beyond the reach of his drone all the way to the motte and the dense, broad, brooding stretch of Mungrid Woods that seems to be almost flickering in the distance through a fresh pelt of rain and an angry gust and then faster than he can understand what's happening; he's falling, tumbling, the spin of earth, sky, ground, cloud, earth, then a judder, an error message, a black screen, and his phone telling him his drone is dead.

OLDER AFTERNOON,
OLDER GENERATION

As Simon gets back to Burrowhead police station, the sun is sinking down into grey and Ricky Barr is just arriving in his ancient Land Rover. So, this is how it's going to go then. Simon is going to deal with Ricky Barr. He walks straight past him to the front door; Ricky's out the Land Rover like a flash, standing up close behind him.

The door swings open and Simon steps inside, taking his time along the corridor before pausing outside the room for questioning and gesturing Ricky inside. He's not inviting him into the office, that's for sure.

'After you,' he smiles. Making it look polite enough. 'So, what can I do for you, Rick?'

'Cut the crap. You've got my son locked up in here, right?'

'Andy's under arrest, yes. It seems—'

'Why?'

'It seems he's been involved in an incident at the Spar.'

'Involved how?'

They're sitting either side of the table now, facing each other, though Simon's leaning back, trying to keep it relaxed. Ricky Barr's brittle, everyone knows it, and there's no point in aggravating him more than he aggravates himself. It is highly unlikely he's here to help Andy, but he won't like thinking anything is happening behind his back.

'It's under investigation,' Simon says, 'but as far as we know at this stage, he's one of a group of boys who've been sending racist threats to some of the villagers. Notes, that kind of thing. Throwing eggs at windows.'

Ricky scoffs, but says nothing.

'Then last night things escalated. They vandalised the Spar and attacked Ms Silva. Dislocated her shoulder.'

'Nothing serious then.'

'We are taking it very seriously, I assure you.'

'You.'

He doesn't say any more, just leaves the word hanging between them. Doesn't need to say any more, not with the way he's looking at Simon – and Simon knows the expression on his face. He's not going to rise to it, but he knows it alright. He runs his hand through his hair.

'Never wanted Andy doing work experience here,' Ricky says. Simon reckons he's trying to make himself look bigger now, what with the way he's leaning forward and squaring back his shoulders, but it's useless really – he's not got the frame for it. Muscle, sure, from the farm work, but he's all vein and sinew. 'Didn't think it would be a good influence on him, hanging round with you lot.'

'Us lot?'

'That's what I said.' He clears his throat with a rough cough. 'He's easily led, that boy. Always has been. Got a habit for telling lies and all.' His voice is gravel and he turns, suddenly choking, the sound of it harsh and painful.

'Are you—'

He stops Simon with a scowl and wipes his mouth with the back of his hand. 'He was a scrawny kid, and now he's a lanky boy. I need him to stand up and help round the farm but he's no use, no bloody use at all.'

'Well, he's got himself in some trouble now.'

Ricky laughs, the bite of his cough still rasping in the back of his throat.

'Got himself in some trouble, aye.'

Simon hears Georgie out in the hall.

'Here's DI Strachan, if you'd like a word with her?'

'No, I'm sure you'll be letting me know when the trial is. That right?'

'Could be a while.'

'Always is.'

Simon doesn't know what that's even supposed to mean. To be honest, he doesn't know why Ricky even came here, except to let them know he was watching. Yeah, that must be it, like marking territory. They have his son, and he is watching.

'By the way,' he says, nice and casual, 'what were you doing up near the Warphill flats on Wednesday?'

'Shortcut into the village.'

'Only if you're coming from the coast road.'

'Aye. I was visiting.'

'Who?'

'I'd say that's my personal life. But I can ask her if she's willing to come make a statement, if yous really want.'

'Girlfriend then.'

'I'm done here.' Ricky's up and heading for the door, looking left and right, and Simon wonders if he wants to catch a glimpse of Andy, if just to judge him, just to kick the boot in.

'Mr Barr,' Georgie says, arriving at the door as Ricky is walking out – she even holds out her hand to shake his. Simon hadn't done that, and he is damn glad. No one's put the lights on in the corridor yet, and night seems to have fallen while Ricky Barr was speaking, while Ricky Barr was glaring at him – and now they're standing in the gloom, all three of them. 'We're waiting to see what charges will be pressed,' Georgie says, 'but Andy will need—'

'Lock him up,' Ricky says.

'What?'

Simon thinks maybe Georgie genuinely didn't hear, though perhaps it's just that she can't understand his words in this context.

She's like that sometimes, Georgie. So taken aback by nastiness it doesn't compute. He doesn't know how she manages to stay that way, after all these years of police work.

'It'll do him some good, I reckon,' Ricky says, and he's seen the cell, gone striding up to the door and beating on it and he yells, 'You mind your behaviour, you hear me? You watch what you say.' Then he's off storming down the corridor and out of the station with a smug look on his face like he's done exactly what he came here to do.

TOO LATE TO SEE

It's dark on the beach, middle-of-the-night dark even though the sun's only just skulked away and there's nothing here, Frazer has to admit that. Nowhere to go, nowhere to hide, just miles upon miles of desolation in this spitting cold hell of a place.

He'd thought maybe there'd be caves or something, traces along sand he could follow, but the cliffs are as solid as they are steep, jagged and harsh, offering no cover to the beach and certainly no help to a desperate woman on the run. Anyone in their right mind would have scaled the path back up to the clifftop. They've got their torches out now, those who have them, but it doesn't help much. Pools of yellow light make the rocks look even more treacherous than they were in the dim grey of the dusk. There's already one twisted ankle, could be a possible suit of some kind – not that he imagines these villagers would think of that – and the grumbling's getting worse as the tide edges up to their feet. It is bitter, and there's nothing here. There is fuck all down here.

'Right,' he says, and they gather round him in a sort of circle, torches pointing inwards. Faces looming out of the dark behind. He's always hated that effect. 'Does anyone know any place along here where someone could have sheltered. A crack in the rocks. A beach hut maybe?'

Whispering and moving of torches, a sort of shuffle as they shake their heads and a few manage a low mumble. The rain's getting even worse, biting and spitting straight out of the sea. 'Nothing round here,' says one. 'We don't come to the beach much, round here.'

He can bloody see why.

'Here's what we're going to do.' He claps his hands, for some kind of encouragement, but in his gloves they make a dull thud and he feels like an idiot. 'We're going to head right up to the cliffs there, walking along the edge far as we can, checking for *anything* – clothes, food, blood.'

One of them whispers something under their breath at that. Something hits him right in the eye, rain or sand or grit.

'I'm thinking she might have cut her feet... But then we take the path back up to the playground, get you all home and dry. Alright?'

Without really saying much at all, they follow him, their lights marking a shaking path up to the cliffs where the villagers of Burrowhead tend never to go. It's not that they really believe the old stories. Not one of them would say they thought it was actually true, about the minister and that girl he killed. Unless. Trouble is, the marks on the rocks, holes in battered pebbles, the layers of sediment ground together – in this torchlight it all looks a bit like splatters of blood. Lines and shapes in the dark, maybe just threads of quartz and iron oxide giving the cliffs that ruddy colour, but brown twisted seaweed and clumps of human hair look the same, on this kind of night. They stop occasionally, though, as they make their way along the cliffs, kick at something till it turns over or squelches beneath their boots. And one by one they all see it, and not a one of them says so: a girl, lace up to her neck, skin blacker than night, her long dress ripped and soaking, pressing herself back into the rocks until she disappears. Just the eyes left, staring out at them. Torches down. Torches out to the sea. Keep walking. The trail of them, lit by a jagged row of tiny lights, keeps moving on until the shape of the swings leers back out of the clouds above the clifftop.

'Here we go,' Frazer calls out, though he's started to wonder if he needs the sound of his own voice just to keep him going. 'Follow me.'

And he leads them up, one step at a time, careful not to slip, careful to keep his mind alert to the here and now until they are all gathered by the strange-shaped scaffolds that are the swings and the frames of the creaking animals which move and groan in the wind that howls through Burrowhead playground.

'Everyone can go home,' he says, and he feels defeated as he says it.

One by one, the villagers creep away with their quiet shame, and again he is left standing alone.

There's nothing here. He's lost his suspect, and in a way he doesn't even care. He pulls his arms close around his body and tries to deny the fear that's creeping its way through his veins but by God this place is something dead and cold and he wants nothing more right now than to go back home.

FORGIVENESS AFTER DARK

Trish can still remember that day she was suspended from school. Trudging home in the afternoon's gloom and the rain, with her fists clenched and her schoolbooks chucked in the mud for nothing but swearing and fighting, pulling posh Matty's hair so hard the teacher thought she'd broken her neck, and how with every step further away from the school and closer to home and Uncle Walt her anger shifted a little into something tinged with dread and guilt until she was standing outside the door unable to let herself in, standing with her drenched hair dripping down her neck until Uncle Walt saw her out there. What you doing, Trish? he'd asked, opening the door, and she'd shoved past him and stormed up the stairs and waited for the shouting to start. Waited all afternoon, she did. Waited through the phone call from the school to report on her, the pacing of Uncle Walt downstairs like he was working out how to punish her, the heavy tread of his footsteps up the stairs. She'd stood by her window looking out with her back to the door and he'd come up behind her and she'd cringed away from him, and then he'd wrapped his arms around her and held her in a bear hug until the tension and the rage dissolved into tears and something began to change.

And now she's thinking about Andy in that cell. What are they going to do, lock him up with a load of kids ten times worse than he is, teach him yet more violence, allow the anger to grow and spread – what's the point in any of that really? But there's Georgie looking angry and stubborn and guarding Andy's cell like she's never going to let him out.

'You're the one who says we should always try to understand,' Trish says.

Something's happened to Georgie though, because of this case, the things that have happened this week, and Trish isn't sure exactly what's caused it but somehow she's on a different side of things to where she normally is. Georgie's given up on Andy, while Trish wants to go in and help him, talk to him, give the boy a hug. He didn't mean it, she's sure of that; he took a wrong turn is all. He's just a kid.

'You were right in the first place,' Georgie says. 'We should lock them all up.'

'No, I didn't mean—'

'Didn't mean people like Andy? Who exactly did you mean then?'

'I'm supposed to be the angry one,' Trish says, with a smile. 'And here I am, keeping my temper, showing a bit a sympathy.'

'Think about who you're showing it to,' Georgie says.

'That's not fair.'

Georgie doesn't reply to that.

'I just want to try,' Trish says. 'I'll take responsibility for him. Please?'

Georgie sighs. After a minute, though, she steps away and passes Trish the key, and Trish opens the door to Andy's cell. It was just a room once, back when there was one police officer for the village and the station was his family home as well. Criminals would have been locked up in a barred corner of his living room till they were either let off or sent to the bigger courthouse at Crackenbridge, sentenced to lashes or stocks or whatever other cruelties the town's ancestors might have come up with. Andy's sitting down against the far wall, legs bent and head on his knees, looking for all the world like a daddy-long-legs. Such gentle creatures they are, gentler than people, Trish has always thought. So vulnerable. She sits down beside him.

'Do you understand?' she says. 'Do you understand how badly you hurt Pamali?'

Andy says something muffled into his knees. When he looks up, there's something resentful in his eyes, something like Trish felt once, when her mum was gone and she slept on a camp bed in Uncle Walt's living room and she had to wear second-hand uniform to school; when she got suspended for fighting but no one ever asked her what she was fighting about.

'Did you want to hurt Pamali?'

'No,' he says, 'I told you already.' There's the anger, like he thinks he's got a raw deal, but Trish waits it out. His hand rises to his mouth, he bites at a nail.

'I'm listening,' she says eventually.

He looks into her eyes at last.

'I'd never want to hurt nobody,' he says, and his shoulders drop a little and he sniffs and he's Andy again, and Trish thinks maybe there's a way through.

'Do you understand that those racist notes you were sending hurt people?'

'Yes.'

'Did you know they were going to hurt people before you sent them?'

He takes a deep breath. 'Yes.' Then lets out the sob he's been holding back since she sat down. 'I'm s-sorry,' he stammers, 'I didn't think I … everyone was saying… I didn't want to look like, like what people say, weak and that…'

'Did it make you feel strong then, to hurt Pamali?'

He shakes his head miserably.

'Do you think Lee is strong, for dislocating Pami's shoulder?'

'No.'

'And your dad now. Do you think he's strong?' Trish pauses for a beat. 'Is it strong to bully people?'

Andy's cheeks are wet with tears now.

Trish gets up, and Andy puts his head back on his knees. 'Time to stand up now, Andy. You think you can do that?'

She reaches out her hand to him and he takes it. Looks over at the open door. The fluorescent strip has come back on and light's spilling into the cell.

'What's happening?' Andy says. He's up now, lanky as he is, but his face looks soft and sad and sorry. 'We going somewhere?'

'You have a choice to make, Andy. A choice about your life. Don't you think it's about time you made some changes? Started making some better decisions for yourself?'

Andy just nods, head down. He's like a wee boy is all.

'Well, you can stay in a cell getting angrier all the while. Or you can promise me you're going to stay in the village and we'll let you go home tonight. What's it going to be?'

'You'd do that?'

He wipes his eyes with the cuff of his hoody. Frayed sleeves, his thumb sticking right through a hole there.

'I believe there's good in you, Andy. But there's going to be charges brought against you. There'll be a trial. You're underage, so you might get community service. Maybe a stint in young offenders. But for now, I'm opening this door and I'm trusting you to start making things better. What do you say?'

'I'd... I'd like to go and say sorry to Pamali. At the weekend. Would that be okay?'

'If we go together,' she says, 'I think it might.'

WEEK'S END

As DS Frazer gets back to the station he sees DC Mackie standing outside giving Andy Barr a hug. He hangs back, out of sight of them till the boy's wandered off in the direction of the farm and DC Mackie is leaning back against the station door watching him go.

'You've decided to forgive him then,' he says, as she notices his approach.

'I don't know.' She shakes her head.

'Easy for you, I guess.'

A frown flits across her forehead, but it's hurt he sees in her eyes.

'He seems sorry. He fucked up—'

'He certainly did.'

'Didn't you make any mistakes when you were a kid?'

He smiles at that despite himself. He's made his fair share, and he's not sharing them with DC Trish Mackie, that's for sure.

'Find anything then, on the search?'

He opens the door for her, and she kind of hesitates like she's about to argue then walks through ahead of him.

'Absolutely nothing,' he says. 'Except the knowledge that the locals don't particularly want someone like me around here.'

'I wouldn't be too sure about that.' She strides ahead and gets to the office door first, opens it for him with a flourish. 'Folk round here take a bit a time adjusting to something new, that's all. I wouldn't give up on them just yet.'

'But we've got nothing,' he says.

'We've got Mrs Helmsteading...'

PC Simon Hunter turns round from his computer to look at them both.

'No sign of Dawn then?' he says quietly.

'Whatever it is she's guilty of, she's gone now. A suspect in two, maybe even three murders, if we count her dad's death as suspicious, and we've lost her.'

'You don't think it was her, do you?' DC Mackie says, and she's got a point – he's not behaving like someone who's just been told the killer of his partner has escaped. 'What do you know that we don't?'

'Nothing, it's just... You'll think I've lost it.'

'Try me.'

'I was down on the beach earlier, and it was so beautiful. You ever feel like that here? A moment when it's you and this coast, the golden-red rocks and this never-ending sea...'

And it's strange, but somewhere below the sympathy Frazer feels for him – and he can see the pain, within his eyes, hovering behind his words – he feels a pang of jealousy. He wasn't able to see any beauty out on that beach. Felt nothing but threat.

'According to what Mrs Helmsteading said, Bobby should be our main suspect for at least one of the murders,' DC Mackie says. 'And it was Bobby who kidnapped Dawn when she was a kid. Him and some others. Hid their faces to terrify her, threatened to cut her throat, to strangle her.'

'Then it seems more in character to me that Bobby is a killer.'

'Except that it was Dawn's hair we found,' DI Strachan says, from the doorway. Her voice is different to how Frazer remembers it. Colder, more edge to it. Two days ago she'd been the one offering to make a brew, handing out chocolate digestives. Not any more. 'And why was Alexis's car left at the old flats?'

'Maybe Dawn was there,' PC Hunter says at last. 'Maybe ... say she and Alexis were there together, at the flats where Dawn was kidnapped. They walked together to the playground – retracing the way she must have been taken – but then Bobby found them. He could have gone there to confront her. Or to silence her.'

'We've not got enough evidence to prove it either way, that's the point.'

Frazer shifts on his feet. He's not done well here, he knows that much. It's no wonder the DI is frustrated.

'But if Bobby arrived, planning to kill Dawn, then Alexis would have stood up to him,' PC Hunter says. 'Maybe … well, could be Alexis saved Dawn's life.'

Frazer's watching the room through all this, watching the small, mismatched team of police trying to reason their way to an explanation in their dim, outdated office, but none of them are watching him: DC Mackie is watching PC Hunter and PC Hunter's avoiding her gaze and the DI's staring out of the window like there's something threatening to break in. There's a heaviness to the atmosphere in here, no doubt about that. Maybe it's the wood everywhere, the peeling wooden window frames, the unmatched, thick wood desks, old and lined and worn and solid. In contrast to the crisp white furniture of his open-plan office, with its glass-fronted entrance and automatic doors, Burrowhead station feels both alarmingly makeshift and immovably permanent at the same time.

'I think that's…' DC Mackie speaks, her voice strangely gentle, different, almost distant. 'I think that's a good way to remember it, Si,' she says. 'He saved her life.' She reaches over and touches his arm. 'And then maybe Dawn avenged his.'

'We don't have the evidence,' DI Strachan snaps, suddenly turning to face the room. 'You want to give them an excuse to close us down?' She sighs into the silence that follows, straightens up a bit. 'At least we've got Andy and Lee. Pamali's statement, fingerprints, the notes, their own confession, CCTV, physical evidence they were meeting at the church ruin… Should be enough to lock them up. It's time we started to fight back.'

DC Mackie looks like she wants to fight back right now, but she doesn't say anything, and PC Hunter looks lost to his thoughts. Frazer's got that feeling again. Like he's stumbled in on something that's been going on for so long it's become a part of the silence. He's an outsider here, no denying it. And he can leave if he wants to.

'I should, er…'

'Yes?' DI Strachan's eyes snap to his.

'It's late,' he says. 'I'm soaked through. I've been working since first thing. If there's nothing else that needs to be done tonight, I'll head off.'

DC Mackie's chair scrapes back against the floor and almost like a harmony the birds start up outside, there's dozens of them suddenly rising as one, and the racket makes Frazer's teeth ache right through to their roots. DI Strachan looks like she's pained by it, even clasps her hands over her ears at first. A grimace on her face like none he's seen her make before.

'I think there's something rotten been trying to get up out of the ground in this village,' she says. 'But I'm not letting it take me over.'

Frazer stares at her, and DC Mackie does the same. The quiet that settles across the office is like a knowledge that's going to be spoken for the first time.

'The graves are pushing their way up, right out of the ground. In the old churchyard. Coffins rising up after hundreds of years buried. You've seen it.'

'It's the soil, Georgie.' DC Mackie's voice is lower than usual, barely more than a whisper as a shudder passes through the room.

'It could be a fault line in the ground,' PC Hunter says. 'Or a sinkhole maybe?'

'It's not a sinkhole, Si. And it's not finished yet.'

'You're as bad as Uncle Walt.' And all of a sudden DC Mackie is crying and she's leaning down, her head pressing tight into her knees.

'He's not come home, has he?' says the DI.

'I don't think he's planning on coming home.' DC Mackie's voice is muffled. 'He's gone and the bees are gone and I just… I just…'

There's a bike outside. No wonder the birds scattered; someone just cycled up to the station, left their bike leaning against the low wall in the car park.

'What do you want?'

At first Frazer thinks the DI is glaring at him, but she's not, she's looking behind him, so he turns and sees Fergus – there'd been no sign of him after the search.

'You've found something?' Frazer steps towards him, suddenly hopeful.

'I'm not… I mean, I don't…'

'What *is* it?' The DI overtakes him, and Fergus steps back. Maybe between them they'd made him feel surrounded. He seems like such a gentle sort of bloke.

'I think there's a – I'm not one hundred percent – but I think there's a fire out in Mungrid Woods.'

'A forest fire, in this weather?'

'No, no, I mean … more like a campfire. I saw something with the drone, but then it ran out of charge and it's been taking ages to … and I just thought maybe I should, well, here I am.'

'You think Dawn's camping in the woods?'

'Erm, well actually my first thought was—'

'Walt,' the DI says.

'Where?' DC Mackie is closer now.

'It was away from the main paths, far as I could see. And the flames were … it was a funny colour.'

'It's him. I have to go.'

'Hold on, Trish.'

'Now!'

Frazer can almost feel himself fading out of view. He'd like to help, but Uncle Walt and camping and graveyards are not what he does, not by a long way. But as he steps out of the room, coat in hand and ready to leave, he hears footsteps follow him out into the hall.

'I see it,' says the DI. For a second he's not sure what she means but he turns, looks her in the eye. 'I see what's happening in these villages. I want you to know that.'

He nods, just once.

'You have my number, Georgie.'

And walks away.

WHAT CAN BE FOUND
WHEN YOU LOOK RIGHT

There are no cars on the road. Rain battering the windscreen and the wipers struggling against it. Georgie is driving, Trish beside her, hood up. Fergus is sitting quietly in the back seat. In the headlights, the rain looks like slashes of metal. As they approach the dark shape of the motte she remembers that iron figure he pulled out of the ground and foreboding curls around her neck like the cold. The road curves past the hill and down an unlit track, pitch-black and smoother than water until her front wheel hits a patch of gravel, then another, water splashing right up to the windows as the road disintegrates into deep puddles and gravel and muck. They judder to a stop and Trish is out fast, racing to the broken metal gate. It's beside the faded sign that was put up twenty years back to encourage tourists to visit, though Georgie's never seen a tourist out here, nor ever heard about one being spotted. Still, they had their big ideas: a woodland trail, an untouched beach, a sleepy village, a quaint playground on the clifftop. None of it quite true, or quite right. When she turns the headlights off the scene is plunged into darkness, but no matter. She swings her legs out of the car and over the puddle she's parked in, makes her way to the sign through the lashing rain.

There's not a word on it can be read any more, even in daylight. Bleached away in the sun seems unlikely, more chance it's been gritted away by the salt in the air, rubbed raw with it like sandpaper on fresh-grown skin. The lichen is making its way up and over, the edges of the sign mottled with it like the tree trunks hereabouts. Except that as the lichen retreats, it is replaced by the grey and brown of hardened globs of guano. The gulls spend plenty of their time here, though there's not a one of them in earshot now. Trish is testing the strength of the fence with her hands, then planting her foot on the middle rail and swinging her leg up and over. Georgie follows, Fergus behind her, but then they all stop. The woods are vast, largely unmarked; they don't even know where to start. Except for Fergus. He steps past her, treading gingerly in the mud, nods to Trish, holds his torch out in front of him and starts to lead the way across the patch of drowned grass and mud that leads to the edge of the deep, tangled woods beyond.

'I think it was... I think north. A mile in, at least. Away from the main path.'

'Are you sure?' Georgie frowns in the rain.

'All I could see was a flickering,' he says as they reach the trees. 'And it was hard, on the phone screen, to make it out.'

'You're right though,' Trish says. 'This was where they found him before, wandering out of the woods. I should have thought...'

'There's been a lot going on,' says Georgie, and somehow her voice silences the others, though that wasn't her intention. Her shoes are filled with the squelch of wet mud already and her trousers are clinging around her shins. Water is seeping up from the ground and pouring from the skies. Big storm on the way, no doubts about that. Fergus doesn't say any more, he just starts to walk, carefully, and they both follow, their torches picking out fallen branches and raised roots before they fall.

The track winds through the trees, for a while, dotted with puddles and stones and edged with gorse – Georgie wonders if it's a deer path, though something stops her from voicing the question. There's something about the feel of it beneath her feet, the soft fur of the ground that's making her queasy, but as the woods get denser and Fergus leads them further in, the track disappears altogether and is replaced by the unpredictable depth of sodden heather. All around them, between them, tall oaks twist and rise as they edge their way around beech and ash. Georgie reaches out a hand to a trunk and is met by the sting of nettles. She thinks she can hear the rustle of aspen in the distance. Fergus stops. Turns. There's not been an oak for a while, it's all birch trees here, the older trunks reaching far overhead, branches knotting together, saplings filling in every gap they can find on the ground. They don't even have their leaves yet, still just spindly branches and tight little buds like promises.

'This way,' says Fergus, his torch pointing down a fresh track curving away to the left. He sounds more confident than he did before, and reasonably so – she can see something's been down there, animals maybe, or a man. But she's just seen a clump of snowdrops that's been planted by one of the trunks over to the right. Someone must have done that. Someone's come out here in autumn to plant bulbs for the spring.

'Georgie!' Trish shouts. 'This is it.'

Georgie, though, is reaching down to the snowdrops, letting her fingertips brush through their stems. Walt is waiting for her.

'Come on!' Trish shouts. 'We're close, the smell...'

Georgie can hear their feet running through mud, but her own won't follow.

'I'm going to check this way.' She says it quietly, and there's no reply, and that's okay with Georgie.

You can see it, in the rocks, Walt had said to her two days ago. In the ancient rocks and stones of the land. You're sensitive, aren't you Georgie?

The cup and ring. That's what he'd meant – the old stone carvings buried somewhere in these woods. The thought of them both draws her in and repels her, like the night itself, the dark velvet of it heavy and rich and thick. Now the others have gone, there's no sign of life. Just the deep blackness of the air, and the ancient symbols and marks calling out to her through the night.

She doesn't know how far they are, she just starts walking through the dense birch woods, letting Walt guide the way. She can see him as clearly as if he was in front of her, his dressing gown flapping back in the wind, his shoulders hunched. Maybe that's why she hasn't given up yet. It hasn't been a complete failure, this case – she isn't a complete failure. There's nothing she can do for Dawn now, or Alexis, but she's going to find a way to help Mrs Helmsteading. An innocent person shouldn't take the blame, so that's something Georgie's going to see to. She straightens up, determined again, keeps walking through the trees, through the undergrowth until she can see a break in the woodland ahead and she stops dead in her tracks; there is something, or someone – a dark shape, low down and slumped, in the middle of the circular clearing where the stones are waiting.

She walks through the rain, her legs heavy as dread, the mud pulling her down, until she can see that the figure is a man, that he's wearing a dressing gown, that it must be Walt, and that he's laid out on the ancient stone carved with the circles and lines of the cup and ring. His eyes are open, reflecting the ghostly light out here. They swivel over to her when she kneels down.

'It's me, Walt,' she says.

He doesn't get up. He doesn't move. He is lying flat out on the stone slab like a sacrifice. No lenticular clouds up there tonight, no beams of starlight, only cumulonimbus swirling into a great mass overhead. He must be frozen in just his soaking dressing gown and pyjamas. She touches his wrist, locates a pulse.

'It's Georgie.'

Suddenly his fingers clasp her hand and she is pulled forward through air and night, she is weightless, she is lying above the ancient stone of the cup and ring and they have come. Everything is darkness except for them. She can see ghastly light reflected in the whites of their eyes. More, in every direction. Faces obscured, cloaked with layers of fabric, their hoods rising to sharp points; she knows them. They are getting closer. Ten of them, more, a dozen, more with every second she looks, encircling the stone, and their voices chanting in a strange language, words she can't translate but that she understands nonetheless. They have come to kill her. Dawn. They've come to kill Dawn. Walt's hand is tight on her wrist. What is he doing? They are closer, their voices rising, chanting, inhuman through the masks they wear, they've surrounded her, they're everywhere and the birds – circling overhead, hundreds of them, the noise of beating feathered wings and Walt is gone and her brother is beside her, his wound already seeping blood, his lungs gasping for breath and at last she can feel the cold of rock beneath her head, her hands are free and she screams, she screams at the figures to get back, she sees them, she'll fight them and there: her torch. Her fingers curl around it. She points it towards them.

Trees. Grass. The swirl of low-lying cloud and her own footprints in the mud. This case has been too much. Got under her skin. She needs sleep, food, rest. On the stone, Walt's eyes are wide with terror. The quiet, though. The silence around them, it is something extraordinary.

'It's me, Walt,' she says again, calmer now. 'It's Georgie. Can you sit up for me?'

Slowly but surely Walt pushes himself up until he is sitting on the stone slab with his legs hanging down the side. Georgie takes a breath. He is okay. She is okay. There is nothing here but the dark and an ancient stone.

'You know people have been looking for you?' Georgie says, soothing as she can, gentle and soft. 'Me, Trish, Fergus, we're all out here looking.'

His shoulders slump, his face in his hands. His whole body like a shadow, undefined and billowy in the wind. Trish and Fergus will be here soon, following their voices, but Georgie knows there are things that need to be said first. She pulls out her gloves.

'Do you want to wear my gloves, Walt? They're good ones.'

'No, Georgie,' he says, as though the speaking costs him some effort.

'I'll put them on myself then, I think,' she says. 'They're good gloves, these. And it's always easier to think when you've got warm hands.'

'They didn't come, Georgie.' He looks up at her then, his eyes swimming, but that could just be the way the darkness is shimmering now.

'Why are you here, Walt?'

'I was trying to call them again. I thought if I could summon them here... We need their help, don't we?'

Georgie wants to say no, but can't bring herself to speak.

'This is the most powerful place we have – you can feel it too, I know you can. But they didn't come.'

'I did, though,' Georgie says.

A crack of thunder is followed a second later by a sharp burst of light that fractures the sky.

'The bag was a sign,' he says. 'Found it by the sea, left it in the church weighed down with my pebbles. Just like the birds told me.'

The rain is pelting the stone, their skin, their faces.

'You knew Jack Helmsteading, didn't you, Walt? You were friends?'

'We were once. Long time ago now. We used to protect the village, you see. But he didn't speak to me much, after...'

'What happened?'

Sheets of water are being hurled at them from the sky but neither of them moves.

'I was out walking the cliffs, like I often did back then. Twenty years ago now. It was dark and late and at first, when I saw them, I was drawn in; I could hear voices on the wind and I felt the presence of the Others – at least I thought I did. Till I got closer.'

'Who was it?'

Walt shakes his head. 'I don't know. There was a gang of them, in masks, twisted into something spiteful. And they had little Dawn – I could hear her sobbing before it all went quiet.'

'You were there,' Georgie says, though her voice sounds more like a sigh.

'I couldn't have fought them all off, there were too many of them. But I shouted and yelled, so they'd run after me and leave her alone. It worked too. I drew them away and lost them in the village, but by the time I'd looped back round to the cliffs little Dawn was gone. And Jack had arrived.'

'Did you call him?'

'Not me,' Walt says. 'But he told me he knew where Dawn had gone, and that he was going to get her, to save her. That she'd be okay. He promised that. And…'

'What?'

'He said that I mustn't tell anyone. Please go home and don't say a word, he said. Like he was desperate.'

'My God, Walt, why didn't you call the police?'

'He begged me not to. Said it was all in his family and he had to be the one to put it to rights. I figured it was up to him. Besides, by the next morning she was home and safe, and we villagers, we take care of our own. In our own way, Georgie. That's how it's always been.'

Georgie feels a shiver climb up her arms, scratch at her neck.

'I don't understand.'

'It's our way,' he says again, and something stubborn settles around his jaw despite the chattering of his teeth. 'But I didn't see much of Jack after that, and then he passed away and things started to turn … and poor Alexis… The village needs help,' he says eventually.

'This is where the Others arrived before. Our ancestors drew it, you see? On the stones.'

'We need to get you home, Walt.'

'I don't want to live here any more,' he says. 'Don't want a be a part of this world no more, Georgie.'

'I know, Walt. I know. Sometimes I don't either, and there's the truth of it. But we keep on going, Walt. People like you and me, we find a way to keep on going.'

'You think they'll come for me, one day?'

His watery eyes are full of hope now.

She sits on the stone beside him, an old man crying streams on an eight-thousand-year-old carving on an ancient stone in a muddy clearing in the middle of the woods. She gives him the time he needs, waits silently while the stream slows and the rain starts to get lighter again. It can never last all that long, rain that heavy, dies down as fast as it arrives usually. Clears the air.

'Come on, Walt,' she says, eventually. 'Come on now. You're soaked and you're freezing, and Trish will be here in a second. Her and Fergus, I think they found your campsite.'

'Trish doesn't believe in the Others.'

'That's true.'

'S'why you were the only one I'd trust with my bees.'

Georgie realises something then, and it's a good realisation, because all she has to do is tell the truth.

'Trouble is, Walt, I don't like bees.'

'What do you mean?'

'I hate the noise they make, the scurrying indoors, and the buzzing when they fly.'

'But they protect us, they're—'

'Well, I hate the thought that they might sting me. I haven't been able to sleep with them in the house at all. I'm scared of them.'

'You're scared of my bees?'

He looks distraught, but Georgie carries on.

'Afraid so, Walt. I don't want them in my home, that's the truth of it. There is someone who loves them, though, just as much as you do.'

'Who's that?'

'Your Trish, of course. She loves those bees.'

'She does,' he says. 'You're right, Georgie. She loves them, just like me.'

'Uncle Walt?' Trish's voice rings through the air, out of breath and desperate.

'Through here,' Georgie calls back.

'Uncle Walt, I'm coming!'

Walt nods and stands up, like he always knew this would be how it would end.

'But you believe me, don't you, Georgie?' he says under his breath. 'You do understand?'

She holds his hands, standing still in the mud by the stone, and looks into his eyes by moonlight. Those heavy clouds have gone, replaced by glitter and satin over the village and she feels it, the sky pulling her back to the job, rooting her again, reminding her there's something here worth saving.

'Yes, Walt. I believe you,' she says. 'I understand.'

Trish runs through the clearing and Georgie steps aside, watching as she throws her arms around her uncle and holds him in a tight hug.

'It's okay,' Walt is saying.

'Uncle Walt, don't you ever—'

'I'm okay.'

'I was so worried.'

'I'm okay.'

'I love you, you know? I...'

Georgie steps further away to give them a moment, and notices Fergus standing at the edge of the clearing. He shines his torch low towards her, the light making a diffuse circle on the ground, and she raises hers towards him.

'You did well,' she says quietly.

He stays where he is.

The rain running down his face almost makes it look like he's been crying.

LATE-NIGHT SAILING

There will be no more going home for me. I'm nearly there. I can see the orange lights in the dark of the harbour up ahead and the rest is far away and free and never coming home again. No wrong faces painted into my dreams any more, and maybe that's a step towards something. Or maybe it's just the storm and an ocean crossing.

And look, there's a boat, a big ship, the cruise liner with round windows winking yellow lights shining out into the dark. The coast smells of seaweed that's more rotten than fresh but I breathe it in anyway, since it's to be the last time. I hand over some money. The man nods. I walk on board. Easy as mince and potato.

Such a big cruise ship, with all these tourists stopping off to see my little patch of coast. Strange thing that they should want to see it, but who am I to question their motives? It should be simple enough for me to get lost among all these faces. Already I'm blending in, see, walking more slowly, turning my own face into a smile. They even have showers on this boat. I'll take a shower, soon as we leave the harbour. And then we'll sail on round the coast, round the country, through the night, and on to France and on to Spain. Maybe I'll get off the boat in Spain. I like the idea of that. Think of all the sunshine. I've never been to Spain before but I have a good picture of it in my mind, with big blue sky and a bright golden sun and no faces in it at all. There can't be anything too bad going to happen to me, in that kind of sunshine.

EYES OPEN

Georgie drives slowly away from Burrowhead, Fergus in the passenger seat beside her. She flicks on her full beams and watches the tiny moths fluttering in and out of her path. Trish and Walt are back home, where they belong, and she's glad of it. But now Georgie's got to go home, with Fergus, and for the first time in her life she doesn't think she wants to. She pulls into the drive and turns the lights off and sits there for a minute, in the darkness.

'Are you going to come in?' Fergus says, eventually.

It's like neither of them is able to move.

'You know, I do understand,' he says. 'I'd be frustrated with me, too. I'd be—'.

'I'm not frustrated.'

'Angry, then. I know this has been a long time coming.'

A part of her wants to deny it, but she can't.

'I'm sorry I wasted all that money on my master's a few years back.'

'It wasn't wasted—'

'Well, what use was it? All I got was six years of unemployment.' He tries to laugh, then stops. His face looks serious, his eyes deeply sad. 'This is your house, Georgie. I'll move out.'

'That's ... oh, Fergus. Come on. Let's go inside and talk.'

They walk together to the door, into their home and through to the living room, where he's been laying out newsletters and posters and what looks like home-made bunting covered with photos of the standing stone alternating with triangles of bright glittering fabric. It's the spring fair tomorrow. She'd forgotten. She doesn't know how anyone could have remembered, but this is the village spring fair and Burrowhead doesn't cancel its village fair for anything. She feels nauseous.

'What do you think?' he says.

'It's...'

'Pami helped me.'

'Pamali?'

'She had lots of spare fabrics, so she brought them round, and I think it was good for her to have the company. She's going to join the archaeological society. She's my first member.'

'Pami...?'

Georgie kneels down on the floor and holds a triangle of silver-threaded purple satin in her hand.

'She said she wanted to come tomorrow,' Fergus says, quieter now. 'Forget about...'

Georgie stares at him.

'I thought we could all go together. I mean, if you want, if you feel up to it... I love you, you see.'

But Georgie is pulling the bunting through her hands and on the photo she's holding there is a close-up of the side of an old iron pot, its sides carved with figures of men wearing long cloaks and awful, threatening pointed hoods.

'What is this?' she says, suddenly throwing it away from herself.

'That's the cauldron they found during the motte excavations. I told you there were some amazing artefacts...'

'But the carvings, those hoods.'

'I know, love. They reminded me of the Spanish Inquisition.'

'The Klan,' Georgie frowns.

'But it's older than that. It's Iron Age, see. Celtic. They'd have worn hoods and cloaks like that for all their ceremonies, maybe.

Rites of passage and the harvest, I guess and… They're basically our ancestors. The ancestors of the village, I mean, from thousands of years—'

Her phone starts ringing. It's Cal.

'Bit of good news for you, Georgie,' he says cheerfully. 'We compared Mrs Helmsteading's DNA sample with the blood trace we found on the knife. It was hers, Georgie. She was the one who killed Bobby. You've got a good case after all. HQ will have to be pleased. Stay of the executioner and all that. Result, eh?'

Result. Station might survive another year. She might get some sleep. Case closed. But not. Very much not.

She ends the call while Cal's still talking. They can charge Mrs Helmsteading with Bobby's murder, her confession backed up by forensics, the motive revenge for what Bobby did to Dawn and Alexis. They can charge Lee and Andy for attacking Pamali, the motive racism, Bobby the ringleader now deceased. So why does she feel like this has only just started? Why does she see it every time she closes her eyes – the circle of bodies tightening around her, eyes glaring out of slashed fabric, a rope held out to her neck and the graves in the old church pushing their last few inches out of the ground. She drops the phone. Fergus is trying to talk to her now, asking her what's wrong, saying she can tell him, but she needs to think—

'I know,' he's saying, 'I know you can't give me details, but if you want to talk…'

She sits back on her heels. There is bunting on her living-room floor, figures in masks and hoods, but her anger's gone and that's good because there's something she's trying to work out.

'Georgie,' he's calling to her. 'Georgie?'

'Be quiet!' she shouts, and there's shock on his face, total unguarded shock, but she needs quiet—

'I'll try harder to find a job somewhere,' he's saying. 'Maybe when they open up that new Tesco outside Crackenbridge…'

The hate in those notes, the shattered look on Pamali's face, Kevin Taylor's throwaway bigotry, Georgie's own brother lying dead on the street with blood spilling out of his neck.

'I want to make things better, Georgie.' He puts a hand gently on her face, and she looks at him at last.

'There's danger here,' she says. 'I know it. I can sense it.'

'Surely no one's going to hurt us,' Fergus says.

'You mean *you*.'

'What?'

'You mean no one's going to hurt you. They could very well be planning to hurt me.'

Fergus looks horrified. Worse, he looks shocked.

'Surely not...' he stammers. 'They ... they're our...'

But it wasn't just Bobby who attacked Dawn when she was a little girl. He was the one holding the knife, but there were others. A circle surrounding her. People from the village, probably people she knew.

'Come with me tomorrow, love. All our friends are going to be there...'

Like the story of Mary and the minister, passed down from parents to children over generations: the circle of villagers surrounding them.

'The forecast says the sun's going to be out and everything,' Fergus is saying, with his big hopeful eyes.

Of course Andy and Lee are not the only ones reading that racist hate on the internet, passing it on. Then Walt's words, about how they used to protect the village, to take care of their own, but what did he mean? Protect it from whom? And Ricky Barr, there's something spiteful about Ricky Barr.

'It's going to be beautiful.'

And at last Georgie can see them, on her own terms, in their long robes and hoods. They're not just the thugs attacking Dawn, they're not hidden in the dark and they're not her own memories either.

They are people from the village. They are old and young, women and men; they are surrounding her but she is not afraid. She is calm. She is thinking. She is watching them now, and their masks are slipping.

ACKNOWLEDGEMENTS

I am deeply grateful to my outstanding editor, Jenny Parrott, who believed in my writing at a time when I truly needed it. Jenny, your insight and skill turned my wild idea into a meaningful reality. Thank you!

My agent, Cathryn Summerhayes, is such an inspiration that words of gratitude don't seem to be enough. Cath, you are extraordinary. I am so lucky to have you both as my agent and as my friend.

To the team at Oneworld and Point Blank: you are all amazing. Sarah Terry, my wonderful copyeditor, Paul Nash, Margot Weale, Jennifer Jahn, Tom Sanderson, Ben Summers, Aimee Oliver-Powell, Mark Rusher, Anna Murphy, Thanhmai Bui-Van, Bala at Geethik Technologies, and everyone who has been involved from brainstorming titles to bookselling, thank you.

To everyone at Curtis Brown, with a special shout out to Alice Lutyens, Irene Magrelli and Luke Speed: you are a shining light among literary agencies.

I completed the first draft of this book at beautiful Moniack Mhor. How lucky we are in Scotland to have such a gorgeous creative writing centre. Scottish Book Trust also provides the most exceptional support for writers, and I will be forever grateful.

To my friends and family who have provided feedback, encouragement and invaluable support in all sorts of ways – Viccy Adams, Jane Alexander, Margaret Callaghan, Merryn Glover, Mandy Haggith, Kirsty Logan, Aoife Lyall, Mairi and Seamus MacPherson,

Katy McAulay, Laura Morgan, Philip Paris, Ally Sedgwick, Kate Tough, Liz Treacher, everyone at Highland LIT, my mum and dad – love and thanks to you all.

This book is dedicated to my daughter, Hazel, who showed remarkable patience and understanding (for a one-year-old) while I edited it.

Michael, none of this would have been possible without you. My love, always.